THE DAEMON'S CURSE

THE JOURNEY BEGINS...

Since birth Malus Darkblade has been taught the most important lesson in dark elf society: do unto others before they do unto you. Even in the treacherous land of Naggaroth, Malus soon became infamous for his ruthless and evil nature. Little does the dark elf know that he's about to meet a creature as evil as him, maybe even more so.

Legends of a powerful magical artefact hidden deep within the nightmarish Chaos Wastes are too much for Malus and he sets off with his retinue in a quest to capture more power and influence. Deep within the Wastes, the daemon Tz'arkan has very different plans for Malus...

A WARHAMMER NOVEL

THE DAEMON'S CURSE

A Tale of Malus Darkblade

DAN ABNETT & MIKE LEE

A Black Library Publication

First published in Great Britain in 2005 by
BL Publishing,
Games Workshop Ltd.,
Willow Road, Nottingham,
NG7 2WS, UK

10 9 8 7 6 5 4 3 2

Cover illustration by Clint Langley
Map by Nuala Kennedy.

A CIP record for this book is available from the British Library.

ISBN 13: 978 1 84416 191 1
ISBN 10: 1 84416 191 9

Distributed in the US by Simon & Schuster
1230 Avenue of the Americas, New York, NY 10020.

See the Black Library on the Internet at
www.blacklibrary.com

Find out more about Games Workshop
and the world of Warhammer at
www.games-workshop.com

*To Lindsey and Marc at Black Library for
taking a chance on a first-time novelist in
the States, and to Dan Abnett for his
insights into the dark corners of Malus's
mind.*

*Many thanks to Jon Butler, for a promise
made almost nineteen years ago.*

*And most especially, to Janet, who keeps on
showing me the way.*

−ML

THIS IS A DARK age, a bloody age, an age of daemons and of sorcery. It is an age of battle and death, and of the world's ending. Amidst all of the fire, flame and fury it is a time, too, of mighty heroes, of bold deeds and great courage.

AT THE HEART of the Old World sprawls the Empire, the largest and most powerful of the human realms. Known for its engineers, sorcerers, traders and soldiers, it is a land of great mountains, mighty rivers, dark forests and vast cities. And from his throne in Altdorf reigns the Emperor Karl-Franz, sacred descendant of the founder of these lands, Sigmar, and wielder of his magical warhammer.

BUT THESE ARE far from civilised times. Across the length and breadth of the Old World, from the knightly palaces of Bretonnia to ice-bound Kislev in the far north, come rumblings of war. In the towering World's Edge Mountains, the orc tribes are gathering for another assault. Bandits and renegades harry the wild southern lands of the Border Princes. There are rumours of rat-things, the skaven, emerging from the sewers and swamps across the land. And from the northern wildernesses there is the ever-present threat of Chaos, of daemons and beastmen corrupted by the foul powers of the Dark Gods. As the time of battle draws ever nearer, the Empire needs heroes like never before.

NAGGAROTH

Karond Kar

Sea of Chill

The Annulii

Vampire Hills

Horeth's Column

Black Tower

Clar Karond

Anul's Anvil

Doom Glades

Grasslands

Arnheim

Sea of Serpents

Chapter One
BLOOD AND COIN

THE SHADOWBLADE RODE the Sea of Malice with a winter gale at her back, her indigo-dyed sails of human hide stretched to their limit and the slate-grey sea hissing along her sharply-raked hull. Her druchii crew knew their trade well, gliding effortlessly along the pitching deck like hungry shades at the sibilant orders of their captain.

They wore heavy robes and thick leather kheitans to keep out the icy wind, and their dark eyes glittered like onyx between the folds of dark woollen scarves. They were racing before the storm with a full load of cargo chained below, but the craggy southern coastline and the mouth of the river leading to Clar Karond lay only a few miles off the bow. The wind howled hungrily in the black rigging, singing an eerie counterpoint to the muffled cries rising from the hold, and the sailors laughed in quiet, sepulchral tones, thinking back to the revels of the night before.

Malus Darkblade stood at the corsair's prow, one gauntleted hand resting on the ship's rail as he watched the sharp towers of the sea gate rise before him. A heavy cloak of nauglir hide hung from his narrow shoulders and wisps of black hair spilled from the confines of a voluminous hood to twist and dance in the wind. The cold clawed at his face and he bared his teeth at its touch. The highborn elf pulled a carefully folded token from his belt and held it to his lips, breathing in its heady perfume. It smelled of blood and brine, setting his senses on edge.

This is the smell of victory, he thought, his lips twisting into a mirthless smile.

The raiding cruise had been a gamble from the outset, and he'd pushed his luck every step of the way. With only one small ship, an equally small crew and a late start hindering his efforts, it wasn't enough to merely succeed; nothing short of a rousing triumph would impress his reluctant allies back at Hag Graef. So they had lingered along Bretonnia's western coast weeks after their peers had set course for home.

The captain had complained bitterly about the turning weather and the damnable Ulthuan Seaguard until Malus had put a knife to his throat and threatened to take command of the *Shadowblade* himself. When a gale blew up in the dead of night off the shores of Couronne all had seemed lost, and six sailors had vanished into the black waves while fighting to keep the wind and the sea from dashing the corsair against the rocks. But by dawn their luck had turned along with the wind; the Bretonnian coastal patrols had fared far worse than they, having been cast up on the rocks or blown down the long inlet towards the free city of Marienburg.

In swift succession, the raiders struck three villages along the coast and sacked the battered fort at Montblanc in four days of pillage and slaughter before escaping out to sea with a hold full of slaves and two chests brimming with gold and silver coin.

He would see to it that his backers were well paid for their efforts; to risk the ire of his family by borrowing the funds he needed for the voyage from other sources had been a risky gambit. After being stalemated for so long, it was tempting to let the money flow through his hands like spilled blood, hiring assassins, tormentors and vauvalka to revenge himself on his brothers and sisters. Part of him yearned for an orgy of revenge, of torture and death and agonies that lingered beyond death. The need was sharp, like steel on the tongue, and sent a shiver of anticipation along his spine.

The darkness awaits, brothers and sisters, he thought, his eyes alight with menace. *You've kept me from it for far too long.*

The darkly-stained deck creaked slightly and heeled to starboard as the corsair settled onto a course for the narrow river mouth leading to the City of Ships. Closer now, Malus could make out the tall, craggy towers of the sea gate rising on both banks of the narrow approach; a heavy iron chain stretched between them, just beneath the surface of the swift-running water. Cold mists, shifting and swirling in the wind, clung to the rocky shore and the flanks of the towers.

From high in the corsair's rigging, a sailor blew a hunting horn, its long, eerie wail echoing across the surface of the water. There came no reply, but Malus's skin prickled as he studied the thin arrow slits of the citadels, knowing that predatory eyes were studying him in turn.

The highborn's ears caught a subtle change in the sound of the corsair's hissing wake, as a faint hum like a chorus of mournful spirits rose from the water near the hull. He peered over the rail and his sharp eyes caught sleek, dark shapes darting swiftly just beneath the surface of the water. They passed in and out of view, vanishing into the icy depths as silently as ghosts, only to reappear again in the blink of an eye. As he watched, one of the figures rolled onto its back and regarded him with wide, almond-shaped eyes.

Malus caught a glimpse of pale, almost luminous skin, a smooth belly and small, round breasts. An eerily druchii-like face broke the surface with barely a ripple, water gleaming on high, sharp cheekbones and blue-tinged lips. *Aaaahhh*, it seemed to sigh, a thin, wavering sound, then back it sank into the depths, its lithe body surrounded by sinuous strands of indigo-coloured hair.

'Shall I catch a fish for you, my lord?'

The highborn turned to find four cloaked figures standing just beyond sword's reach – proper hithuan for lieutenants and favoured retainers. The dual hilts of highborn swords rode high on their hips and fine silver steel mail glinted in the weak afternoon light over black, grey or indigo kheitans. All of the druchii had their hoods up against the punishing, icy wind, save one.

She was taller than her companions, her long, black hair woven in a multitude of long, thin braids and bound back into a corsair's topknot. Fine, white scars crisscrossed her oval face, from her high cheekbones to her pointed chin, and the tip of her right ear had been sliced away in a battle long ago. Three livid red cuts, fresh from the night's revels, ran in parallel lines down her long, pale neck, disappearing beneath the gleaming curve of a silver steel hadrilkar, etched with the nauglir sigil of Malus's house. As ever, there was a glint of mockery in Lhunara Ithil's appraising stare. 'Will you have her for your plate, your rack or your bed?' she asked.

'Must I choose?'

The retainers laughed, a sound like bones rattling in a crypt. One of the hooded highborn, a druchii with sharp features and a shaven head save for a corsair topknot, arched a thin eyebrow. 'Do my lord's tastes run to beasts, now?' he hissed, drawing more cold chuckles from his companions.

The druchii woman shot her companion a sarcastic look. 'Listen to Dolthaic. He sounds jealous. Or hopeful.'

Dolthaic snarled, lashing out at the woman with the back of a mailed gauntlet that the tall raider batted easily aside.

Malus laughed along with the cruel mirth. The years of inaction had soured the spirits of his small warband to the point where he'd begun to wonder which of them would try to assassinate him first. A season of blood and pillage had changed all that, sating their appetites for a time and promising a chance for more. 'Arleth Vann, how fares the cargo?' he asked.

'Well indeed, my lord,' spoke the third retainer, his sibilant whisper barely audible above the keening wind. The druchii's head was bald as an egg and his face and neck were cadaver-thin, like a man rendered down to corded muscle and bone by a long and merciless fever. His eyes were a pale yellow-gold, like those of a wolf. 'We had a small amount of spoilage on the return crossing, but no more than expected. Enough to keep the cook busy and give the survivors some meat in their stew to see them through the march to the Hag.'

The fourth retainer pulled back his hood and spat a thin stream of greenish juice over the rail. He was the very image of a druchii noble, with fine-boned features, a mane of lustrous black hair and a face that looked merciless even in repose. Like Malus, he wore a cloak made of nauglir hide, and his kheitan was expensive dwarf skin, tough but supple. The silver steel hadrilkar around his neck looked dull and tawdry against the fine craftsmanship of the noble's attire.

'That's still good coin lost needlessly,' Vanhir said, his rich and melodious voice at odds with his stern demeanor. 'If we'd made port at Clar Karond your backers would already have their investments repaid, and us besides,' he said, showing white teeth filed to fashionable points. 'The slave lords will not be pleased at the breach of custom.'

'The Hanil Khar is two days from now. I have no time to waste haggling with traders and flattering the whipmasters at the Tower of Slaves,' Malus hissed. 'I intend to stand in the Court of Thorns at the Hag, in the presence of my father and my *illustrious* siblings,' he said, the words dripping with venom, 'and present the drachau with a worthy tribute gift.' And show the court that I am a power to reckon with after all, he thought. 'We march for Hag Graef as soon as the cargo is ready to travel.'

Dolthaic frowned. 'But what of the gale? It will be a hard march to the Hag in the teeth of a winter storm–'

'We'll march through snow, ice and the Outer Darkness if we must!' Malus snapped. 'I will stand in the City of Shadow in two days' time or every one of you will answer for it.'

The retainers growled an acknowledgment. Vanhir studied Malus with narrowed eyes. 'And what then, after you've made your grand entrance and showered the drachau with gifts? Back to the blood pits and the gambling dens?'

Dolthaic grinned like a wolf. 'After four months at sea I've got a thirst or two I wouldn't mind quenching.'

'I shall indulge myself for a time,' Malus said carefully. 'I have an image to maintain, after all. Then I shall begin putting my new fortune to good use. There's much to be done.'

They were close enough to hear the booming of the waves against the shoreline. The citadels of the sea gate loomed high above the *Shadowblade*, barely a mile ahead and to either side of the corsair's rakish bow. The gusting wind carried the sounds of a struggle aft. Malus looked back and saw three druchii warriors wrestling with a manacled human slave. As the highborn watched, the slave smashed his forehead into the face of one of his captors. There was a crunch of cartilage as blood sprayed from the warrior's nose. The druchii staggered a half-step back with a bubbling snarl and raised a short-handled mace.

'No!' Malus cried, his sharp, commanding voice carrying easily over the wind. 'Remember my oath!' The druchii warrior, blood streaming down his face and staining his bared teeth, caught the highborn's eye and lowered his weapon. Malus beckoned to the struggling guards. 'Bring him here.'

The slave wrenched his body violently, trying to tear free of his captors' grip. The mace-wielding druchii gave the human a shove, pushing him off his feet, and the other two warriors lunged forward, dragging the man across the deck. Malus's four retainers slid aside to let them pass, eyeing the slave with cold, predatory interest.

The warriors forced the slave to his knees; even then, he rose nearly to Malus's shoulders. He was powerfully built, with broad shoulders and lean, muscular arms beneath a torn, stained gambeson. He wore dark woollen breeches over ragged boots, and his hands were crusted with scabs and blue with cold. The man was young, possibly a yeoman or a Bretonnian squire, and bore more than one battle-scar on his face. He fixed Malus with a hateful glare and began bleating something in his guttural tongue. The highborn gave the human a disgusted look and nodded to the two warriors. 'Remove his chains,' he told them, then turned to Arleth Vann. 'Shut the beast up.'

The retainer glided across the deck, swift as a snake, and grabbed the slave with a claw-like grip at the point where his neck met his right shoulder. A steel-clad thumb dug into the nerve juncture there, and the slave's heated words vanished in a sharp hiss, his whole body going taut with agony. There was a soft rattle of metal, and the two druchii warriors retreated, holding a set of manacles between them.

Malus smiled. 'Good. Now tell him what I have to say.' He stepped before the slave, staring down into his pain-filled eyes. 'Are you the one called Mathieu?'

Arleth Vann translated, almost whispering the thickly-accented Bretonnian into the man's ear. Grunting with pain, the slave nodded.

'Good. I have a rather amusing story to tell you, Mathieu. Yesterday, I stood at the entrance to the slaves' hold and announced that, as a gesture of charity, I would release one of your number, unharmed, before we made port in Naggaroth. Do you remember?'

A tumult of emotions blazed behind the slave's eyes: hope, fear and sadness, all tangled together. Again, he nodded.

'Excellent. I recall you all talked among yourselves, and in the end you chose a young girl. Slender and red-haired. Green eyes like eastern jade and sweet, pale skin. You know of whom I speak?'

Tears welled in the slave's eyes. He struggled vainly to speak, despite Arleth Vann's terrible grip.

'Of course you do.' Malus smiled. 'She was your betrothed, after all. Yes, she told me this, Mathieu. She fell to her knees before me and begged for you to be set free in her place. Because she *loved* you.' He chuckled softly, thinking back to the scene. 'I confess, I was astonished. She said I could do anything I wanted with her, so long as you went free. *Anything*.'

He leaned close to the slave, close enough to smell the fear-sweat staining his filthy clothes. 'So I put her to the test.'

'Clar Karond was only a day away, and the crew deserved a reward for their labours, so I gave her to them. She entertained them for hours, even with their unsophisticated ways. Such screams… surely you heard them. They were exquisite.'

Malus paused for a moment as Arleth Vann struggled for the right translation, though by this point the slave's eyes had glazed over, fixed on some distant point only he could see. His muscular body trembled.

'After the crew was spent, they returned her to me and I let my lieutenants take their turn.' Off to the side, Lhunara grinned and whispered something to Dolthaic, who smiled hungrily in return. 'Again, she did not disappoint. *Such* pleasures, Mathieu. Such sweet skin. The blood sparkled across it like tiny rubies.' He held out the token in his cupped hand, unfolding it gently and reverently. 'You were a very lucky man, Mathieu. She was a gift fit for a prince. Here. I saved you her face. Would you like one last kiss before you go?'

With a shriek of perfect anguish the slave surged to his feet, but Arleth Vann lashed out with his other hand and sank his fingertips into the nerve juncture beneath the thick muscle of the human's upper right arm. The slave staggered, unmanned by blinding pain. His eyes were wide, and Malus could see the darkness there, spreading into the human's mind like a stain. The slave let out a despairing wail.

'Wait, Mathieu. Listen. You haven't heard the really amusing part yet. By the time the crew was done with her she was begging, *pleading* to be set free instead of you. She cursed your name and renounced her love for you again and again. But of course, I had my oath to consider – I said I would let a slave go unharmed, you see, and that hardly applied to her any more. So in the end her love won out, and oh, how she hated it!' Malus threw back his head and laughed. 'Enjoy your freedom, Mathieu.'

All at once Arleth Vann changed his grip on the man, seizing him by the neck and the belt of his breeches, and with surprising strength the lithe druchii picked the large man off the deck and threw him over the side. He hit the water with a loud, flat slap and disappeared into the freezing depths. The druchii slid along the rail, watching intently. The wind whistled and howled. The sighing of the mere-witches had fallen silent.

When the man surfaced, gasping for air, he was no longer alone. Two of the sea creatures clung to him, wrapping their thin, pale arms around his chest. Ebon talons sank deep, drawing blooms of crimson across the white fabric of the man's gambeson. Thick indigo strands – not rich hair, but ropy, saw-edged tentacles – wrapped around his wrist and throat, sloughing off long strips of skin as they wound tight around their victim. Mathieu choked out a single, gulping scream before one of the mere-witches covered his open mouth with her own. Then they sank beneath the surface and were lost in the *Shadowblade's* wake.

A rattling, ringing sound filled the air ahead – the citadels were lowering the great chain barring entrance to the river. Tendrils of icy sea mist, drawn by the corsair's passage, rolled in on either side of the river mouth, whirling and tangling in the ship's wake.

High atop the tower to the left, Malus could see lithe figures in dark robes and billowing scarves appearing at a small cupola to observe the corsair's progress. They offered no sign of greeting, no gesture of welcome, merely watched in stony silence. As the ship cleared the river chain, one of the figures raised a horn to his lips and blew a long, wailing note, warning the City of Ships of the bloody-handed reavers heading their way.

Malus Darkblade turned back to his retainers, a slow, heartless smile spreading across his face.

'It's good to be home.'

Chapter Two
PROCESSION OF CHAINS

THE WIND SHIFTED, blowing from the north-west, and the cold one's nostrils flared as it caught the scent of horseflesh. Without warning the one-ton warbeast snapped at the harbour lord's warhorse, its powerful, blocky jaws clashing shut with a bone-jarring crunch. The horse shrieked in terror, rearing and dancing away from the nauglir and drawing a stream of curses from the harbour lord himself. Malus pretended not to notice, drawing Spite up short with a jerk of the reins and a good-natured kick to his flanks as he opened the letter the harbour lord had delivered to him.

The *Shadowblade* rode uneasily at its moorings as the leading edge of the winter storm reached up the Darkwine River and lashed Clar Karond with gusts of sleet and freezing rain. The black masts of scores of druchii corsairs crowded the skies along the water-front, bristling like a forest of black spears – fully two-thirds of Naggaroth's nimble fleet anchored at the City of Ships during the long winter months, when the straits to the Sea of Chill were frozen solid.

The city lay in a broad valley bounded by the forbidding crags of the Nightsreach Mountains. Dry docks, warehouses and slave quarters dominated the eastern shore of the river and the city proper with its walls, tall manors and narrow streets rose to the west. The highborn citizens of the city kept their own docks on the western shore as well, and Malus had paid the harbour lord a substantial sum, in silver and young flesh, for the privilege of temporarily claiming one of the highborn docks as his own.

Three bridges of stone and dark iron connected the two halves of Clar Karond, and it was well known that highborn in the city paid bands of thugs to extort 'tolls' from travellers crossing in either direction. Any other day Malus would have relished such a confrontation, but not with almost two hundred human slaves in tow.

It was a fortune in flesh and blood that stumbled and shuffled down the *Shadowblade's* gangway, hobbled by chains that bound them at the wrist and ankle and linked them in two long coffles of a hundred slaves each. Malus's small warband of a dozen nobles mounted on cold ones and a company of spear-armed mercenaries surrounded the shivering slaves on the granite quay.

A handful of taskmasters kept the humans in line with the flickering tongues of long whips, while the troops turned their gaze outwards, watching the three narrow approaches leading to the quay and the narrow windows of the surrounding buildings. Nearly four hours had passed while the ship's hands had offloaded the volatile nauglir, the slaves and finally the warband's baggage. Night was drawing on, and every passing minute set Malus further on edge. The sooner he was out of the city and on the road to Hag Graef, the better.

The letter had been waiting for Malus when the *Shadowblade* arrived, delivered by the harbour lord, Vorhan, when he'd come to collect his bribe. The highborn turned the little packet over in his gloved hands, absently checking for hidden needles or razor edges. It was fine, heavy stock, sealed with a blob of wax and a sigil that was faintly familiar. Frowning, Malus pulled a thin-bladed dagger from his boot and sliced the package open. Inside was a single sheet of paper. Malus stifled an impatient snarl and held the paper close to his face, trying to make out the barely-legible handwriting.

To the Esteemed and Terrible Lord Malus, honoured son of the Dread Vaulkhar Lurhan Fellblade, greetings:

I pray this message finds you flush with victory and your appetites whetted after a season of blood and plunder off foreign shores. Though we have not met before, cousin, your name is well-known to me. Recently I've come to possess certain family secrets that I daresay would be of great value to a clever and capable lord such as yourself.

I await your pleasure at the Court of Thorns, dread lord. Great power lies for the taking if your heart is cold and your hand is sure.

Fuerlan, scion of Naggor

The highborn's eyes narrowed angrily when he reached the letter's signature. With a hiss of disgust he crumpled the paper in his fist.

'Word from the Hag, my lord?'

Malus looked over to see Lhunara nudging her cold one alongside his. Like him, she had added an articulated breastplate of silvered steel over her coat of mail, and her swords were buckled to her high-canted saddle for an easy draw.

Her nauglir, Render, was a giant beast, fully a third again as long as Malus's Spite and half a ton heavier. Much of the creature's weight lay on thickly muscled rear legs; when coupled with a long, powerful tail, a cold one was capable of swift sprints and even long leaps at its rider's command. Its slightly smaller forelimbs came into play when walking or trotting for long distances, and to pin larger prey to the ground while the cold one's massive jaws and razor-edged fangs sliced flesh and pulverised bone.

Render's thick, scaled hide was a dark greenish-grey, with a ridge of larger, broader steel-grey scales running from its blunt, squarish snout to the tip of its tail. A pair of heavy reins ran from a ring on the saddle and clipped to steel rings that pierced the cold one's cheeks; though impressive-looking, they offered little real control over the huge creature. Nauglir were powerful and nearly impervious to injury, but they were also typically slow-witted.

Riders steered their mounts with sharp kicks from their knobby spurs and occasionally the butt of their lances, and used the reins more as a handhold than anything else. Lhunara held her lance upright, couched atop her right stirrup, dark green pennons crackling in the stiff wind.

'Just the croaking of a toad,' Malus growled, swaying in the saddle as Spite shied a bit from the presence of the larger cold one. 'That lickspittle Fuerlan has kissed every boot in the Hag, and now he's set his sights on mine.'

Lhunara frowned, throwing a knobby scar at the corner of her eye into sharp relief. 'Fuerlan?'

'The hostage from Naggor. My cousin,' Malus sneered, 'as he was so careful to mention.' A thought occurred to him and he turned to the seething harbour lord. 'Lord Vorhan, when did this letter arrive?'

'Two days ago, dread lord,' Vorhan said, his words clipped and carefully neutral. 'Delivered by special messenger, direct from the Hag.'

Lhunara raised an eyebrow at the answer. 'A toad, but a well-informed one,' the retainer mused.

'Indeed,' Malus said. 'How long until we are ready to depart?'

'The slaves and the rest of the baggage have been unloaded,' Lhunara replied. 'Vanhir is still in the city, gathering provisions.'

Malus let out a curse. 'Sating his appetites for courva and soft flesh, more like it. He can catch up with us on the road, and I'll have a strip of his hide for every hour he's late.' He stood in the stirrups. '*Sa'an'ishar!*' He cried, his voice pitched to carry across the quay. 'Make ready to march.'

Without a word, Lhunara heeled her nauglir about and sent it loping towards the rear of the slave coffles. Practiced over weeks of raids and marches, the warband shook itself out into marching order quickly and professionally, with the company of spearmen splitting into two files and marching along the flanks of the shuffling slaves. Half the cold one cavalry formed a rearguard under Lhunara, while

Malus took the other half at the head of the column. 'Up, Spite!' Malus called, prodding his mount in the direction of the Slavers' Road. As the great beast stalked forward, the highborn reached back behind the saddle and lifted a black repeating crossbow from its carry hook.

The harbour lord's horse stamped and tossed its head, but this time its rider brought it under control with an angry hiss and a sharp twist of the reins. 'Does my dread lord require anything more?' he asked, fingering his long moustache. 'Casks of spirits for the cold nights? A butcher, perhaps? You'll lose a few of your stock before you reach the slave pits, I warrant.'

'My provisions are attended to,' Malus replied, cranking the complicated mechanism that drew back the crossbow's powerful bowstring and levering a steel-tipped bolt into the track. 'And my raiders are well-skilled at separating flesh from bone. You will, however, have the honour of escorting us across the city to the Skull Gate.'

The harbour lord's eyes widened. He was a young druchii for such a high-ranking position, which spoke of his cunning and ambition. Judging by the cut of his robes, his fine, red-dyed kheitan and the jewels glinting from the pommels of his swords, he'd already grown wealthy lining his purse with bribes from the river trade. 'Escort you, dread lord? But that's not my responsibility…'

'I know,' Malus said, laying the loaded crossbow across his lap. 'But I insist. Without a guide, I and my valuable stock might come to mischief, and that would be… tragic.'

'Of course, dread lord, of course,' Vorhan stammered, his lean face turning slightly pale. Reluctantly, he kicked and cursed his skittish horse along in the nauglir's wake.

The streets of Clar Karond were made to kill the unwary. Like all druchii cities, high-walled houses loomed over narrow, twisting streets lost in shadow. Narrow windows – crossbow slits, in fact – looked down on passers-by. Each home was a citadel unto itself, fortified against trespassers in the streets, and against the neighbouring families to either side. Many streets and alleys led nowhere, coming to an end in cul-de-sacs riddled with murder-holes, or leading down into the poisonous sewers beneath the city. It was a place where strangers trod lightly, and Malus fought to keep from betraying his unease as the column worked its way slowly along the Slavers' Road.

The awnings of the houses kept much of the sleet and rain at bay, but the wind howled like a daemon down the narrow streets, driving many of the denizens of the city to seek their pleasures indoors. There was barely enough room for three men to walk abreast, packing the column tightly together. Lord Vorhan was between the spearmen guarding the slave files and the menacing phalanx of the nauglir leading the way; every now and then Malus stared back at the harbour lord, scrutinising his face for any telltale sign of treachery. Such a thing was to be expected when so much wealth was at stake.

Their best chance was to escape the confines of the city before the gates were shut at nightfall. If the column was trapped inside the city overnight, Malus had no idea where they could find a large enough place to encamp and keep watch on their stock. They would be at the mercy of every gang and cutthroat in the city, fighting in an environment where their cavalry would be at a disadvantage. Malus didn't care much for those odds.

Despite the risks, they had made good time, crossing most of the western half of the city in just over an hour. With Lord Vorhan at their side they'd made good time, avoiding costly detours. The sun was very low in the sky, creating a deep twilight in the shadow of the tall buildings. Pale green witchlight, streaming from the high windows, gleamed on the pointed helmets of the infantry and along the glittering edges of their spears. But the Skull Gate was close – Malus had begun to catch brief glimpses of the spiked ramparts in gaps between the buildings and their peaked roofs.

He gritted his teeth. If there was to be an ambush, it would have to be soon. Twisting in his saddle, he reviewed the order of the column, but the line was so long he couldn't see more than a third of the way along it until the rest was lost out of sight around a turn. There had been no sign of Vanhir and the provisions at all; he could have joined up with Lhunara's rearguard or could be stretched out in a stupor in one of the city's flesh houses for Malus knew.

Malus admitted to himself he'd been too clever by half when he'd accepted the highborn's oath of service rather than tearing out his guts. Lingering humiliation and a means to blackmail another highborn family had seemed like a cunning idea at the time. Now he vexes me at every turn, Malus thought balefully.

Lord Vorhan straightened in the saddle, mistaking the intent of the highborn's glare. 'Not long now, dread lord,' he called. 'Just around the corner up ahead.'

'Indeed?' Malus said. He raised his hand, and the column staggered to a halt. 'The vanguard will proceed,' he ordered, loud enough so his assembled retainers could hear. 'And you–' he pointed to Vorhan– 'will accompany us.'

Without waiting for a response, Malus spurred his mount forward.

The road continued for another thirty yards and turned abruptly right. The vanguard came around the corner in two columns, lances held high. Malus led the way, his hand resting lightly on the crossbow's grip. Around the turn, the road opened into a small square, the first Malus had seen since leaving the quay. Directly ahead lay the city gates, still open. A detachment of guards stood in the relative shelter of its high arch.

There was no one on the square. Malus surveyed the scene warily. The tall windows were shut tight against the building storm, and a thin coating of ice on the cobblestones revealed that no large body of men had passed through the square recently. The Dark Mother smiles on me today, Malus thought. He signalled to one of his riders to head back and call the column forward.

Lord Vorhan edged his horse forward. The harbour lord cleared his throat. 'The gate captain will expect a token of… courtesy… in order to keep the gate open long enough for the column to depart. I would be happy to facilitate the transaction of course–'

'If there's a bribe to be paid you'll pay it yourself,' Malus snapped. 'As a *courtesy* to me, you understand.'

Lord Vorhan bit back his reply, but there was no mistaking the hatred gleaming in his eyes. You may prove to be trouble next season, Lord Vorhan, Malus thought. I believe your career is going to come to a tragic and sudden end.

Perhaps reading the intent in Malus's gaze, the harbour lord blanched and looked away.

'On, Spite,' Malus commanded, giving the beast a kick. As one, the vanguard moved forward.

If the gate commander entertained any thoughts of enriching himself, the sight of a troop of highborn cavalry and the grim look of the young noble at its head quickly persuaded him otherwise. At the captain's urging, the guardsmen stepped out into the sleet and rain to give the cold ones a wide berth as they entered the echoing tunnel between the inner and outer gates.

The Skull Gate opened onto a road at the far end of the valley, passing through rock-strewn fields for a quarter of a mile before disappearing into a forest of black pine and hackthorn. From experience, Malus knew the road ran through the woods for another few miles before opening onto farmers' fields and pasture land. There, a branch of the road turned north and west, beginning the weeklong march to Hag Graef. Once out from under the ominous weight of the gatehouse, Malus nudged Spite out of the column and onto the roadside to watch the rest of the warband pass. He idly fingered the hilt of the skinning knife at his belt, hoping to see Lord Vanhir and the pack train trailing in the rearguard's wake.

Lhunara's cavalry troop was almost clear of the outer gate when Malus heard a furious bellow from one of the cold ones in the vanguard, now almost a hundred yards away. Suddenly, Spite jerked as two sharp blows struck the cold one's shoulder with a meaty *thunk*.

Malus was struck on the shoulder plate of his armour by a small, sharp blow. The missile ricocheted, buzzing within an inch of his nose. *Crossbows!* His mind raced as he twisted in the saddle, trying to look in every direction at once.

Pandemonium reigned all along the column. Slaves shrieked and wailed as more projectiles buzzed through the air. The taskmasters bent to their whips and cudgels with a will, battering the stock back into line, while infantry officers on either side of the road sang out orders to their men. More bellows of rage echoed from the vanguard – the cold ones likely smelled fresh blood. There were two black-fletched bolts jutting from Spite's right shoulder, the small wounds leaking a thin stream of ichor. The beast's scaly hide had clearly stopped much of their impact.

There! Malus caught sight of a small knot of figures crouching among the boulders along the right side of the road, firing bolts at the column in ragged volleys. They wore dun and grey robes that blended perfectly with the rocky terrain.

With a smooth motion, Malus stowed his crossbow behind the saddle and drew his sword from its scabbard with a ringing hiss. 'Lhunara! Crossbows to the right!' He pointed towards the attackers with the tip of his sword.

The druchii retainer caught sight of the attackers and her face twisted into a mask of savage glee.

'*Sa'an'ishar!*' She called to her rearguard. 'Ambushers to the right. Open order… *charge!*'

The air rang with the bloodcurdling war-screams of the cold one knights as they kicked their scaly steeds into a lumbering run across the rocky field. Lances still pointed skyward, they fanned out into a loose formation, dodging around large boulders and leaping small ones in their path. Malus hung back, looking along the length of the column.

The taskmasters had forced the slaves face down on the icy ground, and the twin files of spearmen had grounded their shields, facing outwards away from the road. A bonus for their captain, Malus noted. There were shouts and roars coming from the direction of the vanguard. More crossbowmen somewhere up there, he decided. The knights in the vanguard will take care of them. With that, he slapped Spite's flank with the flat of his sword and the huge predator leapt after Lhunara's knights with a hunting roar, sensing prey in the rocks ahead.

There was a score of the robed crossbowmen lurking in the rocks, and they stood their ground to fire a volley into the face of the thunderous charge. The light bolts sprouted from the snouts and shoulders of the oncoming nauglir, but the huge warbeasts had their blood up and nothing could stem their headlong rush. The knights, skilled riders all, waited until the last moment to level their pennoned lances, and drove their steel points home with a rending sound of torn flesh and splintered bone.

Lhunara, in the lead, bore down on a cluster of crossbowmen, trying to load their weapons for one last volley. Too late, they realised their mistake. Their

leader let out a wild scream and grabbed for his
sword as Lhunara's lance struck him full in the chest.
Eighteen inches of hardened steel punched through
cloth and light mail as though it were paper, splitting
the druchii's sternum and ribs with a brittle crunch.
The lance tip and the first two feet of a blood-soaked
pennon burst from the man's back and struck
another crouching ambusher in the side of the head.
The druchii's skull burst like a melon, showering his
fellows with a spray of blood, bone and brain matter.

The weight of the two bodies dragged the lance
downwards and Lhunara let the weapon fall, drawing
her two curved highborn swords as Render bit
another shrieking crossbowman in two.

Malus caught sight of another small knot of
crossbowmen slipping behind the cover of a large
boulder, heading in the direction of the city walls.
Gripping his sword tightly, he guided the cold one
right at the cottage-sized stone. At the last moment
he crouched low in the saddle, dragged back on the
reins and shouted 'Up, Spite, up!'

The nauglir gathered its powerful hindquarters and
jumped, landing for a heart-stopping moment atop
the boulder before leaping down the other side.
Malus caught a momentary glimpse of a cluster of
pale, terrified faces staring up at him and picked one
as his target, rising in the stirrups and holding his
curved sword high.

Spite landed on two of the men with an earth-shak-
ing crash, and Malus brought his sword down in the
same motion, striking the druchii full in the face and
splitting the man from crown to groin. Hot, sticky
blood sprayed across the highborn's face and the

stink of spilled entrails filled the air. Spite slipped and slid over a slick mush of mud, flesh and pulped intestines. A severed head bounced like a ball across the icy ground, leaving splotches of bright crimson in its wake.

A thrown spear hit Malus full in the chest, striking sparks as it glanced from his heavy breastplate. Two surviving ambushers were running flat out for the city walls and Spite needed no prompting to charge after them. The cold one covered the distance in three bounding strides, clamping his jaws on one of the men and shaking his scaled head like a huge terrier. The druchii literally flew apart, arms and legs cart-wheeling off in every direction. The man's lower torso hit the city wall with a gelid slap before sliding to the earth.

The second druchii veered sharply to the right, howling in wide-eyed terror. Without thinking, Malus vaulted from the saddle and sprinted after him, a lusty howl on his blood-spattered lips. They ran for nearly twenty yards across the rocky field before the druchii turned at bay.

Malus saw the man suddenly whirl, and without thinking, swept his sword in front of him, knocking the thrown dagger aside even before his mind had fully registered it. He lunged in, quick as an adder, but the man met Malus's sword with his own. Silvered steel rasped and rang as Malus blocked a low cut aimed for his thigh and then answered with a backhanded slash that nearly opened the druchii's throat. Malus pressed his advantage, hammering at his opponent's guard with heavy blows aimed at shoulder, neck and head. Suddenly the man ducked and lunged forward, his sword aimed for the high-born's throat. Malus twisted sideways at the last second and felt the flat of the cold blade slide along the surface of his neck.

The druchii looked down and screamed, registering the length of cold steel jutting from his thigh. Bright red arterial blood spouted from the wound in time with his beating heart.

Malus pulled his sword free and the druchii crumpled to the earth. With a snarl he drew back his blade for the killing blow – and a mighty impact sent him tumbling through the air. His trajectory was cut short by a large rock, and for a moment the world went black.

When he could see and breathe again, Malus saw Spite chewing the wounded druchii to bits. The nauglir's eyes rolled wildly in their armoured sockets and the warbeast shook its heavy head as though wracked with pain. Suddenly the cold one threw back its head and let out a wild roar, revealing rows of crimson-stained teeth as long as daggers. The nauglir spun in a circle, snapping at the air, then its nostrils flared and it charged off towards the road, bellowing in rage.

Malus felt his body go cold. He staggered to his feet. Something was wrong. Terribly wrong. He staggered around the rock he'd struck and looked toward the road.

The cold ones had gone wild.

The huge beasts were lost in a frenzy of bloodlust, bucking and snapping at the scent hanging in the air. Every one of the dozen cold ones had thrown off their riders and turned their jaws on every living thing

they could find. The knights themselves were safe –
they coated their skin with the poisonous slime of the
nauglir so the fierce beasts would think them pack
mates – but every other man and woman within
reach was fair game.

The spearmen had tried to make a stand against the
berserk animals, but their shield wall shattered like
glass under the impact of the raging beasts. Dozens
of mercenaries were crushed or torn apart, their
armour useless against the nauglirs' powerful teeth
and claws. The broken hafts of spears jutted from
their heaving flanks, but the beasts were oblivious to
pain or injury.

Then the cold ones fell in amongst the coffled
slaves and the orgy of slaughter truly began.

'No!' Malus screamed as the roadway turned into a
churning abattoir in the space of a dozen heartbeats.
The slaves' cries mingled into a single, shattering wail
of terror as the cold ones tore them to pieces, biting
through bone and manacle with equal ease.

The highborn raced towards the carnage, dimly registering his retainers doing the same. His eye caught
the black fletchings of the crossbow bolts jutting
from Spite's shoulder. Poison, he thought. Something to drive the nauglir wild. The ambush had
never been meant to make off with the slaves, but to
eliminate them.

Malus ducked the lashing tail of a nauglir and
darted to Spite's blood-streaked side. The cold one
had its snout buried in the torso of a dead slave. With
a quick leap, the highborn grabbed the hafts of both
crossbow bolts and pulled them free with a wet pop.
Spite shuddered and turned on Malus, and for a

thrilling moment the highborn feared that the slime no longer protected him. Then the huge creature bolted for the field to the left of the road and began to pace in circles, sniffing at the air. After a moment he settled onto his haunches, flanks heaving, his energy spent. The highborn raised the bolts in one blood-stained hand and shouted angrily, 'The bolts have poisoned the cold ones! Pull them out, quickly!'

Around him the other knights began attending to their mounts, pulling at the bolts sticking from their hides. Malus staggered into the field after Spite, stopping when he reached the nauglir's side before turning to face the devastation behind him.

For a hundred yards, the roadway was a red mass of churned meat. Bits of pale bone or glittering chain shone in the misty rain. The armoured forms of dead spearmen littered the ground, their bodies twisted into unnatural shapes. The cries of wounded men filled the air.

Two years of scheming, three months of hard raiding and a prince's ransom in flesh swept away in just a few minutes. Someone had ruined him in a single stroke, and it had been expertly done.

The rattle of armour and weapons carried across the field from the direction of the city gate. A contingent of the city guard made their way towards him, spears ready. Lord Vorhan walked his horse alongside the troops, his expression inscrutable. He reined in and studied the scene a mere ten yards away.

'A terrible turn of fate, dread lord,' he said darkly, shaking his head at the carnage. He looked at Malus. 'Perhaps your luck will turn next season.'

The highborn considered the harbour lord. 'Perhaps,' he said evenly, then plucked the crossbow from his saddle and shot Lord Vorhan in the face.

Chapter Three
GAZING INTO DARKNESS

LIGHT FROM BEYOND the living world seeped through the great crystal skylight of the audience chamber, bathing the inner court with a boreal display of shifting, unsettled light. High upon a circular dais in the centre of the vaulted room, the drachau of Hag Graef, merciless fist of the Witch King, loomed like a nightmare before his subjects.

He wore the ancient, sorcerous armour of his station, an intricate harness of blackened ithilmar plates, sharpened, fluted edges and cunningly-forged hooks. Fiery light and bitter steam seethed from the seams in the armour and the eyes of the daemon-mask carved into his ornate helm, and when the drachau moved, the joints of the armour cried like the souls of the damned. Three freshly-severed heads hung from trophy hooks at the drachau's waist, and the heavy, curved sword in his left hand steamed with clotted gore. His right hand was enclosed in an armoured gauntlet tipped with barbed talons and carved with thousands of tiny, glowing sigils. In that clawed, vicelike grip a highborn noble writhed in his own blood and filth, his eyes gleaming with fear and pain between the drachau's armoured fingers.

The noble saw only darkness, agonising and absolute, but he uttered not a single sound. The pale faces of the court shone like ghosts in the chamber's unsteady light, bearing witness to the highborn's brush with ancient night and waiting for their own turn to come.

This was the culmination of the Hanil Khar, the presentation of tribute and the renewal of the oath of fealty to the drachau, and through him, in turn, the Witch King. The inner court was packed with the true highborn of the city – prominent nobles rich in gold, slaves or battle honours, with hoary lineages and titles. The families clustered in discrete groups, maintaining a wary distance from rivals and even allies – assassination attempts were a matter of course during public gatherings, especially on such ceremonial days. Every family member was further insulated by a circle of favoured retainers, leaving each high-ranking druchii lost in his own solitary thoughts.

Malus watched the highborn suffer on the steps before the dais and wished that he were the one wearing the dreadful gauntlet. The need to lash out, to slice into skin and muscle and spill sweet blood was so intense it set his teeth on edge. He could feel the eyes of his former allies upon him, those nobles who'd invested in his scheme and risked the wrath of his siblings – to say nothing of his dreaded father.

They were watching him like wolves, waiting in the shadows for the right moment to sink their teeth into his throat. And they could do it. They knew exactly how weak he was.

He'd broken with ancient tradition, going outside his own family for the funds and alliances to embark on his late-season raid. Worst of all, he'd returned empty-handed. Now there was a large debt to be paid, and his father could easily disavow any obligation in the matter. The Vaulkhar hadn't yet, but only because the druchii lords hadn't yet pressed the issue. Of course. they would when they sensed the time was right. He had little support to draw on; the survivors of the mercenary spearmen had left his service as soon as they'd reached the Hag, and Malus had been forced to pay them in full or risk a blood feud he could ill afford. That left him no more than a score of retainers and twice that many household servants.

He'd only brought three retainers with him to court: Lhunara, Dolthaic and Arleth Vann. The retainers stood in a tight semicircle behind him with their hands on their swords. It was a token guard at best, but against the massed strength of his debtors his entire complement of warriors wouldn't have been enough. Better to keep them guessing at his display of bravado than confirm their suspicions with a phalanx of bodyguards.

The children of the Vaulkhar were arrayed in order of age and ostensible power, though gauging the relative strengths of a highborn family was a murky business in the best of times. There was a conspicuous gap between the tall, armoured figure of Lurhan Fellblade and his second-oldest child, Isilvar.

Bruglir the Reaver, eldest son of the great warlord, was still at sea with his raiding fleet, filling his holds with plunder and the choicest slaves from Ulthuan and the Old World. He would not return until the first of the spring thaw, spending most of the year at sea. It was a feat that only a handful of corsair lords could accomplish, and his favour with the Vaulkhar was such that Lurhan made it plain that none of his siblings was fit to take Bruglir's place, regardless of circumstance. It also had the effect of focusing the resentment of Lurhan's other children, chiefly on Bruglir, a fact that had not escaped Malus.

There were no fat druchii – like their debased cousins, the elves of Ulthuan, the peoples of Naggaroth were typically lithe and muscular, hard and swift as whipcord. Isilvar was *fleshy*. His skin had the greenish pallor of the libertine, pouchy and swollen from too many years of potent spirits and mind-altering powders. He wore his black hair braided with dozens of tiny hooks and barbs, and his long, drooping moustache hung like two thin tusks past the line of his pointed chin. His long-fingered hands, with their sharpened, black-lacquered nails, were constantly in motion; even when folded before him, the fingers riffled and danced like the white legs of a cave spider. Isilvar had made no raids past his own hakseer-cruise; indeed, he often disdained to carry a sword in public, relying on a large contingent of lavishly-appointed retainers for protection.

At some point in the past he and his elder brother had reached an agreement of sorts – Bruglir reaped a harvest of flesh and coin from the spineless kingdoms beyond Naggaroth, and Isilvar oversaw its investment at the Hag and elsewhere across the Land of Chill. This kept Bruglir at sea spilling blood and gave Isilvar all the gold and slaves to sate his prodigious appetites.

At the heart of this strange arrangement were Isilvar's relentless cravings, or so the rumours went – his apartments in the Vaulkhar's tower were said to be a charnel house, rivalling the Temple of Khaine elsewhere in the city. So long as he could bathe in the blood of the tormented each and every day, he was loyal to his brother the provider. Isilvar was surrounded by a score of heavily armed and armoured druchii, each of them resplendent in plate armour lacquered in shades of ruby and emerald. They formed a horseshoe-shaped formation around him, taking care not to deny their lord an unobstructed view of the excruciations occurring on the dais. Isilvar watched the agonies of the highborn with rapt attention, his eyes fever-bright. His long hands, spotted with drops of old blood, spasmed greedily at each of the supplicant's convulsions.

If Isilvar wore his hunger like a rich, stained robe, Lurhan's third child wore a mask of cold, perfect marble, revealing nothing of her inner thoughts. It was said that Lurhan's long-dead wife had been a creature of stunning, lethal beauty – stories recounted duels fought over a single, passing caress offered at court, or rivals torn apart by eager young nobles who lived and died at her whim.

Her daughter Yasmir was said to be her living image. Tall and effortlessly poised, lithe and muscular as one of Khaine's blood-draped brides, Lurhan's eldest daughter wore a gown of indigo-coloured silk beneath a drape of delicate, yellowed finger bones bound together with fine silver wire. Her thick, lustrous black hair was pulled back from the perfect oval of her face. She had large, violet eyes, the mark of an ancient bloodline stretching back to drowned Nagarythe; they added an exotic air to her otherwise classical features.

A pair of long, bone-handled daggers hung from a narrow girdle of nauglir hide, and it was well-known that she could use them as well, or better, than any man with a sword. She was closely guarded by a dozen retainers, each one a rich and powerful son of one of the city's highborn families.

Yasmir was a living, breathing treasure to them – a wealth of power, influence and beauty, seemingly ripe for the taking. Malus knew better. *They* were *her* baubles, to be toyed with and expended to suit her needs. And for the few months he was at the Hag, Yasmir and Bruglir were inseparable, taking up residence in his spartan quarters in the Vaulkhar's tower. So long as she held her brother's undivided attention, no other man would dare press a challenge of marriage for her.

Other druchii tended to fade into the background when in the presence of Yasmir's glimmering beauty, but none more so than her younger sister. Nagaira was more the child of her brooding father: her skin was duskier, her frame smaller and her figure fuller and less athletic. She had Lurhan's black eyes and strong nose, and her thin lips were often compressed in a fine, determined line.

Unlike her sister, Nagaira preferred robes of indigo and deep red over a lightweight kheitan worked with the cold one sigil of the Vaulkhar's house. She wore her black hair in a thick braid that hung only to her waist; it was streaked with strands of glistening grey and white, the telltale sign of one who trafficked in dark lore. Rumours of her secret pursuits had circulated through the court for many years, but if she were troubled by the hint of scandal she took no steps to mitigate it. Like her siblings, she was well-attended, though her retainers were less a show of strength or vanity than a nod towards function and propriety.

The ten druchii that surrounded her were a motley crew, a mix of priests, rogues and mercenary swords, but she chose her tools well and knew how to use them when she put her mind to it.

But if Nagaira was the shadow to Yasmir's cold radiance, Lurhan's youngest true child was a patch of deepest night. Urial stood straight and tall, nearly of a height with his father, but the heavy black robes masked the withered right arm and bent leg that had marred him from birth. The druchii had no place in their houses for cripples; the malformed were slain at birth or the males given as a sacrifice to the Temple of Khaine.

The infant Urial had been cast into the Lord of Murder's cauldron, and if the stories were true, the ancient brass split with a thunderclap that knocked the priestesses senseless. It was not unheard of for a sacrifice to survive the seething cauldron; such children were seen as marked by the Lord of Murder and taken in by the Temple to be trained in the arts of assassination. But Urial's body was too deformed to make him a holy warrior. He had been raised in the temple as an acolyte, though what he learned there was a mystery oft-speculated.

After fifteen years the maidens returned him to the Vaulkhar's household without explanation, and since then he had occupied a tower all to himself, attended to by a handful of anonymous retainers. Half a dozen of them stood in a tight cluster behind their lord, wearing nightmasks of polished steel fashioned in the shape of skulls. Like their lord, they wore black robes over fine hauberks of blackened mail and carried great, curved swords in scabbards of leather and bone strapped across their backs. They were still as statues.

Malus noted that they made no sound when they moved. He couldn't say for certain that they even breathed. Urial's skin was so pale it was almost blue, his features too gaunt to be handsome, and his long hair was almost entirely white. It was well-known that the only thing that aroused the druchii's passions, besides his studies and the ceremonies of the temple, was his sister Yasmir, but it was just as well known that she loathed the sight of him. For many years Malus had expected Yasmir to take her stories of Urial's clumsy advances to Bruglir, who would tear his malformed brother apart in a jealous rage – it had happened to other misguided suitors before. Yet despite Bruglir's famous temper, the eldest son of the Vaulkhar had never raised a hand to his youngest true brother.

Urial the Forsaken, Malus thought, cast aside by your father and vomited up from Khaine's own cauldron. You make no raids, you hold no influence at court and your retainers are faceless and few. And yet the drachau favours you. What gifts do you place at his feet?

As if sensing his stare, Urial's head turned slightly in his direction. Eyes the colour of molten brass, bright but devoid of feeling, locked with his own. A chill ran though Malus, and he was unnerved to discover he could not meet Urial's stare. The man has dragon's eyes, he cursed inwardly.

That left him. The bastard child born of a witch. Even Urial held more of his father's favour, or at least a surfeit of fear. Malus was simply a burden Lurhan had to bear, or so the highborn had come to believe. It was the only explanation he could think of for why he hadn't been strangled at birth. His half-brothers and sisters seemed to sense it as well; they were all much older than he and could have murdered him at any time. Instead, they were content to monopolise the household's wealth and leave him to wither on the vine.

One of them had laid the trap at Clar Karond. Of that Malus was certain.

He'd been a fool to think that they would be too busy with other intrigues to take an interest in his sudden absence. But how did they know he would land at the City of Ships? The question had tormented him on the long journey home. Custom – and commerce – required every corsair to make port at the Slave Tower of Karond Kar and auction his cargo to the slave lords who resided there.

Avoiding the tower and sailing directly to Clar Karond had been another rash and unorthodox act, and yet his enemies had been waiting for him. There was even that damned letter, he thought with disgust.

Karond Kar was hundreds of leagues to the north-east, one of the most distant and isolated citadels in Naggaroth. Could a messenger have outrun the *Shadowblade*, riding horses to death along the coastal road as the corsair crossed first the Sea of Chill and then the Sea of Malice? Was such a thing possible?

If he did learn who was responsible, what could he *do* about it?

Whatever I must, he answered himself. He still had his swords and a handful of loyal highborn. It would be enough. Let the wolves come, he thought. I will prepare a feast for them.

'Malus, of the House of Lurhan the Vaulkhar!'

The voice ground through the air, reverberating in his bones. Shaped by the power of the drachau's armour, the voice sank into him like a slow, dull knife, reaching for his heart. At the dais, the vassal lord collapsed from his ordeal, his feet slipping in the congealing blood staining the marble steps, and tumbled bonelessly to the audience chamber's floor. His retainers moved quickly to drag him from the drachau's presence, back to the outer court where the lesser ranks waited.

A poor showing, there at the end, Malus noted. That will go hard on him in the year to come. He straightened and shrugged out of his cloak, handing it to Dolthaic. Like Nagaira, he wore only a light-weight kheitan of human hide over black woollen robes. 'Here I am, Terrible One,' he said, providing the ritual response. 'Your servant awaits your bidding.'

'Come before me, and present me with your gifts.'

Eyes turned his way. He could feel their hungry scrutiny. Was he predator or prey? Malus squared his shoulders and approached the dais. Knots of highborn and their retainers stood aside to allow his passage. For a brief moment he found himself face-to-face with Lord Korthan, one of the cabal of ambitious lords he'd convinced to invest in his raid. The druchii fixed him with a glare of pure hate, and Malus returned the stare defiantly as he slipped past.

The pool of blood at the base of the dais was starting to dry, sticking to his heels as he walked through it and ascended the steps to stand before the drachau. The drachau held the power of life and death over every druchii in Hag Graef; one or more lost their head at the end of every Hanil Khar. Some died for crimes, others for insulting the drachau with paltry gifts. Some died simply because the drachau wished to demonstrate his power.

Three steps below the dais Malus stopped, placing his neck within easy reach of the huge, curved sword.

'Another year has passed in exile, another debt of blood for the usurpers in Ulthuan,' the drachau intoned.

'We do not forgive, and we do not forget,' Malus answered.

'We are the people of ice and darkness, sustained by our hate. We live for the Witch King, and to set the ancient wrongs aright.'

'Through fire, blood and ruin.'

The drachau loomed over him, his eyes hidden behind the red glare seething from his visor. 'The loyal vassal offers tribute to his lord. What gifts do you lay at my feet, loyal one?' The drachau's hand tightened fractionally on the hilt of his sword.

Malus met the drachau's fiery stare with one of his own. A thought occurred to him: does he know of my failure? Will he seek to embarrass me before the court? He fought down a surge of murderous rage.

'Great and Terrible One, all that I have is yours: my sword, my household, my hatred. They are all that I possess.' And you would do well to fear them, his defiant stare implied.

For a moment, the armoured figure was silent. This close, Malus could hear the drachau's breath, rumbling like a bellows through the breathing slits in his helmet. 'Every year the answer is the same,' the drachau rumbled threateningly. 'Other lords lay gold and flesh and wondrous relics at my feet. They serve the city and the Witch King and bring torment upon our foes. Naggaroth has no place for the weak or the craven, Malus Darkblade.'

A subtle tremor reverberated through the crowd. Malus stiffened at the age-old slight. 'Then strike me down, Terrible One,' he snarled. 'Water your silvered steel with my blood. But the severed hand cannot strike at the enemy or uphold the laws of the kingdom. It cannot serve the state.'

'Except as an example to others.'

'My lord and master does not lack for those, I think. But devotion is a precious thing, and the wise lord does not squander it. We druchii drink deep of the world. We stand at the edge of the outer darkness and revel in it as no one else will. We spill oceans of blood and harvest kingdoms of souls to suit our wishes, but we do not waste things that are of use to us.'

The drachau considered Malus in silence. For the first time in his life the highborn sensed he rode on a razor's edge, teetering towards the abyss. Then, abruptly, the druchii overlord extended the great, taloned gauntlet. 'I accept your pledge of fealty, Malus, son of Lurhan. But it is not enough to be loyal; the slave must also fear his master, and know to respect the touch of the lash. Since your gifts are meagre, your taste of suffering must be that much greater.'

Malus gritted his teeth. With an effort of will he forced himself to take another step towards the drachau. You've spared my life but named me prey before the entire court, he seethed inwardly. Well then, let's show them what manner of beast I am.

'Do your will, Terrible One,' he said, going so far as to place his head into the drachau's grip. 'The darkness awaits.'

And I will learn from it, Malus thought, his mind boiling with hate. I will sup from it. I will fill my veins with blackest poison and sow my muscles with hate, and in time you will squirm and foul yourself and cry for mercy before me.

CONSCIOUSNESS FLOWED BACK like the tide, filling in the corners and crevices of his mind. He was walking, his stride numb and halting. His robes were soaked in sweat and piss and blood. The taste of blood was in his mouth, and his tongue was swollen where he had bitten into it. Crowds of people passed by on either side on him, their pale faces blurred and floating at the edges of his perception.

There were shadows in his mind, receding stealthily from his consciousness. Dark, cold, taloned things, ancient beyond understanding. They tantalised him and unnerved him. If he concentrated too much on the memories he felt his tenuous hold on his body start to fray.

Abruptly he stopped. He sensed figures very close by, surrounding him on three sides. They did not touch him, offering no hand to steady him. Malus took a deep breath, and the world drew back into focus. 'Did I scream?' he whispered.

'You made not a sound,' Lhunara murmured in his ear, her breath close and warm. 'Nor did you stumble.'

Malus straightened and faced the doors leading to the outer court. Distantly, he could hear Urial's voice addressing the drachau in turn.

'How long?' Malus asked.

Lhunara paused. 'The longest I've ever witnessed. I heard Isilvar tell one of his men that he thought you were going to die from it.'

The highborn managed a wolfish grin. 'Then I am pleased to disappoint once again.'

His steps stronger and more purposeful, Malus strode toward the great doors of blackened oak, which opened before him without the slightest sound. Beyond, the multitudes of low-ranking nobles and their households waited. Their turn to face the drachau would come, but the touch of the gauntlet was not for them. Instead they inflicted their own forms of self-mortification, slicing and piercing their flesh to show their fealty.

The air was electric with the smell of so much blood. Among the lower ranks there was more of a festival atmosphere in the outer court, with servants carrying trays of food and wine or suffering at the whim of their masters. Laughter, sighs of pleasure and sharp cries of pain rose like grace notes over the general buzz of conversation.

A long processional, flanked by the city guard, was cleared through the crowds so the highborn could come and go without hindrance. Druchii nobles thronged along the aisle, watching the haunted faces of the departing highborn and whispering in one another's ears. Malus surveyed the assembled faces with disdain, forcing his body to function as he walked the length of the processional.

At the end of the line another, smaller group of druchii waited. After a moment, Malus noticed that one of the three nobles in particular was eyeing him with considerable interest. He forced his brutalised mind to try and recognise the face, but no name came to mind.

The noble was of average height and somewhat scrawny, as if the gangly time of his youth had never fully given way once he finally reached adulthood. His head was shaved except for a corsair's topknot, and rings of silver glittered from his pointed ears. His narrow chin was shadowed with a thin goatee, and his dark eyes were wide with excitement and glittering with hidden knowledge.

Who does this fool think he is? Malus frowned. The druchii's robes and kheitan were of some quality, but had a rustic cut, the leather reaching nearly to the man's knees. The dark red hide was worked with the sigil of a mountain peak. Malus stopped cold.

Fuerlan. Of course.

'Well met, my lord,' Fuerlan said unctuously, bowing low. Before Malus could respond, the Naggorite rushed up to him, ignoring any pretence of propriety.

His two men, evidently local knights with no other prospects, or possibly mercenaries, followed reluctantly in their master's wake. Lhunara hissed threateningly, but Malus stayed her with a slight wave of the hand.

'Did my lord receive the letter?' Fuerlan asked quietly. 'I went to no small expense to deliver it to Clar Karond ahead of your arrival.'

Malus studied the Naggorite hostage carefully. His presence at court was meant to ensure the peace between Hag Graef and Naggor, a recent development after decades of bitter and bloody feuds. As such, the fool enjoyed a degree of protection few others at court did. Caution warred with black rage in Malus's heart. 'Oh, yes. I received it,' he said coldly.

'Excellent!' Fuerlan leaned closer, his voice taking on a conspiratorial tone. 'There is much for us to discuss, dread lord. As you know, I've been among the court and your kinfolk for some time, and–' he attempted a self-effacing smile– 'I flatter myself that I have some skill at the art of intrigue. I have learned of some things, some *very interesting things*, that I think you would find of import.' Fuerlan laid a hand on the highborn's arm. 'There is much we could both profit from if we were to form an alliance of equals– *urk!*'

Malus's left hand closed around Fuerlan's throat in a blur of deadly motion. The Naggorite paled, his eyes bulging. One of his retainers rushed forward with a shout, reaching for Malus's wrist, but Lhunara's sword sang through the air, severing the knight's head in a fountain of gore. Fuerlan's second retainer staggered back, raising his hand in surrender and then fading quickly into the crowd.

'Oh, yes, Fuerlan, you and I have some things to discuss,' Malus hissed, tightening his grip. Fuerlan's face was now turning a pale shade of red, his hands scrabbling futilely at the highborn's iron grip.

'After I've flayed the skin from your scabby chest and flensed the muscles away with fine, sharp knives, after I've spread your ribs and shown you your shrivelled organs. After I've reshaped that pitiful face with my hooks and barbs and worn it before you like a mask, *then* you will tell me how you knew when and where I would return to Naggaroth. You will tell me who gave you that information and why. You will tell me everything. And then you will pray through ragged lips that I forbear showing you just how deep the darkness in me truly goes.'

No one knows, Malus thought savagely. But oh, I will show them.

Chapter Four
MIDNIGHT PACTS

MALUS DARKBLADE RECLINED in a carved chair of black ashwood, a leg thrown over one of the chair's curving arms, and studied the twitching, pulpy shape hanging from hooks in the centre of the small room. Each convulsion set the iron chains softly clinking, a soothing sound after the heated exertions of the previous hours. Sensing their master's urges were spent, the half-dozen slaves slipped quietly from the shadows around the perimeter of the room and stood a respectful distance from their lord.

'Bathe him in unguents and stitch him shut, then feed him wine and hushalta and return him to his quarters,' Malus said, his voice hoarse from shouting. The weakness and fugue he'd felt after the drachau's ordeal was gone, replaced by a dark, oily calm. In the past the horrors of the ordeal always faded swiftly, arising only later in nightmares or moments of great passion; this time had been different somehow. He had outdone himself with Fuerlan. Such an exquisite tapestry of pain, such horror, such *darkness*... he'd learned many things, gained many important insights that he'd never known before. And Fuerlan had, too. Malus could see it in his eyes. Whether the glimpse into the abyss had provided wisdom or madness only time would tell, but that mattered little to him.

He'd learned all he needed to know. That, and much more besides.

Footsteps echoed across the floor behind him. A tall druchii wearing a polished steel breastplate and greaves stepped to Malus's side. He was a young man, handsome and unscarred, wearing the hadrilkar of Malus's house. His eyes were troubled as he considered the artful ruin of Fuerlan's body. 'That was unwise,' he said, offering Malus a goblet of steaming wine.

Malus accepted the goblet gratefully. His hands and arms were painted crimson up to the elbows, and streaks of gore glistened against the hard muscles of his bare chest. 'I was careful, Silar. He'll live, more or less.' He smiled darkly around a mouthful of wine. 'Nothing in the treaty says I can't be... *entertained*... by my guests from time to time.'

'He isn't your guest, Malus. Fuerlan belongs to the drachau, who wants the feud with Naggor ended. Trifling with that is dangerous, especially now.'

Malus gave Silar a sharp look. Most retainers would never dare speak so frankly to their master – it was a good way to wind up hanging from a set of chains like Fuerlan, or worse. But Silar Thornblood was a druchii of considerable skills and bafflingly little ambition, and so Malus afforded him a little more latitude than most. 'Why are you in your armour?'

'We caught an assassin in the tower while you were at court.'

The highborn's eyes narrowed. 'Where?'

'In your quarters.' Silar shifted uncomfortably, glancing at the floor. 'We still don't know how he got in. The… precautions… your half-sister placed on your bedchamber warned us of his presence, but he still managed to kill two men before we could corner him.'

'You took him alive?'

Now Silar looked even more uncomfortable. 'No, my lord. He hurled himself into the bedchamber's fireplace when we pressed him hard. Naturally, I take full responsibility.'

Malus waved his hand dismissively. 'He's dead, I'm not. It sounds as though he was exceptionally skilled.'

Silar caught his master's eye, reading the implication in the highborn's words. 'He was from the temple. I'm certain of it.'

There were no deadlier assassins in Naggaroth than the acolytes of the Temple of Khaine. Malus took a thoughtful sip of wine. 'My former backers have deeper connections – and purses – than I imagined. Unless…'

'Unless?'

Malus pursed his lips, considering. 'Fuerlan, much to my surprise, turned out to have quite a few interesting things to say. Some of it might even be true. And if so…' All at once, the vague notion of a plan began to take shape in his mind.

Do I dare? Then – there was an assassin from the temple in my quarters. What have I to lose at this point? To hesitate is to die!

The highborn drained the goblet in great, thirsty gulps and sprang from the chair. 'Get me two guards,' he commanded, handing the cup back to Silar. 'I'm going to see Nagaira.'

Silar's eyes widened as Malus swept purposefully across the room, already belting his robe in place. 'Don't you wish to clean yourself up a bit first?' the retainer asked.

Malus laughed coldly. 'Conspiracies thrive on spilt blood, Silar. It tends to focus one's mind on the business at hand.'

THE CITY OF Hag Graef lay at the bottom of a narrow valley, like a nauglir crouched over its prey. Its broad streets, conducive for the heavy industry that was the city's main source of wealth, radiated out from the huge Plaza of Conquest that lay at the foot of the drachau's fortress. The fortress, a mighty collection of spires, courtyards and deadly cul-de-sacs bound by an inner and outer perimeter of high walls, contained not only the households of several high-ranking druchii lords and ladies, but also the city's convent of witches and the cold one stables of the city guard.

The apartments of the Vaulkhar and his children occupied an entire set of spires on the eastern quarter of the huge castle, overlooking the three mountain entrances to the East Foundry and the broad avenue of crushed cinders leading north to the caverns of the Underworld.

Many of the towers belonging to Lurhan's children were connected by narrow bridges, allowing the highborn to come and go without troubling themselves with a long descent to the public levels of the castle and then back up again. Such was the theory; in practice the children of the Vaulkhar saw the bridges as an invitation to murder and avoided them scrupulously.

Except for tonight. Malus moved swiftly along the delicate-looking stone bridge connecting his spire with Nagaira's, his cloak billowing like a spread of ebon wings in the gusting wind. The auroras seeping from the Chaos Wastelands in the far north had subsided, leaving tattered clouds scudding fast across the face of a single moon. Arleth Vann moved several yards ahead of him, Lhunara several yards behind. Lhunara held a crossbow ready and scanned the nearest overlooking spires, while Arleth Vann tested his footing on the bridge with each heavy tread.

It took ten long minutes for the three druchii to work their way across the vaulting reach. At the far end there was a recessed door lit from above by a flickering globe of witchlight. Arleth Vann paused, and Malus was surprised to find a sentry waiting for them, sheltered in the doorway's small niche. He was one of Nagaira's pet rogues, and watched the trio with hooded eyes as he played at cleaning his fingernails with a wicked-looking stiletto.

'If you've murder in mind, red-hand, you'll find no welcome here,' the rogue drawled with a sly grin. Yet there was nothing frivolous about the set of his shoulders, or the careful, precise movements of his knife.

'If I'd meant you murder, Dalvar, I'd have had Lhunara put your eye out from back at the other end of the span,' Malus hissed. 'Now get that door open, you half-penny thug. I've a mind to speak to my beloved sister before I freeze to death.'

'Beloved *half*-sister,' Dalvar corrected, pointing with his knife for emphasis. 'And it's not within my power, bloody fingers or no. You'll wait here on my mistress's pleasure.'

'Suppose I have Arleth Vann cut you into pieces and we feed you to the night-hawks?'

'It won't get the door open any faster.'

'No, but it will be a pleasant diversion in the meantime.'

'About as pleasant as a knife in the eye, I suspect.'

Both sides grudgingly conceded the other's point and then settled down to wait.

Nagaira kept Malus out on the bridge long enough for the cold to have settled deep into his bones. It was an effort of will to keep his teeth from chattering or his limbs from shivering. Dalvar continued to work on his nails, seemingly oblivious to the conditions. Finally, there was a dull thud of bolts being drawn back, and the door opened a finger's width. Dalvar leaned back and shared a few whispered words with whoever was on the other side, then bowed deeply to Malus. The stiletto had magically disappeared. 'My mistress will see you now, dread lord,' he said with a grin. 'Pray accompany me, but leave any thoughts of ill intent at the threshold…'

'Against Nagaira, or you?'

'…for there are spirits within these walls who would take such things amiss,' Dalvar finished, his eyes dancing with black mirth.

The retainer led the trio inside, past a bowing servant and down a short passage into a small guard chamber. Four guards in full armour sat at a small, circular table, eating a late meal of bread and pickled eels and eyeing Malus with casual menace. Globes of witchfire flickered from sconces on the walls and racks of spears and crossbows sat ready to repel an assault from the bridge or the levels below. A flight of stairs curved both upwards and downwards along the curving outer wall of the room, and a stout oak door stood in the wall opposite the passage.

Malus knew the way as well as, or better than, Dalvar. The highborn pushed past the retainer, who offered a token protest, then turned right and leapt lightly up the tower's curving stair. Up and up he climbed, and with each step he felt the light touch of invisible forces caressing his face and lingering along his gore-stained hands. They flowed in and out of him on the tide of his breath, touching his heart with icy fingers. He'd made light of Dalvar's warning, but he knew all too well that it was no idle boast. Nagaira did not suffer uninvited guests lightly.

The stairs finally ended at a small, dark landing. Icy wind whistled through a number of arrow-slits set into the thick stone walls. Two retainers in glittering mail and thick robes glistening with frost stood to either side of a pair of tall oak doors. They regarded him coldly from behind golden caedlin worked in the shape of snarling manticore faces. Their gauntleted hands rested easily on the pommels of unsheathed great swords, but they made no move to hinder Malus as he pushed the double doors wide and rushed into Nagaira's sanctum like a rising wind.

It was the law of the Witch King that magic was forbidden to the druchii, save for a select group of women who dedicated their lives to him and spent their days in convents in the cities and citadels across Naggaroth. The Dark Brides of Malekith, or the hags as they were commonly known, served their local overlord as needed, but ultimately they answered to none other than the Witch King himself. Any other druchii – especially a male – who was caught pursuing the dark arts was bound in red-hot chains and delivered to the Witch King's fortress at Naggarond and was never seen again.

Naturally, there were exceptions. Minor hedge-sorcerers, practitioners of curses and the secretive shade-casters, all of whom took the coin of the lowborn in exchange for their meagre services. The priestesses and blood-witches of the Temple of Khaine and the hierophants of the Temple of Slaanesh kept sorcerous traditions that were old when lost Nagarythe was young, rites that not even Malekith dared trifle with. And then there was Balneth Bale, the self-styled Witch King of Naggor, who had encouraged the studies of his sister, Eldire, and kept them secret in hopes of profiting from them himself. Instead he'd received a bloody rebuke by Malekith in the form of Vaulkhar Lurhan and the army of Hag Graef, who defeated Naggor's army and made Bale and his people a vassal city to the Hag.

By the same token, it was an open secret that Nagaira, the second daughter of the fearsome Lurhan, was a scholar of the dark paths. Not necessarily a practitioner, but someone who studied the ancient ways and the arcane lore for her own personal ends. No one had ever seen her cast a spell or bind a spirit to her will, nor had anyone ever successfully claimed to have been a victim of her enchantments. Thus she kept herself poised on the razor's edge, dabbling in forbidden knowledge that lent her power and influence without allowing it to be her undoing.

That said, Malus suspected that Nagaira's sanctum contained the sorts of arcane tomes, debased scrolls, potions, idols and artefacts that any sorcerer would sell the remainder of his tattered soul to possess. It was also, the highborn noted, thankfully warm. A small circular hearth rose in the centre of the room, giving off hissing flames of green and blue that turned the curved walls into a swirling chiaroscuro of dancing, threatening shadows. A sinuous, scaly creature with tightly-furled leather wings darted into the shadows at his sudden entrance and hissed threateningly from behind an overflowing bookshelf.

As far as Malus knew, he was the only member of the family Nagaira had ever permitted to enter the room.

His half-sister looked up from a low divan set near the fire. A short table had been pulled up to the divan; sitting atop it was a huge, dust-covered book propped on a small lectern and a curious tripod of copper wire supporting half of a human head. The head had been sheared cleanly through just below the nose, and the grisly trophy rested in the tripod with the open brainpan pointing towards the ceiling.

Nagaira had pulled back the left sleeve of her woollen robe, exposing her sleek, pale forearm which was covered in an intricate tattoo of tightly woven loops and spirals, stretching from her fingertips to her elbow. As Malus watched, she took a fine, brass-handled brush and dipped it carefully in the gaping brainpan. She shot a glance at Malus. He wasn't sure if it was a trick of the shifting light, but her eyes appeared to be a vivid, pale blue. Nagaira looked pointedly at her brother's hands. 'Are those your idea of tattoos?' she asked, using the brush to touch up one of the lines on her arm. 'If so, I think my brushwork is much better than yours.'

'I grew cold waiting on the bridge outside, so I warmed my hands around Dalvar's beating heart,' Malus snarled.

'Liar,' she said with a sly grin. 'That man's blood runs colder than the Sea of Chill. Why else would I take him into my household?' Finished, she licked the tip of the brush with a dainty pink tongue and set the instrument in a felt-lined box. She reclined gracefully on the divan, ostentatiously admiring her work. 'I'm very displeased with you, Malus,' she said lightly. 'Running off on your little raid without warning me. While you were gone that worm Urial tried to practise his charms on me, as though that would make Yasmir jealous. I had to fend off his disgusting advances for months on end.' At the mention of her brother's name Nagaira's face darkened. The lines on her arm seemed to sharpen, then shift, like coiling snakes. Malus found he couldn't take his eyes off them, even though the sight set his heart to hammering and sent cold spasms through his guts.

'I... I'm certain you disappointed him at every turn,' he stammered, then grit his teeth against the show of weakness.

'I told him I was saving my heart for another,' she said, her voice smooth and cold as polished steel. 'It made him very angry, I think. He seems to think he's entitled to salve his frustrations with me, the twisted little creature.' Nagaira lowered her arm and glared at Malus. 'You could at least have the decency to sound jealous.'

With an effort, Malus crossed the room and settled on the divan next to her. 'I had to sneak away, dear sister. You and Bruglir and the rest left me no choice. Surely you didn't expect me to sit in my tower and wait for some noble to put his knife in me?'

Nagaira sighed. 'It's the law of the wolves, Malus. The biggest wolf cub gets the most milk, and so on down the line. Bruglir gets the biggest share, and the rest of us have to fight for what's left. I get barely enough wealth to survive on, and naturally I make sure Urial gets as little of the cut as possible.' She shrugged, but her cold eyes were intent. 'Unfortunately, the temple takes care of their own, even the forsaken ones like him. If you are to blame anyone, blame him for taking your rightful share.'

Malus considered his sister for a moment, contemplating his next move. Beneath her diffident façade, he could sense an insatiable curiosity. What he didn't know was how still and deep her malice towards him ran. If she were truly displeased about his absence, there was every possibility he wasn't getting out of her sanctum alive. 'As it happens,' he said, 'I have more than just my pathetic allotment of gold to hold against dear, twisted Urial.'

'Oh?' Nagaira said, arching one slender eyebrow. Her eyes had darkened to a stormy grey. Faint lines and spirals coiled in their depths.

'Do you know Fuerlan? The hostage from Naggor? A craven little sack of skin with an exaggerated sense of his own worth?'

'I hear that's a common failing in Naggorites, you know. A weakness in the blood, perhaps,' she said, her smile full of sweet poison.

Malus ignored the jibe. 'Fuerlan and I had a long, energetic conversation this evening,' he said. 'He'd been entertaining the delusion of making an alliance with me.'

'An alliance? Against whom?'

'Does it matter? He was most eager, though. He sent a letter by special messenger to meet me when I got off the boat at Clar Karond.'

Nagaira frowned. 'Clar Karond? But how?'

'How did he know I hadn't disembarked at the slave tower? How else? No rider could have made the journey from Karond Kar faster than my ship. So that leaves—'

'Sorcery,' she said.

'Just so,' Malus answered. 'That same sorcerous knowledge enabled someone to arrange a cunning little ambush for me on the Slavers' Road.' He leaned close to Nagaira, his voice dropping to a silken whisper. 'And now I hear that my beloved sister has been using my name to spite the one magic-wielder in Hag Graef who isn't locked up in the local convent.' His hand shot out, closing around Nagaira's pale throat. 'So now *I'm* the one who is most displeased.'

Nagaira's breath caught in her throat at the touch of his sticky, clammy grip – but then she smiled, and began to laugh. The sound was rich and smoky, mocking and seductive. 'Clever, clever little brother,' she breathed. 'But why would Urial the Forsaken entertain the likes of Fuerlan?'

'The little toad grovelled to get an audience, no doubt,' Malus said, 'just as he's grovelled before each of you, in turn. I'm sure Urial agreed to see him to find if he'd learned anything of interest about you or the others.' The highborn tightened his grip minutely, feeling the hot pulse of blood in his half-sister's throat. 'Fuerlan, it seems, was given to believe that Urial possessed a magical relic of some kind, supposedly a source of terrible power.'

'A relic? Where would Fuerlan hear such a thing?'

Malus pulled Nagaira close, his thin lips mere inches from her own. 'Why, from you, sweet sister. I didn't believe it myself at first, but Fuerlan went to great pains to convince me.'

For a moment, she was silent. Her breath was warm and fragrant against his skin. Then she smiled. 'I confess. I hoped Urial would eat the little hostage's heart, and then even the temple couldn't protect him. The drachau would have had him unravelled one nerve at a time, and I would have savoured every moment.' She frowned. 'Sadly, it appears that the Forsaken is repulsive, but not a fool.'

'Indeed.' Malus let his lips brush her cheek. Her breath caught in her throat, and for an instant his mind was full of worms, writhing, spiralling shapes of darkness that wove in and out of his brain, leaving long tunnels that filled with inky shadows in their wake. He shuddered and leaned back against the divan, his hand jerking back from her as though stung. Nagaira regarded him with depthless black eyes.

'Is it true, then?' Malus asked. 'Does Urial have such a relic?'

Nagaira smiled. She, too, leaned back, increasing the distance between them. She tapped a tattooed finger thoughtfully against her lower lip. 'So I have been led to believe,' she said. 'My spies tell me that Urial has been seeking it for some time now, and acquired it recently at great expense after numerous failed expeditions. Why do you ask?'

Malus took a deep breath. 'Because I find myself wanting in power and surrounded by enemies. If the relic is useful to him, why not me?'

'Urial is a sorcerer, Malus, and you are not.'

'Great power finds a way to make itself felt, sister. Sorcerer or no, I can bend it to my will.'

Nagaira laughed, and it seemed the shadows on the walls danced in time to the sound. 'You are a fool, Malus Darkblade,' she said at last. 'But I confess that fools sometimes succeed where other mortals fail.'

'So what of this relic?'

'It is not, in fact, a source of power – at least, not in any sense you would understand. It is a key that, legend has it, will open an ancient temple hidden deep within the Chaos Wastes. The power you want for lies within that temple.'

'What is it?'

Nagaira shook her head. 'No one knows for certain. It was locked away in the days when Malekith fought alongside foul Aenarion in the First War against Chaos,' she said, 'many thousands upon thousands of years ago. It's possible that the temple no longer even exists, or lies at the bottom of a boiling acid sea.'

Something in Malus quickened, like a spark on dry tinder. 'But if the temple and its treasure were beyond reach, the magic of the key would be affected, would it not?'

The druchii woman smiled approvingly. 'Indeed. You are more canny than I thought, brother dear.'

'So the temple and its treasure still lie within reach,' Malus said. 'It could lie within *my* reach, if I had a way to steal the key from Urial and seek the place out myself.'

'You wish to pit yourself against the forsaken one in his lair? Your foolishness borders on the suicidal.'

'Urial doesn't spend his every waking hour in his tower. In fact, the temple has rites of its own to observe in the wake of the Hanil Khar. He will be in the city every night for the next few nights, will he not?'

'True,' Nagaira agreed. 'But that leaves his servants, his guards and most importantly, his web of protective wards and traps.'

Malus leaned forward and rested his fingertip lightly in the hollow of her throat. 'I'm sure you have ways of getting past his many enchantments.'

Nagaira chuckled. 'And why should I help you?'

'To hurt Urial, of course. And to share in the power once I've brought it out of the Wastes.'

She smiled. 'Of course.'

'Now can you get me and a small group of my retainers into the tower?'

Nagaira's eyes roamed the crowded bookshelves and tables around the room, as if taking a mental inventory. 'I can get a small group inside the tower,' she said after a moment's thought. 'But I will have to accompany you as well. I expect some traps will require more than a protective amulet to slip past.'

Malus thought it over. He didn't like the idea, but he didn't see that he had any choice. At least with her along he could be certain she would do everything in her power to ensure they got out alive. 'Very well.'

'And we share in whatever power you bring out of the Wastes?'

'Of course,' he said, the lie sliding smoothly off his tongue.

His half-sister smiled, reclining languidly on the divan. 'Then linger with me here a while, dear brother,' she said. 'It's been so long since we've seen one another, and you and I have much to catch up on.'

Chapter Five
STRATAGEMS

THE ICE-COLD WATER was a shock to his skin, enough
to make Malus catch his breath as he scrubbed the
dried blood from his chest and arms, but not quite
enough to banish the crawling sensation of worms
coiling through his flesh. He fought to keep his gorge
down against the squirming sensation filling his
mouth and caressing his tongue.

'I do not like this,' Silar Thornblood said. 'It's reckless.' The tall druchii stood by his lord's side, his long
face grimmer than usual. 'How do we know she can
be trusted?'

Unable to stand it any more, Malus plunged his
face into the freezing, pink-tinged water. The searing
cold banished the lingering memories of his sister's
embrace, if only for a moment. He came up for air
gasping, unsettled, but for a moment the master of
his own skin. 'She *can't* be trusted,' he said, wiping his

face on a towel offered by Silar. 'But for the moment she and I have a common objective – stealing Urial's precious relic and seizing the power it protects. Nagaira can be counted on to ensure her own interests are met, and no more.'

The highborn's bedchamber was a crowded place in the wake of the evening's assassination attempt and the sudden meeting with his sister. Along with Silar, Lhunara and Arleth Vann paced or brooded at different points around the small, dimly-lit chamber, clearly unhappy with the outcome of the night's events. The druchii woman stood at one of the chamber's narrow windows, watching the night begin to fade in a slow ebb from black to grey.

Hag Graef was called the City of Shadows for a reason – surrounded by steep mountainsides, the bottom of the valley felt the direct touch of sunlight for only a couple of hours each day, and even then only on rare, cloud-free days in the summer. For much of the year Hag Graef was wrapped in a perpetual twilight. Far below in the city proper, she could see the faint, flickering gleam of witchfire globes, guttering like stars amid the currents of caustic night fog roiling in the streets.

'Silar is right,' she said thoughtfully. 'You are being too hasty, my lord. There are too many unknowns, too many things that can go wrong… We do not even know where this temple is. Somewhere in the Chaos Wastes? We could be gone for years – if we ever come back at all.'

'Nagaira claims that the relic will point to the location of the temple,' Malus said, 'and I would rather be raiding the Wastes than waiting here for the next temple assassin to take my head.'

'But surely we can wait for a few more days at least? Spend some coin and see what we can learn about Urial's tower to make a better plan–'

'We don't have a few days. We have to strike while Urial is out of his lair. We think he'll be at the temple for the next several nights, but the only night we can count on for certain is tonight. Isn't that right, Arleth?'

Arleth Vann stirred from the shadows in the far corner of the room. With his heavy black cloak pulled about him and the top of the broad cowl hanging down over his face, he was nearly invisible in the darkness. 'Yes,' he said reluctantly. 'Every supplicant in the city must attend the veneration ceremonies tonight, which last from sunset to sunrise.'

Malus caught Lhunara eyeing Arleth speculatively. Many in the warband suspected that the retainer had been involved with the temple at some point in his past. Arleth had good reason not to discuss his life before coming to Hag Graef, and Malus kept what he knew to himself. It was a worthwhile trade to gain a retainer of Arleth's particular skills.

'So you see, we've little time to prepare,' the highborn interjected, 'and my enemies are moving against me. If things get too far out of hand it's possible that Lurhan will exile me – or worse – rather than risk drawing the entire family into a blood feud. I do not have the resources, the *power*, to fight off these threats. It will be difficult enough just to equip this expedition, much less fight a house war against an alliance of petty nobles.' Malus pulled on a sleeping robe and went to the polished ashwood table near the foot of the bed. He picked up a jug of looted Bretonnian wine and filled the goblet standing alongside it. 'If this... relic... is half as fearsome as Nagaira seems to think it is, things will be very different here upon our return.'

'Do you truly plan to share it with her?' Silar asked.

'Only if I must,' Malus admitted, sipping his wine. 'And only until I'm certain I can master it myself. If I think I can wield it without her... well, the Wastes are a dangerous place, aren't they?'

Lhunara nodded to herself, spinning a web of stratagems and contingencies in her mind. 'How many men will she take with her?'

'Six, including that throat-cutter Dalvar. I'll be bringing six as well, including you and Vanhir. Silar, Dolthaic and Arleth Vann will remain here with the rest of the warband to keep watch over what little property I have left. I don't doubt Urial will retaliate in some fashion once he learns of the theft.'

'Don't take Vanhir,' Silar growled. 'He'll betray you if he can.'

'I agree,' Lhunara said, 'especially after your retribution on the road from Clar Karond. He hates you more now than ever.'

'Precisely why I want him where I can keep my eye on him,' Malus replied. 'He will keep his oath to the letter, to the last minute of the very last day. That's more than a month away. If we're still in the Wastes by then, it might be easier just to kill him, but until then he's one more sword I can use to achieve my ends.'

Lhunara folded her arms and turned back to the window, clearly unhappy with the idea. 'Do we take the nauglir, then?'

'Yes,' Malus said. 'I'll take teeth and claws over a horse's hooves any day. Besides, they can carry more gear and move further each day than a pack train of horses.'

'They'll also need to eat a lot more,' Lhunara pointed out.

Malus chuckled. 'Where we're going, I don't think we'll lack for bodies to feed to the cold ones. Dolthaic will have them saddled and ready in the stables as soon as we emerge from Urial's tower. I don't plan on staying here one more minute than I must once the deed is done.'

'I'm more interested in hearing how you're going to get in and out of Urial's tower,' Silar said.

Malus poured a second cupful of wine. 'No one knows for certain how many servants Urial has, nor how many retainers. He gets many of them from the temple, and they all wear those heavy robes and masks. He could have twenty or two hundred. Worse, Nagaira is certain his lair will be heavily guarded by magical wards and bound spirits. Even monsters, perhaps.'

The highborn glanced at Arleth Vann. The two locked eyes for a moment, then the retainer shrugged. 'It is possible,' Arleth Vann said. 'None but the priestesses know how far Urial has progressed in the mysteries of Khaine. He could be capable of a great many terrible things. It is even possible that his lair may no longer be… entirely of this realm.'

Lhunara took a step towards the cowled retainer. 'What does that mean?'

Arleth Vann's head bowed. Malus could see the tension in the line of his muscular shoulders and the stillness of his frame. 'Go, on, Arleth,' the highborn prodded.

'I can't say for certain. I don't even understand it fully, myself. But… there are places in the great temples, deep places where only the most holy may go, that bear witness to ancient rites and observances. Only the finest sacrifices are made there; there is no word spoken in that place that is not an offering to the Lord of Murder. It is a place where the highest priests go to look upon the visage of Khaine and his realm of slaughter. They thin the weave between worlds, until sometimes it becomes difficult to tell what is of this realm and what is not.'

Lhunara frowned. 'Now you're speaking in riddles.'

No, Lhunara, he isn't, Malus thought. But it's for the best that you don't understand, else I might have a mutiny on my hands. Considering the implications was like a cold knife twisting in his gut. 'Are you saying that his sanctum could be such a place?'

Arleth Vann looked up at the highborn's voice. The face beneath the hood was guarded, except for the eyes. They were bleak. 'It is possible,' he said. 'Nothing is certain with one such as him. He is bound by no law, in this world or the next.'

'From what you're both describing, this sounds like a fool's errand,' Lhunara snarled.

'Not so,' Malus said. 'Nagaira knows of a hidden way into the tower from the burrows–'

'The *burrows?*'

'Enough, woman! She will lead us into the burrows from an entrance elsewhere in the fortress, and then up into Urial's storerooms. She says she has talismans that will allow us to pass unnoticed through his wards and calm his unnatural sentries. Since she will be with us the entire time I have no doubt that she is certain of their power.'

'And if she's wrong, my lord?'

'Once inside,' he continued, ignoring her question, 'we will kill any servants or guards we encounter on the way to Urial's sanctum. If the Dark Mother smiles on us, that won't be necessary. Ideally, we will be able to slip in and out with no one the wiser. Nevertheless, once we get inside the sanctum we will have to move very quickly. Now, Nagaira does not know exactly what this relic looks like–'

Lhunara started to speak, her eyes going wide, but Malus silenced her with a sharp glare.

'But she is certain she will know it when she sees it. We will search the sanctum, locate the relic and depart the same way we arrived. With luck, we should not be inside the tower more than half an hour at most. Once we are back in the burrows we should be able to reach the stables within minutes, and be out of the Hag and on the Spear Road within the hour. By the time Urial returns and finds the relic gone we will be leagues away.'

'Leaving us to bear the brunt of his wrath,' Silar said, his voice full of dread.

Lhunara shook her head. 'I do not like this, my lord. It stinks too much of misadventure. If one thing goes wrong the whole plan could unravel, and then where would we be?'

'Not much worse off than we are now, Lhunara,' Malus replied coldly. 'The temple has been promised my head, and if my suspicions are correct, Urial was responsible for the ambush on the Slavers' Road. No,

I will not sit here and wait for the kiss of the axe. Urial owes me a debt of ruin, and I mean to collect it tonight. If I die in the attempt, then I will do it with a blade in my hand and blood in my teeth! Now go,' Malus said, draining his cup once more. 'Rest yourselves. We meet at Nagaira's tower tonight after the rising of the fog.'

As one, the retainers bowed and moved to the door. Silar was the last to depart. 'Do not tarry long in the Wastes, my lord,' he said with a rueful grin. 'There may be nothing left of us upon your return.'

'I know, noble Silar,' Malus answered. 'But fear not. I have a long, long memory and a pitiless heart. Whatever evil Urial wreaks on you I will repay him a hundredfold.'

Silar paused at the doorway, considering the highborn's words. Then, reassured, he left to see to his duties.

Chapter Six
FORSAKEN HALLS

THE NIGHT BROUGHT heavy clouds and a cold wind whistling through the spires of Hag Graef. More than a hundred feet above the castle courtyards, a heavily cloaked figure leaned slightly from a recessed doorway and studied the two bright moons gleaming over the eastern horizon.

After a moment, a patch of iron-grey cloud slid across the face of the moons, plunging the fortress into abyssal darkness. Without a sound the cloaked figure leapt from the doorway and glided like a spectre across the narrow stone bridge. Seven similarly cloaked figures followed, seemingly heedless of the vast gulf yawning beneath them. By the time the moons had shed their gauzy shroud the procession had disappeared into the tower at the other end of the span.

Once inside Nagaira's tower, Malus pulled back his woollen cowl and scrutinised the small group waiting for him in the passage just beyond the doorway. Tonight, he and his retainers were dressed for war: beneath the heavy, dark cloaks each druchii wore an articulated breastplate and a mail skirt over his dark leather kheitan. Pauldrons protected their shoulders, lending them a bulkier, more imposing silhouette, while their arms and legs were sheathed in articulated vambraces and greaves. Each piece of armour rested on a layer of felt to muffle the rattle of joints and plates and to help insulate the body from the cold steel. Malus and two of his retainers carried repeating crossbows under their cloaks along with their customary swords.

Nagaira's warriors were similarly equipped, surrounding their mistress like baleful crows. Several carried short throwing spears of a type Malus had never seen before, while others carried small repeating crossbows. They eyed the heavily-armed interlopers with clear suspicion – all but Dalvar, who spun one of his stilettos on an armoured fingertip and grinned mockingly at the newcomers.

Like Malus, Nagaira wore plate armour over her kheitan and robes and carried two swords at her hip. The bookish diffidence was gone, and Malus was surprised to see how much she resembled her fearsome father. She held out a gauntleted hand draped with seven leather thongs; from each thong hung a glittering object of silver and crystal the size of a druchii thumb.

'Wear these somewhere against your skin,' Nagaira said, her voice sharp and commanding. 'Once we are inside the tower, touch nothing unless I say so.'

Malus took the talismans without a word, picked one for himself and passed the rest on to his companions. On close inspection, each talisman was a small silver fist clutching a ball of crystal. The irregular crystal had somehow been fractured in such a way as to create a complex spiral within the centre of the stone. The silver hand was etched with dozens of tiny runes that defied easy identification. When he tried to focus on one, Malus's eyes began to blink and water as though someone had blown a handful of sand into them. He gave up trying after a moment and slipped the thong around his neck, then carefully tucked the talisman under the lip of his breastplate. It dug into his chest just underneath the armour plate and felt like a piece of trapped ice.

Nagaira watched carefully to make sure that each of the druchii followed her instructions. Once she was satisfied, she said, 'The entrance to the burrows is fairly close by. Once we're in the tunnels, stick close and keep your weapons ready. There are wild nauglir roaming down there, and worse. It won't take long to reach the tunnels underneath Urial's tower, but we may have to do some digging once we get there.'

The last part brought Malus up short. 'We *might* have to do some digging? You don't know anyone who's used this approach before?'

Nagaira shrugged. 'I don't know for certain that the entrance even exists. In theory, it should.'

'In *theory*?'

'You would rather storm the ground floor entrance, or climb the tower wall in full view of half the fortress?'

Dalvar's mocking grin widened. Malus dreamed of peeling the skin from his shrieking face. 'Lead on,' he hissed.

With a smug half-bow, Nagaira turned on her heel and led the raiding party down the long stairs to the ground floor of the tower. Like all the spires in the drachau's fortress, the tower could only be entered through a single pair of reinforced double doors that opened onto a short corridor leading deeper into the castle complex. When they reached the doors, Malus was surprised to find four of Nagaira's retainers in full armour, holding naked swords in their hands. Nagaira caught the expression on the highborn's face and gave a wolfish grin.

'I can't guarantee that Urial doesn't have agents of his own in my household,' she said, pulling her cowl over her head. 'So Kaltyr and his men are going to ensure that no one leaves the tower until dawn.' With that, she led the party out into the castle proper.

Over hundreds of years, the drachau's fortress – also referred to as the Hag by residents of the city – had grown almost like a living thing. Dwarf slaves were expensive and relatively rare, so many years could pass between opportunities for needed repairs and additions.

When a part of the castle fell into ruin, other sections were built over and around the wreckage, creating a madman's labyrinth of chaotic passageways, abandoned towers and walled-off courtyards. What had begun as a relatively small citadel with a single octagonal wall now covered more than a square mile of land and possessed four concentric defensive walls, each one built to enclose a new wave of expansion. It was said that no one person knew the fortress in its totality; new servants were often sent on errands into the sprawling grounds and not found again for days, if at all.

Nagaira led the cowled procession quickly and assuredly through a series of courtyards and execution grounds, swiftly leaving the more-populated precincts of the fortress behind for a region that showed signs of progressive abandonment. The farther they went, the more desolate and decrepit the surroundings appeared. They crossed over cracked, vine-covered flagstones and under leaning piles of rock that used to be walls or spires. At one point they were forced to climb over a pile of broken stone that was all that remained of a span linking two old towers. Small creatures scuttled through the shadows around them. At one point, traversing a larger, overgrown courtyard, something large hissed a warning at them from a pile of vine-covered rubbish. The druchii levelled their crossbows, but Nagaira waved impatiently for them to continue.

After a time, the raiders reached a section of the fortress that had clearly been abandoned for many decades. Crossing through a doorway stained with mould, Malus found himself in a large, rectangular space dominated by what appeared to be a huge hearth. After a moment he realised that he was standing in an old forge – the bellows and other wooden tools had long since rotted away.

Suddenly there was a flare of blue-green light; one of Nagaira's retainers handed her a shuttered lantern burning with pale witchfire. She held it aloft and turned in a quick circle, gaining her bearings. 'There,' she said, pointing to a corner of the room. 'Shift the rubbish aside. You'll find a trap door.'

For a moment, no one moved. Nagaira and her rogues eyed Malus and his band.

'Tired already?' Malus sneered, impatient at the petty contest of wills. 'Very well. Virhan, Eirus – open the trapdoor.' The men moved at once, throwing black looks at their erstwhile allies. Aided by Nagaira's lantern, the two retainers quickly located a pair of iron rings set into the floor. After several min-utes' effort, they managed to heave one of the doors open with a shriek of rusted hinges. Below was a nearly perfect circular tunnel that sank like a well deep into the earth.

According to legend, the burrows had been made several hundred years after the Hag was first built. One winter the earth trembled beneath the castle from sundown to sunrise each night. Flagstones heaved and sank and towers swayed beneath the moon. Nobles and slaves brave enough to venture into the castle cellars claimed to have heard a slow, deep groaning reverberating through soil and stone, and sometimes clouds of noxious fumes seeped through cracks in the ground and poisoned the unwary.

The strange episode ended as abruptly as it had begun on the first day of spring; later that summer a work crew rebuilding a collapsed tower discovered the first of the tunnels. Nearly perfectly round and bored through solid rock, the passages ran for miles, turning back on themselves again and again as though formed by a monstrous worm. No one ever found the creature – or creatures – that had formed the tunnels, though over the centuries a multitude of vermin had made the labyrinth their home.

There were small, crescent-shaped iron rungs bolted to one side of the tunnel wall. 'Remember: stay close,' she said, then stepped to the edge of the hole and started descending the rungs, holding the lantern below her as she went. Dalvar stepped quickly up behind her, but Malus froze him in his tracks with a forbidding look and went next instead, crossbow held ready.

After about twenty feet the passage began to curve back towards the surface, until finally the rungs came to an end and Malus could stand upright. He stood beside Nagaira as they waited for the rest of the band to make their way down. The only sounds in the echoing space were the scuffing of boot heels on iron and the distant echo of dripping water. At one point he stole a glance at his half-sister, but he could see nothing of her expression in the shadowy depths of her cowl – only the tip of her chin and a flash of her pale throat. The edges of her spiral tattoo now crept up the side of her neck – in the unsteady light it seemed to pulse and shift with a life all its own.

As the raiding party sorted itself out, Malus organised his retainers with subtle nods and gestures to intermingle themselves with Nagaira's men. If the two sides couldn't extricate themselves from one another very easily, they couldn't sacrifice the other at the first sign of trouble.

It was clear to Malus that the burrows were not made by a thinking being – or at least, not a sane one. They were rarely level, plunging and ascending, curving, intersecting and re-intersecting themselves again and again to no evident purpose. Progress was slow, though Nagaira seemed to know exactly where she was going. If there were clues or markers that pointed the way, Malus could not fathom them. A slow tide of unease began to eat at the edges of his steely resolve, but he fought it back with a surge of black hatred. I will prevail, he thought angrily. So long as I have my sword and my wits about me I will not fail.

The raiding party worked their way through the tunnels in silence, their nerves taut and their senses sharp. The air was musty and damp, and a gelid slime covered many of the curved walls. Frequently their booted feet crunched over piles of old, brittle bones. Malus bared his teeth at every sound, wondering what creatures might be drawn to investigate the noise.

There were numerous points where the burrows rose towards the surface and encountered the foundations of the fortress above. Sometimes the tunnel passed through an abandoned cellar or dungeon – in such cases Malus saw the remains of crates, tables and ironwork crushed flat along the burrower's passage. They crossed through several such chambers, each one as deserted as the one before, and the highborn began to relax a little. That was when they nearly stumbled into a deadly trap.

The raiding party had stumbled onto yet another large chamber – it was so wide Malus thought at first that the burrow had intersected a natural cavern, until he noticed the fitted paving stones underneath his boots. The flare of Nagaira's witchlight could not reach the walls or ceiling of the huge space. The parts of the floor Malus could see were strewn with refuse almost ankle deep. He saw bits of bone and old clothes, rusted tools, leather goods and scraps of what might have been withered flesh, plus many more less recognisable items.

Nagaira led the party deeper into the chamber, stepping carefully through the piled debris. She paused to get her bearings, which was when Malus heard the rustling. It was very quiet, almost like the patter of many small feet, but there was something very strange about the sound that the highborn couldn't place. He raised his hand in warning. 'No one move,' he whispered. 'There's something here.'

The druchii paused, their heads turning this way and that as they strained to detect the slightest movement in the darkness surrounding them. The rustling came again – a rapid patter of tiny feet somewhere ahead of them. A pile of refuse was knocked over, scattering what sounded like bits of crockery and loose rock across the chamber. Small feet but a large body, Malus thought. And it's trying to circle behind us. Then the pattering sounds came again – but from the other side of the group. More than one, the highborn realised. But how many?

Now the druchii were shifting uneasily, the wary looks on their ghostly faces suggesting that they were thinking along much the same lines as Malus. Lhunara edged slightly closer to the highborn, her twin swords held ready.

Malus heard the rustling again, much louder and quicker this time – only it came from *directly overhead*.

Nagaira let out a cry, and her globe of witchlight suddenly flared like a bonfire, driving back the darkness. Malus's eyes narrowed against the glare, and he saw that they were standing in an expansive cellar nearly twenty yards to a side, piled with the rotting remains of casks, crates and shelves. Pale, hairy cave spiders the size of ponies scuttled amongst the refuse or reared up aggressively at the sudden burst of light. Their eyes were the colour of fresh blood, and dark fangs as long as daggers dripped with venom as the scent of fresh meat drove them wild with hunger.

Shouts of alarm went up from the druchii, and Malus tried to look in every direction at once as he struggled to get a sense of how many spiders there were. Five? Six? They were moving too fast, and there were too many pools of shadow to keep track of them all. The highborn raised his crossbow and sighted on the nearest one – but the shot went wild as Lhunara knocked him forwards and out of the path of the spider who pounced from the chamber's high ceiling.

Malus rolled onto his back as the rest of the spider pack charged the druchii. Lhunara had gone down beneath the body of the falling spider, and the highborn watched as the creature's mandibles jabbed again and again at the retainer's armoured form, looking for a weak spot to inject its load of venom. He dropped the crossbow and drew his sword just as the point of one of Lhunara's blade's punched through the back of the spider's thorax. The second sword flashed in a short arc, severing one of the creature's fangs in a spurt of greenish poison. The spider seemed to constrict into a ball, its legs closing around its prey, but Malus leapt forward, severing three of the limbs with a single, sweeping cut. Lhunara's swords flickered again in the witchlight, and the body of the spider, now missing the rest of its limbs, fell off to one side.

The highborn reached down and grabbed his retainer by her forearm, pulling her roughly to her feet. 'Are you wounded?'

'No,' Lhunara said, shaking her head. Blobs of venom ran down the front of her breastplate. 'It was close, though.'

Malus looked about wildly, searching for the other spiders. Once the druchii had recovered from their initial surprise, they had reacted with customary savagery. Two of the spiders had fallen prey to the short spears of Nagaira's warriors, pierced through and through in their headlong charge. Two others had been surrounded and hacked to pieces, their soft bodies no match for steel blades. The fifth spider lay at Nagaira's feet, slowly dissolving into a steaming pile of mush as Malus's half-sister stoppered a now-empty flask and returned it to a pouch at her belt.

The encounter had lasted less than a minute, and none of the druchii had been injured, but had it not been for Nagaira's flare, things might have turned out very differently indeed. She turned away from the dissolving spider and sought the tunnel leading out of the chamber. 'That way,' she said, pointing across the room, and set off as though nothing untoward had happened.

Malus retrieved his crossbow and reloaded it. 'Everyone stick close,' he said to the assembled druchii. 'And don't forget to look up.'

THEY WALKED ON for nearly an hour more, cautiously traversing several more dark and abandoned cellars and storerooms. Finally, at the opening to one such chamber Nagaira stopped, her hand raised in warning. 'We are here,' she said quietly.

Malus drew back his hood and shrugged the cloak over both shoulders. The rest of the raiders did the same, exchanging stealth for visibility and ease of movement. Swords hissed from their scabbards.

Nagaira extended her hand, palm out, towards the opening, moving in a widening circle as if getting the sense of the shape of an invisible structure. Slowly, as if pushing against a strong wind, she crossed the threshold into the room. Malus turned back to the raiders. 'Remember, touch nothing. Kill silently, and leave no witnesses behind.' Then he stepped across the threshold.

The highborn fought down a gasp at the shock of cold – and the sense of profound unease – that washed over him as he stepped through the portal. It was like pushing through a caul of living flesh, a barrier that yielded to his will yet somehow seemed alive and aware.

When he came to his senses, he was standing in a room that must have once been a cellar. Like the other chambers, there was a path of crushed furniture and masonry outlining the course of the maddened burrower, but otherwise the room was bare. A spiral stair wound around the perimeter of the room, ending at a small landing and a door of dark iron.

There was something wrong about the room. Malus couldn't quite place it at first. Then, as the next druchii stepped into the room with an audible cry of surprise, he realised – there were no echoes in the stone room. The sound was simply swallowed up, as if they stood at the verge of an endless abyss. When he studied the walls, formed of huge stone blocks, he could not shake the sense that they were somehow porous – as if he could poke through them with his finger into something just beyond. He could not shake the sensation, no matter how solid the stones appeared to his eyes.

One by one the raiders crossed into the room; each one was affected in the same fashion. Only Nagaira seemed untouched. 'We are through the tower's first set of wards,' she whispered as she began to climb the stairs, I expect there will be one or two others as we near Urial's sanctum. Beyond each threshold things will be more... unsettled... than the one before.'

Nagaira reached the iron door. Centuries of disuse had turned the door handle and hinges to barely recognisable lumps of rust. The druchii pulled a small vial from a pouch at her belt and scattered droplets of a silvery liquid across the door's surface. Where they struck, stains of crimson bloomed, spreading rapidly like great wounds across the pitted metal. There was a brittle tinkling sound, and all at once the door collapsed in a darkening pile of rust.

As she was returning the vial to her pouch, Malus moved nimbly past his sister and took the lead on the stair that rose beyond the doorway. Nagaira's head came up, a sharp rebuke on her lips, but Malus shook his head. 'We can't afford to have you walk into an ambush,' he said gravely. 'Better you keep to the centre of the group.' And leave me to issue the commands, Malus thought smugly. 'Dalvar, look to your mistress.'

Before she or Dalvar could reply, Malus turned and crept up the stairs. The climb lasted more than a minute, passing several landings along the way – if Nagaira was any indication, he expected Urial's sanctum to be at the top of his spire – until the stairway ended in another door. This one was in far better condition than its companion in the lower cellar.

Just as he was reaching for the door's iron ring, it swung open from the other side.

A human slave, his emaciated face covered in scars and open sores, saw Malus and opened his mouth to scream. The highborn moved without thinking, raising his crossbow and firing a bolt point-blank through the startled 'O' of the man's scabbed lips.

There was a crunch as the steel head of the bolt punched through the man's spine and part of his skull, and he collapsed without a sound. There was a gasp just beyond the dead slave, and Malus caught a glimpse of a female slave raising a trembling hand to the spatters of blood and brain covering her face. Without hesitation Malus worked the steel lever that drew back the crossbow's powerful string and loaded another bolt into the track. Just as the slave overcame her shock and turned to run, a scream bubbling from her lips, Malus took aim and buried a black-fletched bolt between her shoulder blades. The highborn was readying another shot even as he leapt past her fallen body into the space beyond the door.

He was in a small, dimly lit chamber, with a stone floor incised with carvings of skulls and intricate, sharp-edged runes. What illumination there was seemed to seep from the walls themselves – a dark, crimson glow like banked embers that plucked at the corners of his eyes and seemed to ebb and flow like the surge of blood in some great heart. Silhouetted in the bloody light were smooth-featured faces shaped of some silvery metal inset into the walls. Some snarled, others leered, still others exuded a soulless calm. Their eyes were nothing more than black pits, yet Malus could feel the weight of their stares against his skin. The feeling sent a chill down his spine and set his teeth on edge.

There were three sets of double doors, all closed, and another flight of stairs leading higher up the spire. Malus suspected that they were at the ground floor of the tower, but he was disturbed to discover that his sense of direction had failed him. He could not tell where he was in relation to the rest of the fortress, something he'd never experienced before.

Nagaira stepped over the bodies of the slaves and dashed across the room. 'Did they see you?'

Malus frowned. 'Who?'

'The faces! Did they see you kill the slaves?'

'Did they see me? How should I know, woman?' Damned sorcery! He'd already had his fill of the place.

Nagaira eyed the silvery faces warily. Her eyes shifted from one to the other, almost as though she were following something that moved behind the wall, peering out at them through the black eye sockets. 'We must be very careful how we spill blood in this place,' she whispered. 'The wards here are very potent. If we draw attention to ourselves the tower's guardians may see through my protective talismans.'

Malus hissed in aggravation. Two of the raiding party were rolling the bodies of the slaves down the spiral staircase, but there was no way to know how quickly they would be missed. An alarm could be raised at any time. I wonder if Urial would feel such a thing, all the way over at the temple? He bit back a curse. No time to worry about that now. Malus reloaded his crossbow and hurried for the stairs.

The stairs curved upwards into darkness. Malus pressed his back to the inside wall of the staircase and moved stealthily ahead, his ears straining for the sounds of movement. The stone at his back was warm, like a living body. He could feel it seeping through his cloak and the back plate of his armour. The highborn continued his ascent, past two landings with dark, ironbound doors.

Between the second and third landings Malus heard a door open and the sound of footsteps descending the stairs. He shifted the crossbow to his left hand and froze, raising his right hand to warn the column. Moments later, a slave came around the bend of the staircase, hurrying on some errand. Quick as a snake, Malus grabbed the slave's right sleeve and pulled, dragging the human off his feet. The slave's body tumbled down the stairs past him, bouncing off the stones. The highborn heard the sounds of steel against flesh, and then silence. After a moment, Malus pressed on.

The staircase ended at the third landing. Malus saw that the doorway here was more ornate than the ones he'd seen before, carved with numerous sigils and inset with three of the silvery faces along the arch. He felt their empty gaze upon him as he took the door's iron ring in his hand and pulled it open. The space beyond was even more dimly lit than the landing itself. Holding the crossbow ready, he eased through the doorway – and passed through another protective ward.

This time the magic caul was even harder to push through. When it parted, the transition was so sudden he stumbled forward several steps and felt the surface of the floor give slightly under his weight. The air was close and humid, but the moisture didn't settle on his skin. The stench of rotting blood hung in the dimness. Distantly, he thought he could hear screams, but when he tried to focus on them he could not make out where they were coming from. The walls of a narrow corridor closed around him, yet he felt as though he stood on the edge of a great plain. His mind warred with the conflicting sensations, and he swayed on his feet.

Nagaira stepped through next. Malus noticed that her small strides made a thick, squishing sound, as though she stepped over rain-soaked ground. She seemed unaffected by the forces at work around her. Her lantern was shuttered, yet Malus could see her face quite clearly in the gloom, as if she stood apart from the darkness around her. The other druchii staggered through the doorway, and the highborn found he could see them clearly as well.

'Hurry now!' Nagaira commanded the dazed retainers. 'We are nearly there.' She once again resumed the lead, heading off down the passage, and Malus found he hadn't the presence of mind to protest. He felt a flash of anger – and surprisingly, his mind became clearer. Very well, he thought. Let hatred be my guide.

Malus focused on Nagaira's back as she led them through the gloom. He had a sense of walls and doorways, of turning corners and ascending steps, but they were only vague sensations, dimly felt. With every step he focused on his age-old hatreds, on all the different ways he dreamt that his family would suffer for the insults they'd done to him. With every step he dreamt of the glory that was his due. I will be Vaulkhar. Not Bruglir. Not Isilvar. I will destroy them all and pluck the scourge from my father's stiffening fingers, and then this city will learn to fear me as they have no other!

He saw Nagaira float through an archway made of bleached, blood-streaked skulls. Malus followed her into a small, octagonal room formed of huge blocks of basalt. Another set of double doors stood at the opposite end of the room, the pointed arch crowned with a trio of snarling, silvery faces. The screams were louder here, punctuated by a chorus of ringing tones, like the sound of steel striking bone. The floor was awash in congealing gore, sticking to the soles of his boots.

Nagaira crossed the room and grasped the door's iron ring. She turned to say something to him. Suddenly the air shook with ululating howls as three misshapen figures emerged from the inky depths of the very walls.

Chapter Seven
FLIGHT FROM THE TOWER

THE MONSTERS WERE scabrous, bloody things, with lashing, segmented tails and an odd number of clawed, disjointed legs. They hurled themselves at the invaders, their bulbous, blind heads splitting wide to reveal rows of jagged, saw-edged teeth.

The druchii cried out as one, and at that moment the room seemed to snap into focus. Crossbows thumped, and black fletching sprouted from the chests of two of the twisted creatures. Malus raised his crossbow and shot one-handed, burying a bolt in the third monster's misshapen skull before the beasts were among them. The highborn dropped the crossbow and drew his sword just as the creature he'd shot leapt at him.

Jagged teeth slicked with poisonous slime snapped shut mere inches from his head as Malus ducked to one side and drove the point of his sword into the monster's flank. Black ichor bubbled from the wound, and the beast let out a discordant howl as it flashed past. Its stinger-tipped tail smashed into his left pauldron, half-spinning him around. A gob of venom struck the armour and began to sizzle, filling his nostrils with an acrid stench.

The creature landed, gathered itself and spun – but Malus leapt at it, slashing for its head. The beast shied to one side, and the keen sword sliced through one of the monster's forelegs instead. Again the tail flicked out at him, but the creature's aim was off; the black stinger, long as a dagger, blurred past the highborn's face.

Howling, the monster began to circle to his right, dragging the stump of its foreleg across the gore-stained floor. Steeling himself, Malus feinted with a thrust to the beast's head. The tail flicked out and the highborn pivoted, letting it slide past, and then severed it with a backhanded stroke of his sword. Ichor pumped from the gaping wound, and the creature roared and gibbered with rage.

Pressing his advantage, Malus rushed at the beast, and in an eye blink the blind head ducked low and closed its jaws on Malus's armoured calf. For the moment the curved plates held. Malus shouted a vicious oath and brought his sword down on the monster's thick neck. The blow sliced halfway through the thickly-muscled trunk, and he felt the beast's jaws slacken their grip. Another blow and the creature's headless body was thrashing in a spreading pool of black ichor. Another stroke cracked the monster's jaw and he shook the head loose from his leg with a savage kick.

Reeling a little, Malus took in his surroundings. One of the raiders had pinned a monster to the floor with one of his short spears and two other druchii were methodically hacking the creature apart. Lhunara stood over the second beast, wiping her ichor-stained sword on the monster's hide. One of Nagaira's men leaned against one of the walls, pressing his palm to a wound in his side.

The highborn turned to Nagaira. 'What now?'

'Urial's sanctum lies just beyond,' she replied, still holding the door's iron ring. Malus realised with a start that she hadn't moved so much as an inch during the whole struggle, and the sorcerous creatures had somehow ignored her. 'There is one last ward,' she continued. 'Things beyond will be... unnatural. Perhaps it is best that I go on alone.'

'No,' he said, surprised to find his voice had grown hoarse. Had he been shouting? 'If you go, dear sister, then so do I. The others may remain here.'

Nagaira's face showed a momentary flash of anger, then she quickly composed herself. With a mocking flourish, she pulled the double doors wide. Beyond was nothing but darkness.

'After you,' she said coldly. 'We can't afford for me to be injured, after all.'

The sense of disorientation was returning as the druchii's anger began to wane. Malus's fist tightened on the hilt of his sword. 'Do not tarry, sister,' he said through clenched teeth, and then rushed through the doorway.

THE PAIN WAS like nothing he had ever felt before.

There was no sensation of resistance; he crossed the threshold and felt himself tear from within. Malus fell to his knees with an angry cry, and blood pooled from the spongy floor around his greaves.

The pain went on and on. Trembling, he clenched his fists, focusing on them – and saw a drop of crimson splash on his right knuckle. He brought his hand to his face, and it came away slick and red. Blood was weeping from his skin, soaking through the robes beneath his kheitan.

The chamber was suffused with reddish light. Pillars of bloody skulls stretched from floor to ceiling, framing more than half-a-dozen alcoves around the irregularly-shaped room. Directly ahead of him, Malus could see an altar formed from severed heads. As he watched, he saw mouths gape and mumble, trying to form words of fear or exaltation. Upon the altar rested a huge tome bound in pale leather. Its pages, made from fine human parchment, curled and rustled in a nonexistent wind.

He could not see the walls of the chamber. Malus knew, even as his mind rebelled against it, that space had no meaning in the place where he now stood. His guts clenched, and he vomited blood and bile.

A hand twisted in his hair. Nagaira pulled him roughly to his feet. 'I warned you, brother,' she said, her voice reverberating in his ears like the clashing of cymbals. 'We stand at the edge of a whirlwind that hungers for the living. Only those anointed by the god of slaughter can survive here unscathed.' As she spoke, a single, red tear ran down her pale cheek. 'Do not touch the book upon the altar. Do not even look at it. We must pass beyond into the alcoves yonder. The thing we seek lies there.'

Malus shook his head free with a snarl and lurched past the altar. There were three alcoves in a tight cluster just beyond, each one with a shelf populated by a collection of arcane items. On instinct, he staggered to the one in the centre. There, resting on a tripod of iron, sat an ancient, misshapen skull. The yellowed bone was covered in hundreds of tiny, incised runes and bound with a mesh of silver wire. Even in his wretched state, Malus could sense the power radiating from this artefact – the empty eye sockets seemed to regard him with malevolent awareness. Next to the tripod rested a small book, a quill and a bottle of ink.

'Take it,' Nagaira commanded, her voice strained.

Malus took a pained breath, tasting blood in his mouth, and took the skull in his trembling hands. As he was about to turn away, the highborn impulsively snatched the book as well, tucking the volume into his belt. Nagaira, her face a mask of crimson, had already retreated back to the doorway. 'Hurry!' she said. He noticed that she was pressing something small into one of the pouches at her belt. What had she stolen while his back was turned?

Nagaira leapt through the doorway as he approached, and Malus followed, directly on her heels.

He emerged into the octagonal chamber to cries of alarm from Lhunara and his other retainers. Before he could say a word, however, the air was rent with a chorus of thin, unearthly wails that emanated from the doorway behind him.

Malus spun, his sword ready, but the doorway was empty. Instead, just above his head, he saw three misty shapes streaming from the eyes and mouth of each of the silver masks. As he watched, the mists took the shape of small, thin-limbed figures with long, almost skeletal fingers. Their faces were druchii-like, but their eyes were solid black.

'Blessed Mother of Darkness,' Nagaira whispered, her voice full of fear. 'The maelithii! Run!'

At the sound of their name, the maelithii howled like the souls of the damned, showing mouths full of glittering black fangs. The very air reverberated like a struck gong. An alarm, Malus thought wildly. One of us triggered it. Was it you, Nagaira? Your greed may be our undoing! He swung his sword at one of the spirits. The blade passed harmlessly through it, but a shock of freezing cold shot up his sword arm, as though he'd plunged it into an icy river. The maelithii hissed hungrily at him, and Malus turned on his heel and ran. Nagaira was already moving, fleet as a deer, and the rest of the raiding party bolted after them.

It was all Malus could do to stay focused on Nagaira's retreating form as she plunged through the gloom. A quick look over his shoulder revealed that they had either left the maelithii behind or the spirits had abandoned their pursuit. Hardly daring to trust his luck, the highborn plunged on, feeling sensation return to his numbed arm.

They reached the second ward in minutes. Nagaira stopped at the threshold and put out a warning hand to Malus as he approached. 'Send another through,' she said. 'I don't care who.'

Malus turned to the first retainer who caught up to them, one of his own druchii named Aricar. 'Go!' he commanded, pointing at the doorway, and without hesitation the warrior dove through.

The maelithii pounced on Aricar just on the other side of the door. It was the masks, Malus realised. The spirits could travel from mask to mask throughout the tower.

Aricar staggered as the spirits sank their obsidian teeth into his face and neck. He spun, hands lashing at empty air, but Malus could see the skin around where the spirits bit turn bluish-grey, like a corpse left out in the snow.

'Now!' Nagaira shouted. 'While they're feeding! Run!'

Without hesitation, the highborn plunged across the threshold. At once, it felt as though a crushing weight slipped from his shoulders. Aricar had fallen to his knees, his eyes wide. His breath came in choking, misty gasps through cracked, blue-black lips. Malus pushed past the dying man, thinking of all the silver masks lining the walls at the bottom of the tower. He hoped there were only the three maelithii.

Malus bolted down the curving staircase, hearing shouts echoing from below. Four silver-masked retainers came around the turn, swords in hand. The highborn barrelled into them with an angry cry, hacking left and right with his sword.

Urial's retainers were as swift as nighthawks. With preternatural agility they halted their charge up the stairs and gave way slightly in the face of Malus's charge. They weren't retreating, however – merely opening the distance enough to bring their swords to bear on the highborn. Malus lashed viciously at the retainer to his left, aiming savage blows at his head and neck, but the man blocked one blow with a ringing stroke of his sword and ducked the other, then struck like a viper at one of the articulated lames in the highborn's breastplate. At the last second Malus twisted his whole body, causing the retainer's sword to glance along his breastplate instead of digging in and sinking into his stomach.

There was a glint of silver to his right, followed by the sharp scratch of what felt like a red-hot claw just above his temple. His sudden motion had saved his life from more than one blow, as the retainer to his right had been aiming for his forehead.

Blessed Mother, they're fast, Malus thought. Whatever else his faults may be, Urial knows how to choose his men. The highborn feinted at the retainer to his left, jabbing at the man's eyes – and then Lhunara was beside him, her twin blades flickering like lightning at the man to Malus's right. No longer forced to deal with both men at once, the highborn grinned savagely and bent himself to the destruction of the man on his left.

The narrow staircase rang with the sounds of clashing blades. The silver-masked warrior was a master with the sword, blocking the highborn's every attack with fluid speed and power. Despite Malus's slight advantage of fighting from a higher step and raining blows on the retainer's head, neck and shoulders, the warrior had a countermove for the highborn's every tactic. Well, he thought, as Surhan, his childhood swordmaster had often said: when they're better at the game than you are, change the rules.

Malus let out a roar and brought a vicious blow down towards the top of the retainer's head. The warrior easily blocked the blow – and Malus kicked him hard in the face. The silver mask crumpled beneath the blow and the man staggered backwards. Pressing his advantage, Malus lunged forwards and sliced open the retainer's sword arm from wrist to elbow. A stream of bright red blood sprayed across the stones of the stairwell, but the retainer made no sound.

Another body went tumbling down the stairwell – Lhunara's foe collapsed, blood pouring over his hand as he clutched futilely at his slashed throat. She advanced a step towards the next man in the group, and in passing lashed out with her left-hand sword. Malus's opponent saw the blow at the last moment and twisted away from the sword, catching only a glancing blow against the side of his head, but it was a fatal distraction. Malus brought his sword down on the opposite side of the man's neck, shearing deep and severing the retainer's spine. He collapsed in a heap, his sword tumbling end-to-end down the stairs.

The retainer behind the dead man had to dodge to the side to avoid the falling corpse, and Malus took advantage of the moment, stabbing his sword at the man's eyes. The warrior dodged the blow with a jerk of his head and chopped viciously at Malus's knee. The blade slammed into the armoured joint of his greave, and a thrill of fear raced along the highborn's spine as he thought the metal might fail. But the joint held, and Malus brought his sword down on the retainer's sword wrist, shearing neatly through the limb. Blood sprayed across Malus's legs and feet, but the retainer didn't give up the fight.

To Malus's surprise, the retainer grabbed for his lost sword with his other hand, all but oblivious to the terrible wound he'd received. Moving swiftly, the highborn stepped on the flat of the retainer's blade and thrust his own sword into the warrior's neck. Steel grated on bone and the warrior collapsed, sliding down the stairs in a welter of his own blood. Lhunara was drawing her right-hand sword from the chest of her second foe, and for the moment the way ahead was clear. Raising his sword, Malus rushed down the stairs.

At the next landing a knot of slaves leapt from his path, wailing in fear. He sped past, but just as he turned the next curve he slowed abruptly. Ahead, just out of sight around the turn, he could hear the thin keening of the maelithii – not just three of them but, judging by the sound, a whole pack.

The highborn's mind raced as Nagaira and the rest of the retainers caught up with him. The wailing of the spirits and the cries of the slaves at the landing above made for a discordant chorus. Malus gritted his teeth in irritation. He was half-tempted to send one of the men back upstairs to start cutting throats so he could hear himself think–

Malus straightened. He turned back to the assembled raiders, seeking out Lhunara's scarred face. 'Take two men and bring me those slaves,' he ordered. She gave him a sharp nod and took two of his men back up the stairs. Within moments the wailing of the humans changed pitch, turning from fear into near-hysterical terror.

Rough hands pushed the humans down past the group of raiders. The lead slave, a scrawny human with wide, stupid eyes, tried to recoil from Malus as the highborn reached for him, but the druchii was much too fast. He took the slave by the shoulder, plunged his sword into the human's chest, then hurled the body down the stairs. The wounded man plunged out of sight, and the keening chorus below went silent.

'That's it!' Malus said with a feral grin. 'Cut their throats and hurl them down the stairs! Quickly!'

In moments the bodies of the rest of the slaves tumbled down the stairs. 'Now run!' Malus cried, rushing after them.

The corpses made a bloody pile at the bottom of the stairs, their blood freezing into a black sheet of ice as almost a dozen maelithii swarmed over their rapidly-cooling forms. Malus leapt off the stairs into the room and bolted for the first set of double doors.

'What are you doing?' Nagaira cried. 'The burrows–'

'The burrows be damned!' Malus snarled, dragging the doors open. Beyond lay a short corridor that, to his relief, led into the drachau's fortress. Praying the maelithii could not travel out of Urial's tower, he bolted down the passage.

The far end of the corridor opened onto a small courtyard. A light snow was falling, blowing in fine drifts across the cobblestones. Malus paused, gasping in the freezing air. A pair of druchii highborn conversing at the other end of the courtyard reached for their swords as the raiding party came to a halt outside Urial's spire, but one look at the raiders' stained armour and frenzied expressions convinced them that this was something they wanted no part of. They faded quickly into the shadows as Nagaira and Dalvar appeared, bringing up the rear.

Malus gave his half-sister a baleful look. 'You stupid witch!' he snarled. 'What did you take from the sanctum?'

'I took what I pleased, brother,' she shot back. 'Is that not the right of the plunderer? If anything triggered Urial's trap, it was most likely your theft of the skull!'

'Does it matter at this point?' Lhunara cried. 'Urial could be here at any time, with a troop of the drachau's guard with him. We need to get to the stables and get out of here before someone orders the gates closed.'

'She's right,' Nagaira said. 'If you move quickly you may just escape–'

'Me?' Malus said. 'What about you?'

'I have to get back to my tower,' Nagaira replied. 'Urial will waste no time uncovering who attacked his sanctum and made off with his prize. He'll call upon all the forces at his command to try and recover the skull. If I stay behind I can call on forces of my own to conceal your trail and at least slow any pursuit.' She eyed her men. 'Dalvar, you will take the rest of the men with Malus. See to it that he reaches the temple. Do you understand?'

'Of course, mistress,' Dalvar replied, clearly unhappy with the order.

Malus's mind whirled. Things had gotten completely out of hand. Was Nagaira abandoning him to Urial's wrath? His brother would find Aricar's body, and that would lead him to Malus. Nothing as yet pointed towards Nagaira's involvement in the raid. Malus considered his options. Did it matter?

Let her go, the highborn thought. I still have the skull. 'Go then,' he spat. 'I will reach the temple and return when I can. Then we'll meet again.' By then I'll have thought of a hundred ways to make you pay for this, he promised.

If Nagaira sensed the hatred in his voice, she gave no sign of it. 'Until then, Malus. I will be waiting.' Then she turned and raced off towards her tower, quickly disappearing from sight.

Malus straightened wearily, his bloody cheeks stiff from the cold. In the distance he could hear shouts and the blowing of the horn from the Hag's city gate. Someone was coming through in a hurry. He sheathed his sword and resettled his cloak around his shoulders. 'To the stables,' he ordered, pulling his cloak over his head. 'I want to be a league from the Hag before Urial realises who trespassed in his tower.'

of mist that attacked his nostrils and eyes.

Chapter Eight
RIDERS ON THE ROAD

THE AIR REEKED of scorched iron and the seared flesh of slaves. The caustic night fog of Hag Graef swirled and eddied in the roads and alleys, a thick greenish-yellow pall that oozed down into the valley from the chimney vents of the forges on the mountain slopes above. Silver steel, the precious, semi-magical metal prized by the druchii, was difficult and expensive to make, and thousands of slaves died every year around the great crucibles, their throats and lungs ravaged by the poisonous fumes.

Malus wore a nightmask of black iron worked in the shape of a snarling nauglir, his cloak pulled close around his head to keep the fog from his neck and scalp. His cold one, Spite, loped along the Spear Road at a steady, ground-eating pace. Occasionally he would toss his head and snap at the stinging clouds of mist that attacked his nostrils and eyes.

They had slipped from the drachau's fortress without incident, swinging into the saddles and setting off as soon as they reached the stables. Malus knew that the drachau would take no personal interest in a family feud – the highborn were encouraged to fight amongst themselves, ensuring that the strongest and smartest survived to fight for the Witch King. Yet it was possible that Urial had enough influence at court to order the gates of the city closed against him. Trapped within the city, he could much more easily be located and retaliated against. Urial could conceivably turn him over to the Temple of Khaine, ensuring an agonising death for his half-brother and gaining increased favour from the priestesses besides.

Speed was of the essence. Right now, Malus imagined Urial restoring order and having the entire tower searched while he rushed to his sanctum to ensure that his most precious relics were safe. When he realised the skull was missing, Urial would spare no effort to keep the thieves from escaping.

How long, Malus wondered? How long until his brother realised what had happened? How quickly will he react?

The city's north gate, also known as Spear Gate, was just ahead. Normally reserved solely for military traffic heading north to the watchtowers near the Chaos Wastes, it was the closest way out of the city. Malus turned in his saddle to look back along his small column of riders. The druchii who'd been stung by one of Urial's guard beasts, a man named Atalvyr, was getting steadily worse as the creature's poison ravaged his body. They'd stuck a cloth in the wound and lashed Atalvyr to his saddle. He hoped the guard-captain at the gate wouldn't inspect the warriors too closely and wonder why they were leaving for the frontier with a wounded man in the column.

Snow was still falling from the leaden sky, turning to mist as it descended through the currents of warm night fog. The city wall gained definition as they approached, resolving itself from a looming, dark grey band into a smooth, black barrier some thirty feet high and crowned with spiked merlons all along its length. The north gatehouse was well lit with witchfire globes, gleaming like the eyes of a huge, patient predator. The maw-like opening of the great gate was shut against the darkness outside.

Malus was nearly beneath the gatehouse's massive overhang when a muffled voice from above cried, 'Halt! Who goes there?'

The highborn reined in Spite, raising a hand to halt the column. 'I am Malus, son of Lurhan the Vaulkhar!' Malus shouted up at the invisible sentry.

For a moment, there was no reply. Then: 'The gate is closed for the night, dread lord. What is your business?'

Malus gritted his teeth in aggravation. 'My father has ordered me to lead a party of men north to the Tower of Ghrond, and to go with all haste.'

This time the silence stretched uncomfortably long. They're trying to make heads or tails of the situation, Malus thought. On the one hand, it meant they have no specific orders concerning him. On the other hand, the longer they dithered, the greater the chance that such orders could arrive. He straightened in the saddle. 'Will you make me wait here until dawn?' he cried. 'Open the gate, damn you!'

The echoes of his shout were still reverberating from the walls when there was a rattle of metal at one of the gatehouse's doors, and a guard captain in full armour stepped into view. Spite hissed menacingly and took a half-step towards the man before Malus jerked the nauglir's head aside with a pull of the reins. 'Stand,' Malus ordered, and the cold one settled onto its haunches. The highborn slid smoothly from the saddle, throwing a glance over his shoulder to Lhunara, who was second in the column. Her expression was inscrutable behind her nightmask, but her hands hovered close to the crossbow hooked to her saddle.

Malus walked over to the guard captain, pulling aside his iron mask so that his impatience was clearly evident. 'I've had men skinned alive for making me wait this long,' he said with an air of casual malevolence.

The guard captain was no callow recruit, however; his pale, scarred face regarded Malus impassively. 'We don't open the gate after nightfall, dread lord,' he said calmly. 'Orders from your father the Vaulkhar. It's been that way since the start of the feud with Naggor.'

The highborn's eyes narrowed appraisingly. You could have told me that from behind a firing slit, he thought. What are you really after, captain? 'I'm certain Lurhan is well aware of the standing orders, captain. I'd also say that if anyone can make exceptions to those orders, it would be him.' He lowered his voice. 'Is there anything I can offer you as proof?'

The captain inclined his head thoughtfully, studying the gatehouse overhang. They were both outside the line of sight of the guards above. 'Well,' he said, running his tongue along carefully filed front teeth. 'If you could show me some written orders, dread lord... or some other proof of authority...'

Malus smiled mirthlessly. 'Of course.' I ought to ram my dagger through your eye, he thought brutally, but that wouldn't get the gate open.

Just then a high-pitched, querulous piping floated through the snowy air overhead. Malus looked up in time to see a long, almost snake-like shape furl broad, leathery wings and arrow through one of the gatehouse's narrow windows. He caught a glimpse of long, indigo coloured jesses dangling from the reptile's taloned feet. The guard captain frowned. 'That's a message from the Hag,' he said. 'Perhaps that's word from your father there, dread lord.'

My father? No, the highborn thought. Malus reached into a pouch at his belt. 'Here is proof of my authority, captain.' He pressed a ruby the size of a bird's egg into the man's palm. It was one of the last pieces of treasure left from his summer raid.

The guard captain held the gem up to his eye and his face went slack with wonder. 'That'll do,' he breathed, tucking it into his coin purse. 'Of course, you'll need proof of authority to get back into the city upon your return as well.'

The highborn laughed at the sheer audacity of the man. On one hand, he had to admire such implacable avarice. On the other hand, extorting money from above one's station demanded a brutal reprisal. 'Don't worry, captain,' he said. 'I've an excellent memory. When I return to the Hag I'll make certain you're amply attended to. You have my oath on it.'

The guard captain smiled. 'Excellent. I'm always at your service, dread lord. If you'd kindly mount up, I'll have the gate open in a moment.' The druchii spun smartly on his heel and stepped back inside the gatehouse, closing the ironbound door behind him.

Malus fought the urge not to run back to Spite. One man is ordering the gate opened, he thought. Another is reading the letter from Urial and deciding what to do. Which one will trump the other? 'Make ready!' Malus hissed to the column as he swung into the saddle.

From within the gatehouse came a rattle of enormous chains. Slowly, slowly, the enormous iron gates began to pull back, revealing the tunnel leading to the outer portal. At once, Malus kicked Spite into motion, waving the column to follow. We could get trapped inside, he thought, gritting his teeth. They could shut the inner gate, trap us between the two portals and rain fire down on us if they wish.

He made a snap decision: if he couldn't see the outer gate starting to move he'd wheel the column about and race into the city. We'll climb the wall at another point if we have to, he raged inwardly. I will not be caged here like a rabbit!

Spite's leathery feet slapped along the cobblestones, eager perhaps for the open country and relief from the biting fog. The gate swung ponderously on its ancient hinges; it was just wide enough to allow a nauglir to pass. Malus spurred his mount forward, his eyes straining to pierce the gloom beyond. Was that a shaft of grey light? Yes!

'Ha!' Malus cried, jabbing sharply with his spurs. Spite lurched into a run. The sounds of heavy footfalls reverberated through the narrow passage beneath the gatehouse, an echoing rumble like sullen thunder. Malus could see a bar of wan moonlight just ahead and bared his teeth triumphantly. Too late, brother, the highborn thought. Spite leapt through the yawning gates with a rumbling growl, his clawed feet slipping on the snow-covered road.

There was a shout from above and a sharp thump as a bolt as long as Spite's tail punched into the frozen ground a hand span to their left. There was a whickering sound and another shaft blurred past the cold one's scaly snout, causing the nauglir to snap its jaws and shy to the side.

The druchii in the tower had evidently reached a compromise: let the riders out onto the killing field before the gate and present a pile of corpses to Urial when he arrived. Corpses thoroughly picked clean of valuables, of course.

'Faster!' Malus cried, applying the spurs. Another bolt went wide, ricocheting off the hard surface of the road and skimming its icy surface like a steel-headed viper. The highborn stole a look over his shoulder: most of the warband was already clear. Two of the riders were looking back over their shoulders as well, aiming their crossbows one-handed and firing bolts at the narrow embrasures mostly for Spite's sake.

Already the walls of the city were losing focus, their edges going grey behind gusts of snow as the highborn sped farther down the Spear Road. There was another thump from the gatehouse, and Malus watched the black diamond shape of a heavy bolt swell in his vision. But the gunner on the wall had misjudged the range, and the bolt fell short, striking a rider a yard behind the highborn.

The armour-piercing point punched through the rider's breastplate with a loud crack and plunged on into the back of his nauglir's thick skull. Rider and mount tumbled end for end, kicking up a spray of blood-tinged snow, then fetched up in a broken heap in the middle of the road. Malus steeled himself for another shot, but when he glanced warily back at the gatehouse he saw that Hag Graef was just a ghostly smudge, grey against the winter night.

Malus gave a wild, vicious laugh, hoping the guards at the gatehouse could hear him. That was your best chance to catch me, brother, he thought. Now, every league will carry me further from your grasp. Soon there will be nothing more for you to do than wait in your twisted spire and dread my return. 'Run, Spite!' the highborn called to his mount. 'Tireless beast of the deep earth! Carry me north, where the tools of vengeance await!'

THEY'D COVERED HALF a dozen leagues in the darkness and the snow before Atalvyr toppled from his saddle.

The first indication Malus had of a problem was the change in the sound of the loping nauglir. The steady run of a dozen cold ones was not quiet; even on the snowy road they moved with a low rumble of heavy-footed thunder. Suddenly, the rumble slackened. Looking back, Malus could not at first discern why the column had stopped.

He reined Spite around and headed back down the road until he found Dalvar and the rest of Nagaira's men clustered around their fallen comrade. Atalvyr's cold one had wandered off the road and rested on its haunches in a snowy field nearby. Lhunara had kept the rest of the warband mounted, eyes scanning the road and the surrounding countryside. Malus slid from the saddle, seething with impatience. The snow had slackened as they'd moved north, and he was counting on it to cover their tracks as much as possible. 'What's this?' he said to Dalvar.

Dalvar looked up from Atalvyr's writhing form. 'That damned poison! He had some kind of spasm and snapped his lashings, then fell from the saddle. I thought the venom would have run its course by now, but it's getting worse.'

The wind shifted, and the highborn's nose wrinkled. 'He's putrefying,' Malus snapped. 'The venom is eating him from within. Cut his throat and have done – we've many more miles to go before dawn.'

Nagaira's men studied Malus coldly. Dalvar slowly shook his head. 'I have some potions in my saddlebag. Let me see if I can slow the poison's work, get him back in the saddle–'

'And what then? Ride another few leagues before he collapses again? Speed is our only ally now – we must make it past the watchtowers before Urial can organise a pursuit.'

Dalvar stood, folding his arms. 'Would you squander a fighting man for a few minutes' riding time? We'll need every sword we can muster in the Wastes. Surely you know that.'

Malus ground his teeth, fighting the urge to strike the man's head from his shoulders. A move against Dalvar would bring out the knives from every quarter. When the dust settled, his warband would be cut in half, no matter the outcome. 'Ten minutes,' he said, then headed back to Spite.

He heard the leathery tread of a nauglir sidling up behind him. Malus looked back to see Lhunara and Vanhir pacing him back along the road. 'He's going to be a problem,' Lhunara murmured, the wind whipping long strands of dark hair about her pale face.

'They're *all* a problem,' Malus replied sourly. 'I trusted Nagaira to keep her thugs in line once we'd left the Hag – her greed for the power hidden in the temple would have ensured her cooperation, at least to a point. Dalvar is another matter. If we move against him, no matter how subtly, the rest will turn on us. And I expect he's right; we'll need every sword we can muster where we're going.'

'Has my lord never hunted in the Wastes?' Vanhir's tone was utterly cold, his formerly melodious voice now flat and portentous as a dirge.

Malus glared over his shoulder at the highborn knight, but the warrior was watching the forest opposite their side of the road. Vanhir had suffered every night on the weeklong march from Clar Karond to the Hag; he'd lost enough skin to make Malus a fine pair of boots, all told. Since then the knight's hatred had crystallised into a cold hardness that Malus couldn't quite fathom. It was as if Vanhir had reached a decision about something, and was only just biding his time. Was the knight ready to cast aside his famous honour for the sweet wine of treachery?

'I have not,' Malus said evenly. 'I took a turn with the garrison at Ghrond, during my father's misguided attempts to get me killed in some border raid. But no, I have never travelled into the Wastes. Have you?'

Vanhir turned to regard his erstwhile master. His dark eyes were like polished basalt. 'Oh, yes, dread lord. The best hunting can be found there, just a week's ride or so from the frontier. My family made its wealth ambushing nomadic raiders along the steppes.' He straightened in the saddle and shot Malus a challenging look. 'It is not a place for the brash or the foolish, or warriors of poor mettle.'

Before Malus knew it, his sword was naked in his hand and he'd crossed half the distance to Vanhir when Lhunara let out a sharp hiss. 'Horse's hooves! Someone's riding fast up the road from the Hag!'

Malus restrained himself with an effort of will. He cocked his head, straining to hear over the restless wind, but heard nothing. But the highborn knew better than to doubt Lhunara's keen senses. He leapt into the saddle, blade still in hand. 'Off the road! Quickly!'

The three druchii spurred their mounts back to the rest of the warband. Malus quickly sized up the terrain. They were in the foothills north and west of the Dragonspines, a place of dense woods and treacherous marshes. Off the road to the left were stagnant pools and stands of tall thorngrass, leading back to dense woods and underbrush on the other side of a shallow pond. 'That way!' he pointed with his sword. 'Into the tree line across the pond!'

Dalvar was kneeling by the fallen warrior, whose convulsions had eased but who still seemed incapable of moving. 'What about him?'

'Put his sword in his hand and leave him, or stay behind and die at his side!'

For a moment, Dalvar looked ready to protest, but the sound of distant hoof beats galvanised him into action. He drew the man's sword and pressed it into the druchii's palm, then scrambled into the saddle and joined the warband as they dashed across the fen.

The cold ones handled the terrain with ease, something a horse would have been hard-pressed to emulate. They nosed into the thick undergrowth, panicking small animals in their path and brushing aside thickets of brambles without slowing their stride. Once out of sight, the druchii dismounted, and Malus led them back to the edge of the trees. 'Crossbows ready,' he ordered as they settled down behind fallen logs and thick underbrush. 'No one fires unless I give the word.'

Malus took cover behind a broad oak tree. Dalvar settled into a crouch beside him. 'Another minute and he'd have been ready to move,' the retainer growled.

'Then it's fortunate for us that our pursuit came early and Atalvyr could still serve us as bait.'

Before Dalvar could reply, a group of riders swept into view riding tall black warhorses. They wore heavy black cloaks with full hoods, and held long, ebon-hafted spears in their hands. One of the riders surveyed the area surrounding the fallen druchii, and Malus saw moonlight glint on a silver steel night-mask. Urial's men all right, Malus noted. They must have left right on our heels to have caught up with us so quickly. He counted only five riders, however, which surprised him. Possibly an advance force, hurriedly dispatched ahead of a larger hunting party? He and his men would make short work of these riders, and hide the bodies in the fen.

Until he noticed that something wasn't quite right about the men and their mounts. Steam curled from the horses' muscular flanks, and they pranced and pawed at the earth as though fresh from the stables, not at the end of leagues of hard riding. And there was something strange about the riders themselves – the way their masked faces turned first one way and then another, like hounds searching for a scent.

Suddenly the air shook with a deep-throated roar as Atalvyr's cold one rose from its haunches and crept up onto the road. The slow-witted beast had finally caught the horses' scent; nauglir loved the taste of horseflesh.

Malus's concern deepened when none of the horses panicked at the nauglir's hunting roar. The riders reined their mounts around to face the approaching cold one, moving as though driven by a single mind. Malus felt the cold touch of dread run a talon down his spine.

The cold one leapt, and the riders spurred their mounts to meet it. At the last minute they split to either side of the beast, but one horse was not as fast as its mates and the nauglir knocked it to the ground with its powerful shoulder, then locked its jaws around the animal's neck. The horse screamed – not a cry of fear or pain, however, but of rage. Its rider rolled easily out of the saddle and sprang to his feet, readying his spear.

The other riders struck at both of the cold one's flanks, driving their spears deep into the beast's side. The nauglir roared and lashed its tail, catching one rider full in the chest. There was a splintering sound and the rider flew backwards out of the saddle, landing in a misshapen heap almost fifteen feet away.

'That's one!' Dalvar hissed triumphantly.

'No,' Malus said. 'Look.'

The broken, twisted shape was still moving. As they watched, the man pushed himself to his knees, then climbed to his feet. One arm hung limp, and the man's ribcage was clearly smashed – yet he stood, and drew his sword, and rejoined the fight.

Even the horse the cold one had bitten had scrambled back up and bolted away from the creature, blood pouring from its neck.

The cold one thrashed and spun in a wide circle, trying to attack all its tormentors at once. Its flanks bristled with long spears, and a huge pool of crimson melted the snow beneath its scaly body. The first dismounted rider was edging closer, his spear levelled at the nauglir's right eye, waiting for the right moment to strike. Sensing his opportunity, he leapt forward – right into the creature's gaping jaws.

The beast had not been as oblivious to the man's approach as it had appeared. It moved like a striking snake, taking man, spear and all into its fanged mouth up to the rider's waist. It bit down with a shattering crunch, spraying blood in a wide fan, and shook the man in its teeth like some great terrier with a rat.

The other riders paused, seemingly considering their next move – then suddenly the cold one let out a strangled cry. It shook its head fiercely once more, then swayed on its feet. Suddenly Malus saw the creature's skin start to bulge slightly, just behind the eyes, and then with a sharp cracking sound, a silver steel spearhead punched through the nauglir's skull from the inside out. Blood and brain matter stained the sharp point. The beast gave a shudder, then collapsed.

'Blessed Mother of Night,' Dalvar said, his voice strained. 'What are those things?'

'They are… murder given form,' Malus said, struggling to believe what he'd seen with his own eyes. 'Urial must be very, very angry.' Or possibly afraid, he thought with a start. If so, the treasure that awaits must be very great indeed.

While they watched, the remaining three riders dismounted and drew their swords. One began cutting into the nauglir's side, while the others started hacking the beast's skull apart to free their companion. Within a few moments' time the spearman staggered free, his entrails spilling from his ravaged belly and catching on the beast's jagged teeth.

The third swordsman pulled the nauglir's steaming heart from its chest and held it up to the sky. The other four lurched over to him, and one by one pressed the great organ to their bodies, sluicing gouts of sticky blood across their chests. The two wounded riders seemed to gain strength from their enemy's lifeblood; their wounds did not heal, but neither were they any longer a hindrance. Suddenly moonlight glinted on a spinning blur of metal and a dagger sprouted from the throat of one of the riders. Atalvyr let out a fevered howl of challenge, holding his sword before him as he swayed on unsteady feet.

The riders turned to face the warrior as if noticing him for the first time. The stricken rider reached up and slowly pulled the needle-bladed knife from his throat.

As one, they advanced.

Malus considered the odds and bit back a curse. 'That's it. I've seen enough. We're getting out of here, as quickly as we can.'

'But our crossbows–' Dalvar began.

'Don't be a fool, Dalvar. It wouldn't make any difference.' The highborn's hand went to the cold lump of metal and stone beneath the lip of his breastplate. 'The only reason we're still alive right now is because of your mistress's talismans, but I'll wager that if these hounds get much closer they'll be able to sense the skull no matter what, and then we'll be finished.'

There was a clash of steel back by the road. Malus turned away. Dalvar watched, his eyes widening. 'Where are we going to go?'

'Back through these woods, for a start, and then up into the hills. These... killers... are going to be searching the Spear Road for us, all the way to the Tower of Ghrond and possibly beyond. We must find another way across the frontier and into the Wastes.'

Dalvar's eyes widened. 'Back into the hills? But they're full of Shades!'

'That's what I'm counting on. If anyone can get us through the mountains unseen, it is they.'

The retainer's face twisted in fear. 'You're mad! The things they do to trespassers–'

'I would rather try my luck with a foe that dies when I pierce his heart!' Malus snarled. 'If we stay here, we die.'

The highborn pulled back deeper into the woods, and one by one, the rest of the warband followed. The screams of the man they'd left behind echoed through the snowy trees long after he was lost to sight.

Chapter Nine
FELL SHADOWS

SPITE LOWERED ON his haunches and leapt again, rear legs clawing for purchase on the frozen, leafy ground. The talons of his left hind leg caught on a thin sapling. For a moment the green wood held, then splintered under the huge beast's weight. The cold one started to slide again and Malus threw himself against Spite's hindquarters, pushing for all he was worth. The weary nauglir leapt as though stung, whipping about and snapping at the highborn in irritation.

Dagger-like teeth clashed shut less than a foot from Malus's face, spraying him with thick tendrils of poisonous slime. Malus snarled and punched the cold one full on the nose, and the beast whipped back around with a roar, stomping further up the slope. The highborn wiped his face and thanked the Dark Mother that they'd at least managed to climb a little further up the hill.

It had been two days since the terrible encounter on the Spear Road, and Malus doubted that they'd covered more than ten miles in the rugged, densely-wooded terrain of the Dragonspine foothills. Each night the warband made camp wherever they happened to be when the weak sunlight faded from the cloudy sky. Each time they built a small fire and roasted some of their precious store of meat, and each time they laid out a generous portion on a plate in a place of honour, hoping that one of the hill-druchii would accept the invitation and enter the camp. So far, the Shades had kept to themselves.

Malus was certain they were out there. The legends said that when the druchii came to Naggaroth, some two thousand men, women and children turned their backs on the great Black Arks and the nascent great cities, travelling instead into the mountainous wilderness to live according to their own laws.

No one knew how many had survived those first few years in the pitiless Land of Chill, but it was well known that the Autarii – the Shades – claimed much of the mountain country north of Hag Graef as their own, and did not suffer intruders lightly. At various times he'd felt his scalp prickle with the undeniable sensation that they were being watched, but not even the nauglir smelled any threats nearby. For whatever reason, the hill-folk were keeping their distance.

Privately, Malus hoped that the Autarii would take their invitation soon. After only two days in the hills he'd begun to seriously consider heading back for the road and taking his chances with Urial's riders. Hour after hour of steep slopes, frozen ground and treacherous underbrush had sapped the warband's strength.

The nauglir were hungry and irritable because Malus had been forced to ration their meat. Each beast could easily consume a full-grown deer or a human body each day, and the highborn was very leery of sending out hunting parties when the risk of ambush was so great. The warband bore the conditions stoically, though more than once Malus had caught sight of Dalvar whispering quietly among Nagaira's other retainers. It could be nothing, but he couldn't afford to take that chance. The question, Malus thought, is what could he do about it?

Spite paused, and Malus suddenly realised that they had reached the top of the slope. He reached out and tugged on the beast's thickly muscled tail. 'Stand,' he commanded, a little breathlessly, and the cold one eagerly complied, snowflakes steaming off its scaly hide.

Malus clambered up alongside the cold one and saw that the trees were considerably thinner on the reverse slope, affording a good view of the next hill over and the small vale in between. In the far distance, he could see the dark, broken teeth of the Shieldwall, the huge east-west mountain range that marked the beginning of the frontier. Leagues and leagues away, Malus thought tiredly. It'll take a thousand years to get there at this pace.

The crackle of brush behind him brought Malus's head around. Dalvar clambered up alongside him using a roughly carved cedar stick for support. The druchii's normally smug face was flushed and worn. 'It will be dark soon,' the retainer said, leaning a little on his makeshift staff. 'The men are exhausted, dread lord, and the nauglir besides. If we make camp now, we might have a little light left over to hunt for some fresh meat.'

Malus shook his head. 'No hunting, Dalvar. I'll not lose men to Autarii crossbows.' He indicated the vale below. 'There is some clear ground down there, and what looks to be a stream. We'll set up camp there.'

Dalvar surveyed the vale wearily. 'We'll get weaker every day at this pace. Soon the Autarii won't need to pick us off one by one – they'll just send their striplings in to round us up with willow switches.'

'City living has made you soft,' Malus said with a snort. 'Right now the Shades are testing us, gauging our strength. Each day sees us a few miles deeper into their domain. As long as we keep our force together and afford them no opportunity for easy ambushes, the Shades will have to choose a different tactic – and accepting our invitation is the simplest and easiest option available. They know we're interested in talking with them,' Malus said confidently. 'Sooner or later they're bound to become curious.'

It was well known that, like any druchii, the Autarii had a mercenary streak. Shades served wealthy warlords as hired scouts and skirmishers, and when the Witch King rode to war, entire tribes of Shades marched in the vanguard and claimed their share of the plunder.

'Or they could simply wait until we're too weak from hunger to fight back and take us all captive. Your man Vanhir says that the Autarii bargain only when they have no other choice.'

You've been talking to Vanhir, have you? How disquieting, the highborn mused. *I'll have to have a talk with Lhunara about that.* 'If they ambush us as a group, we can fight them off – possibly even kill one or more of them. They're excellent woodsmen, but they lack good armour and we have the nauglir on our side. The cold ones will warn us if they catch the scent of a large ambush party. No, I think we still hold a slight advantage here if we stay disciplined.'

Dalvar gave Malus a long look that was frankly doubtful, if not outright challenging. 'Then I suppose we'll see what the night brings,' he said, then turned and made his way carefully back down the slope.

Malus watched him go. 'Tread carefully, Dalvar,' he said. 'The footing here is more dangerous than it appears.'

'Thank you for the warning, dread lord,' the rogue replied over his shoulder. 'You'd do well to remember that yourself.'

You're going to have to die, Dalvar, Malus thought. And it is going to have to happen soon, unless I can find a way to discredit you in the eyes of your men. But how?

'Up,' Malus commanded, slapping Spite's flank. 'It's downhill from here, and then you can rest.'

The nauglir lurched forward, muscles bunching in its shoulders and hips as it negotiated its way down the slope. Malus had to jog to keep pace, until suddenly the cold one let out a barking roar and broke into a run. 'Spite! Stand!' he called, but the nauglir sped on, head low and tail stiff as a spear. He's hunting, Malus realised. What's he got wind of? A deer?

Then, farther upslope, he heard the other nauglir take up the roar as well, and Malus suddenly realised he was in the path of a multi-tonne stampede. Thinking quickly, the highborn cut to the left and slightly back upslope, knowing that there weren't any trees or boulders large enough to protect him from an out-of-control cold one. He could only get out of the way as much as possible and hope for the best.

The hillside shook with dozens of pounding feet. The nauglir, being pack animals at heart, thundered down the slope in a single, lumbering mass, kicking up a huge cloud of powdery snow as they went. In their wake scrambled their owners, clambering down the hill and shouting ineffectual commands at the galloping beasts. Under other circumstances it might even have been amusing, but suddenly Malus felt very vulnerable indeed.

A deer wouldn't have set them off like this, he reasoned. Not the entire pack. They only responded like that when they were hungry and there was blood in the air. Someone's baited them, he thought. There's probably a fresh deer kill in the copse of trees, its body opened to the cold air.

Malus felt his guts turn to ice. He saw that the nauglir were already halfway across the small meadow at the bottom of the hill, galloping for a small copse at the far end. The druchii were in hot pursuit, running lightly across the snowy field.

The warrior in the lead suddenly stumbled and fell. A heartbeat later the druchii behind him collapsed. Then the third warrior in line spun in a half circle, and this time Malus caught the blurred flight of the blunted crossbow bolt that struck the man in the centre of the forehead and dropped him to the snow. The ambushers were firing from the dense tree line on the opposite side of a winding streambed, and Malus's men had nowhere to hide.

There was a faint scuffling sound behind him. Malus whirled, his sword springing from its scabbard, and caught the knobbed end of the Autarii's club right between the eyes.

SOMEONE WAS FORCING a thin, bitter liquid down his throat. Malus gagged and spat, jerking his head violently away from the wooden tube that was being pushed between his lips. The motion set a flare of agony blooming behind his eyes and his stomach roiled. A calloused hand grabbed him by the jaw and despite the awful sickness he jerked his head once more and snapped at the offending hand, sinking his teeth deep into the flesh between forefinger and thumb. He tasted blood and his stomach finally betrayed him. The hand pulled free as he retched a thin stream of bile, and then the blackness behind his eyelids exploded with white fire as a fist smashed into his cheek.

The next thing he felt was a blade against his cheek. It was cold, rough and sharp, and he cried out in fury as it was slowly drawn against his skin, slicing easily through into the flesh beneath. The white-hot pain sharpened his senses into full awareness. He blinked his eyes as warm blood leaked down his face and when he could focus he saw the silhouette of a short, lean-limbed druchii standing before him.

The Shade's sharply-angled features were covered in spiral tattoos of indigo and red, giving him a snarling, daemonic expression even when in repose. When he leered at Malus, his face was the very image of otherworldly hate. The man wore layers of loose robes and soft, leather boots, and an assortment of daggers protruded from a wide belt at his waist. He was backlit by a roaring fire that illuminated a small clearing surrounded by a circle of trees. More of the Shades crouched or paced around the roaring flames, most wearing cloaks of mottled greens and browns that blended artfully with the shadows of the forest. Each druchii in Malus's warband was tied to one of the surrounding trees, as he was himself.

It was difficult to focus, despite the pain. It was full dark, with both moons shining in an unusually clear sky. Malus tried to think. How long was I out? Hours? Days? He tried to concentrate, tried to summon up the fires of his anger. 'Misbegotten runt,' he snarled. 'Is this how you treat an embassy from the great Vaulkhar of Hag Graef?'

The Shade cocked his head at the highborn's outburst, then with a smile he brought the knife to his lips and licked the blood from its edge. His eyebrows rose appreciatively, and he turned to his compatriots, speaking in such thickly-accented druhir that Malus couldn't understand a single word of. The men around the fire laughed, and the highborn didn't like the sound.

'Have a care, my lord. The short one likes the way you taste.'

With an effort, Malus forced himself to turn his head towards the sound of the voice. Vanhir was bound to the tree immediately next to Malus, his face a mass of purple bruises. He spoke with effort through swollen lips. 'The blood and flesh of highborn warriors is a delicacy to the hill clans, so I wouldn't mention your father quite so forcefully if I were you.'

'You're mad!' Malus exclaimed. 'They wouldn't eat their own kin-'

Vanhir managed a pained laugh. 'We *aren't* their kin,' he said. 'We're city folk, and prisoners besides. We're just meat to them, fat and soft, like those Bretonnians were to us.'

There was a rattle and clink of metal near the fire. Malus looked and saw one of the Shades unfolding a roll of soft leather sewn with a number of different-sized pockets. A bone or wood handle protruded from each pocket. As the highborn watched, the short Autarii drew forth a pair of flensing knives and a well-polished bone saw.

'If you're lucky and they've eaten recently, they might settle for just a hand or a forearm,' Vanhir said. 'They're very good at taking only what they need and keeping the victim alive for later.'

The short Autarii spoke, and several of his fellows went to work. One shook out a length of rope and looped it over a sturdy branch hanging near the fire. Another Shade took the end of the rope and walked over to Malus, looping the cord around the highborn's ankles in a few swift, practiced strokes. Two others untied the bonds that held Malus to the tree, leaving his hands bound tightly behind his back.

'You wouldn't dare!' Malus roared. 'Touch me again with your filthy knives and by the Mother of Eternal Night I will call a curse down on you that will blight these hills for a thousand years!'

The short Autarii made a disgusted sound and barked a short command. Two of the Shades hauled on the rope and Malus was hoisted upside down, his body swinging perilously close to the fire. Rough hands stopped his pendular motion, and another Shade set a large brass bowl underneath his head.

Malus watched the short Autarii pull a sickle-shaped knife from the leather cloth. His body was trembling like a plucked wire, seething with white-hot rage. 'Kill me and the Vaulkhar of the Hag will hunt you and your kind to extinction.'

The Shade stepped close and smiled, showing a mouth full of jagged teeth. 'You are nothing but smoke, high man,' the Shade whispered. 'In a moment – puff! You will be gone, as though you had never been. Your Vaulkhar will never know what became of you.'

The knife was cold as ice against Malus's throat.

Chapter Ten
TRIALS AND TORMENTS

SUDDENLY THERE WAS a shout from the other side of the roaring fire, and the Shade paused. A harsh voice barked commands in rustic druhir, and the short Autarii answered in rapid-fire retorts that Malus couldn't follow.

Without warning, the highborn was dropped to the ground, landing painfully on his shoulder and neck. Malus rolled onto his back, craning his head around to try to see what was going on.

There were a number of Shades standing at the edge of the firelight, led by a broad-shouldered Autarii with tattoos on both his face and hands. The other Shades who had been slinking about the fire backed away from these new Autarii, treating them with a mixture of deference and fear.

The heavily-tattooed Shade surveyed the bound druchii and rattled off a long query to his shorter cousin, who spat a quick reply. The newcomer asked another question, and this time got a longer response. The Shade rubbed his chin with a tattooed hand.

They're haggling over us, Malus realised. And the prospective buyer doesn't much care for the price.

The bigger Shade turned as if to say something to his fellows – and abruptly tackled the shorter Autarii. The two men rolled back and forth over the damp earth, and firelight glinted from the knives that had appeared in their hands. I see some things are still the same between us and the hill-folk, Malus noted.

There was the sound of steel against flesh, and the bigger Shade snarled in pain, but then Malus saw a tattooed hand shoot up and plunge its knife down with a meaty smack. The larger Autarii stabbed again and again, and the shorter man let out a single, bubbling cry before the struggling finally ceased.

The victor staggered to his feet, blood oozing from a cut to his arm. One look at the remaining Shades set them to work cutting Malus's retainers from their trees.

A pair of rough hands hauled the highborn to his feet, and a knife slashed through the bonds at his ankles. The broad-shouldered Autarii spared him a single, appraising stare, then nodded in satisfaction and began looting the body of his dead foe. Before Malus could speak, he was spun around and propelled forward with a hard shove, towards the deep shadows beyond the fire.

Malus staggered a few steps, then regained his balance. Suddenly he spun, and in a few swift strides he reached the spot where his former captor lay. The highborn bent as close as he could to the Shade's tattooed face; he was pleased to see the fading glow of life still there. 'Savour your feast of blood and cold steel, runt,' he hissed. 'I warned you what would happen if you trifled with me.'

There were angry shouts behind Malus, and the burly Shade reached up with a broad, scarred hand and shoved the highborn backwards with surprising ease. Malus crashed into two strong bodies. Hands grabbed his arms and a dark sack smelling of sweat and vomit was thrown over his head and tied loosely around his neck.

HE MARCHED FOR hours in stifling blackness with a rough hand clasping each of his arms, keeping him upright no matter how many roots he stumbled over.

Over time his head cleared, and Malus strained to hear every sound emanating around him. He could hear the footfalls and curses of his warband, strung out in a line behind him. From the quiet conversations around him, he suspected that he'd been taken by a large group of Autarii, easily twice the size of his small band. From the relaxed way they talked, they were somewhere within their home territory, and thus had no fear of being attacked. He was further shocked to hear the somnolent groan of a nauglir far to the rear of the column; how the Shades had managed to handle the volatile cold ones was a mystery to him.

Time ceased to have meaning. The Shades seemed tireless, never pausing in their swift, ground-eating march. Malus concentrated on making his legs work, putting one foot in front of the other, until finally his whole world boiled down to a cycle of simple, rhythmic motion. Thus, he was surprised when his senses registered the smell of wood smoke and new voices penetrating the darkness of his hood.

Without warning, his minders came to a halt, and there was a brief exchange between them and their broad-shouldered leader. Just as abruptly the men were moving again, this time leading him off to the side and away from the rest of the group. They walked for several yards, and then a hand at the base of his neck bent him in an awkward bow and he was hurled unceremoniously forward. His foot hit something soft and he sprawled headlong, landing in what felt like a pile of furs or blankets.

There was another curt exchange of words behind him, and then the sounds of movement. Strong hands grasped him and turned him over, and then nimble fingers plucked at the ties around the hood. The vile sack was pulled away, and Malus greedily gulped at the smoke-tinged air.

His eyes, already accustomed to blackness, quickly took in his surroundings. He lay on his back amid a pile of furs, in what looked like a tent with a curved roof. There was a banked fire nearby, reflecting a wan, orange light against bent wood poles with rawhide lashings. There were three figures crouched over him, their hands gliding over his face and body. Fingertips brushed his head, lingering briefly at the swollen lump on his forehead, then floating over his patrician nose and down across his lips. Their touch was feather-light, unnaturally gentle. Then someone stoked the embers of the fire, and as the fire bloomed back into life Malus saw why.

Three druchii women crouched over him, each one dressed in a simple tunic of doeskin. Their heads were bald and tattooed with identical glyphs on their foreheads. Collars of beaten iron rested around their necks. Their ears were gone; nothing but lumps of gnawed scar tissue remained. The tips of long, ropy scars peeked from beneath the top and bottom of their collars, showing how their vocal chords had been crudely cut. The faces of the slaves hovered above him in the wavering light, their expressions seemingly rapt. Pools of darkness swallowed up the light in the holes where their eyes had once been.

'You lie in the tent of Urhan Calhan Beg,' croaked an old, implacable voice somewhere near the firelight. 'You are to be treated as a guest, but first you must make the guest-oath.'

The blind slaves reached down as one and pulled Malus upright. He fought, but could not quite suppress, a shudder of loathing. To cripple a person – a druchii – in such a way, to rob them of their essential strength and then deny them the release of death was cruel beyond belief.

Once he was sitting up, Malus caught sight of the crone sitting by the fire. She was ancient, her alabaster features grown lustreless and still, like cold marble. The old woman moved slowly and carefully, as if each motion threatened to crumble her into dust. She reached out a long-fingered hand and fetched an object from a low shelf next to her.

The crone whispered a command and one of the blind slaves moved silently and surely to take the object from the crone's hand and hold it before

Malus. It was a statue, shaped from a dark rock that
swallowed the light and was as cold as death itself.
The carving was of a woman, sharp and slender as a
blade, with cruel, cold features and deep-sunken eyes.
The age of the thing surrounded it like a mantle of
frost. It could have been carved in lost Nagarythe,
thousands of years past.

'Swear upon the Dark Mother that you will make
no attempt to escape from this camp, nor do any
harm to your caretakers while you are a guest here.'

Malus considered for a moment, then nodded.
'Before the Mother of Night, I swear it,' he said, and
pressed his lips to the ancient stone.

The crone nodded solemnly as the slave returned
the statue to her frail hands. 'Undo his bonds.'

Two of the slaves undid the ropes around his wrists.
Malus stretched his shoulders and tried to massage
the feeling back into his hands. 'Where are my men?'
he asked.

The crone shrugged.

'Was it the Urhan who brought me here?'

'No. That was his second son, Nuall. I expect you
are intended as an offering to appease his father's
wrath.'

'His wrath? Why?'

'Enough questions,' the crone hissed. 'You are hungry. Eat.'

While he and the crone were talking the slaves had
retreated to the other side of the tent. Now they
returned, bearing a platter of bread and cheese and a
goblet of spiced wine. The highborn ate swiftly and
methodically, taking only small sips of the wine. The
crone watched in funereal silence.

By the time Malus was done, a man's face appeared at the entrance to the tent. 'Come,' the Autarii said, beckoning to him. The highborn bowed respectfully to the impassive crone and stepped carefully into the night.

Once outside, Malus discovered that the night was all but gone; the sky above was paling with the touch of false dawn. Through the dimness, the highborn could see that he stood at the end of a narrow, wooded canyon that ended in a sheer wall of rock. Numerous other domed tents crouched amid the tall trees, surrounding a large, permanent structure of cedar logs and piled stone built out from the sheer cliff face – the longhouse of the Urhan. The Autarii headed for the building and Malus squared his shoulders and followed.

The air in the longhouse was raucous and smoky. Two large fireplaces dominated the long walls of the building, and a blue haze of pipe-smoke curled and eddied among the cedar rafters of the ceiling. Piles of furs and floor pillows were thrown over a thick carpet of rushes, and the Autarii lounged about the single great room like a pack of wild dogs.

At the far end of the longhouse the Urhan Calhan Beg presided over his clan, sitting in the building's single chair on a raised dais while attended by three female slaves. The druchii women had been blinded and rendered mute like the others in the Urhan's tent. Malus watched as one of the slaves carefully served Beg a goblet of wine; he noted that the wretched creature was missing both of her thumbs.

Calhan Beg was an old, grey wolf of a man. He was lean and wiry and bore a multitude of scars from a lifetime spent battling man and beast alike. Half of his left ear had been gnawed away at some point, and a sword had cut a deep notch from the top of his prominent nose. Intricate tattoos covered face, neck, hands and forearms, speaking volumes of his deeds as warrior and chieftain. Beg had a long, drooping grey moustache and piercing blue eyes as cold and hard as sapphires. At present that pitiless stare was fixed on the man standing at the foot of the dais – his second son Nuall.

Malus's guide picked his way across the crowded floor and the highborn passed in his wake, carefully ignoring the looks of challenge aimed his way. When Nuall caught sight of them, he indicated Malus with a sweep of his arm.

'And here is another mighty gift to you, father – a highborn prisoner, son of the Vaulkhar of Hag Graef. He will fetch you a great ransom from his decadent kin.'

The Urhan shot Malus a cold look of contempt before refocusing his ire back on his son. 'Did I tell you to go fetch me slaves and hostages, Nuall? Is this my tribute day, that you seek to shower me with gifts?'

Several of the Shades in the hall laughed derisively. Nuall's jaw clenched. 'No, father.'

'No, indeed. I sent you to reclaim our family's honour and return to me the treasure of our household. But where is it? Where is the medallion?'

'It… I know where it is, father, but we couldn't reach it! The river–'

'Be silent, whelp!' the Urhan roared. 'Enough of your witless puling! You think to excuse your failure with gifts, as though I'm some tent-wife? You're no fit son, not like your brother,' Beg growled. 'Perhaps I'll have a dress made for you and see if I can get you married off to some blind old Autarii in need of a bed warmer.'

The assembled crowd howled with laughter, and Nuall's face went chalk-white with rage. His trembling hand went to the long knife at his hip, yet his father made no attempt to protect himself, frankly challenging Nuall with his stare. After a moment's hesitation the younger man snarled and spun on his heel, staggering clumsily through the crowd of jeering clansmen and slamming the door of the longhouse in his wake.

Beg watched his son's retreat with evident disdain. 'All muscle and no guts,' he grumbled, drinking deeply from his cup. 'Now I'll have to watch for vipers in my boots or stray arrows on the hunt, or some other such callow thing.' He eyed Malus balefully. 'No doubt you found that entertaining.'

Malus took his time before responding, considering the situation carefully. 'All fathers want for strong sons,' he said at length. 'In that, we are not so very different, great Urhan.'

'You have children?'

The highborn shook his head. 'No, I am a son with something to prove to his father.'

Beg cocked his head to one side and studied Malus closely for the first time. 'So you're one of Lurhan's sons, eh? Not his eldest, and not that twisted thing he gave to the temple. The middle son, perhaps?'

Malus smiled coldly. 'No, great Urhan. Lurhan's late wife had no part in my making.'

At that, Beg's eyes narrowed. 'Then you're that witch's whelp. The one they call Darkblade.'

'My name is Malus, great Urhan,' the highborn replied. 'Dark blades are flawed things, objects of scorn. That's a name only my enemies use.'

'Well, then, Malus, what ransom will your father pay for you?'

The highborn laughed. 'About half as much as you'd pay if he had Nuall as his prisoner.'

The Autarii laughed, and even Beg managed a sour smile. 'Then that bodes ill for you, my friend. I have no use for a guest who cannot enrich me in some way.'

'Ah,' Malus raised a cautionary finger, 'that is a very different matter entirely, great Urhan. I believe my stay here can profit you very well indeed.' He folded his arms. 'I believe you mentioned that you'd lost a certain precious heirloom, is that not so? A medallion?'

The Urhan straightened in his chair. 'I did. What of it?'

Malus shrugged. 'I came into the hills looking for a guide who could show me a path to the frontier. You are keen to reclaim your family's honour. It seems that we both have something to offer one another.'

Beg snarled impatiently. 'Cut to the heart of it, city-dweller. What do you propose?'

'I will retrieve this medallion for you, great Urhan, if you will free me and my men and guide us through the hill passes to the frontier.'

The Urhan laughed coldly. 'Suppose I just start cutting pieces off you until you'll fetch the moons from the sky if I wish it?'

Malus smiled. 'In the first place, I've sworn the guest-oath before the crone in your very tent. Raise a hand to me now and you tempt the Dark Mother's wrath. In the second place, I've seen how you practise your art, great Urhan, and it isn't the sort of thing one fully recovers from. I expect I'll need to be at my best if I am to reclaim your family's honour. Or–' the highborn indicated the assembled Shades– 'perhaps you should ask your clanmates for help instead.'

Beg shifted uncomfortably in his chair.

That's what I thought, the highborn mused. You don't want anyone else getting their hands on your lost medallion, lest they crown themselves Urhan in your stead.

Malus spread his hands, acting the conciliator. 'All I ask is a simple service, something you and your clan are justly famous for. In return, you regain your family's precious honour. It is an arrangement clearly to your benefit.'

The Urhan rubbed his chin thoughtfully, but Malus could see in his eyes that the Autarii chieftain had already made up his mind. 'So be it,' Beg declared. 'But on one condition.'

'Very well. But I will name a condition in return.'

'You have until dawn tomorrow to recover the medallion and bring it to me. If you have not returned by then I'll hunt you through the hills like a stag.'

Malus nodded. 'Done. In return I want my warband out of your slave pens. Since we're allies now they are your guests just as much as I, and bound by the same oaths.'

Beg grinned. 'Clever. Very well, they go free. But no weapons.'

Malus affected an elaborate shrug. 'I can hardly blame the great Urhan if he fears for his safety with ten armed highborn in his camp.'

The great longhouse fell silent. The Urhan's eyes narrowed in irritation. Then Beg threw back his head and laughed. 'By the Dark Mother, you're a reckless one!' he cried. 'I can see why your father wants no part of you.'

Malus smiled mirthlessly. 'My father's loss is your gain, great Urhan. Now tell me of this medallion, and where I might find it.'

YET IT WAS not so simple as that. The Urhan insisted on breaking bread and sharing wine with his new 'ally', and made a show of having the highborn's warband brought into the hall and given places of honour. More of the Autarii made their way to the hall in the meantime, and it was clear that word of Malus's deal with the Urhan was racing like wildfire through the camp. It wasn't long before Malus caught sight of Nuall, surrounded by a half-dozen men, muttering darkly to one another at the far side of the great hall. *The old wolf is laying out an unspoken challenge to Nuall*, Malus reckoned, struggling to conceal his irritation.

The meal stretched for more than an hour. Finally, Nuall seemed to reach a decision of sorts, and he and his men slipped out of the hall. Not long afterward, the Urhan clapped his hands, and an Autarii stepped from behind the dais and presented Malus with his weapons and sword belt. As the highborn quickly buckled his sword belt in place, the Urhan leaned back in his chair and spoke.

'Understand, friend Malus, that this is no simple trinket that I ask you to retrieve. It is the Ancri Dam, a potent talisman that my ancestors claim was given to them by the Dark Mother when they migrated to these hills. It is a symbol of our divine right to rule this clan, and has been passed down from father to son for generations. As the eldest son reaches manhood the medallion becomes his, to show that he is to be the next Urhan. So did the medallion pass from me to my eldest son Ruhir.'

The Urhan's face darkened. 'Then, a week past, Ruhir went hunting as was his wont, and went missing in a storm. We went searching for him, and eventually we found one of his boots by the shore of a nearby river. This river is home to many black willows, and one in particular has an evil reputation. We call it the Willow Hag, and it has claimed many lives.'

'Including Ruhir's,' Malus said.

'Even so.'

Malus's mind raced. *Your thick-witted second son can't fetch a medallion from the roots of a willow tree? What else aren't you telling me, Beg?* Malus waited for the Urhan to continue, but after a few moments it became clear that his tale was done.

'Well, since the sun is now well on its course to mid-morning, perhaps I should be about my appointed task. And since forty pounds of silver steel isn't the wisest thing to wear by the banks of a treacherous river–' he rapped a knuckle on his enamelled plate armour. 'I'll leave my harness in the care of my warband. Now, how shall I find this Willow Hag?'

Beg studied him carefully, his expression inscrutable. 'Walk out of my hall and turn west. Cross the hills until you come to a swift-flowing river, then walk upstream until you find a great riverbend. The Willow Hag waits there.'

Malus nodded. 'That seems simple enough. I shall return with the Ancri Dam before sunrise, Urhan Beg. Then we will discuss my journey north.'

With that the highborn stepped from the dais and crossed quickly to his warriors. Lhunara, Dalvar and even Vanhir rose at his approach. 'Get this armour off,' he said quietly, unbuckling his recently secured sword belt.

Lhunara's nimble hands worked at the buckles of his armour, while Dalvar leaned in close. 'He means to betray you, dread lord.'

'I can see that, Dalvar,' Malus hissed. 'He's using me as a goad to push Nuall into more forceful action. I expect his stupid son will wait until I've recovered the amulet and then try to kill me for it.'

'What do we do?' Lhunara asked, as she pulled his breastplate free.

'For now, nothing. We still need the Autarii to get us to the frontier. But–' As the armour was pulled away and Malus still had his back to the dais, he ran his thumb along the outside of one of his sword scabbards. A thin blade of dark iron popped out of a hidden sheath. With a deft movement, he slipped the tiny weapon into Dalvar's hand. 'If I don't return by dawn, make your escape any way that you can. Get to the nauglir and try to make it back to the road. Though, if possible, leave that piece of iron in the Urhan's skull before you go.'

Dalvar pocketed the blade. 'You have my oath on it,' he said darkly.

Lhunara watched the exchange with hooded eyes. She glanced meaningfully at Malus. 'I hope you know what you're doing.'

The highborn gave her a wolfish grin. 'Right or wrong, Lhunara, I always know what I'm doing.'

The retainer watched her lord and master stride confidently from the hall, throwing a hard stare at any man with the temerity to meet his gaze. 'Somehow that doesn't reassure me one bit,' she muttered.

like fans to soak up the feeble warmth

Chapter Eleven
RIDDLES OF BONE

MALUS LEANED AGAINST the rough bark of a thorn oak and once again gauged the light seeping through the overcast sky. It was late afternoon. By his estimation he'd covered barely three miles from the Autarii camp and he hadn't even seen the river yet, much less the Willow Hag.

Birds called shrilly across the hilltops, and back the way Malus had come he saw a black-furred stag creep stealthily among the trees. Without a large pack of nauglir and a rattling column of knights frightening the wildlife out of their path, the highborn found that the undergrowth teemed with creatures large and small. Hunting cats yowled in the shadows, hoping to frighten their prey into the open, and hawks swooped low over the brush. Winged serpents sunned themselves in high branches, their leathery wings spread like fans to soak up the feeble warmth.

Malus had learned early on to stay close to the trees, moving in short hops from bole to bole. Almost two hours after he'd left camp he'd begun to hear the sounds of something heavy pushing its way stealthily through the brush to his right. When he stopped, it would stop. The highborn found himself wishing for his crossbow as he pressed on, listening as the sounds of his pursuer grew slowly but steadily closer to his own path.

Finally, Malus reached the bottom of one of the hills and discovered a small clearing just ahead. His first urge was to dash across the welcome patch of light brush, but his pursuer was close behind him now, and instinct prompted him to choose a different tack. Drawing his sword, the highborn leapt nimbly into the low branches of a hackthorn. Quietly as he could, he scrambled more than a dozen feet up, settling carefully on a large branch that was still covered in a mantle of reddish leaves.

He sat there, controlling his breathing, for several long minutes. Then, without warning, the brush beneath him parted. A huge, humpbacked shape crept into view. It was a boar, a huge, black-skinned animal with a scarred, bristly hide and two cruel, dagger-like tusks. It stood beneath the tree for several heartbeats, sniffing the air and seeming to listen for Malus. Then, looking left and right, the great beast moved cautiously into the clearing.

Malus leaned his head back against the trunk of the hackthorn, cursing his skittish nerves. A boar, he thought, fighting the urge to laugh. Treed by a pig!

Suddenly there was a rushing sound in the air and the entire tree swayed like a sapling. Malus fell from his branch and only just stopped his plunge with a desperate grab for a nearby limb as a dark shadow swept before the sun. There was a heavy thud in the clearing and then the air was filled with shrill squeals and grunts. Eyes wide, Malus climbed back onto his branch and watched the scene below.

The boar was squirming in the talons of a huge wyvern, its long, reptilian head clamped around the animal's thick neck. Blood scattered across the grass, then there was a crunch of bone as the boar's neck snapped. Its limbs drummed a brief tattoo, then went still.

As Malus watched, the wyvern raised its head and surveyed the clearing, its gaze lighting briefly on the highborn in the tree. It was in the branches above me the entire time, he thought, waiting for its next meal to stumble through the clearing. He smiled weakly at the huge predator. 'I'm too lean and full of gristle,' he said to the beast. 'Be content with the great ham in your talons and don't waste your time on a morsel like me.'

The wyvern studied Malus for a moment longer, its expression flat and devoid of mercy. Then it bunched its shoulders and leapt into the air, carrying the boar effortlessly beneath it. The highborn listened to the flapping wings receding in the distance, but it was some time before his hands were steady enough to hazard the climb down and resume his hunt for the river.

Once again, he'd underestimated the difficulty of traversing the steep slopes and rough terrain of the foothills, even without the heavy weight of his armour. Malus was starting to think the Shades didn't bother walking along the ground – they just climbed the trees and swung from limb to limb like Lustrian gibbons. The notion was beginning to sound pretty appealing.

At this rate it will take me most of the night just to get back to camp, Malus thought angrily. Providing of course I don't get lost in the darkness. Or killed by Nuall and his men.

Malus pushed away from the tree trunk and resumed his climb up the steep hillside. One way or another, Nuall is going to die, he vowed to himself. If this fool's errand gets the better of me, I'll be damned if that idiot is going to profit from it!

The climb to the top seemed to take an eternity as he struggled for footing on the slick, icy soil and worked around tangles of brambles and thick under-brush. When Malus finally reached the top, however, he was rewarded with the sight of a fairly wide valley, curving away slightly to the north-east, and a rushing black ribbon of water running along its base. The river bend that Beg described was nowhere in sight. About a mile to the river, Malus calculated. Another couple of hours at least, and the light is fading fast. The prospect of digging around the roots of a willow tree in freezing water and at night didn't appeal to him in the least. The sun, however, wasn't going to linger at my convenience.

Gritting his teeth, he began his descent.

As IT HAPPENED, Malus made better time than he expected, reaching the river in less than an hour by virtue of losing his balance and tumbling, head over heels, down the bramble-choked hill. His face and hands were raw and bleeding, and the stumps of broken thorns still jutted from his cheeks and chin. What light remained needed to be used for covering ground, not tending trivial hurts.

Unfortunately, the undergrowth only thickened as he drew closer to the river, weaving into tangles so dense that for a time Malus feared he wouldn't get to the riverbank at all. When he did at last find a break, he soon saw that there was no stretch of bare shoreline he could walk along between river and brush. The highborn stood for a moment, watching the river go by, and reached an abrupt decision. Slipping one of his scabbarded swords from his belt, he tested the depth of the water at its edge. Satisfied it wasn't too deep, Malus stepped into the swift-flowing water up to his knees and started to work his way carefully upstream.

Malus's boots were nauglir hide, expensive and well made, and for a short time the freezing cold water didn't have a significant effect. The strong current was something different entirely, but he was certain that he was still making better time than he would fighting through the thick scrub on land.

An hour passed. Then another. The sky began to grow dark. He was getting very tired from fighting the current, and his calves and feet were numb. Malus rounded another bend in the river, and there, about a half-mile ahead, the river took another sharp turn around a narrow bend. Rising up from that narrow talon of land was a broad, black stain against the iron-grey sky. It was a huge, old black willow, rising high above its stunted cousins along the riverbank. Even from this distance, Malus could see the twisted mass of cable-like roots that spread like a tangled net down into the icy water. Battened on the flesh of the dead, the highborn thought grimly. Someone should have taken an axe to the thing years ago.

With his objective in sight, Malus forced himself to pause and consider the terrain – though, after a moment's study it was clear that there was very little to see. The thick brush along the riverbank obscured the land beyond; Malus could see the tops of trees, but nothing of what lay beneath. The good news, however, was that unless Nuall had a lookout high in one of those very trees he couldn't see Malus, either. It would almost be worthwhile to leave the same way I got here, he thought, but for the fact I'm half frozen to death as it is. Nevertheless, the highborn sank a little lower in the current, suppressing a sharp hiss as the freezing water stung his thighs. Moving slowly, so as not to generate any more noise than the river itself, Malus worked his way towards the great tree.

Night came on swiftly as he approached. The Willow Hag seemed to stand out against the blackness of night, swathed in its own inky aura of malevolence. There was a smell on the wind – the stink of fleshy rot, wafting from the tree. Then the wind picked up, and Malus realised that the tree's branches weren't stirring in the breeze. It seemed to crouch motionlessly over the riverbend, waiting like a predator for its next meal.

The sound of rushing water increased the closer Malus came to the tree, and in the wan moonlight he could see thin traces of foam marking whorls and eddies of churned water on the downstream side of the tree.

The swift water was being forced through the tangled roots in such a way as to create strange crosscurrents. Malus reckoned there would also be a sharp undertow on the upstream side. No wonder this Hag eats men, he thought. After a moment's consideration, he decided that he would first try to penetrate the tangle of roots on the downstream side. Better to fight something pushing him away from the tree than let hilself get dragged inside.

Malus soon discovered that the water grew deeper the closer he got to the tree, until he was forcing himself to wade in water that rose above his waist. The current lashed at him from first one direction, then another, trying to spin him around. He forced himself ever closer to the great tree until finally he could throw himself forward and grab one of the thick willow roots. His hands closed around a root as thick as a ship's cable, its springy core sheathed in a slick, almost viscous skin. The highborn fought a shudder of revulsion. It felt just like rotting flesh, he thought. Icy rotten flesh, at that.

Using the slimy roots for leverage, Malus began to probe his way deeper into the mass of roots. Almost at once, his sword scabbards became entangled in the convoluted mass. This is an invitation to disaster, Malus thought. Reluctantly, he undid his sword belt and tied it securely around a thick root near the edge of the mass, then pressed ahead.

Soon he was up to his neck in freezing water, crouching low under overhanging roots that pressed him closer and closer to the water's surface. He'd penetrated perhaps an eighth of the way into the root complex and he was entirely swallowed up in the malignant labyrinth. As he proceeded deeper, he was surprised to find a pale green luminescence emanating from the larger roots, glowing like grave-mould and providing a faint illumination. So far there were no signs of bones, but Malus figured he still had a way to go.

A few minutes and as many feet later, he came to a place where his way was blocked by a thick root broader than his leg. The only way ahead was to swim beneath it, and for the first time the idea gave him pause. The dank air beneath the tree smelled like a crypt, and a palpable aura of dread hung over Malus's head like a funeral shroud. I didn't come this far to drown beneath some damned old tree, he thought angrily. At the same time, he wasn't about to leave his warband to be mutilated at the hands of Beg and his savages.

No one steals my property from me, he thought grimly. With a sharp intake of breath, he slipped beneath the water and pushed his way under the great root, trusting that there would be another pocket of air on the other side.

There was – but the space was much tighter than he'd imagined, barely enough to hold his head. He gasped at the agonising cold, only dimly aware that the narrow space was brightly lit by the greenish mould. Malus filled his lungs and dived again, pushing himself ahead.

He came up – and his head struck a springy net of roots. Further, he thought. With an effort, he pushed himself lower and farther on, running his hand along the tangled mass above him.

Two feet. Three feet. Still nothing. His lungs began to burn. Do I turn back? He fought the first stirrings of panic.

Four feet. Five feet. No end in sight. The burning in his chest became an ache. It was hard to resist the urge to press his face against the ceiling of roots, hoping to find a mouthful of air.

Six feet – and the ceiling of roots began to curve sharply downwards. It was all he could do to keep from opening his mouth and gasping for air that didn't exist. Mother of Night, Malus thought, help me!

Malus turned around, struggling to keep his bearings in the darkness, when suddenly his ears filled with a slow, torturous groan. The entire mass of roots around him shifted – and the current shifted with it. The powerful force he'd been pushing against abruptly pulled him downwards and deeper towards the centre of the tree.

He tumbled in the vortex, striking roots that were tough as iron. His hands and feet caught in loops and sharp bends and were just as roughly yanked free. There was a buzzing in his ears, and the last breath in his lungs burst from his mouth and nose in a thin stream. Succumbing to panic, his eyes snapped open in the tumult – the pain was sharp and numbing, causing him to blink fiercely – and he caught a glimpse of greenish luminescence ahead of him. He struck another root, and this time he grasped it with a drowning man's iron grip. With all his failing strength he worked his way hand over hand towards the grave-glow, his eyes squeezed shut with the effort.

Malus's head burst through the surface of the churning water with a whooping gasp for air. It reeked of the sickly sweet taste of decay, but the highborn drank it down all the same. For a moment it felt as though he couldn't possibly inhale enough.

And then a pair of cold, rotting hands closed about his throat.

The highborn's eyes snapped open in shock. The glow came not from grave-mould, but from the figure of a woman. Rotting skin sagged like melted wax from her bones, which themselves were stained dark with age, like the bark of the tree.

Much of her hair was gone, and beneath her shrivelled cheeks her lips had rotted completely away, leaving only a death's-head snarl. Her eyes were empty sockets, but Malus could still see the burn scars around the edges, and the remnants of a rusted iron collar around her withered neck.

Silent and hateful, the Willow Hag pushed him downwards, until the raging water was roaring in his ears. She was not strong, but she had leverage and she was tireless as death. Malus beat at her rotting arms, feeling the bones flex like willow roots. His strength was failing fast, and her bony fingers closed inexorably tighter around his neck.

Desperate, Malus pulled at the hands until he could draw a thin stream of breath. 'Hateful wight, release me!' he gasped. 'I am a druchii of Hag Graef, not a Shade like those who blinded you! Let me live, and I'll give you another chieftain's son to pour your hate upon!'

For a terrifying second, nothing happened. Then there was another groaning sound, and Malus felt his surroundings shift once again. The churning water grew still. With eerie slowness, the fingers loosened their grip on his throat. As soon as he was free, Malus pushed away, putting as much space between himself and the wight as possible.

He was in a hollow of sorts, possibly directly under the tree itself. Walls, ceiling and floor were shaped by an impenetrable web of strong, layered roots. Skeletons, dozens of them, were enmeshed there, held together by tatters of clothing.

The stench of rot hung like a haze in the air, coating the inside of his nostrils and throat. At the same time this realisation struck home, Malus's backwards-reaching hand sank into a soft, pulpy mush. Gelid body fluids oozed around his splayed fingers. The highborn turned and found his hand buried in the rotting goo of a dead Autarii's stomach. Well met, Ruhir, Malus thought, pulling his hand free of the mess with a frown of disgust. Beg's son was splayed on a rack of tree roots like the Hag's other victims; beneath the mangled throat hung a silver medallion worked with the image of a rearing stag.

Malus turned back to the Hag, his mind working furiously. Clearly the wight was the hate-filled spirit of an Autarii slave who'd escaped her captors, only to stumble blindly into the river and die beneath the tree. Studying the rotting form, he saw by the ragged kheitan she wore that she'd once been a noble. In the uncertain light, it appeared that the tree's roots pierced the body in dozens of places; indeed, it was difficult to tell where the tree ended and the Hag began.

'Hear me, fell spirit,' Malus said hoarsely. 'Even now, another chieftain's son waits nearby to murder me when I emerge from your chambers. He means to make slaves of my warriors, just as he enslaved you. I mean to see him dead, and it would please me to deliver him into your hands. If you allow me to leave here with the medallion around this corpse's neck, I'll give him and his men to you. That's seven lives for the price of one, and sweeter prey besides. I give you my oath as a highborn.'

The wight regarded him silently for long moments. Dark water lapped gently at the tree roots, and insects crawled and chattered through Ruhir's decaying corpse. Then, suddenly, the hollow shifted again, elongating and contracting, pushing Malus inexorably closer to the Hag.

She stood less than a foot away when the movement finally stopped. Cold air wafted down from above. Malus looked up to see that a channel had opened through the roots at a slight angle, opening to the dark sky a dozen feet or so above. With a creak of old sinew and leather the wight pointed silently upwards.

Malus bowed his head to the Hag. 'Your wish is my command,' he said with a cruel smile.

SHIVERING IN THE cold wind, Malus looped his sword belt over an overhanging branch that stretched out over the river on the upstream side. With a grunt of effort, he pulled the limb back until he could reach it, then hung the Ancri Dam from it and carefully returned it back to its original place.

The black willow's overhanging branches and long, black tendrils created a curtain of foliage that encompassed a space larger than a campaign tent. Plenty of room to manoeuvre, he thought. Next, he concealed his swords amid a cluster of roots close to

the water's edge. Once all was in place, he turned
and ran inland, bursting through the curtain of
foliage into full view.

'Nuall!' he shouted, having no difficulty sounding
tired and hurt. 'Show yourself! I know you're out
here! I have a bargain for you!' Malus walked a few
yards from the tree and sank to his knees.

Wind whispered in the bushes and shook the
branches of the trees. Malus peered warily into the
darkness. Then, without warning, seven Shades coalesced out of the shadows, surrounding him with
bared blades. Nuall grinned at the shocked look on
the highborn's face. '*I'll* make *you* a bargain,' the chieftain's son replied. 'Give me the medallion and I'll kill
you quickly.'

'I don't *have* the medallion, you fool,' Malus said
contemptuously. 'Your father neglected to mention
that the Hag was haunted. I'm lucky to have gotten
away with my life.'

Nuall took a step forward, extending the point of
his sword until it was scant inches from Malus's eye.
'Well, your luck just ran out.'

'Wait!' Malus cried, holding up a warding hand. 'I
saw the medallion. I know where it is. Let me live and
I'll take you to it. You can have the Ancri Dam and my
warband besides. I've had enough of your damned
hills.'

The chieftain's son thought it over, clearly struggling with the competing urge to please his father and
sate his bloodlust. Finally he nodded. 'Very well.'

'I want your oath, Nuall!'

'All right, my oath on it! Now show me the medallion!'

Malus rose painfully to his feet. Surrounded by the Shades, he turned and walked back to the tree. The Autarii hesitated when they reached the curtain of black tendrils, but when the highborn passed through without harm they quickly followed suit.

He led them up to the base of the old tree. Nuall looked around. 'All right, now what?'

'The medallion is hanging from a limb on the opposite side. We'll have to work our way over across the tops of the roots–'

'You're mad, highborn!' Nuall exclaimed.

'Or you're a coward,' Malus answered. Before Nuall could respond, the highborn stepped onto the tangled mass of roots. 'It's slick, but not impossible to cross. Now, are you coming?'

Nuall gave him a glare of pure murder, then set his jaw stubbornly and followed Malus onto the roots. As he did, he turned and pointed at three of his men. 'You go around the other way and meet us.'

Reluctantly, the Autarii obeyed. Malus turned and walked carefully along the roots, working his way around the wide bole of the tree. Nuall followed closely, growing bolder with every step. Finally, Malus pointed to the medallion, turning gently on its chain out over the river.

'There it is,' he said. 'If two stout men can climb onto the branch enough to bend it back towards the tree, a third man could grab the medallion.'

Nuall nodded. 'A good plan.' Just then, the retainers who'd made the journey on the opposite tack around the tree stepped carefully into view. Nuall pointed at them. 'Two of you get up on that branch and start

bending it towards us. You–' he pointed at Malus–
'grab the medallion and hand it to me.'

Malus nodded, trying to look fearful. 'If you insist.'

The two Autarii climbed nimbly up the bole of the
willow and began edging their way along the limb.
Slowly but surely the branch dipped, bending closer
and closer to the trunk. Malus crouched, as though to
steady himself. His right hand felt between the roots
beside him and closed on the hilt of one of his
swords.

The medallion inched towards him. Malus
stretched out his left hand, while the other loosened
the sword in its scabbard. *Just a little bit more…*

'Ha!' Nuall cried, lunging forward without warning
and closing his fist around the medallion. 'Kill the
highborn!'

Just as I expected, you oath breaking bastard, Malus
thought scornfully, and leapt a heartbeat after Nuall.
He grabbed Nuall's wrist and heaved downwards,
drawing his sword in the same motion. The chieftain's son let out a yell, and the branch cracked like a
thunderclap, spilling one of the Shades into the river.
Nuall overbalanced and fell in as well, dragging
Malus with him.

All around them, the Willow Hag groaned hungrily,
and the undertow at once became a ravenous vortex.
Malus pressed back against the roots, held momentarily in place by the force of the undertow rushing
through a gap just beneath his boot heels.

The Shade disappeared beneath the surface with a
startled gasp. Nuall thrashed about, groping for the
shifting tree roots. He held the Ancri Dam in a white-
knuckled grip. 'Release me!' he roared, threatening to

pull Malus away from the roots and into the undertow.

'As you wish, fool,' Malus snarled. His sword flickered in the moonlight, slicing through Nuall's
forearm just below the highborn's own clutching
hand.

The chieftain's son screamed, bright blood pump-
ing from the severed limb. Broken ends of bone
gleamed pale white in the moonlight. Malus reposi-
tioned himself carefully, digging his boots into the
network of roots for support.

'Your brother is waiting below, Nuall,' he said
coldly, 'along with a serving girl eager to take you into
her arms!'

Nuall screamed as Malus brought his blade down
on the Autarii's other wrist. Blood bloomed darkly
beneath the water, and then the chieftain's son was
gone.

Suddenly there was a sharp blow along the top of
Malus's head, tracing a line of fire along his scalp. The
highborn cried out in pain as hot blood poured down
the side of his head. The second Autarii still clung
from the overhanging branch directly above Malus,
swinging down at him with a short, broad sword.
Much of the man's body was protected by the dark
wood, an advantage the Shade was trying to use to its
fullest effect. Of the other Autarii, nothing could be
seen, though the Hag's roots were writhing hungrily
like a bed of snakes.

Malus pushed against the roots beneath him and
hacked upwards, getting a shower of wood chips for
his efforts. He struck again, and this time the Shade
took the opportunity to slash at his forearm, leaving

a deep cut just behind the highborn's sword wrist. Malus thrust at the Shade's leering face, but the distance was too great, and the tip faltered well short of its target. The Autarii lashed downwards again with a stroke that left a shallow cut on the back of the highborn's sword hand.

The highborn let out a roar and slashed his long blade in a backhanded arc that buried the blade in the tree branch – and widened the crack made earlier. With a grinding crash the limb broke away, plunging the terrified Shade into the river. Autarii and limb hit the water with a flat slap, but only the limb surfaced again, spinning lazily along the surface of the river.

With a supreme effort, Malus pulled himself up onto the mass of writhing roots. His left hand still clenched Nuall's severed forearm; its hand still held the medallion in a death grip.

Unwilling to let go of his sword and lose it in the roiling mass of roots, Malus sank his teeth into Nuall's stiff fingers and pried each one away from his prize. The medallion fell away, and the highborn hurriedly tossed the severed limb into the whirlpool at the base of the tree. Immediately, the palpitating tendrils fell still. Malus rolled onto his back and managed a breathless laugh. 'Such an appetite,' he said to the tree stretching above him. 'That's the kind of epic hate I can truly admire.'

He lay there in the cold for some time, catching his breath and contemplating a nap. Just a short one, he thought. The roots aren't so bad. Just a short nap, to get my strength back. But finally a tiny, strident voice in the back of his mind pushed itself to the fore and warned him that if he paused to rest for much longer he would never get up again.

Groaning, Malus pushed himself upright, then clambered carefully to his feet. He buckled on his sword belt and fumbled the medallion over his blood-caked head. The cut on his scalp ached and burned, and he focused on the pain, drawing strength from it. The wisdom of the Dark Mother, he thought, his mind turning back to the catechisms of his childhood. In pain, there is life. In darkness, endless strength. Look upon the night and learn these lessons well.

Malus worked his way carefully around the tree. There was a cold wind blowing down into the valley, and the branches of the Willow Hag rustled and whispered above him.

Wait, Malus thought. This tree doesn't shift in the wind–

The highborn turned just as the Shade leapt onto him from one of the willow's broad branches, and the knife stroke meant for Malus's heart tore a ragged furrow along his back instead. Both men went down, howling for one another's blood.

Malus snarled like a wolf and drove the pommel of his sword into the Autarii's face, crushing the man's left cheekbone like brittle wood. He pushed away from the Shade and hacked down with his sword in the same motion, but the man threw up his left hand to protect his exposed throat.

The sword rang like a struck chime as it hit the soft flesh between the man's middle fingers and split his hand down to the wrist. Runnels of bright blood poured down the Shade's forearm, but incredibly the berserk Autarii clenched his fist and twisted his hand, pinning the sword in his grip. The man rolled onto his back and stabbed wildly with his knife, scoring another bloody line across Malus's cheek. Another quick stab sank the point of the Shade's knife two inches deep in the highborn's shoulder. Roaring, Malus grabbed the Shade's knife wrist and leapt atop him, trying to pull his sword free for the killing stroke.

There was a rumbling beneath the Shade, and the ground began to sink around the combatants. Sensing what was happening, Malus let go of his sword and grabbed the Autarii by the throat, pressing him down into the earth's embrace. Then the ground parted, and both men were plunging down a chute of pulsating roots.

The plunge stopped as swiftly as it began. The chute had narrowed, and the Shade was at the bottom, wedged headfirst down the hole. Without warning the chute constricted and the Shade began to scream and thrash, his feet beating desperately against the glistening roots. The walls of the chute closed in around Malus as well, pushing the two men apart. The screams rose to a crescendo amid the creaking of pliant wood. There was a sound like a melon dropped onto cobblestones and the Shade spasmed, then went still.

More creaks and groans filled the chute, and the walls continued to constrict. Malus felt a surge of anger, but it guttered like a candle in a gale. He was all but spent. With his last burst of strength he grabbed at the hilt of his sword and drew it firmly into his grip.

It took a few moments to realise that he was being pushed steadily upwards. Malus glanced down and saw the soles of the Shade's boots disappearing amid the tangled roots. Soon his head was in the open air again, and he weakly managed to push himself the rest of the way out of the hole.

His ravaged body cried out for rest, but he was wary of that siren song now. The highborn forced himself to his feet, facing the old, black tree. Wearily he raised his sword in salute. 'You keep your oaths better than the living, hateful wight,' he said. 'If it lies within my power, I'll see you're well fed for years to come.'

Malus carefully sheathed his stained sword and staggered into the night. The branches of the Willow Hag rustled faintly in a nonexistent breeze, and then settled down to savour its fleshy feast.

IN PAIN THERE is life. In darkness, endless strength. Or, as Malus's childhood sword master was fond of saying: as long as you're hurting, you're still living.

Malus had stopped hurting some time ago. He wasn't exactly sure when. He crawled like an animal up the slopes, over the brambles and around the many trees, and then tumbled down the opposite sides. Sometimes the climb took longer than usual – he'd be climbing and then realise that for a while he hadn't been moving at all, just staring down at his bloodstained hands.

When he finally hit level ground the change was so profound it left him stunned for quite some time. It was only when he noticed that he could see the blue tinge to his hands that he realised false dawn was colouring the sky overhead. Malus looked up and saw the round shapes of tents not far away, and the long-house beyond. He took a deep, shuddering breath and forced himself to stand. There were the shadows of men lingering at the corners of his vision – sentries, his exhausted mind supposed, trailing along behind him but unwilling – or afraid – to lend him aid.

The next thing he knew, he was pushing the long-house doors open. Inside, the Autarii were sprawled about on their pillows, and the Urhan passed out in his chair. Malus's retinue sat in a tight knot near the hearth, their eyes wide upon seeing their lord's return. The warmth of the room touched the high-born's frozen skin, and now his body awoke in a grinding onslaught of pain.

Malus let out a roar that was born of triumph and agony intertwined, and the Autarii leapt to their feet with steel in hand, believing themselves under attack. The highborn laughed wickedly at their distress, then fixed his eyes on the astonished face of Urhan Beg.

Slowly, painfully, Malus pulled the Ancri Dam from around his neck and tossed it at the Urhan's feet.

'A gift from the Willow Hag,' Malus said, 'plucked from the gold and pieces of jewellery scattered upon her cold breast. There is a king's ransom down there among her roots, but this was all I escaped with. Much good may it do you.'

Pandemonium erupted in the great hall, but Malus was already falling, down into oblivion's waiting arms.

Chapter Twelve
THE WIGHTHALLOWS

THE OLD, WEATHERED skull had the chill of the grave about it, even in the fire-lit warmth of the Autarii tent. The delicate silver wire felt like a thread of pure ice beneath Malus's slender finger as he traced its convoluted path. During his first, tortured glimpse of the relic he'd believed that the wire was meant to hold the skull and the lower jaw together, but now he could see that this wasn't so. It was one continuous loop that turned and twisted upon itself again and again, enclosing the bone within a weave that had a pattern and a purpose to it that was maddening in its complexity.

The skull itself felt like cold, unyielding stone – it leeched the heat from his hand, leaving it numb and aching even as the rest of him sweltered in the tent's hot, smoky air. Worst of all were the skull's empty eye sockets. The black pits swallowed up the firelight and revealed nothing of their depths, yet for all that Malus could feel the cold weight of the skull's penetrating stare. It was as if some remnant of the owner's malignant intelligence still haunted the empty braincase and studied him with cold, reptilian interest.

Damned sorcerous thing, Malus thought. I'd just as soon take a mallet to it. He knew next to nothing about sorcery, and what Malus didn't know, he didn't trust. Not for the first time he wished he'd forced Nagaira to come along and take charge of the relic. She would have had its riddles unravelled in a moment, leaving him to focus on getting to the temple and reaping its hidden treasures.

Malus sat propped against a pile of floor pillows near the tent's fire pit, with a weight of furs and wool blankets lying over his lower body. The cuts to his hand, forearm and scalp had been neatly stitched, and the healing skin itched fiercely despite the soothing ointment covering the wounds. A wooden tray dusted with crumbs and an empty water flagon lay on its side close by, next to the highborn's swords and his saddlebags. The journal of Urial the Forsaken lay in Malus's lap, the parchment pages opened to the book's final entry.

There was the sound of rustling leather, and Malus glanced over to see Lhunara stooping through the entryway of the tent. She let out a grunt of surprise at the sight of him. 'Awake at last!' she said, clearly relieved. 'We were starting to fear you'd sleep through the winter, my lord.'

Malus frowned. He knew from the aches in his muscles and joints that he'd been lying asleep for some time. 'How long?'

'Nearly four days, my lord.' She shuffled across the tent and began adding fresh sticks to the fire. 'The first day was the worst – you were like ice, and nothing we did would warm you up. The Autarii who were guarding the camp said you looked like a vengeful spirit when you came staggering down out of the hills. Even the Shades in the longhouse thought you were a ghost come back to haunt them. That's what they're calling you now: *An Raksha.*'

The highborn chuckled. 'The Wight, eh? If only they knew.' Unconsciously, his free hand went to his throat, where he could still feel the long bruises left by the Willow Hag's implacable grip. 'Is it morning or night?'

'Night, and late at that. I've just got back from checking the men keeping watch on the nauglir. Dalvar and Vanhir are drinking with Urhan Beg in the longhouse.'

Nothing good can come of that, Malus thought. 'Whose tent is this?'

Lhunara shrugged. 'Yours now, my lord. It was Nuall's, but Beg ordered his things moved into Ruhir's old tent, since he's now the eldest surviving son. Not that anyone has seen Nuall in the last four days or so.' The retainer gave Malus a pointed look. 'The Urhan wants to talk to you as soon as you've awakened.'

'Yes, I imagine he does,' Malus said, ignoring the implication in Lhunara's tone. 'I expect he wants to fulfil his part of the bargain and be rid of us just as quickly as he can.'

Lhunara poked at the embers with a short length of kindling, then indicated the skull with the stick's smoking end. 'Has it given up any secrets yet?'

'No,' the highborn said reluctantly, reaching for his saddlebags. 'And there's very little that makes sense in Urial's journal.' Malus pulled a thick scarf from the saddlebag, wound it tightly around the relic and carefully placed it back in the bag. 'Unless I'm much mistaken, I don't think Urial knew much more about the skull than we did.'

'Why do you say that, my lord?'

Malus leaned back against the pillows, concealing a sigh of relief. He was startled at how weak he felt after the ordeal in the hills. A small part of his mind reeled at the thought of how close he'd come to dying. No, he thought fiercely. It proves that if my will is strong, nothing can stop me.

He picked up the journal, flipping back through the delicate sheets of human parchment. 'Urial's notes make reference to a number of sources – *The Saga of Crimson*, *The Ten Tomes of Khresh*, and others – but very few direct observations about the skull itself. No insights about the runes or the silver wire. Either he was already familiar with the runes and what they said, and knew what the wire did, or–'

'Or they weren't relevant to the mystery of the temple and its contents, which leaves us with nothing to go on.'

Malus suppressed a smile. You're almost too clever sometimes, Lhunara, he thought. Good thing for me you have nowhere else to go.

'That's true. But,' he said, raising a long finger, 'the journal does mention a few possible clues.' The highborn searched the entries carefully. 'Here we are. There's a note here that reads "Kul Hadar in the North", and describes "a wooded valley, haunted by beasts, in the shadow of a mountain cleft by the axe of a god". Then–' he flipped through a few more pages– 'there's a reference here to "the key to the Gate of Infinity, and the temple beyond"'.

Lhunara frowned. 'And this Kul Hadar is the name of the valley?'

'Or the temple perhaps,' Malus said. 'I'm not sure.'

The retainer poked at the fire some more, considering her next words carefully. 'I thought Nagaira said the skull would lead us to the temple.'

'She did.'

'And yet…'

'And yet it's doing nothing of the sort,' Malus replied. 'It's possible that Nagaira didn't know as much about the skull as she let on.'

Lhunara nodded slowly, her face carefully neutral. 'Perhaps so, my lord. That being the case, is it wise to continue at this point? As weak as you are–'

'Weak? *Weak?*' Malus flung the furs and blankets aside. Anger burned along muscle and sinew in his chilled limbs, propelling him to his feet. He leapt at Lhunara, one hand snatching a half-burned stick from the fire while the other closed about his retainer's throat. 'I should put a red coal under your tongue for such insolence! Do not presume to judge my strength, Lhunara. I will find this temple and reap whatever treasures it holds and *nothing* will stand in my way – least of all you.'

Lhunara had gone rigid at Malus's touch. She met her lord's eyes with a cold, black stare of her own. 'No one questions your terrible will, my lord,' she said with preternatural calm. She eyed the red-hot ember hanging scant inches from her face. 'Shall I quench the hot coal with my tongue?'

With an effort, Malus reined in his temper. He dropped the stick back in the fire. 'And how would you give orders to the men afterwards?' The highborn gave her a rude shove that sent her sprawling. 'Go to the Urhan and tell him I am coming,' he said. 'And don't question my strength ever again.'

'Yes, my lord,' Lhunara replied, her face carefully neutral. She rose smoothly to her feet and slipped gracefully from the tent.

Malus waited for the space of two more deep breaths and then collapsed onto the blankets. His arms and legs quivered in the wake of the sudden burst of energy. His mind roiled with a tumult of thoughts. It was bad enough that he'd taken such a gamble with Lhunara – she could have handled him like a kitten if her anger had gotten the better of her, as his had. Worse, it was foolish to make an enemy of one's own lieutenant on an expedition as risky as this one.

But worst of all was the suspicion that now festered like poison in the back of his mind. If Nagaira knew less about the skull than she'd let on, perhaps she had other reasons for remaining back at the Hag. Had she made a cat's paw out of him?

The notion did little to improve his humour, but the anger soon quelled his rebelling muscles and returned a little fire to his veins. Slowly and deliberately the highborn rose to his feet and started to dress.

As DRAINED AS he was, Malus still felt more at ease with his armour on and his swords belted in place. It was indeed well past midnight, and one moon shone full and bright in a sky crowded with tatters of high-flying cloud. The pale light glimmered on a carpet of freshly-fallen snow. He drank in the cold air gratefully, a little surprised at how pleasant it felt. Not so cold as the Willow Hag's embrace, Malus thought ruefully as he made his way to the long-house.

The great hall was practically empty; a light dusting of ash from the fireplaces lay on the tumbled floor pillows and rugs. Dalvar, Vanhir and a half-dozen older Shades sat near the Urhan's dais, passing a wineskin between one another and smoking from pale clay pipes. Neither of Malus's men appeared drunk, though it was clear that several of the Shades were deep in their cups. Urhan Beg had evidently declined the wine, and instead reclined in his great carved chair, brooding over a pipe of his own. Lhunara was nowhere to be seen.

Vanhir rose silently to his feet as the highborn approached the dais, his expression calculating. Dalvar finished off a long swig from the skin and raised it in salute. 'My lord An Raksha walks the world of the living once more,' he said with a roguish grin. The other Autarii chuckled respectfully. The Urhan made no reply.

'My thanks, great Urhan, for your hospitality,' Malus said, 'and your generosity to my men. I trust they haven't been seduced from their duties by your fine wine and warm hearth.'

The Urhan shrugged. 'It's no affair of mine if they have.'

'As it happens, my turn at watching the nauglir is almost at hand,' Vanhir said smoothly, then offered

Malus a short bow. 'With your leave, my lord, I will depart.'

Malus nodded severely, but the knight made no reaction, instead bowing to the Urhan and striding quietly from the hall.

'And you, Dalvar?' the highborn inquired.

Nagaira's man shrugged expansively. 'The morning watch is mine, dread lord, but there's plenty more night left for sleeping. In the meantime, I'm learning what I can at the feet of these old ghosts.'

And what are they learning from you, I wonder? Malus thought. Since his realisation about Nagaira, his mind had started to boil with suspicions. The sooner they were in the Wastes the better. Fighting for one's life left little time for treachery.

'What brings you walking in the snows so late at night, city-dweller?' Beg asked, his gaze hard and appraising.

The highborn bowed to Urhan Beg. 'My lieutenant informed me that you wished to speak with me as soon as I awoke, great Urhan. I did not wish to keep you waiting.'

'Your *lieutenant*,' Beg sneered. 'A woman bearing swords and armour in peacetime? It's unseemly.'

Malus shrugged. 'The brides of Khaine bear arms all year long, and no one faults them. Lhunara Ithil went to war and found she liked the taste of it. What's more, she is very, very good at it. I would be a fool to overlook such skills simply because Naggaroth is not at war now. Regardless, as you so clearly pointed out, my retainers are no affair of yours. Now what did you wish to speak to me about?'

Beg leaned forward in his chair, his hand going to the medallion at his neck. 'The Ancri Dam is a powerful relic,' the chieftain said, rubbing the polished ithilmar thoughtfully. 'With it, I know when a man lies to me. I haven't seen my son Nuall for almost four days, not since you left to visit the Willow Hag. Did you see him that night?'

Malus considered Beg carefully. He could be bluffing, Malus thought. Do I take that risk? 'Yes. I saw him,' the highborn said after a moment's thought. 'He waited until I left the tree and tried to steal the medallion from me.'

Several of the Autarii shook their heads at the news. They didn't seem much surprised. The Urhan eyed Malus balefully. 'Did you kill him?'

'No, I didn't.'

'Did you hurt him?'

Malus smiled, holding up his stitched arm. 'I gave as good as I got, great Urhan. But there were seven of them.'

'Then what happened to Nuall and his men?'

'I can't say for certain,' Malus replied. 'I had the medallion, they tried to take it from me, and I escaped. Beyond that, I don't know.'

For a long time the Urhan said not a word, staring into the highborn's dark eyes as though he could pore through them like a book. Eventually he gave a snort of disgust and leaned back in his chair. 'Stupid boy,' he muttered, half to himself. 'What's the point of having the medallion if there's no one to pass it on to?'

You should have thought of that before you set him against me, Malus thought, suppressing a smile.

One of the Shades spoke up as he reached for the wineskin. 'What about the story Janghir told, about those dark horsemen near Seven Tree Hill?'

'Horsemen!' Beg spat. 'Who brings horses into these hills?'

Malus saw Dalvar stiffen. He shot a surreptitious glance at Malus, who kept his face impassive. Dark riders, Beg, filled with Khaine's wrath, the highborn thought. Horses and men who do not suffer from wounds, fatigue or fear. Deathless, patient and relentless...

'I can appreciate your concern for your son, great Urhan,' Malus said. 'And I do not wish to distract you from the search for Nuall and his men. So let us be on our way and create no further distractions for you or your clan.' The highborn drew himself to his full height and folded his arms imperiously. 'I require a guide to the frontier, one who can lead me past the druchii watchtowers and to the edge of the Chaos Wastes.'

'Why not take the Spear Road?'

'I don't recall personal questions being included as part of our bargain, Urhan Beg. It's enough for you to know that I need to get to the frontier quickly and quietly.'

'What part of the Wastes are you trying to reach?'

Malus squared his jaw. 'There is a mountain in the Wastes that looks as though it were split by the axe of a god. Somewhere near the foot of that mountain is Kul Hadar.'

The assembled Shades stirred uneasily, throwing dire looks at one another. Beg gave Malus a bemused look, his eyebrows furrowing in concern. 'You're looking for Kul Hadar? Why?'

'*Questions*, Urhan Beg. Can you get me to that part of the frontier or not?'

The Urhan thought it over for some time, while the Autarii passed the wineskin between them and muttered under their breath. 'Yes, this can be done,' he said carefully. 'In fact, it can be done very quickly, if your heart is up to the task.'

'Now I ask *you* to speak plainly, Urhan Beg. What do you mean?'

Beg tapped the stem of his pipe against his stained lower teeth. 'There is a path through the hills,' he said. 'A... a path that's not entirely of this world. At certain times, it is possible to walk that path from one end to another and cover a hundred leagues in a single night. I did it myself once, many years ago. But it is not for the faint of spirit.'

Malus smiled. 'Believe me, we have no small experience with such places. I'm certain we are up to the journey.'

The Urhan looked Malus in the eye, and for the first time he smiled. 'On your head be it, then. As it happens, the moons and the season are in a very favourable alignment, so the road should be easy to follow. Gather your men, Darkblade; we will leave an hour before sundown.'

'And in the meantime?'

Beg leaned back in his chair, his eyes glittering in the firelight. 'In the meantime take what joy of the sunlit world you can.'

By LATE AFTERNOON Malus had roused his warband and set them to making preparations for travel. Despite Urhan Beg's ominous warnings, he was eager to be moving once more.

Malus uncorked the glazed earthenware jug and poured another dollop of viscous fluid onto the silken cloth in his hand. For an instant, the poisonous slime was shockingly cold against his bare skin, but within moments the affected area had gone numb from the effects of the toxin. Over time, most cold one knights lost all feeling in their skin – in some cases, even the ability to smell and taste – after years of exposure to the nauglir's slime. But those were concerns for the future. Today, Malus needed the use of his nauglir, Spite, and so he paid the necessary price.

Lhunara waited patiently in the dark confines of the tent, holding the backplate of the highborn's armour as Malus shrugged into his robes and kheitan. 'Any sign of Beg?' Malus asked.

'None, my lord. The crone in his tent says she has not seen him since last night. I don't think he's anywhere in the camp.'

Malus pulled the laces on the kheitan tight, then picked up his breastplate and fitted it into place. With the ease of long practice, Lhunara fitted the snug backplate around the highborn's shoulders and waist, and then began to buckle the two halves together. Malus grunted thoughtfully as Lhunara drew the straps tight. 'Possibly out looking for his son, or planning some other sort of mischief. Inform the men to keep their crossbows ready once we set out.'

'Yes, my lord.'

The highborn paused. 'How long until Vanhir's oath runs its course?'

'Three more weeks,' the retainer answered. 'Do you suspect something?'

'I always suspect something, Lhunara. He's been talking a lot to Dalvar, and Dalvar has been talking to the Urhan. His oath doesn't allow him to act directly against me, but that wouldn't stop him from sharing what he knows about me with anyone who will listen.'

Lhunara picked up the highborn's left vambrace and slipped it over his arm, sliding it up to Malus's shoulder like a jointed steel sleeve. 'You never should have accepted his oath,' she said darkly. 'Far better to have taken his life and been done with it.'

Malus shrugged, a gesture mostly lost beneath the weight of his armour. 'He comes from a powerful household. I thought it would be useful to have something to hold over them. And at the time, binding him to me seemed like the most humiliating punishment I could imagine. It was a fair wager, and his pit fighter lost.'

'His nauglir lost,' Lhunara corrected. 'You were wagering on the cold one fights after the gladiatorial games.'

Malus frowned. 'Were we? No matter – he bet against me and lost. And since then he's observed the particulars of his oath with ruthless, hateful punctiliousness. I greatly admire him for that, truth be told.'

'Do you still intend to kill him?'

'Oh, yes. Possibly even today. Keep a close eye on him and Dalvar. If Beg tries any treachery and either of them tries to help the Urhan, make certain you kill them both.'

THE AFTERNOON SKY had turned leaden, and drifts of snow whirled about in the cold air. The cold ones were saddled and drawn up in line, under the wary eyes of their riders – five days in a corral had left them snappish and sullen despite regular meals of venison and boar. It was already getting dark beneath the snow-covered limbs of the forest, and Malus was growing increasingly impatient. Sensing his master's mood, Spite clawed restlessly at the frozen earth and rumbled deep in his throat.

Malus paced down the length of the column, making a show of inspecting the warband as a way of concealing his unease. Lhunara sat in her saddle at the end of the line, her crossbow in her lap, her eyes searching the shadows to either side of the column.

Dalvar and his mount were in the centre of the column. Malus came upon Nagaira's man as he was checking the girth-straps on his saddle. 'I believe you still have something of mine,' the highborn asked, holding out his hand.

The rogue grinned up at Malus, and the small iron knife seemed to magically appear in his palm. 'Are you certain you don't want me to hold onto it?' Dalvar asked. 'We still have Urhan Beg to deal with.'

'Do you think he'll try to turn on us?'

Dalvar shrugged. 'Of course. Don't you?'

Malus plucked the blade from Dalvar's hand. 'You've been spending time in his hall. What do you think?'

'I think he believes you've killed his son. Even if you didn't, you embarrassed him by recovering that medallion of his when Nuall couldn't.' The druchii pulled the last strap tight and turned to face Malus. 'Frankly, he's *obligated* to betray you. They're rustics, but they aren't that much different from us. If he doesn't get the better of you at this point his clan will think him weak. That wouldn't bode well for his future.'

Malus studied the retainer carefully. 'And how do you suppose he's going to do this?'

Dalvar shook his head. 'I don't know. I've tried to get a sense of the man in the last few days, but he's a canny one. If you want my advice, my lord, you'll keep him close at hand once we've started on this path he's been so ominous about.' The druchii straightened and glanced past Malus's shoulder. 'There's the old wolf now.'

Malus turned to see Beg and two of his men standing in the shadow of a snow-covered cedar, speaking quietly among themselves. The highborn looked back at his men. *'Sa'an'ishar!'* Malus called. 'Mount up!'

As the druchii swung into their saddles, the highborn approached Urhan Beg. The Autarii chieftain eyed him with undisguised malice.

'My men are ready, great Urhan,' Malus said. On closer inspection, the highborn saw that the old Shade's boots and breeches were damp. You've been searching by the river, Malus thought.

'Ready? That remains to be seen,' sneered Beg. 'But we'll find out soon enough. Stay close – we've much ground to cover before nightfall.' With that, the three Autarii set off at a silent, ground-eating pace, slipping through the camp and heading north. Malus was forced to jog back to Spite and mount quickly before the scouts were lost to sight.

'Forward!' Malus ordered, grabbing up the reins. He caught sight of the scouts' retreating backs and put the spurs to his nauglir's flanks.

Let the game begin, he thought.

* * *

IT WAS NOT long at all before Malus and his warband were forced to dismount, prodding their recalcitrant mounts up steep and overgrown slopes as they had in days past. After the first hour, however, Malus began to note that the wildlife in the area was much more subdued – if not entirely nonexistent.

With each mile northwards, the sounds of the woods grew quieter, and fewer birds darted between the black-boled trees. The growing stillness conveyed a sense of menace that set the highborn's nerves on edge. He could tell the rest of the warband felt it too, from the way they eyed every deep shadow they passed. Some of the men had taken to carrying their crossbows at the ready, as if expecting an ambush at any moment.

After less than two hours, the light started to fade in the western sky. Strangely, the going became somewhat easier; the trees and undergrowth had grown sparse and taken on a grey, sickly cast. Malus began to notice a chill in the air – not the dry cold of the winter wind, but a kind of clammy stillness that ran along the ground beneath the trees and sank deep into one's bones.

Soon the landscape was painted in hues of inconstant, otherworldly light, as the auroras of the Chaos Wastes lit the northern horizon. Against this unsettling display, Malus could see that the hills ahead were giving way to larger, broader mountains – the old, granite bones of the earth, stripped bare by millennia of wind and snow. The highborn focused his eyes on the dark-robed figures several yards ahead and drove Spite onwards, wondering how much further they had yet to go.

As it happened, when Malus led Spite over the next hilltop, he found the Autarii waiting for him halfway down a long, fairly gentle slope leading to a broad valley. The slope was dotted with dozens of moss-covered boulders and tussocks of low grass. Everything was silhouetted in shifting, pale-green light, making the wisps of fog in the valley below seem to glow with a life of their own.

Beg and his men waited near one of the boulders. Malus hoisted himself into the saddle and urged Spite in their direction. He relaxed minutely, more comfortable in the open terrain than he had been in the overgrown hills behind him.

The Urhan's eyes were hidden in shadow as Malus approached, but the highborn could feel the weight of his stare all the same. 'We've come to the beginning of the path,' the chieftain said. 'We will walk along with you for a way, but the rest of the journey is for you alone.'

'What is this place?' Malus asked, shifting in the saddle.

'It is called the Wighthallows,' Beg answered. 'It is a place where the dead do not rest easy. Does this frighten you, city-dweller?'

Malus glared at the man. 'I've faced one wight already, Urhan. I can face another.'

Beg chuckled. 'We shall see.'

The Shades turned and made their way downslope. Malus paused to make certain the rest of the column had crested the hill and had closed the distance behind him, then sent Spite padding along after the Autarii.

As the column proceeded, Malus noticed that the boulders and the scattered tussocks grew more numerous closer to the bottom of the slope. The boulders themselves were oddly shaped, with a mix of rounded and sharp edges that seemed maddeningly familiar.

Suddenly there was a strange, metallic crunch and Spite's gait stumbled a bit. Malus glanced down and saw that the cold one had stepped on one of the tussocks. The gleam of bare metal winked in the ghostly light. Malus realised with a start that he was looking at a crumpled steel breastplate, covered in a thin layer of dirt and grass.

They had come upon the edge of a great battlefield.

Ahead, the Autarii had all but disappeared into the lambent mist. Malus fought down a rising sense of unease and pressed on.

The fog hungrily swallowed rider and beast, restricting vision and muffling all sound. Spite balked at the change in atmosphere, but Malus nudged him on. Shapes came and went in the mist. Two great obelisks appeared to either side of Malus, carved in the looping sigils of old Ulthuan. Faintly, Malus could hear Spite's talons clicking along bare stone. Were they on a roadway?

More shapes appeared, clustered on either side of the path. Malus took them for more boulders at first, but upon second glance he realised they were elven chariots, their wheels rotted away and their armoured flanks dented and rent. He caught sight of helmets, rusted swords and spearheads, their hafts long gone to dust.

The highborn looked about for any sign of the Autarii. He felt a vague sense of dislocation. It's the fog, he thought. Or was it?

He could just see the shapes of the scouts ahead. Malus kicked Spite into a trot, expecting to catch up with them in moments, but the fog had apparently distorted his sense of distance. It felt like long minutes before he caught up with Beg and his men. 'What happened here?' Malus asked. His voice sounded strange and indistinct, even to his own ears.

'One of old Aenarion's generals built a road here during the First War,' Beg replied, his voice sounding as though it were coming from a long way off. 'It winds through these valleys for many, many leagues – in the daylight you can just see the black stones of the roadway poking up from the earth. Legend says it was built for a siege against a city of daemons, far to the north, but no one knows for certain. If such a place ever existed, it's long gone now.

'The general took his mighty army north and met with tragedy. Some stories say he was betrayed – a rare few even go so far as to accuse your great Witch King of the deed – while others claim the general was simply a fool. Regardless, the great march turned into a bloody, bitter retreat, fraught with sorcery and slaughter. Every mile of this road is soaked in blood, the stories go. The stones of the road are mortared with bone.'

Malus felt a chill sweep across his skin. The wind moaned faintly in the darkness – or was that the sound of a distant horn?

'It is said that such was the power of the daemon host that they fixed the moons in their courses and fought beneath a mantle of perpetual night. The echoes of that power – and the restless spirits of the dead – linger here even now. When the proper season comes around and the moons are in the right phase, that long night resumes once more.'

The fog appeared to be thinning now; it lingered like a pall at the edges of his vision, but at the same time Malus could see more of his surroundings. Piles of armour, splintered shields and notched swords, ruined chariots with the barding of their horses resting in their rotted traces. A banner pole leaned at a drunken angle amid a tangle of breastplates, helmets and mail. The standard was heavy with dried gore, hanging listlessly in the mist. Malus could taste the dread in the air. It had a coppery tang, like spilled blood.

They travelled on. Malus began to notice more details as they went: the elaborate carvings of chariots and armour stood out in sharp relief. Polished ithilmar glowed with a pale, bluish light. He began to see the bones of skeletons amid the piles of armour. Once he passed an upturned helm still holding the skull of the man who wore it. The jaws gaped wide in a silent scream of anguish or rage.

There was a light up ahead. A bluish radiance suffused the mist, growing in intensity as they drew nearer. The sides of the road were crowded with chariots and wagons – the detritus of an army on the retreat. Their sides were raked and torn, hewn and hacked by tooth, claw and blade. The bodies of the dead were everywhere, still clutching their weapons in skeletal hands.

The air trembled. Malus felt the vibration against his skin. It shook with the din of battle, but no sound reached his ears. The highborn reached for his sword, taking some comfort in the familiar solidity of its hilt.

He could feel the presence of others around him – horses and men, moving past him, away from the nightmare they'd found in the far north.

The air quivered with silent screams.

Suddenly there were robed figures on either side of him. The Shades had stopped and he hadn't realised it. Their gaze was focused on the road ahead. As Malus reined in his mount, he saw the horror they beheld.

An army of the dead stood astride the road, gleaming with the unearthly glow of the grave. Enamelled armour shone in the pale, blue light, hanging on the skeletal frames of soldiers and horsemen. Some held spears and swords, while others held up grasping, claw-like hands. Points of cold blue light gleamed from the pits of their eyes, and their jaws gaped in silent cries of despair.

At their head stood a great prince, his armour enamelled in silver and gold. In his right hand he held a fearsome-looking sword, its length etched with runes of power. His left hand held a torn standard. Its ragged hem dripped with fresh blood.

'Who disturbs our rest?' The undead prince cried. His voice was a thin, keening whisper, like the sound of wind whistling over stone.

Chapter Thirteen
FIELDS OF DESPAIR

THE GHOSTLY PRINCE's helmeted head turned to regard Malus, the weight of his burning gaze falling on the highborn like the blow of a sword. He reeled from the wight's baleful stare, feeling his heart turn to ice. Around him he could dimly sense his warband pulling up, the druchii hauling back on their reins in shock and fear. One of the men let out a wail of terror, and the ranks of the dead lunged a half-step forward at the sound, as if hungry to set themselves against a foe who would bleed and die beneath their blades.

Before Malus could master his own tongue and make a reply to the fearful apparitions, Beg took a measured breath and spoke in a loud, strained voice. 'We are but travellers on the road, mighty prince! Forgive us our trespass, and we will honour you with obeisance... and sacrifice.'

Sacrifice! Malus's mind raced. Now the Urhan's scheme was all too clear.

The prince took another step towards the terrified warband with a creak and rattle of harness and ancient steel. 'Sacrifice!' The wight whispered hungrily. 'Who will stand atop my cold, stone bier and warm my bones with a libation of hot blood?'

With a cry of desperate rage Malus tore his eyes from the prince's paralysing stare and ripped his sword from its scabbard. Before Beg could reply, the highborn rose in his saddle and raised his blade high. 'Ride!' he called to his men. 'Ride for death and ruin, warriors of the Hag! RIDE!' The highborn clapped his spurs to Spite's flanks and the nauglir charged at the ghostly horde with a thunderous roar. A heartbeat later the unearthly air rang with the war-howls of Hag Graef as the cold one knights bared their steel and charged the fearsome host at the command of their lord.

The air filled with the shrieks of the damned as the spectral host charged to meet its foes. Malus lost sight of the banner-wielding prince amid a mob of howling wights as the two forces met with a great, rending crash. The charging cold ones ploughed into the elf army in a rough wedge, shattering ancient bodies and flinging bits of armour and bone in a gruesome shower back upon the ranks of their fellows.

Swords flickered and scythed through the frenzied ranks of the dead, shearing through limbs, torsos and skulls. Withered flesh and sinew parted in white clouds of rot; bleached bone was ground to powder beneath the stamping tread of the cold ones. A mortal host would have reeled in shock from the sheer ferocity of the warband's charge, but the howling dead swept around the druchii like a flood. Every warrior torn asunder was instantly replaced by another, all of them hammering at the armoured warriors with blades, spears, axes and claws.

'Forward!' Malus roared into the din, his blade hacking left and right at the frenzied horde. Spite tossed his head and snapped at his attackers, biting rotting corpses in two and scattering their remains in a wide arc. The highborn spurred the beast forward and the cold one charged into another knot of shrieking wights, bearing down on them with a sound like splintering wood.

The nauglir let out a furious bellow as one or more of the foe's weapons bit deep into his scaly hide. A corroded spear point glanced off Malus's left pauldron and scored a bloody track across the back of his neck. Hands scrabbled at the smooth armour enclosing his arms and legs, struggling to pull him from the saddle. With a roar he brought his sword down and smashed through wrists and forearms; rusty mail burst in glittering clouds of split links.

And then the prince was upon Malus, his gleaming blade flickering at him like the tongue of a viper.

Malus twisted in the saddle and brought his sword around in a desperate block that caused the prince's thrust to glance across the highborn's armoured thigh. The highborn chopped down at the prince's sword arm, but the wight blocked the stroke with supernatural speed. The enchanted ithilmar blade licked out again and Malus cried out as its point sliced a line of icy pain across his cheek. Blood trickled down his face and steamed from the frozen edges of the wound.

Malus could hear other screams around him now as the impetus of the warband's charge was spent and the warriors were surrounded by the tide of hungry dead. He leaned forward, slashing at the prince's eyes, but the wight no longer feared the thought of blindness. Instead of flinching back, the skeletal warrior ducked low enough to take the blow on his helm and slashed at the highborn's calf. The enchanted blade carved a neat line through the steel plate, and Malus gasped as his lower leg went numb.

Think, the highborn's mind raged. You can't best him sword to sword! Think of something quickly or you're dead!

The highborn cried out in defiance and slashed again at the prince's face. The wight leaned back fractionally, just beyond the limit of Malus's stroke, then leapt forward, swinging his blade in a brutal arc for the knee joint of the highborn's armour.

But Malus's attack was only a feint; anticipating the prince's blow, he jerked his boot from its stirrup and caught the wight's sword wrist with his heel. With a blood curdling howl, Malus brought his sword down on the crown of the prince's helm, splitting the ithilmar armour in two.

The prince reeled back, his skull wreathed in leaping blue flames and his skeletal jaw gaping in fury.

Malus snarled in reply and hauled on his reins, dragging Spite hard to the left. The nauglir's thickly muscled tail whipped around like a battering ram and smashed into the prince's chest. The wight's body exploded in a cloud of dust and shattered armour, his rune-carved sword spinning end-over-end through the air.

The highborn had barely a heartbeat to savour his triumph before a wight drove his spear deep into Spite's shoulder and the cold one jerked sharply away from the blow. The sudden change in motion caught Malus by surprise. For a dizzying second his numbed leg flailed for the empty stirrup, then clawing hands seized his shoulders and dragged him from the saddle. He landed on his back on the stones of the roadway with a frenzied mob of wights standing over him.

Blows rained down on his armour like a clatter of hail. A spear point found a gap in his left vambrace and gouged deep, causing Malus to hiss in pain. The blow of an axe smashed against his left knee; the armour held, but the joint beneath was wrenched by the impact. The tip of a notched sword sliced across his forehead, spilling a curtain of blood down the sides of his temples.

Malus roared like a man possessed, smashing his sword at the legs of his foes. Armoured foes toppled onto him, their cold hands clawing for his face and throat. Spite roared, and the crowd around him was knocked momentarily back as the cold one smashed them aside with a sweep of his armoured head.

The highborn threw his foes off him with a convulsive heave, shattering the skull of one determined wight with a short, chopping stroke of his sword. He leapt to his feet, propelled by battle-frenzy even as his mind fought a rising tide of panic. Without warning, his wrenched knee gave way and he fell forward against Spite's bloody flank. His free hand closed on one of his saddlebags for support, but the worn leather parted beneath his weight.

He fell, and a blazing skull tumbled into his grasp.

Malus's hand closed reflexively on the wire-wrapped relic despite the sizzling lines of blue fire that arced and snapped along its length. The skull's hollow eye sockets, formerly black pits of shadow, now seethed with globes of fiery light. When the relic settled into the highborn's hand a jolt shot through him, shooting down his arm and causing his heart to clench painfully. His whole body jerked – and words came bubbling up his throat and boiling from his mouth.

He couldn't understand what he was saying – he couldn't even hear the words, just a savage buzzing sound that sawed at the air. But he could *feel* the phrases tumbling from his mouth, taking shapes that were jagged and hard. He tasted blood in his mouth and felt the skin of his lips split from the pressure. With a terrible moan, the wights fled from him, falling back upon one another and clapping their shrivelled hands to their skulls.

As the wights fell back, the sizzling energy of the skull began to wane, but Malus lurched to his feet and willed the fire to blaze brightly again, focusing his anger at the incandescent relic. The terrible words twisted and writhed in his brain like a living thing, resisting his command. Burn brightly, wretched thing, Malus raged. Burn or I'll break you to pieces!

At that, the words surged through him again like a torrent, savaging his throat with their sharp edges and searing heat. The wights retreated still further, fleeing the sound of his voice. The din of the battle subsided, stunned into silence by the highborn's raging tongue.

Malus threw himself back into the saddle. His chest ached. It was as if a hot coal had been put in the place where his heart had been, and his lungs were shrivelling in the heat. The highborn held the relic high and swept his merciless gaze across the horde of the damned. Malus stood in the saddle and roared at the wights. 'Our blood is not for the likes of you! Raise a hand against us and I will scourge the spirit from your worthless bones and hurl you into the Outer Dark! Flee before my wrath, wretched sons of Aenarion! The Dark Mother waits, and if you press me I shall offer your souls up to her!'

The wights howled in fear and pain, their clawed hands raised in supplication. Malus looked back along the roadway and caught sight of the Shades, who'd dared to linger and watch the city-dwellers' demise. The highborn locked eyes with Urhan Beg and savoured the expression of terror on the chieftain's face.

Malus pointed his sword at the three Autarii. 'Slake your thirst on them, foul wights – they who thought to cheat you of your due.'

Beg screamed, and the heads of the malevolent wights turned at the sound. Then the air was rent with eerie howls as the Autarii turned to run and the skeletal warriors took up the chase.

The fire was ebbing again. Malus sought to stoke it once more, but found his fury wanting. His insides felt twisted and torn. Blood leaked from the corner of his mouth and spattered on his thigh. His sword drooped in his hand.

Around him, the druchii of his warband drooped wearily in their saddles or leaned against the heaving flanks of their mounts. The gore that streaked their faces and stained their armour was their own. Two knights lay near the corpses of their cold ones, one pierced with spears and hacked by swords and the other lying in bloody, twisted pieces, his guts shrivelled and blackened with frost.

Spite shuddered beneath him. The nauglir sported a score of wounds from head to tail. None of those who had survived had escaped unscathed.

The druchii looked to their leader, their faces gaunt and pale. Around them stretched a panorama of shattered bones and crumpled armour, broken spears and splintered shields. All of them, even Lhunara, looked upon their lord with an expression of utter fear.

A scream tore through the murky air, then another. The voices of the damned howled in reply.

Malus sheathed his sword and grasped Spite's reins. 'We ride,' he growled, each word a brilliant spike of pain. 'Leave the dead to their feast.'

With that, he turned his cold one north and set off along the road, bones crunching beneath Spite's feet.

MALUS AWOKE TO the hollow moaning of the wind. Slowly, achingly, he opened his eyes. He lay on his back beneath an iron-grey sky, his arms spread wide. The wind rustled through the tall grass in which he lay.

Something large stirred behind him. The highborn rose to one elbow, his whole body leaden and throbbing. Only a few feet away, Spite shifted on his haunches, regarding his master with one blood-red eye. The cold one's flanks were streaked with gravedust and splashes of ichor.

He lay on a grassy hill, facing a line of weathered mountains perhaps a mile away. Malus could see the mouth of a valley winding between two craggy peaks. Was that the end of the Wighthallows? The highborn frowned, trying to think. How did we come to be here? Memories eluded him, slipping away like shadows into the recesses of his mind. It seemed as though he'd ridden for an eternity, always in darkness, hounded by the voices of the dead. When dawn finally came he remembered falling from the saddle and a deeper darkness rushing up to meet him.

Malus tried to stand and bit back a hiss of pain as he put his weight on his wrenched knee. Like Spite, his dark armour was nearly white with grave-dust, darkened in places with splotches of old blood. There were cuts on his face, neck and forehead, and his cheeks were stiff with dried blood. The wound in his arm throbbed painfully, aggravated by a bent piece of metal forced into his skin by the wight's spear point. The cut in his right calf ached, but he was grateful to be able to feel the pain.

The skull was still in his left hand. His fingers were locked in a death-grip around the braincase. Its shadowed eye sockets seemed to be taking stock of him.

After a moment, the highborn noticed other furtive sounds of movement amid the waving grasses. Groans and whispers carried on the wind. A cold one let out a pained cry as someone pulled the point of an enemy weapon free and threw it across the hill, the thin steel ringing as it spun through the air.

Lhunara limped into view, the wind twisting loose strands of her braided hair. Her face was a mask of dust and blood, and the dark lines of fresh cuts marked her cheek and chin. Her eyes were haunted and sunken, ringed with dark circles of fatigue. She held a waterskin in one hand and a naked sword in the other, her gaze sweeping the surroundings with the practiced ease of a long-time veteran. She walked over to Malus and settled on her haunches, wincing at the loud popping of her knees. 'Are you hurt, my lord?' the retainer asked, a little out of breath.

'My damned knee–' the words came out in a horrid croak, dissolving into a string of wracking coughs. The inside of his mouth and throat felt scabby and dry, and his lips were cracked and stiff. Lhunara passed him the waterskin and he drank greedily in spite of the pain it caused. 'My damned knee,' he said in a hoarse whisper. 'That's the worst of it, I think.'

The retainer took the waterskin back and stoppered it. There was a wariness to her movements that Malus hadn't seen her use around him before. She eyed the relic. 'Still holding on to that?'

Malus looked down at the skull. With an effort, he forced his hand open. The metal creaked, and the relic fell onto the grass. At once, his knuckles began to throb and ache.

Lhunara seemed to relax a little. 'How did you do that, back there in the valley? What were the words you spoke?'

The highborn shook his head. 'I don't know. It… it was the skull. It put the words in my head somehow.' Unbidden, his sister's words echoed in his head: *It is not, in fact, a source of power – at least, not in any sense you would understand.* 'I don't know why.'

'Well, it saved us. I suppose that's all that matters,' Lhunara said. 'But we lost Hularc and Savann to the wights. That just leaves Vanhir and myself out of the six you brought from your household. The remainder are your sister's men.' She lowered her voice. 'And there's talk of turning back.'

Malus sat up, his hurts forgotten. 'Turn back? We've barely begun.'

Lhunara shook her head. 'I'd be wary about saying such things, my lord. That ride last night shook the men to their core. If you push them too hard, they'll break, and we can't afford to lose anyone.' She looked wearily to the south, at the mountains they'd only just departed. 'Like you said, we've barely begun.'

The highborn bit back his anger. Part of him wanted the names of the men who questioned his authority, but Lhunara was right. What could he do? He needed every sword he could muster. All he could do was lead them, and deal with a mutiny when it finally reared its head. 'Dalvar and Vanhir charged along with the rest, back in the valley?'

Lhunara nodded. 'They did.'

Malus grunted. The news puzzled him. 'They weren't going to get a better opportunity for treachery than that,' he muttered. 'Strange.'

Lhunara shrugged. 'You're assuming Dalvar is plotting against you. Why should he? I'd think it more likely he'd wait until you'd discovered the temple, then slip the knife between your ribs.'

'Unless he knows that we aren't going to reach the temple, and his orders are simply to ensure my demise.'

The retainer eyed him sharply. 'Why do you say that?'

Because I'm starting to think my sister tricked me, Malus started to say, then thought better of it. 'Never mind. I'm being overly suspicious,' he answered instead.

With an effort, he climbed slowly to his feet. Every part of him hurt in some way, like the day after a great battle. Malus limped over to Spite and slipped the skull into his other surviving saddlebag. As he did, he peered over the cold one's back and saw miles of rolling plains, covered in a rippling sea of brown grass.

Beyond them lay a band of dark green forest, and past that, rising high on the northern horizon, the dark, triangular bulk of a great mountain, its peak wreathed in snow and cloud. A sharp cleft, like the mark of an enormous axe, split the mountain at a shallow angle, stretching two-thirds of its length from tip to broad base. The highborn leaned against his saddle, trying to gauge the distance. It seems so close, he thought. A few days, perhaps? Then we'll see just how much Nagaira really knew.

Malus rested his forehead against the leather saddle for a moment, gathering his strength. Then, with a deep breath, he climbed painfully into the saddle. Spite barked in aggravation, but obediently rose to his haunches. 'Tell the men to mount up,' the highborn said, studying the sky. 'The day is nearly half-done. I want to cover a few more miles before dark.'

Lhunara stared at him. 'But, my lord, the men are tired and injured—'

'We aren't camping here,' Malus interjected. 'Better to reach the edge of those woods, where we can gather some wood for a fire.' And give the men something else to think about instead of plotting a mutiny, he thought. Bad morale was like an infection. It couldn't be allowed to sit and fester.

The retainer started to protest, but quickly regained her self-discipline. 'Yes, my lord,' she replied, and started barking orders to the rest of the warband.

As the warband checked their mounts and got back into their saddles, Malus kneed Spite around until he could face the mountain directly. He surveyed the plains and the dark woods carefully. So this is the Chaos Waste, he thought. Not so greatly different from home. I had expected much worse.

The wind shifted and moaned across the plains, stirring the sea of dead grass. He could not see what would cause such a hollow, funereal sound.

THEY WERE NO closer to the distant line of trees by the time night fell. The cloud cover remained heavy, but the auroras leaking from the northern horizon played across the underside of the clouds somehow in an eerie display of blue, green and yellow light. The shifting colours set a riot of shadows dancing among the windblown grasses, playing tricks on the eyes as the members of the warband kept watch for nocturnal predators. As long as there was enough light to ride by, Malus urged the column on. From time to time he caught himself nodding, his chin drooping to his chest. Fatigue and hunger were starting to take their toll.

There was a sound from up ahead. Malus tensed, his ears straining to hear over the incessant wind. Just when he thought he'd imagined it, he heard the sound again, like a faint scream of rage or pain. The highborn reached back and unhooked the crossbow from his saddle.

Moments later he heard the sound again. Definitely an angry cry, like a druchii war-scream. It was coming their way, but all he could see were dancing shadows and rippling waves of grass silhouetted against the dark horizon. He raised a gauntleted hand, waving his warband forward.

The warriors fanned out to either side of him, their weary faces tense. 'Arm yourselves,' Malus said. 'Something's coming.'

Lhunara pulled alongside him. 'What–'

Then the scream came again. This time it was joined by two others. The sound brought the nauglirs' heads up.

Malus worked the arming mechanism on his crossbow. He was halfway done when the monsters burst from the grasses into the warband's midst.

They looked like great Lustrian lions, but their sleek flanks were soaked in crimson and their faces were broad and almost human. The cold ones roared a challenge and the cats responded with their eerie scream, like a man with a hot iron against his skin. Crossbows thumped and black fletchings sprouted from the lions' flanks, but it only enraged them further. One of the beasts gathered itself and leapt at Spite, crashing into the nauglir's shoulder and knocking the great beast onto its side. Malus tried to leap from the saddle as the lion's wide jaws clamped around the cold one's neck, but his left foot got caught in its stirrup and the nauglir rolled atop his leg.

The lion's face was less than a foot away, its strange green eyes studying Malus even as the creature's jaws clamped down on Spite's scaly hide. The highborn frantically tried to kick his way loose with his one free leg, to no avail. Only the armour encasing his trapped leg had prevented it from being crushed; if the nauglir rolled again, however, nothing would save him.

Malus frantically worked to reload his crossbow as Spite thrashed and snapped at the lion. The cold one's jaws closed on the lion's ribs, and the lion lashed out with its claws, raking deep furrows across the nauglir's shoulder just scant inches from the highborn's free leg. He could feel the cold one twisting, trying to roll onto his back. Suddenly the crossbow's string locked into place with an authoritative clack, and a bolt popped into the track. Malus braced himself with his free foot and fired the bolt point-blank into the lion's eye.

The lion leapt from the nauglir with a strangled cry, its head snapping around in pain. The huge creature spun in a circle, howling in torment, then its legs collapsed beneath it and it fell in a twitching heap.

Spite rolled to his feet, hissing angrily at the creature's corpse, and Malus jerked his trapped leg free from the stirrup. He looked frantically about as he reloaded the crossbow, but the other lions had disappeared. 'Where did they go?' he shouted to no one in particular.

Dalvar's voice answered. 'They ran on past us!'

Malus leapt to his feet, crossbow at the ready. 'But why...' He looked to the north, and suddenly he understood.

The darkness he'd taken to be the horizon swept over them like a thrown blanket, and suddenly the howling wind rose to a terrible roar. Hot rain lashed at his face, running down his neck. He could barely see more than two feet in front of him. 'Circle up!' he shouted over the wind. 'Cold ones on the outside, men inside! Quickly!'

By the time he'd grabbed Spite's reins he could see the dark bulks of other cold ones looming around him. It was a manoeuvre that every knight was taught before he went on campaign as a way to shield themself in a blizzard. Within minutes the great beasts were arranged in a circle and the druchii slumped down against their flanks, shielded somewhat from the worst of the wind.

It was only after Malus had huddled against Spite's heaving flanks that he noticed the cold one was covered in red. Rivulets of crimson ran down his sides and pooled in the grass.

The highborn held out his hand, listening to the rain spatter on his palm. He brought it to his lips.

It was raining blood.

Malus tried to peer through the dark rain, dimly seeing his men huddled in their cloaks against the sides of their mounts. They looked exhausted beyond measure. If they were aware of the strange nature of the storm, they gave no sign of it.

The highborn pulled his own cloak around his shoulders, drawing its hood over his head. Drops of blood drummed against the cloth.

We're well and truly in the wasteland, he thought grimly, and drifted off into a fitful sleep.

Chapter Fourteen
HUNTERS AND THE HUNTED

THE DAMNED PLAINS seemed to go on forever.

They rode from sunrise until well after dark, navigating by the lunatic glow of the northern lights and stopping only after they were too tired to go any further. Yet when they awoke the next day they seemed no closer to the dark mountain and its surrounding forest.

The warband rode beneath a sky of swirling cloud, forever shrouding the light of the sun. Night and day were merely different degrees of grey and black, shading from one to the other in a subtle, stealthy pattern that robbed the mind of any sense of time. Storms came and went, often blowing up without warning and passing just as swiftly. They no longer paused to wait them out, instead just huddling in their cloaks and spurred their mounts forward toward the elusive forest and the hope of shelter.

Food was also becoming a concern. They were down to iron rations now; rock-hard biscuits and thin strips of dried meat, enough for one meal per druchii per day. They saw very few animals during the day – mostly dark shapes like vultures, soaring low over the hilltops in the distance. Once, one of the birds strayed too close to the column and Lhunara shot it out of the air with her crossbow. But when the hungry druchii cut the bird open they found its guts riddled and squirming with pale worms.

There were howls and hunting cries at night. Some sounded like the lions they'd encountered in the past, while others were like nothing the druchii had ever heard before. In camp the nauglir would rise off their haunches and bellow a challenge when one of the creatures came too close – jolting everyone from fitful attempts at sleep and sending them scrambling for their weapons. Finally, Malus had ordered the cold ones' saddles removed and left them free to hunt every night.

The huge beasts had to eat regularly or even their legendary stamina would start to fail, and the high-born couldn't imagine anything on the plains that could fight off an entire pack of hunting nauglir. From what he could tell, however, it didn't look as though they were having much better luck than the druchii. They were becoming increasingly short-tempered, sometimes snapping at their riders when approached with saddle and reins. Unless something changed soon, their aggressive behaviour would become a much more serious problem.

The druchii took to sleeping in their saddles during the day, weaving drunkenly with their mounts' rolling gait. Malus pushed them as hard as he dared, both to reach the forest as quickly as possible and to keep the warband too tired to contemplate rebellion in the meantime.

To the best of Malus's reckoning, it was their fifth day on the plain when they stumbled upon the tribesmen. Spite had been acting tense for close to an hour, sniffing the air and growling deep in his chest, but the highborn had been too tired and hungry to consider the cause. Then he began to hear a faint clatter every time the wind shifted from the north. Finally his fatigued mind recognised the sound for what it was – steel clashing on steel. The sound of battle.

After a quarter of a mile the plain began to slope gently upwards, rising to a low ridgeline another half a mile ahead. The closer they came to the ridge, the louder the sound grew, punctuated now by screams and bloodthirsty shouts. The other members of the warband had heard it as well by this point, and several had their crossbows loaded and ready.

As they ascended the ridge, Malus raised his hand and signalled for the knights to form into line. Just as they crested the top, a small part of his mind observed that they might have been better off sending a couple of scouts ahead to see what was happening before committing the entire force. The highborn cursed quietly to himself; exhaustion and hunger were getting the better of his judgement.

The battle was effectively finished by the time the druchii edged over the ridgeline; more than a quarter of a mile away the victors were surrounding the remnants of their foe and systematically slaughtering them. Bands of horsemen galloped about in the plain below, hemming in smaller groups of riders and bringing them down with thrown spears and axes.

Dozens of bodies, both horses and men, littered the churned earth. The warriors were human, from what Malus could tell, wearing furs and mismatched pieces of armour. They rode stout, shaggy ponies that seemed to make up what they lacked in size with nimbleness and stamina. Near the centre of the swirling mass, Malus made out what appeared to be the remnants of a camp.

The highborn brought Spite to a shuddering halt. The nauglir pawed at the earth, excited by the presence of so much horseflesh within reach. 'Vanhir!' Malus called as he wrestled with the reins.

Obediently the knight swung out of line and wrestled his cold one over to Malus. 'My lord?'

Malus indicated the battle on the plain with the point of his chin. 'What do you make of that mess?'

'Feral humans,' the knight said at once. 'Nomadic tribesmen by the looks of their ponies. We're close to their tribal lands, and I would guess this is a raiding party on their way back to winter quarters.'

Malus frowned. 'Who are they fighting?'

'One another,' Vanhir said disdainfully. 'A falling-out over plunder, I expect. They are close enough to their home range that some must have felt it safe to start cutting others out of their share.'

Not so different from us, then, Malus thought. He tried to estimate the number of tribesmen on the field – at least thirty, victors and vanquished combined. 'Greater numbers, but poor armour,' the highborn mused. 'Do you think they've seen us yet?'

Just then one of the cold ones reared onto his haunches, its patience exhausted, and let out a hunting roar that the rest of the nauglir took up as well. By the time the druchii had their mounts under control the plain was covered in rearing ponies and shouting, gesticulating nomads.

'You were saying, my lord?'

'Never mind,' Malus hissed. 'What will they do now?

Vanhir seemed shocked that the highborn would ask such a question. 'Why, they'll attack, my lord,' he said. 'The nomads worship the Lord of Skulls. You see – here they come now!'

Sure enough, the tribesmen had gotten over their initial surprise, and now the raiders – all of them, apparently united against a common foe – had formed into a loose mob and were trotting their way. They waved bloody axes over their heads and shouted ululating war cries as they rode.

'Very well. Back in line, Vanhir,' Malus ordered, then stood in the stirrups. '*Sa'an'ishar!* Crossbows ready!' he commanded. 'Two volleys on my order, then prepare to charge!'

Malus reached back and grabbed his own weapon just as the nomads urged their ponies into a canter. They were nearly at the base of the ridge. At this distance, he could see that their faces were painted with a white paste that gave them the look of skulls. Thick heads of braided hair flapped wildly in the wind. Each rider, the highborn saw, had a clutch of severed heads tied by the hair to their saddles. 'Make ready!' he cried, lifting the crossbow to his shoulder.

His eyes scanned the front ranks of the oncoming mob, looking for their chieftain. He settled on a huge nomad riding a shaggy black pony and carrying a massive battle-axe in one broad hand. The man's head had been shaved bald and tattooed with crude, red sigils, and his face had more in common with a wolf than a man. As Malus watched, the nomad bared pointed teeth and let out a howl, and the horde spurred to a gallop.

'Fire!' Malus cried, and the crossbow thumped in his hand. The wolf-headed nomad reeled in the saddle as a black-fletched bolt punched into his chest. He clung to the saddle for the space of two heartbeats, then the great axe fell from nerveless fingers and he pitched backwards onto the ground.

The highborn was already working the reloading mechanism with swift, sure movements, honed by years of hard practice. A half dozen tribesmen had fallen, shot from the saddle or thrown from dying ponies and trampled by their fellows. The raiders were halfway up the slope now, streamers of blood trailing from their axes. Malus's crossbow clicked into firing position and he chose another target.

'Ready!' he cried, hearing answering yells from his men. Malus picked a rider at random who was hefting a short throwing spear. 'Fire!' The crossbow thumped and the bolt took the man in the throat, punching cleanly through and severing his spine; there was a bloom of red around the nomad's skull and he toppled bonelessly to the earth.

Malus hooked the crossbow onto the saddle and drew his sword. The humans were almost upon them. Blades rasped from their scabbards along the druchii line.

'Charge!'

The nauglir leapt forward with a frenzied roar. For a moment it was all Malus could do to stay in the saddle as Spite leapt hungrily at the closest pony. The animal shrieked in terror and tried to swerve away, but the cold one caught the pony by the throat and bit through in a fountain of hot blood. The rider was thrown forward by the impact, sprawling across the back of Spite's neck, and Malus buried his sword in the nomad's skull. Another raider swept past on the right and struck the highborn a resounding blow across his breastplate, knocking Malus flat against the back of the saddle and sending his sword spinning through the air. Grabbing the saddle, he spurred the cold one savagely away from his impromptu meal and fumbled his second sword from its scabbard as he pulled himself painfully upright.

Another rider galloped at Malus from the left. The highborn hauled left on the reins, pulling Spite's head into the nomad's path, and the cold one snatched the man from the saddle. The raider screamed in rage and found the strength to hack weakly at the cold one's snout before Spite bit through the man's torso and sent limbs and head tumbling to the ground.

By now the raiders had swept past the druchii and were reining around at the top of the ridge. A dozen nomad bodies littered the slope, and one of the druchii lay in a crumpled heap – his famished nauglir had pounced on the first pony it reached and rolled downslope with its prey, crushing the rider to a pulp. Less than half the raiders were left, but the wild-eyed tribesmen showed no signs of abandoning the fight.

Malus brought Spite around and spurred him back up the slope, and the nomads rushed to meet him.

Once again, Spite lunged for the nearest pony, but this time the nomad was an expert rider and mad with battle-lust to boot. At the last moment he jumped his pony over the cold one's head, and Malus found himself staring wide-eyed at the animal's bunched legs and broad chest as the beast hurtled at him like a falling boulder. Before he could react, Spite caught the hurtling pony's hindquarters in his jaws and suddenly riders, mounts and all were tumbling end-over-end back down the slope.

The nomad's pony struck Malus a glancing blow and sent him flying from the saddle. He landed hard nearly a dozen yards away in a shower of dirt and grass, but the blow had very likely saved his life. Spite and the dying pony crashed past, the animal shrieking wildly in terror and pain. The raider fetched up close by, stunned senseless by the fall, and Malus leapt upon him while he was helpless, severing his head with a stroke of his sword.

By the time Malus staggered back to his feet, the battle was over. Riderless ponies shrieked and galloped in every direction, some pursued by out-of-control nauglir as their riders cursed and wrestled with their reins. A dismounted nomad lurched down the slope at one of the druchii, his left arm hanging uselessly at his side. Malus watched Dalvar pluck a knife from his belt and send it in a glittering arc to bury itself in the back of the raider's skull.

Lhunara caught sight of Malus and trotted over, Vanhir following in her wake. Her own bone-weariness had vanished in the thrill of the charge, and the wolfish grin on her face was the first he'd seen in days. 'A pleasant afternoon's diversion, my lord!' she called.

'Any prisoners?' Malus asked.

Vanhir shook his head. 'The tribesmen aren't the sort one captures,' he said. 'They'll fight with their teeth and the splintered stumps of their arms if that's all they have.'

'Orders, my lord?' asked Lhunara.

Malus snatched a handful of brown grass and started cleaning the blood from his sword as he surveyed the battlefield. 'Dismount the warband and let the nauglir eat their fill. The men can plunder the camp while the cold ones gorge themselves. There are bound to be valuables among the tents, and the men have earned a reward. Then we'll take all the food we can find and be gone from here before nightfall.'

Vanhir frowned. 'If we let the cold ones stuff themselves they'll become sluggish–'

'When the nauglir get hungry enough they turn on the weaker members of the pack – in this case, that's us.' Malus said. 'This was a gift,' he said, taking in the battlefield with a sweep of his sword. 'I want to take as much advantage of this as possible, because who knows when we'll have so much meat on hand again?'

The knight considered this and shrugged. 'As you wish,' he said, and turned his mount back upslope. Lhunara watched him go.

'He looks disappointed.'

Malus shrugged. 'He might well be. With their bellies full and their pouches heavy with gold the men will have less reason for slitting my throat tonight.'

'True enough,' she said, then looked down at the highborn with a wry smile. 'Of course, there's always tomorrow.' The retainer then turned her own mount around and headed off to issue Malus's orders.

THE CITY SEEMED to appear from nowhere. One moment there was nothing but arid plains and a steel-grey horizon, and then they were crossing a low ridge and the ruins were rising into the sky from the plain to the north less than half a mile away. The druchii sat in their saddles on the reverse slope and tried to make sense of the thing. *We couldn't see it before because of the dust,* Malus thought. *Nothing else makes sense. But then, this is the Wastes.*

Malus fidgeted with the scarf pulled over his nose as another gust of wind sent a billow of dust and sand into their faces. It had been days since they'd left the nomad camp behind, and the terrain had gone from grassland to cracked earth and clouds of dirt. The gusts of wind were hot and stank of sulphur, like breaths of air from an open furnace, even though the heavy grey clouds overhead threatened snow. The mountain, at least, appeared closer now. At least Malus believed it did. He was no longer certain.

'Well, Vanhir, what do you make of that?'

Vanhir sat to Malus's right, holding his scarf to his face. 'I don't know what it is, my lord,' he said, shaking his head. 'We never roamed this far north when my household hunted the humans.' He paused, studying the toppled walls and broken towers in the distance. 'It appears deserted – at least, I don't see any signs of activity. Perhaps it's the daemon city Urhan Beg spoke of outside the Wighthallows?'

'If the place is deserted, I don't care who built it,' Lhunara said irritably. She sat her mount to Malus's left, her hood pulled up over her head and her night-mask protecting her face. 'I'd fight a daemon if it meant getting out of this damned dust storm for an hour or two!'

Malus considered his options. The ruined city did appear deserted, but such an impression could easily be deceiving. It looked to be the size of Hag Graef, and a hundred raiders could shelter there with no one the wiser. Still... 'If someone built a city in this place, there must be a well in there somewhere,' he said. 'And we're running low on water.'

The highborn bit back a curse, trying to force his exhausted mind to function. He wished he had enough men to risk a patrol, but their numbers were so few now that risking one or two druchii was tanta-mount to risking the whole party. 'Let's go,' he said, collecting Spite's reins. 'Like Lhunara said, at least we can get out of the dust for a while.'

It took nearly half an hour to cross the dusty plain and reach the broken walls of the city – as ever, dis-tance and time in the Wastes were deceiving. As they drew near, Malus and the druchii saw that the piles of stone – a dark, veined marble all at odds with the bar-ren nature of the plain – were deeply weathered.

Statues that might have stood for thousands of years had been eroded down to vague man-shapes, and only faint shadows remained of the carvings over the high, vaulted gate. Drifts of sand piled in small dunes along the empty streets, and many of the buildings they could see were little more than piles of rubble.

Malus's hackles rose as they rode down the short passage between the inner and outer gates, but the narrow murder holes overhead were long choked shut with sand and dust. Beyond, they emerged into a refuse-strewn courtyard. Weak light gleamed along the cobblestones – they were a dark green, polished to a kind of translucence that gave them the look of ornamental glass.

The highborn pointed towards a cluster of spires near the centre of the city. 'That must be the citadel,' he said. 'That will be the most likely place to find a well or cistern.'

Spite growled, his broad nostrils flaring as he tasted the air. Malus studied the shadowy alleys between the buildings and the gaping doorways, but he could discern no imminent threat. *Too long out on those cursed open plains*, he thought. *The narrow city streets make me feel like I'm threading a needle.*

The small column worked its way through the ruins. The warband was tense; they'd seen enough unexpected danger to become wary of everything they encountered. But their only companion in the city seemed to be the relentless wind, stirring up a pall of choking dust wherever they went.

Navigating the city proved surprisingly difficult. They had gone barely a hundred yards down one narrow street when they found their way blocked by a channel almost thirty feet deep and more than fifty feet wide that ran from left to right as far as the eye could see in either direction.

The sides of the channel were smooth and vertical, and the road they were travelling on met a cross street that paralleled the rim of the channel. Some kind of defensive construction, perhaps, Malus thought? A ditch to delay the progress of invaders? He frowned, unable to see the sense of it. He turned the column to the right and began searching for a way across the gap. After another hundred yards, the druchii found a narrow bridge spanning the gap, though as far as Malus could tell the span would be a poor spot to defend in the middle of an attack.

He led the column over the decaying structure, and his roving eye caught sight of carvings along both sides of the bridge. The marble was carved with the sinuous image of sea dragons, their graceful arcs lending the appearance that they were leaping from one end of the ditch to the other.

Not a ditch, Malus suddenly realised. A *canal*.

The column encountered two more such canals as it worked its way deeper into the city. In the last dried-up watercourse they found the remains of a ship, leaning drunkenly to port with its splintered masts hanging over the far side of the canal. How long ago had this city sat at the edge of a great sea? Malus shook his head in wonder.

Farther into the centre of the city the buildings were in better condition. The streets were narrow and winding, reminding Malus somewhat of distant Clar Karond, and the sheer bulk of the structures seemed to lend them more resilience against the constant wind. There were statues of leaping sea dragons and mosaics of coloured stone depicting underwater scenes – or so the highborn supposed, given all the depictions of fish and eels. One mosaic in particular held his eye: it showed a city beneath the water, its broad streets travelled by fish and serpents and other creatures the highborn couldn't easily identify. The image disturbed him, but he couldn't explain why.

The buildings themselves were expertly constructed, of the same dark, veined marble they'd seen around the city gate. The sheer expense of the construction was staggering, to say nothing of the effort that must have been required to quarry so much high-quality stone and carry it to the site. The structures were made almost exclusively of stone – Malus saw very little wood of any kind, which hinted at a degree of craftsmanship that rivalled that of the dwarfs. Yet no dwarf had lent a hand to the construction of this place – the buildings lacked the broad, squat solidity of their structures. Of course, Hag Graef was built by dwarf slaves to druchii specifications, the highborn mused.

Could not the same thing have happened here? Logically, it was possible, but some instinct told Malus that it wasn't the case. Someone else had built this city by the sea. Perhaps it had been the craftsmen of old Aenarion, but if so, the secrets of their trade had died with them many millennia ago.

It took almost three hours before the column found its way to a large square that lay in the shadow of the city's central fortress. Like the city gates, the entrance to the citadel lay wide open, its defenders long since departed. The castle, with its tall, narrow spires, reminded Malus somewhat of the Hag. Or of a forest of coral rising from the seabed, the highborn realised, somewhat uncomfortably.

The citadel as a whole was in better condition than the rest of the city. The riders emerged into another sand-choked courtyard, but the high walls mitigated the wind somewhat, and Malus recognised an intact barracks and forge set against the inside of one of the outer walls. 'Stand,' Malus commanded, and slid gratefully from the saddle. Spite remained tense, his powerful shoulders hunched and his nostrils flaring with each breath. 'Vanhir,' Malus said as the rest of the warband reined in. 'Take a man and stand watch over the mounts. The rest of us will see if we can find some water.'

They draped water skins over their shoulders and combed the courtyard for more than an hour, searching the barracks and forge and discovering kitchens, stables and storehouses, but no sign of a well.

The silence of the place began to weigh on Malus. Every so often he would catch himself staring up at the narrow windows of the citadel's central keep. The hackles rose on the back of his neck and he was certain that he was being watched. Their steps echoed in the empty buildings; not even rats stirred at their approach.

Finally there was no place left to search but the keep itself. They returned to the cold ones and gathered three lanterns then the five druchii made their way inside.

Past the open doorway the drifts of sand rapidly gave way to a floor of slate tile that echoed with every step. Malus led the way, lantern held high. They walked through a succession of great halls filled with piles of dust and broken statuary. Mounds of old bones lay in some corners, hinting that the citadel had been home to some predator in the past. Pale witchlight from the lanterns picked out mosaics of more underwater scenes lining many of the walls in the great rooms. Once again, Malus saw depictions of undersea cities, this time peopled with vague figures that bore the heads and arms of men but the bodies of fish or serpents. Several mosaics featured rakish sailing ships battling what appeared to be huge kraken. Shining figures in pale green armour hurled lances of fire into the monsters' eyes, even as the kraken wrapped their thorny tentacles around mast and hull.

Every now and then the highborn thought he heard furtive sounds among their echoing footsteps – the shuffle of feet or tentative steps from the deep shadows of a side passage or a branching chamber. Beyond their globe of lantern light, the search party moved through an echoing abyss, its boundaries only dimly and infrequently glimpsed. Lhunara seemed to sense it, too – she walked at the rear of the party with a naked blade in hand, her face a mask of concentration.

Finally they crossed another great hall that might have once been an audience chamber – no throne remained on the dais at the end, if ever there had been one. Beyond they found a series of empty rooms and a flight of stone steps leading down into deeper darkness.

Malus stood at the top of the stairs and took a deep breath, holding his lantern high. Among the heavy pall of dust and mildew the air had a cool, damp feel to it. He turned to pass the news to the rest of the party, but the words died in his throat. They were deep in the citadel, surrounded by stone and echoing blackness, and a part of him feared to speak. He didn't know what else might hear and come looking for the source.

The highborn led the way downwards, sword in hand. The stairs descended into a cavern-like cellar, with columns of veined marble supporting vaulted stone arches. Carvings of sea dragons spiralled sinuously up the columns, and the close-set flagstones were more pieces of dark, polished glass. In the flickering witchlight the floor gleamed like a seascape in the moonlight. Try as he might, Malus couldn't catch sight of any walls – the chamber stretched off in every direction – but he could smell the water now. The moisture hung in the air of the chamber. 'Spread out,' the highborn said quietly. 'And watch where you put your feet.'

Within minutes, there was the sound of shifting stone, then Lhunara whispered, 'Here! I've found it!'

Malus and the other druchii converged on the retainer, who stood by a broad, circular opening in the rock floor. She had pulled aside a stone cover carved with a sea shell design to reveal the water's still surface, only a few inches below the lip. Another of the retainers was taking a tentative sip under Lhunara's insistent eye as Malus approached. The druchii warrior nodded tentatively to Lhunara, who in turn addressed her lord. 'It appears to be safe to drink.'

'Good,' Malus replied tersely, shrugging his water skins off his shoulder. 'Let us fill the skins and be gone. I don't like the feel of this place.'

The water party bent to the task. Malus fought the urge to turn in slow circles and peer warily into the gloom. It wouldn't achieve anything except to make the others nervous, so he forced himself to be still and wait.

As tense as he was, the highborn still didn't hear Dalvar slip silently up beside him. 'My lord?' Dalvar murmured. 'I found something that I think you need to see.'

'What?' Malus asked, but by the time he'd turned around the retainer was already slipping away into the darkness, heading deeper into the chamber. Frowning, the highborn hurried after him, lantern held high.

He followed Dalvar for the space of several heartbeats, drawing farther and farther away from the cistern. Then, abruptly, the retainer came to a halt. 'Watch your step my lord,' Dalvar said quietly. 'The footing is uncertain here.'

Malus stepped to the edge of what appeared to be a large sinkhole. At some point, possibly hundreds of years in the past, a large section of the floor had collapsed into a cavern beneath it. Peering down, the highborn could see piles of glassy rubble and tall stalagmites pushing up from the cavern floor nearly fifteen feet below.

The highborn studied the area with wary eyes. 'I don't see what's so important,' he said.

'That's not what I wanted to show you, my lord,' Dalvar said, nearly whispering in Malus's ear. 'This is.'

The point of the dagger slipped effortlessly into the skin beneath the highborn's right ear. It was an assassin's blade, razor sharp – Malus barely felt the tiny pinprick, but the message it sent was clear: *Don't move. It won't do you any good.*

'It is said that in the city of Har Ganeth, assassination can be seen as a gesture of respect – even admiration,' Dalvar whispered. 'It's also an expression of art. The act itself is not as important as the manner in which it is executed. Of course, such art can only be appreciated by a single spectator, and if the execution is successful, it is the very last experience the spectator ever has. It is sublime, you see?'

Malus said nothing. His sword was in his hand, but Dalvar stood very close, effectively trapping the blade.

'Consider the tableau set before you, my lord. A single twitch of my arm, and the dagger will penetrate into your brain. Death will be instantaneous – and almost painless, if that matters to you. Best of all, the heart will stop, so there will be little or no blood from the wound; a smudge of dirt from my thumb would render it invisible. You then collapse onto the rocks below, and I tell the others you were tired and careless and fell over the edge.'

'Lhunara will kill you,' Malus said.

'Perhaps. Perhaps not. She is loyal, but pragmatic. Each warrior who dies is one less sword to help fight our way back home. Either way, that's my risk to take, not yours. You will be past caring.' The dagger pressed fractionally deeper into the highborn's neck. 'Now, do you appreciate how precarious your life is at this moment?'

'Oh, yes,' Malus replied. He was surprised at how calm he felt.

'Excellent,' Dalvar replied – and the dagger was suddenly gone. 'Now you will hopefully appreciate the fact that I have no interest in taking advantage of this opportunity.'

Malus turned slowly to face Dalvar. The sword trembled in his grip. 'You have an interesting – and possibly fatal – way of making a point,' he said.

The retainer shrugged. 'I could think of no better way to allay your suspicions, my lord. If I had any interest in killing you, I could have done so just then with minimal risk.'

Malus gritted his teeth. It was an infuriating notion, but also an accurate one. 'All right. What is your interest then?'

'Survival,' Dalvar said simply. 'Not to put too fine a point on it, my lord, but I believe you have been deceived. And Nagaira has sacrificed me and my men to lend that deception extra weight.'

The highborn's eyes narrowed suspiciously. 'How do you know this?'

Dalvar shrugged. 'I don't know for certain. But several assurances my mistress made to you – and me, incidentally – haven't proven true, have they? The skull isn't leading us anywhere, and Urial had those riders on our trail almost as soon as we'd left the Hag.'

'So what does she gain from all this?'

'She hurts both you and Urial in one stroke. You've taken one of Urial's most prized possessions and carried it far beyond his reach on a dubious expedition into the Chaos Wastes. Even if you survive, your half-brother will bend all his energies towards destroying you, and you have no allies within or without the Hag who will aid you. This, incidentally, also keeps Urial too busy to continue harassing Nagaira. She was very angry with you for sneaking away on your raiding cruise this summer and abandoning her to his attentions.'

'Urial has to know she helped me invade his tower.'

Dalvar shrugged. 'Perhaps. But you have the skull, and she doesn't. Also, he lusts after her.'

'And she would sacrifice her closest lieutenant and five retainers just for the sake of a deception?'

'As I said, she was *very* angry.'

Malus took a deep breath and composed himself. 'All right, what do you want?'

'Want? I don't want anything. I'm offering you my service.'

The highborn blinked. 'What would I want with a rogue like you?'

Dalvar's mocking grin reappeared. 'Come now, my lord. Your chief lieutenant is a woman, you've got a knight in your service you won on a bet, and if the rumours are true you're sheltering a former assassin who fled Khaine's temple. You've as much use of rogues as the next highborn – and you're not so careless with their lives.'

Malus considered this. 'All right. What can you tell me about Vanhir, then? What treachery is he planning?'

'Treachery? None, my lord.'

'You expect me to believe that, Dalvar?' Malus snapped.

'Of course,' the retainer replied. 'I think you've misjudged that man, my lord.'

'Really? How so?'

'He's not about to betray you, my lord. Vanhir is a proud and honourable man – hasty and impetuous, perhaps, but proud and honourable nevertheless. He's not the sort to slip a knife in your back or slit your throat when you sleep. No, he'll fulfil his oath and return to the Hag, and then dedicate the rest of his life to destroying you, one small cut at a time. And he'll make certain you know he's the one that's doing it the whole time. In that, I suspect the two of you are much alike.'

Malus thought it over carefully, and was pained to admit that the rogue had a point. 'What about your men?'

Dalvar spread his hands. 'They belong to me now, not her. They'll do as I say.'

The highborn nodded. 'Very well. But remember this: as you so cleverly pointed out, *I* have the skull, and I mean to claim the power behind it, no matter how many of you have to die in the process. I'll walk out of the Wastes alone if that's what it takes. Do you understand me?'

Dalvar bowed deeply. 'I live and die at your command, my lord.'

'My lord?' Lhunara's voice echoed across the cavernous space, tinged with mild concern. 'We've filled the water skins. Is everything all right?'

'All is well,' Malus answered, meeting Dalvar's eye. 'We've got everything we need. Let's head back up.'

Malus led the way back up the stairs, alternately seething and calmly considering his next move. His suspicions about his sister seemed to have been confirmed, and the thought galled him to the core. But she'd overplayed her hand. Her retainers belonged to him now, and soon, so would the power in the temple.

His footsteps quickened through the dark and empty halls and he grinned savagely in the blackness. If anything, his position was even stronger than before.

The party was just short of the citadel door when the ambushers struck.

Chapter Fifteen
KUL HADAR

THE CITADEL'S LARGE feasting chamber was separated from the keep's entry hall by a long passageway that essentially took one huge room and separated a third of its length into a separate space opposite the keep's tall double doors. As Malus and the water party cut across this passage, the highborn could see grey sunshine slanting through the open doorway and painting a faint square of light on the sand-strewn floor. The dead light of the Wastes had never looked so welcoming before.

He and Dalvar had just stepped into the entryway when the darkness around them erupted in howls and bestial roars, and broad, bare feet slapped across the slate tiles. Malus caught a glimpse of a huge, horned, muscular form rearing up in the lantern light, then a heavy club smashed into his left vambrace and threw the lantern from his hands. The highborn retreated, raising his sword as the lantern shattered on the tiles, scattering burning oil across the floor.

Malus's attacker let out another inhuman roar and rushed at the highborn with his club held high. The weak light of the burning oil gleamed on a broad, heavily muscled chest fringed with black, wiry hair and powerful, furred legs that terminated in large hooves. The monster was close to seven feet tall and looked far stronger than any druchii, and moved with the speed of a plains lion.

As fast as the monster was though, the highborn was faster still. As the man-beast charged, Malus leapt forwards as well, ducking beneath the monster's thick arms and stabbing his sword deep into its belly. The sword pierced the monster's thick wall of abdominal muscle and the power of its charge forced the blade through its body, grating against its spine as it punched out through the creature's back.

The man-beast bellowed in shock and anger, doubling up around the druchii sword, but its left hand reached over and caught Malus by the hair. It flung him backwards against the nearby wall; the highborn's head struck the stone and sparks exploded across his vision. Then came the creature's club, smashing against his thick breastplate, and Malus thought he'd been kicked in the chest by a god.

Malus bounced off the stone wall and fell to the ground, gasping for air. The armour plate was the only thing that had saved him, and even then he could tell that the tough, flexible steel was deeply dented just to the left of his heart. The club smashed down again, this time striking the wall and part of his shoulder, and the joint flared with a sharp spike of pain. Malus cried out in pain and anger, fumbling a long dagger from a sheath in his boot. When the man-beast lifted his club once more, Malus leapt from the ground and grappled the huge creature, stabbing again and again into the monster's chest and throat.

The monster roared, its mouth right above the highborn's left ear. Malus could smell the thing's fetid breath, and was battered by the tips of thick tusks or horns as the creature tossed its head in pain. Hot, bitter blood washed down the monster's chest, and its bellows turned to a choking rattle.

Once again, the monster's broad, callused hand grabbed Malus by the hair and neck and tried to pull him free, but the highborn snarled in pain and held on, driving the knife again and again into the man-beast's body. The heavy club tumbled to the floor, but the highborn's triumph was short-lived as the beast smashed its right fist into the side of his head, once, twice and then a third time that sent him sprawling across the floor.

Stunned and disoriented, Malus scrambled to regain his feet. There were shouts and screams echoing in the empty room, and the beasts seemed to be everywhere. A fur-covered figure crashed into him, bearing him down, and the highborn sank his teeth into the thing's torn and bloody throat before he realised that it was in its death throes. A moment later, the man-beast died, and Malus rolled the creature off himself. His sword was still buried to the hilt in its abdomen.

The ambush was as brief as it was brutal. As Malus recovered his senses he saw another monster topple onto the still-burning oil, but the dagger protruding from the creature's eye spared the beast the agony of burning alive. Two other creatures sped in front of the flickering light, arms and legs flashing as they ran for the open doorway. 'Stop!' Malus roared as they ran headlong into the courtyard, and the highborn staggered to his feet in pursuit.

A nauglir bellowed a challenge just as Malus reached the doorway. The beastmen – for there was no better term to describe them – stood frozen in place just a few feet from the doors as seven cold ones stalked their way. The cold ones were fanning out in a rough semicircle to surround and pin their prey against the wall of the tower.

'Stand!' Malus commanded, his voice crackling with authority. All seven of the war-beasts paused, their training briefly overcoming instinct.

The beastmen turned at the sound of his voice and fell to their knees, bleating words in a language Malus had never heard before. In the grey light of day, the highborn saw that the creatures were both powerfully built and covered with black fur except across their biceps and chest. Their legs ended in glossy black hooves, and their fingers were tipped in thick, claw-like nails. The beastmen had heads like great rams, with black eyes and heavy, curved horns that sprouted from their foreheads and hung down to their chests. One wore a bracelet of crude, beaten gold around his right wrist, while the other had a necklace of bone and assorted feathers hanging around his thick neck. As far as Malus could tell, the twisted creatures were pleading for their lives.

Vanhir and one of Dalvar's men came from the gatehouse at a dead run, crossbows in their hands. The side of Malus's face throbbed, and blood dripped on his neck from deep gouges in his cheek and ear. The rest of the water party stumbled out into the light, many covered in blood themselves.

'How many attackers?' Malus asked.

Dalvar shook his head, pressing a hand to a cut on his cheek. Lhunara wiped her hair from her eyes. 'Five, all told. Those two ran as soon as they realised they were the only ones left.'

Malus turned to Vanhir. 'What are they?' he said, pointing to the two creatures.

The retainer shrugged. 'Beastmen.' As the high-born's expression paled with rage, Vanhir quickly added, 'The Autarii say they live in loose tribes in the farther reaches of the Wastes, where the mystical energies warp their bodies into blasphemous shapes. They sometimes raid our watchtowers along the frontier, but the Shades slay any that trespass in the hills.'

'Can you speak their language?'

'Certainly not, my lord,' Vanhir replied, offended by the very idea. 'I don't think even the Autarii understand them.'

'Then they aren't of much use to me besides sport,' Malus growled. 'Why do you suppose they are here?'

'I'm a knight of the Hag, my lord, not some damned oracle,' Vanhir said archly. 'If I had to guess, I would suppose they were fugitives of some kind. These beasts typically travel in bands hundreds strong – for one reason or another, these are far away from their litter mates.'

Malus rubbed his chin thoughtfully, wincing as the motion set his torn ear to aching. 'They're from farther north, you said?'

Vanhir nodded. 'Farther north than here, at least.'

The highborn eyed the beastmen speculatively, then strode quickly over to Spite's side. He fumbled through his saddlebag and produced the wire-wrapped skull. Malus returned to the two creatures and showed the relic to them both. 'Kul Hadar?' Malus asked. 'Kul Hadar?'

One of the beastmen let out a cry of surprise. '*Hadar! Hadar!*' it grunted, pointing at the skull, then gobbled out a long string of gibberish.

Malus smiled. 'That's better.' He turned to his men. 'It appears we have a guide,' he said, pointing to the babbling creature. 'That one lives. The other one will entertain us tonight.'

The druchii smiled, their eyes glittering at the prospect of an evening's flirtation with darkness. One night's revelry would be good for morale – tomorrow, Malus felt, they would be at the edge of the forest that skirted the mountain.

And then Kul Hadar, he thought, smiling with anticipation.

'ARE YOU CERTAIN?' Malus asked, feeling a fist close about his heart.

The druchii looked from Dalvar to Malus, clearly nervous at earning the highborn's undivided attention. 'Y-yes, my lord. The nomads wore furs, but these riders had on black cloaks and rode proper horses.'

Malus stepped to the closest gatehouse window. The sun had only just cleared the horizon, and already hot gusts of dusty wind blew against his face. From this height he could see a long way past the broken walls and across the desolate plain. 'How far would you say?'

The retainer shrugged helplessly. 'Half a day, my lord? Less than five miles, I think. I only caught a glimpse as the sunlight silhouetted them along one of the ridgelines. The way distances are warped here. Who can say for certain?'

'Urial's riders must have followed us through the Wighthallows,' Dalvar said, his face paling. 'You don't suppose they *fought* their way through the wights?'

'Perhaps,' Malus growled. 'Or perhaps they're close enough to being dead themselves that the wights couldn't tell the difference. It doesn't matter. We're leaving. Now.' The highborn headed swiftly for the stairs.

Out in the courtyard the warband was saddling the cold ones for the day's travel. For the first time in days the warriors were talking easily among themselves, their humour improved by the entertainment of the previous night.

The beastman hung from an improvised rack they'd built with steel bars taken from the old forge. The creature's prodigious endurance had prolonged the revels well into the early morning hours, until, drunk with torture and running short of time, the warband had adopted much cruder tactics to bring the celebrations to an end. The beastman now resembled nothing so much as a badly butchered slab of meat, its blood staining the sand around the rack. The surviving beastman didn't seem overly troubled by the death of its companion; it had watched the revels with some curiosity once he'd been persuaded that he wasn't about to be the next victim.

Now it stood among the druchii as they loaded the animals, running its hands along its arms and chest with a troubled look on its face. It had taken a large amount of the nauglir slime to cover his scent so the cold ones would accept him. Malus hoped they hadn't accidentally poisoned their guide. Lhunara and Dalvar alike tried to tie the beastman's hands, but Malus had prevented them despite their heated objections. He wanted the creature to think they were potential allies, not captors.

If the beastman thought it had a chance of being released when they reached Kul Hadar, it would be more inclined to cooperate and get the whole thing over with. Plus, the highborn hoped it sent a signal to the creature: *It doesn't matter to us if you try to run. You can't escape us, no matter what you try.*

They were almost ready. Malus considered the dead beastman. It would be easy enough to pull the corpse down and conceal it in one of the buildings. After a moment's thought he shrugged in resignation. Let the riders find the body and traces that they'd been here. With luck they would search the rest of the city for them and waste precious time while the druchii escaped. 'Sa'an'ishar!' he cried. 'Mount up! We leave in five minutes!'

The warband immediately bent themselves to finishing their last-minute tasks. Malus gathered Spite's saddle and headed for his mount. Lhunara was waiting for him, her expression troubled. 'What's happened, my lord?'

'Urial's riders,' he said with a grunt as he threw the heavy saddle over Spite's back. 'The sentry thinks he saw them on the plains, about half a day's ride away. I want to put as much distance between them and us as possible.'

The retainer muttered a curse under her breath. She eyed the beastman warily. 'Do you think you can trust it?'

'I think after what it saw last night it knows that it'll be next unless it gives me exactly what I want.'

'That was a wise decision last night, my lord. The men seem much improved.' Lhunara glanced sidelong at him as Malus tightened the saddle's girth strap. 'Or does this have something to do with the conversation you had with Dalvar underneath the keep?'

Malus grinned. 'Clever girl. A bit of both, I think. Dalvar and I have come to an understanding of sorts. He and his men have sworn themselves to me.'

'To you? What of Nagaira?'

'They've seen enough to believe that my dear sister has washed her hands of them. Thus, they no longer consider themselves in her employ.'

'Your sister will not be pleased.'

'At this point I am beyond caring what my dear sister thinks.' Malus stood and leaned close to her. 'It's possible that this is all an elaborate scheme to punish both Urial and myself. She's sent me out here with my brother's precious relic in the hopes that I'll be lost forever.'

Lhunara looked grim. 'So far I'd say she's succeeding. So why continue this fool's errand? Why not head back for the Hag?'

'Because Urial is there, and my former allies, *and* their contract with the temple,' Malus hissed. 'Nagaira has thought this through carefully. If I stay here in the Wastes, I die. If I return empty-handed, I die. The only way out is through the temple. I must succeed, or I'm finished.'

'You're assuming there even is a temple! All you have to go on is what your sister told you!'

'Not so,' Malus said. He pointed to the beastman. 'That thing knows where Kul Hadar is. And that's where we're going.'

Lhunara opened her mouth to protest, but she knew the implacable look in Malus's eye all too well. 'As you wish, my lord,' she said with a sigh. 'I only hope the rest of us survive to celebrate your triumph.'

The bleak look on Lhunara's face elicited a sharp laugh from Malus. 'Fear not, terrible one,' he said, not unkindly. 'If I want you to die I'll kill you myself. Now mount up and let's be gone.'

THEY REACHED THE outskirts of the city within the hour, navigating ponderously over piles of fallen stone and shifting mounds of sand. There was no northern gate, as it happened – the warband was forced to seek out a large enough section of collapsed wall and clamber their way over the rubble. The dark mountain loomed in the distance, shrouded by drifts of wind-borne dust.

Malus turned to the beastman, who rode on Lhunara's nauglir just behind the retainer's saddle. The highborn wasn't certain who appeared more uncomfortable with the arrangement – the cold one, Lhunara, or their erstwhile guide. 'Kul Hadar?' Malus inquired.

The guide pointed a clawed finger – off to the northwest, seemingly away from the cleft peak. '*Hadar*,' the creature grunted, then added more in his guttural speech.

Malus gazed from the mountain to the direction indicated by the beastman. It made no sense. But this is the Wastes, he thought. Besides, what's the point of having a guide if you don't follow his directions? 'All right,' the highborn said to the creature. 'But remember your packmate back in the keep. That's what happens to those who aren't any more use to me.'

From the look in the beastman's eye, the creature may not have understood the words, but the meaning was clear enough. '*Hadar!*' the beastman replied, more forcefully this time, pointing to the north-west.

Malus tugged on the reins and pointed Spite away from the mountain. 'This makes as much sense as anything, I suppose,' he muttered, and spurred the nauglir into a trot.

THEY REACHED THE forest by nightfall.

For the entire day the mountain rose from their left, never receding but at the same time growing no closer. The warband rode through desolate plains of shifting dust and grit, passing the occasional withered tree or empty lakebed.

As the sun sank low in the west, the terrain began to slope slightly upward and the vegetation became more abundant. The hot, sulphurous wind tapered off, and before they knew it the druchii were riding across rolling hills thick with underbrush and scraggly, black-leafed trees. Unseen animals hissed and chattered in their wake, and once a creature with broad, leathery wings burst from the scrub and soared away to the north, screaming its agitation at the intruders.

Malus was starting to look for possible campsites when Spite crested a tall hill and he found himself staring at the outskirts of the elusive forest. Beyond rose the great mountain, its deep wound standing out as a line of abyssal blackness against the steel-grey of its flanks. For a moment, Malus couldn't believe his own eyes. When had their course begun curving back towards the peak? Try as he might, he could not remember. No matter, he thought. We're here.

Lhunara sidled her cold one up alongside Spite. 'Do we camp here, my lord?'

The daylight was almost spent, but the northern auroras were already boiling across the sky in the most vivid display Malus had ever seen. Streaks and great loops of blue and red and violet arced across the underside of the clouds, casting unsteady shadows among the tall trees. 'We'll press on a bit longer,' the highborn decided at length. 'Urial's riders have no need for sleep, I suspect. I want to cover as much ground as possible while there's light to see by.'

Somewhere deep in the woods, a creature gave out a long, gruff howl. The cold ones shifted uneasily, and Malus could feel Spite gathering his wind for a response until he quieted the beast with a jab of the spurs. He looked to the beastman. 'Kul Hadar?'

The beastman sat with its shoulders hunched, apparently unnerved by the strange howl. Reluctantly, it pointed straight ahead, into the shadowy wood.

'All right, then,' Malus said, raising his hand to motion the warband forward and then reaching back for his crossbow.

There were a number of well-worn paths through the wood, wide enough for even cold one riders to traverse them in single file with ease. The tall oaks and cedars blocked much of the light from the auroras with their spreading branches, but colonies of green and blue fungus climbed the boles of many of the trees and gave off a faint luminescence that revealed enough of the path to navigate by. The small column moved slowly amid a preternatural stillness. No night animals disturbed the silence with their cries, an observation that set Malus's nerves on edge.

They had been riding beneath the trees for more than an hour when they heard the howl again. Once again, it was off to the west, but it seemed somewhat closer than before. Whatever made the long, hungry cry had to be huge, the highborn thought, as loud and as lengthy as the sound was. Something as big as a cold one, or possibly bigger, he thought.

Then another howl came – also from the west, but this time from a different source. It sounded a bit farther away than its predecessor, but still too close for comfort. Now another barking cry – from the east – and Malus grew concerned. A pack, he thought. And they sound like they're hunting. Spite shifted uneasily beneath him, and one of the other cold ones let out a low groan. Malus spurred his mount into a trot, his eyes straining to pick out the path ahead. Perhaps if we can just escape their path...

For a few minutes nothing broke the forest silence save the heavy *pad-pad-pad* of Spite's tread, but then another howl broke the stillness, and less than a mile to the west came a splintering crack, like a tree broken by the passage of something swift and powerful. It was answered by another howl to the east, and then another. Four of them, Malus thought. And they have our scent!

They couldn't go any faster in the darkness. The trees hung too close and the light was too poor. Malus could hear huge forms crashing through the forest on either side of the path behind them – ponderous steps of two-, four- and even three-legged gaits. And then… silence.

Malus halted the column, his senses straining to penetrate the thick shadows all around. There was nothing save the heavy breathing of the cold ones. The highborn turned to look back at Lhunara. The retainer's face was tense, but the beastman behind her looked almost mad with fear.

We can't outrun them, Malus thought. Perhaps we can stand our ground and drive them off. He reined Spite around and began to nose his way back down the length of the column. 'Crossbows ready,' he said to each of the druchii he passed.

The warrior at the end of the column was the same druchii who had stood watch in the gatehouse the night before. Malus edged alongside him. 'See anything?'

The druchii peered back the way they'd come, his face pale. 'No,' he whispered. 'But I can hear them. They're shifting about back there in the darkness behind the trees.'

Now Malus could hear them, too – huge shapes pacing slowly and carefully in the shadows, perhaps fifty yards back along the path. He strained his eyes to penetrate the gloom, but to no avail. The glow generated by the fungus only deepened the shadows beyond the trees, and whatever the creatures were, they were cautious and cunning.

'They're sizing us up,' Malus said, half to himself. 'Trying to decide if we're prey.' Malus straightened in his saddle, and after a moment's thought, put his crossbow away and drew his sword. 'Time to snarl back,' the highborn said to the druchii beside him. 'Keep your crossbow ready. I'm going to try to shake them up a bit.'

The druchii nodded, his eyes wide. Malus took a deep breath and spurred his mount forward. Spite, sensing the presence of the unseen creatures, let out a loud, rumbling growl.

Branches snapped and heavy footfalls echoed from the darkness ahead. Malus walked Spite forward, feeling the nauglir grow increasingly tense. The beast's tail began to lash angrily, and the highborn caught sight of something large nosing through the thick brush almost directly ahead of him. Malus edged Spite closer to the thing. Predictably, the nauglir let out a long, furious bellow at it, a cry that was quickly taken up by the rest of the cold ones in the column. You see? Malus thought. We are not some timid deer for you to slay. Best you seek less deadly prey.

Just then Malus caught sight of a flash of movement off to his right. He turned sharply, but all he could see was a glimpse of something large slipping swiftly through the brush past him, heading for the rest of the party. They're much stealthier than they led me to believe, Malus thought with amazement. That means the one in front of me is just a distraction!

At that moment the creature facing Malus let out a wild shriek and charged forward like a rampaging boar, the sounds answered by thunderous cries further up the path.

Brush and saplings exploded in the monster's path as it charged the highborn, and Malus could feel the air curdle at its approach. Monstrous as it was, the creature exuded an aura of palpable *wrongness* that even Spite's senses picked up on, causing the cold one to shy backwards with a startled howl. Then the monster burst onto the path, and even the highborn cried out in fear and disgust at the abomination that reared before him.

It was huge, easily as large as Spite, its body little more than a lump of cancerous flesh and muscle supported by four trunk-like legs. Long, narrow arms terminating in scythes of exposed bone lashed at Malus, severing tree limbs and tearing huge gouges from tree trunks in their path. There were no eyes nor even a face that Malus could recognise, only a round, lamprey-like mouth at the end of a thick, muscular trunk. Rings of barbed teeth pulsated in ranks down the monster's throat as its sphincter-like oesophagus dilated and expelled a maddened roar at the highborn and his mount.

'Dark Mother preserve us!' Malus exclaimed in horror as he hauled on Spite's reins. The twisted monstrosity rushed at Malus as Spite wheeled around and struck it with his powerful tail. The blow staggered the monster, knocking it into a huge oak that splintered under its weight. Scything limbs lashed at the cold one, but Malus was already putting the spurs to Spite's flanks, heading back up the path as fast as he dared.

More of the twisted creatures had burst from the woods onto the path. Malus could hear the hysterical screams of the druchii he'd spoken to only moments before. One of the monsters had leapt upon the man's cold one, pinning it to the ground with its four clawed legs and slashing it to a bloody ruin with its scythe-like arms. Malus could see the druchii's still-kicking legs as the monster forced the armoured warrior down its fanged throat.

With a furious cry Malus spurred his mount harder, directly at the hideous monster. I can play that game as well, he thought wildly. At the last moment he hauled on the reins and cried 'Up!' Spite leapt onto the monster, taloned feet slashing and scrabbling for purchase. The monster seemed to distend beneath the cold one's weight, flattening out as though it possessed no skeleton at all. Ichor sprayed from grotesque wounds as the nauglir's thick talons ripped away gobbets of putrid flesh, but it was like clawing apart a midden heap.

Malus slashed with his sword, his gorge rising at the stench of rot in the air, and the creature howled and gobbled with rage, slashing wildly with its arms. Finally, Spite's talons gained purchase and the cold one leapt over the monster, just as its packmate came lumbering up from behind. Malus sped along up the path, daring only a single backward glance to see the mortally-wounded monster pushed aside by its packmate so it could continue the chase.

The warband was in full flight, trying to break out of the trap. Malus could see the lashing tails of the running nauglir up ahead, past loping, gelid bodies bristling with bony scythes and talons. The highborn ducked low in the saddle, sword raised, and let Spite shoulder the monsters out of his path. The cold one crashed into – and in some cases through – the monsters' glutinous bodies, showering Malus with evil-smelling fluids, but in moments they had broken free of the pack and were pulling away. Howls of rage and hunger shook the dark trees and seemed to fill the air from every direction.

As surprisingly fast as the monsters were, they were far from nimble, while the cold ones negotiated the twisting paths with ease. In minutes the warband had pulled away from its pursuers, but the monsters seemed tireless, never slacking their pace. Malus worked his way swiftly up to the head of the column. Lhunara rode with a stained sword in each hand, her eyes wild with a mix of terror and battle-lust. The highborn saw that the beastman was gone. 'What happened to the guide?' Malus yelled.

'It leapt for the trees as soon as the ambush started. I couldn't stop it!'

Malus uttered a blistering curse. 'Keep your eyes peeled for branches off the path!' he cried. 'Those things can't keep up with us – if we can turn off we will, otherwise we'll see if they tire and give up.'

But the minutes stretched, and the monsters refused to give up the chase. The nauglir were racing tirelessly along, but Malus knew that even the rugged cold ones had their limits. Why are they still chasing us, the highborn thought? They can't catch us. It should be obvious by now.

Just then Malus was startled by a wash of chaotic light overhead. The path was plunging down into a mountain hollow, the trees receding substantially on either side of a dark, narrow stream. More room to manoeuvre, at least, Malus thought. If I can direct the entire warband as a single unit, we might have a chance against these things.

Malus's mind raced, devising tactics as he waved the column into a ragged line and continued to race up the hollow. They'd covered almost a hundred yards when howls and battle-cries erupted from the woods on either side of them, and a horde of beastmen came charging out of the shadows beneath the trees, waving axes and clubs in the air.

Hounds to the hunter, Malus realised, his heart growing cold. *Those creatures were driving us down the path to their masters.*

In the darkness and chaos there was no way to know how many beastmen there were, but it was clear that the druchii were far outnumbered and pressed from every side. In the thick of battle, Malus made the only decision he could. He raised his blade. 'Forward!' he cried.

The cold ones put their heads down and charged deeper into the hollow. The beastmen closed in behind them and took up the chase, and the wall of foes ahead rushed at the druchii in a ragged line. The charging knights met the beastmen with a crunch of bone and the whickering ring of steel against flesh.

A beastman disappeared beneath Spite's taloned feet with a hoarse scream. Malus slashed at another howling rams-head nearly as tall as himself, severing the horned head from its thickly muscled neck. Blood splashed across his armour, but Malus welcomed its bitter taste after the horrid ichor of the Chaos-spawned monsters in the forest. A heavy blow rang against the left side of his breastplate, and Malus slashed at the head of another beastman, hacking away part of one curving horn. Another foe leapt at him from the right, swinging an axe that missed his thigh and bit into the cantle of his saddle instead. The highborn responded with a backhanded slash across his attacker's eyes. The foe dropped his axe and reeled backwards, his hands reaching for his ruined face.

Malus spurred Spite forward, bowling over the beastmen in front of him and breaking bones with the nauglir's lashing tail. A clawed hand grabbed for the reins and Malus severed it at the wrist. An axe blade glanced from his armoured thigh and a club smashed into his backplate, knocking him forward against the saddle. Then Spite leapt free of the press and charged farther up the hollow, momentarily leaving the beastmen behind.

A quick glance showed that the rest of the warband had fought their way clear as well, staggering up the hollow in a rough line alongside him. Skill, experience and heavy armour had won through, but the enemy was far from finished. Malus pointed to a scattering of boulders up ahead. 'Form a line there and ready your crossbows!' he ordered. The druchii raised their swords in acknowledgement and spurred ahead for the rocks.

They had gained perhaps thirty yards on the beastmen. Malus glanced back over his shoulder and saw that there were close to a hundred left, loping along in a disordered mob and howling at the sky. Worse, he could see the pack of scythe-armed monstrosities shambling up the hollow in their wake. He thought they could break the beastmen with a few sharp volleys and another charge, but even the cold ones were frightened of the misshapen creatures. Still, if we hurl the beastmen back upon their hounds, it might buy us some manoeuvring room, he thought. Though even then, our prospects look grim.

Malus reached the rocks beside his warriors. 'Make ready to fire,' he said. 'Three volleys, and then we charge. We'll try to break the animals and slip past their monsters in the confusion.'

Just then a horn wailed from the bottom of the hollow, a deep, banshee-like howl that echoed through the trees. Malus stood in his saddle and saw another dark knot of beastmen break from the trees to the west, waving torches over their heads. Another fifty, perhaps, he thought grimly. We're going to pay dearly for this one.

Then, to Malus's surprise, he saw the newcomers hurl large sacks or bladders at the backs of the shambling monsters. Torches followed, and suddenly the pack was wreathed in leaping blue flames. An angry shout went up from the beastmen farther up the hollow and confusion reigned as the torch-wielding beastmen charged up the hollow at them.

Several of the druchii cheered in relief. Lhunara turned to Malus. 'What in the Outer Darkness is happening?'

Malus shook his head. 'I have no idea, but I'll thank the Dark Mother for her gift.' Below, the two mobs of beastmen had crashed together, and sounds of battle filled the air. The highborn turned to his warriors. 'Check your crossbows and make certain they're fully loaded! We'll advance at a walk and fire into the melee!'

Lhunara frowned. 'Who do we aim at?'

'Who cares? They could all be foes. We'll kill as many as we can and worry about the rest when the time comes.' Malus sheathed his sword and reached for his crossbow. 'Ready... advance!'

The cold ones made their way slowly back down the hollow. The druchii raised their crossbows, choosing targets. 'Fire at will!' Malus ordered, and the slaughter began.

Crossbows thumped and bolts hissed through the air. In the darkness and the swirling melee, it was difficult to see the effects of their fire. The druchii reloaded and fired again. At the third salvo, the ranks of beastmen seemed to waver. Then suddenly a ripple of cold curdled the air around the creatures, and Malus felt the hairs on his neck stand on end. Sorcery! the highborn thought. Battle cries turned to wails of despair, and a large knot of beastmen threw down their weapons and ran – heading straight for Malus and his warband.

'Fire at will!' Malus ordered. He sighted on a running beastman and put a bolt in the centre of his chest. The druchii worked their weapons with quick, brutal efficiency, loading, firing and loading again. They'd killed nearly a score of the beastmen when they realised the peril in front of them and scattered, running for the safety of the trees to the east and west.

Malus sighted on a running beastman and fired, punching a bolt into the creature's back. 'Cease fire!' he ordered as the beastman crashed to the ground. Farther down the hollow, the torch-wielding beastmen had finished off the last of their opponents and were now advancing uphill. In their lead, Malus could see a huge beastman bearing a massive staff and wearing a heavy robe draped over his sloping shoulders.

The highborn studied the advancing mob carefully. They seemed wary, but not overtly hostile. On impulse, he put his crossbow away. 'I think they're coming to talk,' he said to Lhunara. 'Hold the men here. If something goes wrong, come and get me.'

'Yes, my lord,' Lhunara said, but the choked expression on her face spoke eloquently of her real opinion of Malus's plan. The highborn put the spurs to his mount and trotted across the corpse-strewn ground to meet the newcomers.

The beastman sorcerer grunted a command to his fellows as Malus approached, then he and one other continued their advance. The pair worked their way among the fallen beastmen until they stood approximately ten yards ahead of the torch-wielding mob.

Malus stopped within easy hailing distance and showed his empty hands. 'Well met, stranger,' he called, realising, too late, that the beastman probably didn't understand a word he was saying. 'It appears my enemy is your enemy. Do you have a name?'

At that, the second beastman stepped from behind the sorcerer, and Malus was shocked to see that it was his former prisoner. The beastman raised itself up to his full height and pointed dramatically at the towering sorcerer.

Malus's eyes went wide. He'd been wrong all along. Kul Hadar wasn't the name of a place at all.

The sorcerer tossed his horned head and smiled. 'Hail, druchii,' the sorcerer rumbled in guttural druhir. 'I am Kul Hadar.'

Chapter Sixteen
BONDS OF BLOOD

MALUS'S MIND WAS a-boil as the warband followed the beastman pack through the forest. Kul Hadar, the great sorcerer, had offered little in the way of information at the battlefield in the hollow, saying the time for talk would come once they had returned to his camp nearby. The very idea had set the highborn's teeth on edge, but he was hardly in a position to refuse. The sorcerer's warband had suffered few losses in the battle, and they seemed more than ready for another fight, and Malus had no way to counter Kul Hadar's magical prowess. If the beastman lord lost patience with the druchii, Malus did not relish the thought of open battle.

Kul Hadar's beastmen set quickly to looting the bodies of the dead, and then with swift efficiency began butchering the healthiest and fattest of the corpses. Within an hour, the pack was ready to move, and quickly set off west. On the way out of the hollow, Kul Hadar made a point of leading the warband through the spot where he and his pack had fought the enemy beastmen. In the centre of the piled corpses, Malus saw a ring of pale, withered bodies, their once-muscular forms withered by the sweep of an unseen power that reduced flesh and bone to brittle ash. The bodies collapsed into dust at the heavy tread of the cold ones. The highborn took note and remembered the wave of chill that had curdled the air and broken the enemy ranks. Kul Hadar was giving him a message.

The pack moved overland, disdaining the clear paths, and the nauglir were forced to pick their way slowly through the wild terrain. Their former guide now walked alongside them, pointing out the way with infuriating smugness. Time and again Malus found himself hoping that the creature would wander too close to Spite and lose an arm for his clumsiness, but the opportunity never arose.

After almost an hour the pack turned north, and the warband found itself climbing the mountain's steep slope. The air was cold, but no wind stirred the dark trees. There was a sound – almost like a humming – in the air, so deep as to be almost undetectable. Spite felt it, and occasionally shook his head to try to free himself from the sound. If their beastman guide noticed it, he gave no sign.

Two more hours of hard travel saw them perhaps a quarter of the way up the wooded mountainside. A horn sounded mournfully up ahead, accompanied by faint cries – Malus suspected that they had reached the sentries guarding the beastman camp. Ten minutes later the warband reached a sprawling encampment of crude shelters formed from limbs and pine branches, arranged around the mouth of a large cave that gaped from the mountainside. Malus could just see the back of Kul Hadar disappearing into the cave when their guide grunted and barked, pointing them off to the right.

The guide led them to a reasonably clear area near the edge of the camp, and with gestures and grunts conveyed to them that they were to remain there. Near the centre of camp someone had got a fire going, and a chorus of voices were raised in an eerie, barking chant.

'Stand,' Malus commanded, and slid wearily from the saddle. Every part of him from the neck down ached, and he was covered in dried blood and less savoury fluids. The rest of the warband followed suit, silent and stoic as ever. 'Dalvar,' the highborn called, 'if these beasts have camped here there must be a spring somewhere nearby. Go see if you can find it. I smell like a dung heap.'

'Indeed, my lord? I hadn't noticed,' the rogue said with a mocking grin, then quickly slipped from sight. Malus threw a half-hearted glare at the retreating man, then started fumbling at the buckles of his armour.

'Are you certain that's wise?' Lhunara asked, checking her mount for injuries a few yards away.

'I've had this cursed harness on for three days,' Malus growled. 'If the beastmen wanted to kill us they'd have done it three hours ago. At this rate, the stink might do the work anyway.' His pauldrons clattered to the ground, then his vambraces, then a moment later his breast and backplates. The highborn straightened with a sigh, savouring the cold air on the sweat-soaked sleeves of his robes. He ran a hand through matted and crusty hair and scrubbed bits of gore from his cheeks. Not a bad look for social occasions or the odd negotiation, he mused, but I wouldn't recommend it for days on end. 'What's our situation, Lhunara?' he asked as he tried to untangle his hair.

'One dead. Minor wounds for everyone else. The nauglir are in good shape, but they're getting thin again. A pity we couldn't have fed them back at the hollow.'

'Kul Hadar probably wouldn't have cared, but I didn't think to ask.'

'Ammunition is running low for the crossbows, as well as food and water. Also, we appear to be camped in the middle of an entire mob of beastmen.'

'I'd noticed that last part myself,' Malus answered darkly.

'What, then, are we doing here, my lord?'

'We're here to see Kul Hadar,' the highborn replied. 'It appears that when Urial wrote to take the skull to "Kul Hadar in the north", he was referring to the beastman sorcerer. How he knew of Hadar is a mystery. Perhaps Hadar himself can enlighten me, or perhaps not.'

'Well, what are we going to do now?'

'I'm going to talk to Hadar, of course,' Malus snapped. 'Obviously he's interested in negotiations of some kind, or he wouldn't have brought us to his camp. I suspect he's after the skull, but we'll see. In

the meantime, rest the men and the mounts. I expect
we'll know something before long.'

AS IT HAPPENED, Kul Hadar kept them waiting for
another three hours, while the flames in the centre of
the camp grew into a bonfire and the smell of roasted
meat filled the air. Dalvar found the spring quickly
enough, and Malus took the opportunity to get himself and his warband cleaned and fed. By the time the
beastman guide came and beckoned for Malus to follow, Vanhir and Dalvar were standing watch over the
camp while the rest of the warband – druchii and
nauglir alike – slept on the rocky ground. Once again
buckled into his armour, Malus trooped up the slope
to the cave.

Pale, greenish light flickered fitfully at the cave
entrance. The highborn expected to find more
colonies of glowing fungus, but was surprised to find
the stone walls bare of life. Just beyond the cave
entrance was a small chamber carpeted with rubbish
and stinking of rotted meat. Bitter smoke hung near
the cave ceiling, and the hulking shapes of beastmen
slouched near the walls, eating noisily or swilling
wine from huge leather skins. They eyed Malus with
barely veiled hostility as the guide led him through
the chamber and down a rough, twisting passageway.

The green light came from deeper in the complex of
caves. The illumination grew stronger the deeper they
went. Finally, the passage opened into another, larger
cave. As Malus crossed the threshold, he felt a wave of
coldness pass through his body, as though he'd
stepped through a ghostly wall of ice. He looked
down and saw that the floor was covered in crude

symbols etched with pale chalk. The sorcerer's wards, he thought.

The shaman sat on a broad ledge at the far end of the cave, his large staff close to hand. The sorcerer's dark eyes were studying him with intense curiosity. Something's surprised him, Malus realised. Could it be Nagaira's talisman? Perhaps his magic doesn't work so well against it.

Unlike the previous cave, this chamber was surprisingly clean. Symbols were etched into the walls and ceiling of the space, and several collections of jars, pots, bones and feathers were arranged on rocky shelves around the cave. The chamber was lit with a powerful greenish light emanating from what looked like an enormous, faceted crystal growing from the floor of the cave.

Kul Hadar dismissed the guide with a broad, clawed hand. Up close, the beastman sorcerer was a fearsome sight. He was large and powerfully built even for a beastman – had he stood, his horned head would have scraped the cave's seven-foot ceiling. Necklaces of bone and feathers hung from his thick neck, as well as a number of brass medallions etched with crude sigils. Malus was shocked to realise that they looked strikingly similar to the runes carved on the surface of Urial's relic.

The sorcerer's black eyes studied him dispassionately, his long snout and huge, glossy ram's horns lending him an aura of otherworldly menace. Power reverberated through the air, vibrating against Malus's bones.

'Hu'ghul says you have come to the Wastes seeking me by name, and bearing a skull in your hand,' Kul Hadar said.

Malus considered the beastman's words for a moment. It was disconcerting to hear intelligible druhir rumbling from that bestial snout. More sorcery, Malus thought? Perhaps. Finally, he nodded. 'That is so.'

The highborn caught the slightest tremor in the beastman's powerful frame, and there was no mistaking the fevered gleam in his black eyes. Ah, Malus thought. Interesting.

'And how did a lord such as yourself learn the name of Hadar?' the shaman inquired, his eyes narrowing suspiciously.

Malus affected a shrug. 'I took the skull and some papers from a druchii sorcerer,' he replied. 'The papers spoke of many things I did not understand, but they also mentioned you.'

Hadar considered this. 'And what do you want of me, druchii?'

'I want the power locked in the temple – the same as you.'

The shaman studied him for several heartbeats, then chuckled deep in his chest. 'I have been the Kul – the shaman-lord – of my herd for many years, druchii. I took this mountain for my own and studied the temple when other lords took their herds to pillage the soft kingdoms of men. I know the way past the Gate of Infinity, and the Skull of Ehrenlish is the key. Long have I searched the Wastes for it, making pacts with many dark powers for clues to its whereabouts. At last, I learned of its resting place in an ancient city by the sea, but when I reached the ruins, a band of druchii rogues had got there before me and spirited the relic away.' The shaman's gaze glittered with thwarted ambition. 'But now the Ruinous Powers have brought you – and the relic – back into my grasp.' Hadar chuckled again, savouring some private amusement. 'The gods are fickle beings, Lord Malus. I will help you past the gate, druchii, but my aid does not come without a price.'

And now we get to the heart of the matter, Malus thought. If the skull was all you needed, we wouldn't be speaking to one another right now – you'd be roasting me on that fire outside. 'What do you wish?'

Hadar leaned forward, propping his elbows on his furred knees. 'At first, my herd obeyed my will and served me faithfully as I struggled against the magical defences of the temple. Aside from the great power contained within, the inner sanctum of the temple is heaped with treasure, or so the legends tell it. For a time, the promise of wealth was enough. But as the years went by without glorious raids or the sweet taste of foemen's flesh, my herd drew restless. They began to think me weak and foolish.'

Malus nodded, permitting himself a thin smile. 'I know too well what you speak of, Kul Hadar.'

'When I learned at last of the skull's resting place, I gathered my champions and journeyed to the lost city, but while I was gone, my lieutenant, Machuk, rose up and claimed the herd for his own. When I returned, empty handed, he hunted me through the forest like an animal. The hunting party you fought in the woods was one of several searching the mountain for me.' The shaman indicated the sigils carved into the walls of the chamber. 'My magics and the power of the warpstone here have been enough to conceal myself and my band, but it is only a matter of time before we are found.'

The highborn nodded thoughtfully, folding his arms. He could guess where the conversation was headed. 'You want me to help you regain control of your herd.'

The shaman grunted in acknowledgement. 'Yes. Your numbers are few, but you wear hard shells and have weapons that kill from far away, as well as fearsome beasts that carry you into battle. Machuk has ways of defeating my magics, but he has no defence against you. If we strike swiftly, we can kill him and his champions, and I can regain my control of the herd. More importantly–' Hadar pointed out, raising a clawed finger for emphasis– 'I can regain access to the sacred grove at the heart of the herd's camp. I will need the power contained there to unlock the secrets of the Skull of Ehrenlish and learn how to open the Gate of Infinity.'

At which point you'll throw me to your herd and claim the temple's power for yourself, Malus reasoned. Of course, I am no stranger to treachery myself.

'Very well, Kul Hadar. We have an agreement. I and my warriors will gain you access to the grove, and you will reveal to me the secrets of the skull. And then?'

The shaman smiled, a slow revelation of cruel teeth. 'Why then, the power in the temple will be ours.'

'THIS IS MADNESS,' Lhunara said, leaning against the flank of her nauglir with arms folded and a defiant look in her eye. The rest of the warband had circled the nauglir and now clustered around to hear the news from their lord.

A chorus of guttural shouts went up from the bonfire near the centre of the camp. Evidently Hadar had passed word of his newfound alliance down to his champions. With all the noise, Malus could feel confident that they weren't being overheard.

'The plan is not without risk,' he conceded, 'but we need Hadar to unlock the gate, and he won't turn on us until he's pacified his rebellious herd. They aren't simply going to bow their heads the minute we've killed this Machuk and go on as though the rebellion never happened. Until Hadar has cemented his authority he will still need us, and there are ways we can keep the herd restive until we've learned what we need to know about the skull.'

Vanhir shook his head. 'We're not dealing with other druchii, my lord. It's not as though we can play one lord off against another with promises of succession, or stoke buried feuds to keep this herd at one another's throats.'

'No, but we can keep them angry at Hadar, enough that he remains uncertain of his authority,' Malus replied. 'From what he told me, the herd has resented him for years. They won't be happy returning to his rule, no matter how many warriors he has on hand.'

'But this time he can promise them the treasures of the temple,' Dalvar pointed out.

'He's promised them that in the past. They won't be convinced until he's shown them the treasure – and by that point we'll have learned what we need to know and beaten him to it.'

'And how exactly are we going to do that?' Lhunara inquired. 'None of us are sorcerers.'

'The skull is not leaving my possession,' Malus replied. 'I'll be there every moment Hadar is examining it. What he learns, I'll learn. I've already discovered that his protective wards don't work against me, thanks to Nagaira's talisman–' Malus tapped his breastplate over the spot where the magical orb rested, '–so it's possible I can kill him the moment I've learned what I need. Then we can escape.'

'With a horde of vengeful beastmen howling for our skins,' Vanhir muttered.

'Once I have the power within the temple, they'll have ample reason to howl, believe me.'

'My lord, do you actually know what this great power is?' Lhunara asked. 'Does anyone know?'

Malus fought a surge of anger. 'It's a power that two great sorcerers have spent years of effort and substantial wealth to acquire,' he said coldly. 'What more do we need to know? Great power finds a way to make itself felt, Lhunara. It will obey me as much as it would Urial or Hadar, and I will not hesitate to use it on my enemies. And besides that–' the highborn spread his arms to encompass the warband, 'think of the riches the temple holds. Wealth beyond your dreams. Enough to make each of you a lord in your own right. Think of that. When we make it inside you can take as much as your nauglir can carry. You have my oath on it.'

The gleam of naked avarice thawed the masks of uncertainty on many of the druchii's faces, Vanhir and Dalvar in particular. Lhunara gave a loud snort. 'Gold's not much use to a corpse,' she growled. 'But it's not as though this is open to a vote. You've decided, and that's that, and the Dark Mother be with us all. When do we ride?'

'We ride out tomorrow night, and strike at dawn,' Malus said. 'Until then, sharpen your blades and mend your armour. There's hard fighting ahead.'

Chapter Seventeen
SWORDS AT DAWN

THE SENTRY WALKED a predictable path, shuffling almost invisibly through the undergrowth from east to west and back again. Sloppy, Malus thought. He should be sitting somewhere with a good field of view and using those long ears of his instead of moving. It was clear that the herd felt it had little to fear from Kul Hadar or anyone else on the mountainside.

The druchii crouched low as the sentry approached. It was nearly dawn, and the attackers had been working their way through the woods for hours surrounding the herd's permanent camp. Already they had intercepted and killed a handful of Hadar's former followers; hunters returning with food for the following night and small packs of scouts hunting for Hadar and his exiles. Now it was the sentry's turn, and after that, the real fighting would begin.

The attacking force was split into three smaller, mixed groups of druchii and beastmen. This allowed the force to move more stealthily and cover more of the camp's perimeter, and provided each column with two or three druchii crossbows to silence unexpected threats. Malus, Vanhir and one of Dalvar's men marched with fifteen of Hadar's champions, led by a massive beast named Yaghan. Unlike the other beastmen Malus had seen, Yaghan and his warriors were all clad in knee-length coats of heavy bronze scales and greaves, and each wielded a huge, double-bitted axe. Surprisingly, for all their size and bulk, the champions moved silently and nimbly through the woods.

Hadar had pulled aside Yaghan shortly before leaving the exile camp and grunted a series of orders at the beastman. The champion followed Malus's hand signals and relayed orders to the rest of the champions without hesitation, but never without a burning glare of resentment in its small eyes.

The sentry's movements made little more than a faint rustle among the ferns and bushes beneath the tall trees – someone less alert might have mistaken the sound for the furtive movements of a fox. Malus kept himself still and watched the spaces between the trees carefully. Within a moment he caught a glimpse of the beastman's silhouette as he crossed from the shadow of one tree to the next. He was exactly where the highborn thought he would be. Malus raised the crossbow to his shoulder and waited.

The highborn listened to the scuff of hooves along the forest floor, following the invisible presence of the sentry with his eyes. The beastman crossed

Malus's field of vision, almost to a large bramble bush some five yards away. The sentry took another few steps and stopped. For a moment, there was only silence. Then Malus heard the beastman sniff the air suspiciously.

Suddenly the bramble bush thrashed and shook, and Spite lunged at the beastman. In less time than it took to draw a breath, the nauglir snapped up the sentry and bit through his torso with a muffled crunch of bone. An arm and a head thumped softly across the ground and the cold one settled back on its haunches.

Malus grinned. 'All right. That's the last of them,' he whispered to his men. 'Get to your mounts. We're moving forward.'

The two druchii nodded and slipped silently forward to where their own nauglir waited. Malus turned to Yaghan and waved him ahead. The beastman glared at him and motioned its champions forward with a nod of its horned skull. We can only hope you'll come to a glorious and messy end here in the next few minutes, Malus thought coldly. Otherwise, you might be trouble later.

The attackers worked their way forward through the woods, drawn by the light of the bonfires now burning low in the centre of the camp. The habit of the herd was to eat and drink heavily towards the end of the night and sleep it off during the day. Already Malus could hear groans and low growls as tired, drunk beastmen staggered off to their tents or one of the caves that pocked this part of the mountainside.

According to Hadar, Machuk's tent was surrounded by those of his own champions farther up the slope, near the opening of the great cleft that Hadar called the sacred grove. That was where the attackers would find him just at dawn, and it was the job of the druchii to pave the way for Yaghan and his champions to reach the tents and take the usurper's head in Hadar's name.

Malus reached Spite, running his hand across the cold one's armoured flank. He checked first to make certain the nauglir had finished eating – forcing a cold one to give up his meal was begging for disaster. 'Up, Spite,' Malus whispered, prodding the cold one behind the foreleg with the pommel of his dagger. The nauglir rose to his feet and padded quietly forward.

The edge of the forest was a mere fifteen yards away. Already Malus could see the pale light of dawn brightening the dark sky over the mountain. Faintly, he could hear the shuffling movements of the other cold ones off to his right – they formed a loose line nearly five yards across, but the plan was to tighten up considerably once they'd broken cover. The shock value of the cold ones alone would be enough to keep most of the beastmen back, at least at the beginning, but any organised resistance had to be hit quickly and with maximum force before the enemy could regroup.

Malus climbed into the saddle and looked to the notch in the mountainside. Hadar had said that the first light of dawn would send a shaft of light down the cleft and would serve as the signal for the attack. The highborn twisted his left hand in the reins and slowly, quietly, drew his sword. Much depended on the outcome of the next few minutes. If his plan worked, he would have the upper hand on Hadar. If not…

Darkness faded in thin shades of grey, and a thin shaft of light shone down into the camp. Malus raised his sword and let out a long, ululating scream that was echoed along the line of trees. The highborn put his spurs to Spite's flanks, and the attack began.

The cold ones burst from the forest growth in an explosion of leaves and branches, stretching themselves into a run up the steep slope of the mountainside. Instinctively the knights marked one another's positions and nudged their mounts closer together, until the riders were less than a sword's length apart. Honed sword blades gleamed in the weak light, and a howl of shock and dismay went up from the camp. Malus grinned like a wolf at the prospects of spilled blood and slaughter.

True to Hadar's prediction, many lone beastmen scattered out of the way of the thundering knights, their eyes wide with surprise. Halfway up the slope, however, Malus caught sight of a large knot of warriors racing around the corner of a large tent, weapons held ready. Many looked to be deep in their cups, but they were nevertheless ready for a fight. The highborn levelled his sword at the mob of beastmen and the knights put the spurs to their mounts, going to a full gallop as they rushed to meet their foe.

The beastmen remained resolute until nearly the last moment, when the thundering menace of the charge caused several of the warriors in the front ranks to waver. They turned to their fellows and tried to push through their ranks, spreading more confusion and fear. The mob surged one way and then the other, trying to rally itself with shouts and angry barks, but by then it was too late. The seven knights struck the disordered mass like a hammer on glass.

Lhunara spurred Render to leap headlong into the mob, her two curved swords held high and her face a terrible mask of death. The swords flickered and sang as they sheared through muscle and bone, and beast-men reeled away in an arc before her, dead and dying from gruesome wounds in head, throat and chest. Beside her, Vanhir slew the panicked beastmen with swift, economical strokes, knocking weapons aside and shattering skulls with rhythmic precision. The knights swayed in their saddles as though riding the deck of a storm-tossed ship, fighting their foes as the cold ones beneath them twisted and lashed out at the tempting flesh surrounding them. Bones shattered beneath their powerful paws and bodies were flung into the air with every toss of their armoured heads.

Malus swept his sword in a vicious arc that hacked a beastman's skull open, spraying its fellows with blood and brain matter. Two other warriors were flung through the air by the impact of Spite's rush, and a third lost an arm and much of its shoulder to the nauglir's powerful jaws. A beastman struck the cold one a jarring blow on his left shoulder with a heavy, knotted club.

As the warrior drew back for another blow, Malus darted forward and jammed the point of his sword through the beastman's eye. The huge warrior fell backwards, almost dragging the blade from the high-born's grip, but Malus pulled the sword free with a convulsive wrench, the steel point ringing on bone.

'Forward!' Malus cried to his knights. 'Forward. Press on!' He dug his spurs into Spite's flanks and the cold one leapt ahead, scattering maimed and retreating beastmen left and right.

Hadar wanted to use the druchii cavalry as shock troops, brushing aside any early resistance so Yaghan and his champions would have a clear path to Machuk. Malus had no intention of giving Yaghan or any other beastman the opportunity to slay the usurper. That not only meant brushing aside the enemy as quickly as possible, but also required the druchii to beat the charging beastmen to Machuk's tent and defeat the herd's best troops in the space of a few minutes.

The beastmen scattered, howling in despair. Spite snapped at one retreating warrior and neatly snipped the horned head from the beastman's neck; the body continued to run a dozen paces more before collapsing. The knights broke from the press and carried on up the slope, bloody swords held ready.

Another small group of beastmen tried to block the druchii's path, rushing from behind the shadow of another large tent to take the riders in the flank. But the charge was ill-timed, appearing too soon, and Malus simply angled Spite into the mass, aiming the cold one for the largest brute in the crowd. The nauglir smashed his blunt head into the beast's chest and tossed him through the side of the nearby tent, while Malus leaned out from his saddle and slashed open the throat of another warrior with a swipe of his blade. He hauled on the reins and Spite cut to the left, trampling two more warriors before closing back into line with the other knights.

The usurper's tents were just up ahead – a large, round tent surrounded by a constellation of smaller ones, all made from thick animal hide and wood frames. Machuk and his champions waited there. The rush of the druchii cavalry left little doubt as to their ultimate objective, and the usurper had used his time to assemble his best warriors and arrange them in something resembling a formation.

Malus noted that the lead warriors hefted large swords and battle-axes, just like Yaghan and his men, and the beastmen looked like they knew how to use them. This is going to be grim work, Malus thought. If only I had the time for a few good crossbow volleys first – but that would give Yaghan the time he needs to climb the slope and join the fight, and I can't allow that.

Malus raised his sword and sought out the usurper Machuk among the ranks of beastmen. Hadar's former lieutenant was, if anything, even larger than the shaman, and unlike Hadar, Machuk wore heavy armour like Yaghan, and carried a large sword in his hands. He'll carve me like a roast with that cleaver, Malus thought. I'd best be quick and close if I'm going to beat him.

He pointed his sword at the beastman and howled a challenge, one the usurper angrily accepted. The highborn drew a long, needle-pointed dagger from his belt and let go of the reins just as the knights' charge crashed home.

Machuk's huge sword was fearsome but slow, a near-irresistible force that took time to get into motion. It was a matter of heartbeats at most, but fights were decided in such tiny, crucial increments.

Using his knees, Malus swerved Spite to the left at the very last moment, just as the usurper drew back his sword, and the highborn leapt from the saddle, blades out, right for Machuk's chest.

The din of impact was incredible. The champions held their ground, and the sound of the cold ones smashing against their line was a thunderous crash of flesh and steel. Blood sprayed in the air from friend and foe alike. Malus barrelled into Machuk, throwing his sword arm around the usurper's neck and stabbing at the beastman's throat with his keen dagger. The needle point danced across the thick bronze scales covering Machuk's neck and shoulder, and the huge beastman bellowed in rage, fanged mouth inches from the druchii's own neck.

Dark Mother preserve me, Malus thought. That didn't go according to plan.

The highborn clutched Machuk in a deadly embrace, his feet dangling nearly a foot from the ground as he pinned the beastman's left arm against his chest. Machuk thrashed and heaved with his trapped arm and the highborn's body bucked in the air, his feet going parallel to the ground. Malus held onto the beastman's neck for dear life, still trying to find a weak point with his knife. The point struck a leather and bronze collar guarding the usurper's neck and the tip broke off against a metal boss.

Machuk let go of his great sword with his left hand, grabbed Malus by the neck and slammed his thick, horned skull into the highborn's forehead.

The next thing Malus knew he was crashing to the ground. He landed on his back against the packed earth and skidded several feet, half-blind with pain. It felt like his skull had cracked like a boiled egg. Dimly, he heard a roar, and knew that Machuk was almost upon him, sword held high. Move. *Move*! his mind railed.

On instinct, he rolled to the right, and the beast-man's huge sword struck him a glancing blow across his pauldron; the shoulder guard crumpled under the blow and a spike of searing pain shot across Malus's chest. He roared in shock and anger, and the highborn's vision returned as the red rage of battle-lust consumed him.

Malus rolled again – this time forwards, towards the towering figure of the beastman. Once again he placed himself within the powerful arc of the usurper's massive sword, and the highborn found himself staring up at Machuk's armoured calves and a gap of bare thigh between greave and scale coat. He lunged with his sword and the point bit deep in the beastman's right thigh, severing flesh and muscle and spilling a stream of thick, dark blood.

A less-experienced fighter would have retreated from such an attack, but Machuk was a hardened veteran. He roared his fury at the highborn and brought his left foot down on Malus's chest, pinning him in place. Then the great sword raised skyward and plunged like a thunderbolt.

The only thing that saved Malus was that he was so much smaller than the beastman and presented a poor target in his current position. Machuk struck at Malus's waist, and at the last moment the druchii rolled as far onto his hip as he could. Fully a third of the sword buried itself into the ground, but the blade struck the articulated steel plates covering his hip and bit through them. The blade's edge felt like ice beneath his skin; then the sensation was lost in the shock of the blow and the hot surge of blood and pain.

Malus snarled like a maddened beast, dropped his sword and scrabbled for the pommel of the knife jutting from his right boot. With a convulsive heave he bent far enough forward to snag the small knife and pull it free. As Machuk brought his sword up for another devastating blow, Malus drove the dagger into the back of the beastman's left knee, sawing the blade left and right through the cable-like hamstring.

Machuk screamed in fury and toppled onto Malus, his left knee smashing into the highborn's face. Blood spurted from the druchii's nose and lips, and for a moment he knew nothing but the ringing in his head and a world of red-shot blackness. The beastman's knee was still in his face, and the highborn blindly stabbed upwards with the small knife, plunging it again and again into Machuk's groin. The beastman screamed, now a tortured wail of agony, and fell forward, taking his weight off Malus. The highborn rolled away, blinking in an attempt to restore his vision.

When his sight cleared a moment later, there were two of Machuk's champions standing over him as they tried to reach their stricken lord. One bent down and grabbed a fistful of Malus's hair, pulling his head back and exposing his neck as he raised his ponderous axe one-handed. Suddenly there was a flash of light and a dagger sprouted from the beastman's eye. The champion froze, his expression one of mild surprise, and then he toppled to the side.

The second champion had pushed past and was trying to help Machuk to his feet. Malus snarled in rage and lurched to his feet. His left hip blazed in pain and his leg collapsed beneath him, causing him to fall heavily against the beastman. Before the champion could react, Malus drove his small knife into the beastman's exposed neck, sawing forward to sever the thick veins in a torrent of hot, bright blood. The champion let out a choking gasp and fell to one side, and Malus threw himself onto Machuk's back.

The usurper's wounds were mortal. Arterial blood pumped steadily from the cut to his thigh, and a huge pool of blood and fluids spread from the stab wounds in his groin. Still, Machuk was struggling to regain his feet, his thick arms trembling with effort. He didn't seem to notice the highborn's extra weight at all.

Malus caught sight of Machuck's sword off to the side, and snagged its pommel with his fingertips. He pulled the blade to him and raised its ponderous weight above his head. 'Well fought, Machuk,' he croaked through swollen lips, and brought the sword down with all his remaining strength. The heavy blade cut into the side of Machuk's neck and buried itself in his spine. The usurper gave a gasp from compressed lungs and collapsed face-first onto the blood-soaked ground. With a savage cry Malus pulled the sword free and struck once again, and Machuk's bloody head rolled across the grass.

There was a roar of fury from farther down the slope. Yaghan and his men had arrived, and the champion glared at Malus with undisguised rage. The highborn gave the champion a bloodied, bestial smile. Too late, Yaghan, he thought. Too late. He tangled his fingers in the tuft of fur atop Machuk's forehead and lifted the dripping trophy high.

'Glory to the Dark Mother and the Hag!' Malus cried, and heard his companions take up the shout in the melee around him.

A cry of despair went up from the surviving champions as they realised their leader was dead. Malus sensed rather than saw their ranks waver around him, and then a booming voice echoed across the field. Kul Hadar had appeared, striding up the slope with his staff held high. The highborn couldn't understand a word the creature was saying, but the intent was clear: The king is dead. Long live the king.

The sounds of fighting dwindled abruptly, punctuated by sharp cries from the druchii as they fought to rein in their battle-frenzied mounts. Malus thrust Machuk's sword point-first into the ground and used it to push himself painfully to his feet. He could feel blood seeping down his left leg and pooling in his boot, and his left arm was already swelling and growing stiff. He spat blood onto the ground and took slow, methodical steps towards Kul Hadar.

The shaman was turning slowly on the spot, levelling his fierce gaze at each and every member of the herd he could see. He continued to address the beastmen in low, sonorous tones, clearly laying down the new law of the herd in the wake of Machuk's demise.

Malus stood beside the shaman, raising the usurper's severed head for all to see despite the quaking of his wounded arm. The gathering herd took in the scene with various expressions, ranging from delight to dismay to weary resignation. Their stares alternated between Hadar, Machuk's head, and Malus himself. The highborn kept his gaze neutral, but his bloodied expression was none the less fierce for it.

At length Hadar turned to Malus. The shaman's bestial visage made it hard to discern his expression, but the highborn assumed that Hadar was trying to appear studiously grave for the benefit of the herd. 'This was not the plan, druchii,' the shaman hissed. 'Machuk was to be killed by my champion Yaghan! You knew this!'

Malus met the shaman's gaze calmly. 'Resistance was lighter than expected, great Hadar. I and my men reached Machuk first, and he wasn't in a mood to wait.' He offered the usurper's head to the shaman. 'The end result is the same, is it not? He is dead, and you rule the herd once more.' *Though you rule by virtue of me and my men, and your herd knows it*, he thought. *And that gives me leverage to keep your own treacherous knives at bay.*

Hadar ground his teeth in evident frustration, but within a moment he had mastered himself and took the severed head from Malus's hand. He raised it high before the herd and howled, and the assembled beastmen dropped to their knees, pressing their foreheads to the ground. He then handed it to Yaghan, and began barking orders to his champions.

As the battle-lust faded, Malus became more and more aware of his surroundings. Fully half of Machuk's champions lay on the blood-soaked ground, hacked and hewn or crushed by powerful blows. Two nauglir and their riders also lay amid the bodies of the foe, the armoured druchii and their mounts split apart by the champions' heavy swords and axes. The sun was still not fully risen – in all, perhaps five or six minutes had passed from the moment the druchii's charge began.

Malus turned and sought out Lhunara and Vanhir. They both stood nearby, splashed with blood and bits of flesh, but otherwise uninjured. The sight of them made the highborn feel a peculiar sense of relief. 'Lhunara, gather the men and take the nauglir back down the slope,' he said, the words slurred somewhat by his swollen lips. 'It would be impolitic if they started feasting on the fallen warriors here in the middle of camp. Take Spite as well – I don't know that I can walk so well at the moment.'

Lhunara frowned with concern, starting to realise that much of the blood covering the highborn's armour was in fact his. 'We should tend to your injuries, my lord–'

'Do as I say, woman,' he said, though the command had little heat behind it. At the moment, all he wanted to do was find somewhere to sit and rest, but there was still much to be done. As the retainers gathered their mounts and headed down the mountain slope, the highborn turned to find Kul Hadar waiting nearby. There was an expectant look on the shaman's face.

Malus summoned up a conciliatory smile. 'My congratulations on your victory, great Hadar,' he said, wincing in pain as he limped closer to the beastman. 'I expect you will need some time to sort things out with the herd before we may begin to plumb the secrets of the skull.'

But the highborn was surprised when the shaman bared his teeth and barked a guttural laugh. 'All that needs saying has been said, druchii,' Hadar replied.

'The herd belongs to me once more, and the moment I have waited decades for is at hand. We will not linger a moment longer, lord Malus. No, the time is now. We will go into the sacred grove and attain the key to the Gate of Infinity.'

Chapter Eighteen
TREACHERY

MALUS FORCED HIS mind to concentrate despite the fatigue and the waves of pain that dogged him with every halting step. The climb up the steep mountain slope was torturous, even using Machuk's sword as a makeshift cane. The highborn had recovered the skull from his saddlebag and carried it tucked beneath his left arm. Lhunara and Dalvar had tried to patch his wounds as best they could, but there was little they could do as long as he was buckled into his armour.

Now he and Hadar walked alone, striding purposefully toward the great cleft that split the mountainside. Yaghan and four of his champions walked a respectful distance behind the pair, laughing and boasting of their exploits in their guttural tongue.

He hadn't expected Hadar to move so quickly in the wake of the battle. Was it a matter of greed, or was he intent on catching Malus off-balance? Likely both, the druchii reasoned. He seeks to regain the initiative while I'm tired and injured. A sensible enough tactic, he thought, but it won't avail him much. When Malus had recovered the skull, he'd asked Vanhir for a strip of courva from his dwindling store. He'd chewed the piece of root mechanically, his eyes narrowing at the shockingly bitter taste. His mind was clearing though, moment by moment, growing ever sharper as the stimulant took hold. He forced himself to look around and take in his surroundings, anything to stimulate his numbed mind.

They were high enough up the slope that he had a panoramic view of the forest stretching off to the left and right around the base of the mountain. Malus could also see another, smaller mountain rising farther to the right, and in between a heavily wooded valley, still wreathed in mist. He nodded towards the valley. 'Is that–'

'Yes. The Temple of Tz'arkan lies there,' Hadar said. 'A road of skulls winds through the valley, and at the end lies the Gate of Infinity. Beyond the gate, in a space not entirely our own, lies the great temple.'

Malus stifled a groan. Damn sorcerers and their mind-twisting creations! 'When was the temple built?'

'Millennia ago,' Hadar grunted. 'During the days when your people fought the children of the Ruinous Powers, or possibly even before. Five great sorcerers, mighty servants of the Dark Gods, conspired to bind a great power into their service. They plotted and schemed for more than a hundred years, so the story goes, and in the end they bound the power behind the walls of the great temple and bent it to their will.

With it, they became conquerors, cutting a great swathe across the war-torn world.'

Malus grinned hungrily, his heart quickening with anticipation. Soon, that great power would be his. *And to think I merely sought this place to slake my thirst for revenge,* he thought. *What else could I achieve with this power in my grasp?* He saw himself sitting in the Court of Thorns, encased in the drachau's armour and wearing the Claw of Night, steam rising behind the boiling red glow of his eyes as all the highborn of the city bent their knee and submitted themselves to his tortures.

The highborn saw a great army on the march with him at its head, crossing the waves to blighted Ulthuan and dashing their great cities into ruin. He saw himself in dark Naggarond, fortress of the Witch King, seated on a throne of dragon bone...

'Over time, however, fortune deserted each sorcerer in turn. They were betrayed by their companions, or their own lieutenants, or grew overconfident and were bested on the battlefield. One by one they were destroyed, but the power in the temple remained. When the last sorcerer fell, the Temple of Tz'arkan was forgotten, its secrets guarded by the most terrible of magical wards.' Hadar glanced at Malus, and once again offered him a cruel, fanged smile. 'Until now.'

They had reached the mouth of the great cleft. Up close, it was much broader than Malus expected, and widened even further as it went. Soil had settled into the crevice over the aeons and given life to dark green grass and tall, glossy-leaved trees. There was a deep humming in the air, much as Malus had felt in the exile camp, only much stronger and more intense.

The trees rustled quietly at their approach, though the highborn noted that there wasn't so much as a breath of wind.

Hadar paused at the entrance to the cleft and planted his staff. 'This is our sacred grove,' the shaman said in a reverent voice. 'Here lies the source of all our power. Walk softly here, druchii. Until this day no living thing not of our race has entered here and survived.' The shaman bowed his horned head and rumbled something that sounded like a prayer, and then he pressed on.

There was a faint path of sorts that wound among the trees. Hadar followed it with the ease of long familiarity, and Malus was left to limp painfully in his wake. As they climbed up the cleft, Malus noticed that the great trees were covered in black, shiny vines that sprouted hundreds of needle-like thorns. Clusters of bones lay at the foot of each tree, some weathered by the elements and others fresh and glistening with bits of fat and gristle. Malus eyed the wood with much greater respect than before.

They walked along the path for several long minutes until Malus spied the first of the glowing crystals. The greenish rock sprouted from the ground just like the one in Hadar's cave, and Malus sensed that the formations were the source of the powerful vibrations he felt along his bones. 'What gives these stones such power, great Hadar?'

'They are gifts from the Dark Gods,' Hadar said proudly. 'The herds can hear their powerful song for leagues across the earth, and we seek them out for the power they give us. The stones make us very strong; when we feel their song in our bones we can work great magics, far more potent than your pitiful sorceries. When we stretch forth our hand, the earth and sky bend to our will!'

The shaman swept his hand in a broad arc, taking in the whole of the mountain cleft. 'A tribe is considered mighty indeed if its grove boasts three of the great stones. Here, on the mountain blessed by the God of the Axe, we have nearly a dozen. When I first led my herd here they celebrated for a fortnight, chanting my name to the dark sky. They believed I was favoured of the gods, to have led us to such power.' Hadar chuckled deep in his throat. 'The conquests, the slaughter, the terrible destruction I could have wrought. I could have bent the other herds to my will and ruled as no other of my kind had ruled for thousands of years. But I did not.' The shaman turned his horned head and fixed Malus with one dark eye. 'I did not, because I knew I stood at the threshold of a greater power still.'

The farther they went, the more crystals Malus saw, their luminescence increasing until he could feel it against his bare skin like the warm glow of the sun. The highborn also began to notice crude stone obelisks carved with spiky runes and sigils arranged around the crystal formations, and long poles hung with the rotting figures of beastman sacrifices. Old bones rattled in a nonexistent wind, and the smell of leather and rot hung in the air.

A few minutes later they reached a circle of standing stones, leaning precariously together on the steep slope. Outside the circle was a great bronze gong with a striker leaning beside it. Within the circle lay a stone floor made from slate tiles, its centre stained from years of spilled blood. Long lines of runes ran the length of each of the stones, laid atop the faint lines of carvings that were far older still. Malus sensed that Hadar's herd was not the first to claim this cleft and its power for their own.

Hadar stepped to the gong and picked up the striker. He struck the metal disk three times, slowly and purposefully, then he inclined his head to a point above the standing stones. Malus followed his gaze and saw that the far end of the cleft was surprisingly near, narrowing to a dark opening that appeared to be the mouth of a cave. The echoes bounced along the walls of the cleft and then faded to silence. The dark trees rustled, then fell still.

Moments later Malus caught a glimpse of movement within the cleft. A line of robed and cowled beastmen emerged from the darkness, bearing ceremonial staves and censers of beaten brass, jars of powders and tall coloured bottles of strange liquids. They descended without a sound, seeming to glide effortlessly down the steep slope toward the standing stones. Hadar bowed his head reverently at their approach.

Malus leaned heavily on Machuk's sword, suddenly uneasy. What good were powders and potions when the knowledge they sought was bound up in an ancient skull? 'What do we do now?' he asked.

Kul Hadar glanced sidelong at him, a flash of annoyance in his dark eyes. 'Now we call upon the shade of Ehrenlish, you fool.'

The highborn's brows narrowed in consternation. 'His shade?'

The shaman turned, his lips pulling back in a sneer. 'How did you come so far, knowing so little?' The shaman pointed gravely at the skull in Malus's hands. 'That is the skull of Ehrenlish, the greatest of the five sorcerers who mastered the power of the temple. He, last of his cabal, sensed that soon he would suffer the same fate as his fellows, and sought to cheat death by sorcerously binding his soul to his very bones.'

The shaman chuckled. 'But in the end the fool had crafted himself a most horrible prison. His head was struck from his neck by a rival and his body ground to dust. The great sorcerer then became a trophy to be passed from one hand to another for hundreds of years, his dreams of glory long forgotten.' Hadar took a step forward. 'But the secret to unlocking the gate remains bound within those old bones, and we will make Ehrenlish tell it to us.'

The highborn's mind raced, struggling with the implications. 'How then will you draw out the ghost and make him speak?' he asked numbly.

Kul Hadar smiled, his outstretched hand clenching into a gnarled fist. 'Why, we will give him your mouth to speak with, druchii.'

Bolts of green fire leapt from the shaman's hand. Malus instinctively threw himself to one side, the hair on his neck standing on end as the magical energies sizzled through the space where he'd been standing. Terror and rage seethed through his veins, banishing pain and weariness, and Malus scrambled back down the slope, lurching from one crystal formation to the next. Another volley of magical bolts slammed into the ground in his wake, burning dark holes into the grassy soil. Sorcerous thunder boomed and rattled down the cleft.

Malus ducked close to a crystal outcropping. A green bolt struck it in a shower of sparks, and shouting erupted among Hadar and the robed priests. Think, Malus, think! The highborn's brain worked furiously, trying to think of a way out. He felt a warm lump beneath the edge of his breastplate. Nagaira's talisman. Perhaps that's been throwing off Hadar's aim.

He paused for a moment to catch his breath, listening to the robed priests rushing down the slope after him. Malus considered his options, and none of them were good. The bastard has been planning this all along, he thought ruefully. No wonder he accepted my change of plans so easily. He knew it wouldn't matter once he'd got me up here.

The highborn planted Machuk's great sword in the ground. He pulled out his trusty boot knife with one hand, while the other fished out his sister's talisman. A plan fell into place. Good thing Lhunara isn't here to see this, he thought wildly. She'd tell me this was suicide – as though that weren't perfectly obvious.

Malus leapt from behind the crystal, drawing back his knife hand. He sought out Kul Hadar and hurled the dagger just as the shaman unleashed another storm of magical bolts. The sizzling energies struck the knife and knocked it aside with a bright spark and a clap of thunder. Well, so much for that, the highborn thought.

The priests rushed at him from left and right, their hands reaching for his arms. Malus ducked beneath the first one's clutches and rammed his fist into the beast's gut. The robed beastman doubled over, tumbling into the path of his compatriot, and the two went down in a tangle of limbs. Thank the Dark Mother they aren't all like Machuk, Malus thought. He turned back and snatched up the great sword, swinging it in a vicious arc that kept the remaining priests at bay as he backed swiftly down the slope.

Then the air turned bright green and sizzling energies struck Malus's chest. He went rigid as the sorcerous fire coursed along his limbs. The highborn's lips drew back in a silent scream of agony. The talisman hanging from his neck turned a bright red as it tried to hold off Kul Hadar's power, until the crystal orb shattered in a bright flash of light and a sharp crack.

Malus was hurled off his feet, tumbling a long way down the steep slope before sliding to a stop. The great sword was still in his bloodied hand as he rolled painfully to his feet. Thanks for the boost, the highborn thought wildly, and broke into a lurching run.

He rounded the first turn in the path and almost ran into Yaghan and his champions running the other way. Yaghan saw Malus and roared out a command, and the other warriors immediately moved to surround the highborn. Snarling, Malus leapt at Yaghan, swinging the heavy blade at the beastman's chest, but the champion blocked the blow easily with the broad head of his axe. Another beastman lunged in and clouted Malus on the side of the head with the pommel of his own great sword, and the highborn swayed on his feet, blinking at the stars crowding his vision.

The beastman to the right, emboldened by his friends, rushed at the stunned druchii, but Malus wasn't as disoriented as he had let on. When the champion got close, he drove the point of his sword into the arch of the beastman's foot. When the champion's rush faltered in a bellow of pain, the highborn pulled the sword free and brought it up into the beastman's chin. Blood and teeth flew and the beastman fell backwards with a scream, lashing out wildly with his sword.

Malus ducked the blow easily and slashed at the champion with his heavy sword, tearing open the beastman's abdomen and spilling his steaming entrails onto the ground. The champion collapsed to the grass, clutching vainly at his intestines as Malus broke from the circle, edging around Yaghan so he could reach the downhill path.

He'd taken two steps when something powerful crashed into the centre of his back and knocked him headlong. The point of the great sword lodged in the ground and was wrenched from his grip as he hit the path face first. Pain bloomed from his nose and chin and blood spilled down over his lips, but Malus was already trying to get his legs underneath him and spring back upright.

Another massive blow smashed into his side, flipping him easily onto his back. One of Yaghan's champions stood over him, bellowing a throaty laugh as it wielded a massive club as though it were nothing more than a willow switch. The beastman brought the gnarled length of wood crashing down on the highborn's chest and the armour flexed beneath the blow. Malus felt his ribs bend, and all the air rushed from his lungs.

Leering fiercely, the champion planted a chipped hoof squarely in the centre of the highborn's breastplate and set the knotty end of his club on Malus's forehead. The beastman leaned forward, putting all his weight on the club, and Malus gritted his teeth against the slowly spreading bloom of pain. Drawing back his right leg almost to his chest, the highborn lashed out as hard as he could, driving the heel of his boot into the beastman's groin twice in rapid succession. The champion howled and its knees buckled, and Malus rolled swiftly to the side as the beastman crashed to the ground.

Malus scrambled to his feet and turned back just long enough to kick the downed champion in the face before dashing once more for the path. The moment of spite cost him, however. A broad hand closed on the back of the highborn's neck, and suddenly he found himself being propelled at a dead run towards the black-boled trees on the opposite side of the path. His arms flailed wildly, vainly seeking a target, until his foot struck a half-buried stone and he stumbled forwards, fetching up against the bole of a vine-covered tree. Instantly the dark tendrils slithered like snakes, writhing down the glossy bark to wrap themselves around his throat. The needle-like thorns sank deep into his flesh, and immediately his skin burned with the touch of some insidious toxin. His throat swelled from within even as the vine tightened around him, closing off the passage of both air and blood.

The highborn fumbled for a knife to cut himself free, but already his vision was narrowing. There was a buzzing in his ears. His fingers closed on the pommel of his belt knife and he gripped at it spasmodically, but the weapon refused to come free of its sheath.

There were dark figures floating towards him, hands outstretched. Beyond them he could see a huge, horned figure, green fire playing between his hands, and the coarse, braying laughter of Yaghan and his champions. Malus felt the priests' hands on him, and the vine tightened even more possessively, refusing to give up its meal. With one last burst of strength, the highborn tugged his dagger free, but he could no longer see where to cut.

Malus thrust the knife into the belly of one of the priests just as darkness rose up to embrace him.

Chapter Nineteen
THE GATE OF INFINITY

WHEN MALUS AWOKE he hung within the circle of stones, bound aloft by hissing loops of sorcerous fire. The energies held him immobile and suffused his body with dull agony. His every muscle was tensed, as if unconsciously fighting the forces working on it. His throat was no longer swollen. He'd been arranged so that the Skull of Ehrenlish rested in the palms of his hands, clasped together at his waist. His head was forced slightly back, giving him a glimpse of the sky – from what he could tell, very little time had passed since he'd succumbed to the terrible vines. He could sense the priests forming a circle around him, murmuring a chant in low, guttural tones. The Dark Mother grant there's one less of them than there was before, he thought fiercely.

Then he felt a shadow fall over him, and Malus saw the towering form of Kul Hadar, taking his place at the head of the priests' ritual circle. The shaman had set aside his great staff, raising both hands to the sky. A low growl began deep in the beastman's throat, swelling to a powerful rumble that took the shape of guttural words. Power crackled from the shaman's lips, and Malus could make out the name Ehrenlish.

The skull quivered in Malus's grasp. Though he couldn't see the relic, he could sense that it was beginning to glow with a light of its own as the shaman called the ghost of the sorcerer forth.

The relic grew warm in his hands. There was a buzzing in the air, like an angry swarm of bees. Was it a physical sound, or a vibration trembling along his bones? Suddenly there was a jolt that shook his entire body, then another. A burning, tingling energy seethed against his belly and tried to push its way inside him. The shaman was forcing the spirit of Ehrenlish into his body. It was similar to the sensation he'd felt in the Wighthallows, only slower and more purposeful, like a dagger sinking inch by inch into his flesh. He gritted his teeth in rage and mustered his will against this unwanted invasion, but he was powerless to stop the inexorable violation of his body.

Dark power seeped slowly into his abdomen, staining his guts with the taint of psychic corruption. His stomach rebelled at the cold, gelid touch, but his body could not expel it no matter how hard he tried. Malus shrieked in impotent rage, and the shade of Ehrenlish crept like a spider along his bones.

The spirit soaked into him on a tide of madness and hate. Visions filled the highborn's mind – visions of otherworldly planes that clawed at his sanity and froze his soul. His heart writhed with worms and his veins filled with corruption. The sorcerer leaked inexorably into his skull, twisting and writhing like a serpent and probing into the dark recesses where all his secrets lay.

Then Hadar shouted a command, and Ehrenlish recoiled as though struck by a physical blow. Words clawed their way through Malus's mouth, savage, hateful curses for the animal that dared to command a champion of the Ruinous Powers. Malus raged and wailed in the remote corners of his mind as the battle between sorcerers was joined. Kul Hadar bent his will against Ehrenlish, and every blow reverberated through the highborn's body in waves of brilliant pain.

The struggle stretched for an eternity, with neither side yielding to the other. Ehrenlish roared his defiance with Malus's mouth, and the skies above roiled and thundered in response. The shade spat streams of curses that curdled the air, but each time Hadar lashed back, Malus could sense the fear in Ehrenlish's spirit.

He'd sensed that terror before, back in the Wighthallows, when the skull had fallen into his grasp, though at the time he hadn't know what the savage jolt had really meant. For all the shade's power, it also feared the darkness that waited beyond the confines of its magical prison. Ehrenlish had been an ancient and terrible force long before he had gathered his cabal to bind the power within the temple to his will. He had made many dark and fearsome pacts with things far more ancient and terrible than he, and they still waited for the reckoning that was their due. If Hadar pressed too hard, Ehrenlish would give anything to stave off his dissolution.

Malus wondered if his body would give out before the sorcerer's will finally broke.

Hadar lashed at Ehrenlish with blasphemous words of power, and the shade responded in kind. Malus felt his throat tearing beneath the force of the fearsome curses. Heat shimmered in the air over the standing stones, and Malus could see the strain evident on the beastman's face. But years of obsession lent Hadar a fevered will that seemed to match Ehrenlish blow for blow, and the highborn could sense the sorcerer beginning to weaken.

His fingers and toes were beginning to burn. Malus could feel the heat flowing from his extremities as his body tried to cope with the awesome energies coursing through it. He was being consumed like a candle, burnt from both ends, as the two sorcerers raged on, oblivious to his fate.

Malus heard screams in the air. Screams? At first he thought it was his own maddened thoughts deceiving him, but after a moment, he realised that Hadar's voice had faltered, and the cries of pain warred with Ehrenlish's shouted blasphemies.

A shadow fell across the standing stones – no, not *across* it, but *into* it, rushing up amid the priests from the lower slope. Hadar reared back, shouting in rage, and then one of Urial's riders stepped into the ritual circle, reaching for the skull in Malus's hand.

The world shook and the sky split with a cataclysmic crash of thunder, and Ehrenlish shrieked as the pent-up energies of the ritual exploded in a storm of ravening green fire.

* * *

IN PAIN THERE is life. In darkness, endless strength.

The old catechism echoed from some dark part of Malus's mind. He lay in blackness. His body felt shattered like a pot in a kiln, smoking fragments scattered beyond his reach. And yet, in the darkness, a mote of the highborn's will still lingered. And slowly, bit by bit, gathering strength and speed, Malus knit himself back together.

When his vision returned, Malus found himself lying on his side, fetched up against one of the standing stones. The skull of Ehrenlish lay nearby, the bone blackened and the silver wire partly melted from a blast of intense heat. Many of the stones had been blown apart, jagged shards scything like knives through the bodies of the priests, who lay burned and ravaged all around the circle. Surprisingly, Kul Hadar still stood, his massive form wreathed in smoke. He was stunned and reeling from the blast, but his sorceries had somehow protected him from the worst of its force.

Malus couldn't think of a single reason why he'd survived, but at the moment he had far more pressing things on his mind.

It had been a desperate gamble, brandishing Nagaira's talisman. The moment it was broken he suspected Urial's hunters would be able to sense the location of the skull and then race to claim it. Malus's faith in his half-brother's single-minded hate had been borne out once again. Urial had made his minions well.

Malus had got the violent diversion he wanted. Now he just had to escape it in one piece.

The rider who'd single-mindedly breached the circle had somehow survived – the pale, ravaged figure was pulling its shattered body across the slate tiles towards Malus on the burnt stumps of its forearms. Its clothing and much of its skin had burned away in the blast, but the eyeless, blackened skull was focused on Malus with unerring, murderous intent.

Malus tried to stand, his limbs weak and pitifully uncoordinated. His feet writhed weakly on the steaming tiles as the revenant crept closer. Malus could hear the seared flesh of the rider's arms sizzling on the hot slate. With a savage cry the highborn pushed his armoured body across the stone, burning his own bare hands in the process, and snatched up the blackened skull as he forced himself out of the ritual circle. The more he moved, the more strength returned to his body; after crawling only a few feet across the bare earth, he found that he could stagger painfully to his feet.

Surprisingly, he found that the wounds on his hip and arm didn't pain him nearly as much as they had before. He suspected it was Ehrenlish's doing – the shade's fear of dissolution was so great it might have reflexively repaired the worst of his injuries to ensure his continued survival during the forced possession.

There was a battle raging in the grove. As Malus's senses returned he realised that the beastman herd had reacted violently to the arrival of the riders and their invasion of the sacred grove. Yaghan and his champions had pursued the riders into the cleft and now their great weapons and fearsome stamina posed a real challenge for the revenants. The riders had been stunned by the magical blast, and now the beastmen had them surrounded.

Dark horses reared and lashed out with bloody hooves, and their dismounted riders wove a deadly web of steel with spear and sword, but for each beast-man that fell, a rider took a grievous wound in return. Already two horses thrashed impotently on the ground, their legs sheared away, and one of the riders had fallen once and for all when his head was severed from his neck.

Malus watched a rider surrounded by beastmen plunge his sword through one of the huge warriors, but the mortally wounded beastman only rocked back on its heels and gripped the rider's skull in its massive hands. The beastman squeezed, and blood began to spurt sluggishly between its fingers as it slowly crushed the revenant's skull.

The highborn heard a furious bellow and a savage peal of thunder to his right, and glanced over to see Kul Hadar savaging the crippled rider in the circle with bolts of searing green fire. Arcs of seething energy cut into the revenant like blazing knives, carving the figure into a dozen smoking pieces and scoring red-hot lines into the slate beneath. The berserk fury of the beastmen at the invasion of their grove had eclipsed all pretence of reason, handing Malus an opportunity that he knew would not last for long. The problem was the path down the cleft was packed with a mob of furious beastmen and sorcerous riders.

Malus closed his eyes and took a deep breath, summoning what little strength he had left. His hand fumbled for the sword at his hip. Drawing the blade, he hurled himself forward, running headlong down the slope. He raced past the oblivious beastmen and

plunged full-tilt into the midst of the bloodthirsty
trees that lined one side of the twisting path.

The hungry wood exploded into sinuous motion as
he hurtled between the trees. He leapt every root that
reared up in his path. Once he lost his footing and
threw himself into a long, bouncing tumble, eventually leaping back onto his feet. As long as he kept
moving, part of his mind desperately reasoned, the
vines could not move fast enough to get a grip on
him. At one point he burst from the trees and across
a curving part of the path, running between a crowd
of surprised beastmen before disappearing into the
trees on the other side.

Thorns lashed at his face and hands, their poison
burning across his skin, but to one who'd coated himself in poison for most of his adult life, the force of the
toxin had little effect so long as it wasn't concentrated
around his throat. His wild plunge seemed to last for
hours, but only minutes passed before Malus burst
from the hungry forest at the base of the cleft.

The highborn shoved his way through the crowd of
beastmen gathered below the path and ran on down
the slope, casting about wildly for his warriors. 'Warriors of the Hag!' he cried, his voice sounding high
and wild. 'Mount up!'

Malus heard Spite's familiar bellow at the very bottom of the slope. In moments he had reached his
warband, every one armed and mounted. Their faces
went white with shock as they saw the ravaged, lurching form of their lord. Without a word, the highborn
threw himself into the saddle.

'My lord!' Lhunara cried. 'What happened? We saw
the riders – they swept past us as though we didn't

exist and charged up the slope with the whole herd baying at their tail.' Her face went pale when she saw the look on Malus's face. 'What did Hadar do to you?'

Malus leaned drunkenly in his saddle. His body began to tremble, then quake, and he bent double over Spite's neck. The retainers watched him with deep concern as racking gasps welled up from deep inside his chest.

Then the highborn threw back his head and laughed with the mad glee of the damned. 'Hadar has given me the key to the gate!' the highborn cried. 'The great fool! He'd have been wiser to have cut my throat than give me such a glimpse into Ehrenlish's soul!' He dropped the skull in his saddlebag and grabbed up his reins. 'Quickly now! We must ride for the valley while we can. Once Urial's riders are finished, Kul Hadar will come at us with everything he has!'

Just then a great, angry shout echoed down from the mountain cleft, and Malus knew at once that his diversion was finished as Hadar realised that the highborn had escaped. 'Forward!' Malus cried hungrily, and put his spurs to Spite's flank. With a wild cry the warband leapt after their lord, thinking him mad but also sensing that their long hunt was nearly at an end.

MALUS EXPECTED TO find a well-worn path leading from the camp through the forest to the road of skulls that wound up the valley. As it happened he was mistaken, and it was an error that nearly cost him his life.

The warband skirted the edge of the camp, riding along the tree-line looking for a path. After nearly half a mile the slope of the mountain bulged outwards,

creating a high ridge too steep for the nauglir to climb,
and the forest at that point was extremely thick with
brambles and close-set trees.

With a curse, Malus turned the warband around
and raced back the way they'd come, looking for less
dense woodland to work through. On the way back
he saw the beastmen coming on at a run – the entire
herd, some three hundred strong, led by Yaghan and
the surviving champions. They were all howling for
blood, incensed at the defilement of their sacred
grove. Malus hauled on the reins and cut left, driving
Spite into the first relatively passable stretch of woodland he saw.

Even then, it was slow and difficult going. Spite
bucked and plunged through the undergrowth, and
Malus bent low over the cold one's neck, pressing his
face against the scales of the nauglir's back. The rest of
the warband followed in his wake, plunging blindly
ahead without a clue as to where they were going.
After a time Malus began curving the cold one's path
back to the left, resuming a general course back
towards the valley.

By this time, however, the woods were full of howls
and hunting cries as the herd plunged headlong into
the forest to cut the druchii off from their intended
goal. The shouts seemed to echo all around the belea-
guered warband, and Malus watched along either of
Spite's flanks, fearing they might be surrounded at
any moment.

Fortunately, the thick woods had a similar effect
even on the woods-wise beastmen – in their rage they
plunged into the thick undergrowth and quickly
became scattered, hunting beneath the trees singly or

in small packs. More than once Malus and Spite burst through the tangled foliage into the midst of a group of beastmen; those caught in the nauglir's path were crushed beneath the cold one's feet or smashed from their feet by the beast's head or shoulders. Any the cold one missed felt the edge of the highborn's sword, leaving a trail of bloody bodies and stunned survivors in its wake.

Malus came upon the skull road without warning. One moment Spite was thrashing through brambles and brush and the next he was hurtling past a tall marble obelisk that passed within inches of the highborn's left leg. The transition from dense growth to a broad, open avenue was disorienting, even for Spite, who briefly checked his headlong pace to gain his bearings.

The road leading up the valley had been quarried from pale stone. Each smooth surface had the carved relief of a skull on it. Some were animal skulls, others elf, and still others were miniatures of mythical beasts such as dragons, manticores and chimera.

There were thousands of them stretching in an unmarred white trail through a tunnel of dark greens and greys. No living thing grew up in the thin spaces between the stones – in fact, the lowest overhanging branches were all of a uniform height, creating a tunnel-like effect through the forest. It was as if the sorcery that laid down the stones consumed any living thing that lingered too close to its surface.

Although thousands of years old, the stones looked as if they'd been laid only the day before. Every half mile an obelisk of black marble reared up on either side of the road, carved with the faces of daemons

and inscribed with columns of runes that drew the
eye and tormented the soul.

Once in the open, the warband thundered down
the road, the forest around them erupting with howls
and cries as the hunters reacted to the distinct sound
of heavy footfalls on the paving stones. Malus kept
the knights riding as fast as the nauglir would carry
them, plunging ever deeper into the mountain valley.

The sounds of pursuit dwindled behind them. The
riders raced their mounts for a mile, then two. Malus
was beginning to believe the worst was behind them
when he rode Spite around a bend in the road and
there, just ahead, stood a score of armoured beastmen arrayed in loose order before an arch of
irregular, veined marble. Beyond that stone portal the
air seethed with madness and destruction, the death
of worlds given tangible form. They had reached the
Gate of Infinity at last.

LESS THAN A hundred yards separated the druchii from
the beastman contingent. Whether they had been dispatched hours ago as a precaution by Kul Hadar, or
they had been part of the pursuit and had simply
made for the one place they knew the warband would
head for, Malus could not tell. They waited resolutely
with their backs to the silent, otherworldly storm,
and Malus saw at once that the deadly barrier presented a hazard to the onrushing knights. He raised
his hand, ordering the warriors to slow to a walk.

If they charged full-tilt at the beastmen and met
with little resistance, there was a real risk that the running nauglir would career headlong into the storm
before they could check themselves. Malus didn't like

to think what would happen to anyone unfortunate enough to cross that unearthly barrier. 'Crossbows!' he ordered.

Still at a walk, the riders readied their weapons. 'Fire at will!' Malus said, and shot one of the beastmen in the front rank. The four retainers fired a volley, and another four beastmen fell. By the time the druchii had reloaded the two sides were less than fifty yards apart, and the beastman leading the contingent had grasped the plight it and his warriors were in. Rather than stand by and be shot at, the pack leader let out a howl and the beastmen charged down the road at the druchii.

'One more volley!' Malus cried, and the five crossbows fired as one. Three more beastmen fell, and then the druchii drew their swords and kicked their mounts into a trot. When they were less than twenty yards from their foes, the knights spurred their mounts into a run, and moments later the two sides crashed together.

These beastmen might not have been among Yaghan's chosen warriors, but they still knew a thing or two about dealing with cavalry. The last of Dalvar's retainers was dashed to the ground as two beastmen buried their axes in his nauglir's chest. Before the warrior could gain his feet another beastman stepped up and crushed his skull with a two-handed warhammer.

The warriors facing Malus tried to sidestep Spite's snapping jaws and slash at the cold one's face. One beastman misjudged and had his head crushed like an egg in the cold one's jaws. The other swung his broadsword two-handed and opened a long, ragged gash in the cold one's neck. Ichor sprayed across the beastman's chest and face, momentarily blinding it. Malus leaned over in the saddle and thrust his sword through the warrior's throat.

Beside Malus, Vanhir was sorely pressed from both sides by three of the beastmen. His cold one was already backing away from the warriors, shaking his snout and blowing blood from his nostrils from a deep slash above his mouth.

Malus gave Spite his head and let the cold one pounce on one of the beastmen, while he aimed a vicious blow at the back of another warrior's head. Spite crushed his victim under his clawed feet, while Malus sliced open the back of his target's neck, causing the beastman to bleat in shock and panic. Vanhir chopped off the right arm of the third warrior, and within minutes the surviving beastmen were in full retreat, running down the long road as fast as their feet would carry them.

'Ready your crossbows and form up before the gate,' Malus commanded, mindful of the chorus of howls and roars echoing down the long, wooded tunnel back the way they'd come. The highborn led Spite up the road toward the stone gateway. The cold one got to within ten yards of the gate and the raging energies beyond, and refused to take another step. 'I cannot say I blame you,' Malus muttered, and slid from the saddle.

Lhunara, Vanhir and Dalvar, all that remained of the eleven knights who'd ridden with him from the Hag, reined in their mounts alongside Spite and brought their crossbows to bear down the length of the road. From the wild cacophony echoing down the leafy passage it sounded like all the daemons of the outer darkness were hot upon the druchii's heels.

Malus reached into his saddlebag and drew out the Skull of Ehrenlish. The blackened relic seemed to glare at him with tangible loathing. Once, the feeling might have unsettled him; now, however, he had the measure of the spirit trapped within.

The highborn turned and regarded the raging energies beyond the portal. The very air seemed alternately gelid and charged with rapacious energies; violet and green lightning raged through billowing clouds of red and purple. From one heartbeat to the next the vista beyond the portal warped and shimmered. One moment Malus beheld vast, desert plains red as blood, another moment and it seemed he looked out on a vast, starry sky lit by hundreds of ancient suns. Another flash, and he beheld a flat, endless plain baking under a pitiless, red sun. Vast armies raged across that blood-soaked plain, fighting a war without end. Another flash, and he looked upon a land beneath a moonless sky. Under cold stars a ruined city of cyclopean towers waited for sleeping gods to rise and drown the universe in blood.

Malus watched the mad jumble of images and knew, deep in his bones, that he looked upon lands not of this world. He looked upon planes where even gods feared to tread, and he knew that if he stepped into that raging storm he would be lost for all eternity, like a handful of sand tossed into a stormy sea.

The highborn clutched the Skull of Ehrenlish. He could feel the energies of the relic reverberating through his hands as the shade was brought before the terrible ward it had once helped create.

What you can make, damned spirit, you can also unmake, Malus thought savagely. Steeling himself, he began to walk slowly and purposely through the dreadful gate.

Chapter Twenty
THE TEMPLE OF TZ'ARKAN

You SPOKE THROUGH my body once before, when you feared you would be lost in the land of the dead, Malus thought as he stepped beneath the rough arch of the portal. That peril is nothing compared to the one you face now. Come forth, Ehrenlish! Open the gate or perish in the storm!

The highborn felt a tingle of nascent power wash over his body as he stepped up to the gateway. For all its rough-hewn appearance, he could sense that there were arcane mechanisms inlaid in the stone, waiting for the proper hand to summon them into use again. Malus held the blackened skull before him as he inched closer to the swirling vortex that raged beyond the arch.

Do you think me weak, Ehrenlish? Do you think I will not step into the fire? Then you are a fool. I will burn and you with me! A druchii seeks death in the face of failure. Open the gate or die with me!

There was a buzzing in the air. Malus could feel the skull begin to tremble in his hands. This close to the storm, the highborn could feel its warping pull against his skin, as though it were reaching out for him. Faces came and went in the shifting, nebulous clouds – cruel, twisted visages that leered hungrily through the archway. Whether they hungered more for the soul in the highborn's body or the shade bound in the wire-wrapped skull, Malus could not say.

Blue fire began to lick across the surface of the relic, blowing fiercely over the curves of the skull as though it were being forced into the heat of a forge. Malus could feel the lines of silver wire turn hot in his hands. *The end approaches, ancient shade! Are you ready to face those who wait beyond?*

The back of the skull touched the raging energy beyond the gate, and the black, empty eye sockets blazed with furious life.

Ehrenlish drove spikes of fire into Malus's brain, forcing himself into the highborn's skull like a spear-head and thrashing angrily in the tortured paths of his brain. The highborn's body went taut and his head arched back as it had in the stone circle of Kul Hadar. His mouth opened in a frozen scream, but jagged, blistering curses spewed forth instead.

Malus felt Ehrenlish's spirit clench like a knotted fist inside his skull and felt his body begin to bend backwards, away from the otherworldly storm. *NO!* he raged, grappling with Ehrenlish in a contest of terrible wills. *You think to master this body, foul spirit? Fool! You cannot master me. I am Malus of Hag Graef, and I bend to no one. Do as I command, sorcerer, or meet your doom!*

For a moment, the highborn's body trembled, caught between opposing forces. Then, inch by painful inch, Malus's frame began to straighten again. The stream of raging curses slurred into a wordless growl of determination as Malus forced himself to take a tiny, half-step forward and pressed the skull deeper into the vortex.

An agonised shrieking filled the air. The storm penetrated the skull, lashing at Ehrenlish and by extension into Malus. The spirit of the sorcerer gibbered and wailed at the touch of the storm, and Malus's mind shrank from the impossible vistas that unfolded in his mind. Skies of liquid fire and seas of boiling skin. Terrible creatures with bones of ice and eyes that had beheld the first night of the world. And beyond them more terrible spirits still, ancient beings of incalculable wisdom and cruelty who stirred from their meditations and gazed across the immense gulf of the storm at the two beings struggling fitfully at its edge.

And then the words burst from Malus's bloody lips. Buzzing, shrieking words of power and intent that tried to wake the arcane mechanism of the portal and hold the great storm at bay. The skull jerked in the highborn's hand and he felt more than heard the crack that raced along the curve of the braincase. Molten silver was running in hot droplets down the wire mesh, propelled away from the storm and falling toward Malus, splashing in sizzling droplets against his breastplate.

The highborn dimly sensed the engines of the portal trying to awaken, but something was wrong. They had lain idle too long with no hand to tend them, and now the paths that directed the shade's power were spinning out of control. There was a groaning sound in the air, and Malus saw the irregular arch start to twist and deform like heated wax.

A shudder passed through Malus's soul. The terrible storm was swelling. At first he thought it was because the arch was failing, but then he realised that the raging energies were being pushed aside by the passage of those ageless beings, as sea dragons shoulder aside the freezing waters of the ocean. They were reaching across the storm.

They were reaching for him.

Ehrenlish's cries had reached an agonising crescendo. Bloody froth burst from Malus's throat as the torrent of incantations poured into the air. He could feel the shade's stark terror. It, too, felt the rising of the ageless ones, and in a fleeting moment of clarity Malus caught a glimpse of the fate that awaited Ehrenlish, and even his hardened soul quailed at the thought of it.

The gate wavered in the air and flew apart into molten gobbets of rock that were sucked into the hungry maw of the storm. The great sorcerous engines failed in a clap of thunder and a blaze of terrible light, and a huge, clawed hand coalesced from the energies of the storm itself, closing about the sizzling surface of the skull. The bone turned to dust at the touch of that impossible hand, and the silver wire flared into mist, and the otherworldly storm that had seethed beyond the gate vanished as though it had never been, taking the shade of Ehrenlish with it.

Malus fell to his knees in the place where the Gate of Infinity had once stood. Steam curled from the joints in his armour. It felt like an eternity before he could hear the sound of his own heartbeat again, or put intent into coherent thoughts in his numbed mind.

When he could focus his eyes again, Malus could see a white road of skulls stretching ahead of him to a huge, stone edifice made of enormous slabs of the blackest basalt. It was a square, tiered structure with no windows or carven images that hinted at the glories held within. It was a temple of power, a place built not for venerating the unseen but to serve the ambitions of the worldly. The very sight of it lit the flames of desire in Malus's savage breast.

The highborn rose to his feet, suppressing flashes of pain with a ruthless effort of will. Here was a triumph beyond all imaginings. He could sense it calling out to him. With the power secreted within the temple he would bend the entire world to his will.

Someone was calling his name. Malus turned, trying to focus on the sound.

'My lord! They're coming!'

It was Lhunara. She and the rest of the warband sat astride their cold ones, facing back down the road from whence they'd come. Just at the bend of the road, nearly a hundred yards away, Malus saw the beastman herd had gathered. A tremor went through their massed ranks, and isolated voices howled challenges at the distant riders. Malus guessed the mob had seen the storm come undone, and they were now working up the courage to attack.

The highborn glanced back at the temple. Sure enough, a low wall surrounded the structure, broken by what appeared to be a single gate. Malus raced forward and leapt into Spite's saddle. 'To the temple!' he cried, hauling on the reins. The warband turned as one and raced down the road, and the beastman herd broke into bloodthirsty cries and charged after them.

In moments the cold ones were racing through the plain gate of the temple wall, turning left and right across broad stone tiles worked with runes and carvings of daemonic skulls. 'Bar the gate!' Malus ordered. He checked the height of the walls. There were no parapets, but a druchii standing on a cold one's back could peer over it. 'Lhunara, get the men against the wall! They can fire over it when the herd tries to force the gate.'

Vanhir and Dalvar pushed heavy gates made from basalt slabs into place. Thick iron bars fitted into holes in the bottom of each gate thudded into place into corresponding holes carved into the road. 'This won't hold them forever, not if they bring hammers,' Vanhir told Malus. 'What do we do when they breach the gate?'

Beyond the gateway the road ran straight up to a simple entryway at the side of the great temple. Malus had already slid from the saddle and was walking swiftly towards the shadowy portal.

'Hold them off,' the highborn said simply, and disappeared inside.

MALUS'S FOOTSTEPS ECHOED hollowly down the narrow processional leading into the temple proper. No torches lined the walls, nor ironwork stands holding globes of greenish witchfire – instead the black walls seemed to radiate a kind of power that thinned the darkness somehow, like water added to ink. He could see clearly in any direction, but the weight of abyssal darkness hung about his shoulders all the same.

The silence in the great temple was palpable, like the funereal stillness of a tomb, and yet the highborn could sense a faint tremor of power suffusing the air. It was not so fierce and uncontrolled as the storm that had raged outside; rather, it seemed ruthlessly harnessed and infinitely patient, waiting to be summoned to life.

The processional led to a large, square chamber similarly devoid of ornamentation. Row upon row of humped shapes lined the floor to either side of the aisle, and it took a moment for Malus to realise that they had once been the shapes of servants. In life they had worn metal vestments and mantles of some kind, and those ceremonial clothes still remained, bent in positions of supplication towards the narrow aisle. The highborn wondered what kind of power – or awesome, numbing fear – could drive more than a hundred slaves to bend their heads to the stone floor and remain there, waiting in vain for the return of their terrible overlords, until finally they died there. The same could be said for the two massive suits of armour that still stood to either side of the doorway at the far end of the chamber. Their occupants had long since fallen to dust, but their empty armour still maintained their endless vigil.

Malus passed through the doorway into what appeared to be a large chamber for prayers and sacrifices to the four gods of the north. Great statues stood at four different points within the room, each with its own stained altar. The darkness here was palpable, pressing against him like a hundred clammy hands sticky with blood.

The great statues of the Ruinous Powers glared down at him with implacable hate, demanding his subservience and adoration. Muttering a prayer to the Dark Mother, the highborn crossed the room without sparing the idols more than a passing glance, and stepped through a doorway.

The space beyond was nothing less than cavernous. Heat and the stench of sulphur smote his face and neck. Malus stepped onto a floor of slate tiles that stretched across an open area the size of a small plaza back at the Hag. Ahead, he could see a dim, red glow through the haze of darkness, silhouetting a huge shape that seemed to descend from the vastness of the ceiling above.

Malus walked for nearly fifty yards across the tiles, until he reached the edge of a precipice. The statue of an immense, winged daemon crouched at the very brink, its horned forehead bent to the tiles in a gesture of supplication. Frowning, the highborn stepped around the statue and peered into the abyss beyond. Hundreds of feet below was nothing but fire and seething, molten stone… and a line of flat-topped boulders that seemed to hang in the air above the magma.

The highborn glanced at the large shape hanging above the fiery pit and saw that it, too, was an enormous, rough-hewn pillar of stone, carved with wide stairs that spiralled upwards to the temple's next level. Unfortunately, they were also more than thirty yards away.

Malus stepped back and regarded the statue of the daemon once more. He noticed that its knobby back could also be seen as a set of cunningly carved steps. Carefully, he placed one boot on the top of the daemon's head and took a step up. The stone easily supported his weight.

The highborn climbed the short flight of 'steps' along the daemon's back, until there was nothing but reeking air before him. Peering down, he saw the first of the floating boulders, perfectly in line with the statue's back. A bit ostentatious, Malus thought, staring up at the distant staircase. But effective. The sorcerers were jealous of their power indeed. The question was how to make the boulders rise for him.

Force of will, Malus thought. What is sorcery, after all, but bending the world to one's will? How else did Kul Hadar and Ehrenlish fight one another? How else did I force Ehrenlish to obey my commands?

Malus looked down at the stepping stones. *Rise*, he thought, focusing his will on them. *Rise!*

The stones remained where they were.

Rise, damn you! Malus thought fiercely, adding his rage to the force of his thoughts. *In the name of dead Ehrenlish, obey your new master. Rise!*

Nothing happened.

A growl escaped Malus's lips. He cast about for another name to hurl at the implacable rock. 'In the name… in the name of Tz'arkan, RISE!'

At once, Malus felt the power in the air thrum like a plucked chord. The stepping stones trembled, and then began to rise.

The highborn smiled triumphantly. Tz'arkan, eh? What kind of name is that, I wonder?

The stepping stones rose smoothly and silently through the air, their faceted lower halves glowing from the heat of the magma below. They formed a perfect set of steps that curved upwards and met the stairs high above the blazing pit. Steeling himself, Malus stepped from the daemon's back onto the first stone, and was gratified to discover it was as stable as the very earth.

In minutes the highborn climbed the floating boulders to the staircase. As he stepped from each one, the stone plummeted back to its original position deep in the pit. By the time he reached the curving staircase, Malus felt like a petty god himself. The steps themselves appeared to be carved from alabaster; each riser worked with a cunning relief of dozens of small, naked figures, writhing in torment. Their faces were upturned, pleading for mercy, even as their shoulders and backs supported the weight of each stair. This is a place made for conquerors, Malus thought.

His smug grin faded a third of the way up the stair when he stumbled upon the body. It wore robes of a finer cut and a jewelled mantle that was similar to, but far richer than, those in the entry chamber below, and the hot, dry air had mummified the corpse almost perfectly. Malus was struck by the corpse's gaping mouth, frozen in a rictus of terror. Nor did he miss the curved dagger in the body's right hand, and the long, neat cuts along the withered veins of both forearms.

THERE WERE BODIES everywhere, perfectly preserved by the heat. All of them had died violent deaths, slain by one another or dead by their own hand.

The second floor of the temple was given over to five large sanctums and the smaller quarters of the attendants who ministered to the needs of Ehrenlish and his cabal. Huge, broad columns of basalt, carved in the likeness of terrible daemons, supported the arched ceiling, and cold braziers made of bronze and dark iron stood at regular intervals along the broad corridors. Inserts of dark sandstone had been fitted among the black granite blocks of the walls. Each panel contained a bas relief of corpse-choked fields or ruined cities burning beneath the twin moons.

The doorway to each sanctum was carved with thick bands of magical runes, though the violence that marred the entire floor had made itself felt against these guardian wards as well. The bands of runes were broken by the blows of hammers and axes, though on two occasions Malus also found the blackened husks of the servants who'd tempted their masters' arcane power. The rooms themselves were torn apart; ancient brown bloodstains marked the thick tapestries lining the walls and lay in pools across the marble floors. All of the rooms were piled with riches – urns full of gold and silver coin sat amid broken bookshelves and piles of ancient books. Malus could only imagine the sorcerous wisdom contained within those pages – what would Nagaira or Urial have given for one hour alone in these rooms? Suits of armour and fine weapons lay scattered along the floor, evidently ignored in the frenzy of slaughter that came upon the sorcerers' servants.

At one point Malus stumbled into a servant's room that had been turned into a slaughterhouse. A large, oaken table had been drawn into the centre of the sparsely furnished room and a wide assortment of cleavers and saws had been laid by its side. A

mummified corpse still lay tied to the table, its right
leg and arm sawn away. They ran out of food when
Ehrenlish and his army failed to return, Malus
thought. Why didn't the stepping stones work for
them? Surely they had better knowledge of the
workings of this place than I?

The aura of power was much stronger here. It
pulsed along the walls and hummed along his bones.
Perhaps that is what eventually drove them mad,
Malus thought. Trapped here, slowly starving to
death, and that tremor constantly running through
one's body. It would be enough to drive me to murder.

Seeing the sanctums of the lost sorcerers finally
brought home the realisation that whatever power
the temple contained, it was not meant to travel. This
wasn't some magical sword or arcane relic like Ehrenlish's skull. Perhaps a source of power tied to the
land, like Hadar's crystals? Clearly the cabal was able
to draw upon its strength from a great distance, but if
they had living quarters in the temple, it seemed they
couldn't be separated from it for very long.

The notion vexed Malus. I'll have to find some way
to make it work for me as well, he thought, but
couldn't imagine how. I may have to treat with that
treacherous goat Hadar after all. Give him access to
the temple and the power, and entrust him with its
safekeeping. Putting so much trust in the beastman
seemed the height of lunacy, but what else could he
do?

I'll taste of the power for just a short time, enough
to deal with my family and become Vaulkhar, and
that will be enough, Malus thought. It was a bitter

drink to swallow, but the history of Ehrenlish and his cabal hinted that the power didn't come without cost. Better a brief flirtation and escape rather than the kind of obsession that consumed one from the inside out.

There was a ramp at one end of the level, surrounded by the quarters of the five sorcerers, that led upwards to the third tier of the temple. The ramp itself was carved with skulls and worked with hundreds of runes, and the doors were formed of solid gold. Ten years' worth of raiding wouldn't purchase all that gold, Malus thought with avaricious wonder. *I could pull those down, break them up and return to the Hag a wealthy man. But then, if those are merely the doors, what manner of glories lie beyond?* The great doors were perfectly balanced, and swung open at the lightest touch.

Beyond lay a large chamber dominated by a tall pair of basalt doors, flanked by huge statues of fearsome, winged daemons. The floor was made of polished basalt slabs, blacker than night, and inlaid with an intricate series of interlocking magical wards, worked in gold, silver and crushed gems. The greatest of the wards was only a third of a much greater circle that evidently ran beneath the far wall and encompassed part of the chamber beyond the basalt doors.

At the foot of the great doors lay a heap of mummified bodies – one with its arm still outstretched against a basalt slab. Long brown streaks of dried blood made four perfect lines that stretched from the door's golden handle to the mummy's ragged fingertips.

The air here trembled with power. It tasted like copper and ash on Malus's tongue. He set ripples of it in motion as he stepped across the threshold, like he was wading out into an ocean of invisible energy. It lapped around him, plucking at his hair and roiling with his breath. The feel of it left him giddy with greed, but a small part of him was also troubled. So much strength here. Why couldn't these wretches bend it to their will?

He crossed the lines of the wards with great care, even though they had been worked in such a fashion that no mere man could harm them. When he stepped across the first of the rune-inlaid barriers he felt a new kind of power settle over him, like an iron fist closing around his chest. It was so potent that for a moment he thought he couldn't breathe – and then he realised that his heart wasn't beating, either.

Once, in his early years of flirtation with Nagaira, she had taken him into her sanctum and showed him some of her oldest magical tomes. One of them was about wards of stasis and binding, the magical arts of trapping spirits and objects in one place and holding them there until the spell expired.

He was standing in such a ward now – in *layers* of them, each one supplying energy to the others in a weave of incredible complexity and strength. Standing within the wards effectively stopped his body from one heartbeat to the next. He could stand here for thousands of years and not die.

With a creak of ancient, leathery skin, one of the mummies turned to stare at Malus with yellowed, rheumy eyes.

The highborn drew his sword, watching in horror as five bodies – not living, but certainly not dead – rose awkwardly to their feet. Two of the figures brandished knives, while the rest reached out to him with gnarled, wrinkled hands. They tried to speak, their desiccated mouths working, but only a thin whistle of air leaked from their ruined lungs. They staggered towards him, their faces contorted with a mixture of anger, fear – and greed.

The first mummy to reach him swung its dagger wildly at the highborn's head – Malus rocked back on his heels, dodging the blow, then leaned back in and slashed at the creature's knife arm. The limb tore away in a puff of dust, but the mummy simply dropped its shoulder and rushed at him, knocking Malus off his feet. His sword hand cracked against the basalt tile and the blade went skittering across the floor.

A rotted hand groped for Malus's throat, and the mummy's face was inches from his own, still uttering its thin, whistling cry. The other creatures were on him moments later, tearing at him with their hands. The highborn caught sight of the second knife-wielding mummy circling around to stab at his unarmoured head.

Paper-dry fingers closed around his neck. The other mummy's knife flashed downwards, and Malus pulled the one-armed mummy into its path. The blade plunged into the back of the one-armed mummy's skull with a sound like a cracking eggshell, showering the highborn with stinking dust and flecks of dry skin. Malus pulled his leg up underneath the one-armed mummy and kicked the withered corpse back over his head, crashing it into its knife-wielding companion. Both were knocked off balance and fell backwards – landing outside the boundaries of the wards. They hit the floor and exploded into dust as the stasis effect of the magical barriers deserted them.

The other mummies recoiled from Malus with wordless cries of despair as they saw the fate of their companions. The highborn rolled to his feet, recovered his sword, and remorselessly attacked the ancient figures. Within moments their limbless torsos were hurled across the barrier and dashed into dust.

What madness is this, Malus thought, wiping the brownish powder from his face. They lingered for centuries, trying to open those doors, and yet when I appeared to try the same, they attacked me. Was it out of greed, or fear? Or both?

Malus stepped towards the doors. He felt the power flow past him like a receding wave, retreating into the chamber beyond. There was a faint click, and the basalt doors swung silently open.

The room beyond looked like nothing so much as a vast treasure chamber. Piles of gold and silver, jewels and ornate relics lay heaped everywhere, surrounding an enormous, faceted crystal set in the centre of the room. Unlike the green crystals that the beastmen held sacred, this stone was lit with a shifting, bluish glow, not unlike the ambience of the northern lights. The aura of power coalesced around the crystal, sending arcs of blue lightning flickering over its surface.

At last.

Malus approached the crystal, eyes gleaming with anticipation. You were so certain I would fail, sister. You had no idea with whom you were dealing!

The highborn laughed, gazing at the fabulous wealth that surrounded him. Gold enough to beggar

Hag Graef, he thought. And it is only the beginning. His eyes alighted on a gold ring, set with an oblong ruby almost as long as his finger. The flickering light of the crystal played across its surface, giving it the deep colour of fresh blood. Malus plucked the ring from the pile of treasure, savouring its weight and the rich colour of the gem. A ring of blood befitting a conqueror, he thought. The Dark Mother grant this is only the first of the glories that will be mine!

Malus slid the ring upon his finger. The instant it settled into place the power that surrounded the crystal struck the highborn full in the chest. Fire and ice and black corruption seared along his bones. It was a sensation greater than pain and terror and madness combined.

The power that flooded him was coldly, cruelly aware. It was as merciless as a winter storm, as relentless as an avalanche. The highborn's will wasn't merely broken; it was swept away as though it had never been.

Malus screamed in agony and soul-numbing terror as the terrible power hollowed out his soul in a single, awful instant. He fell to his knees, and only then became aware of the thunderous laughter echoing through his mind.

Darkness threatened to overwhelm him. Then a voice reverberated through his skull, whispering with all the intimacy of a lover.

'It is you who are the fool, Malus Darkblade. For want of a bauble you have become my willing slave.'

Chapter Twenty-one
GRIP OF THE DAEMON

MALUS DOUBLED OVER, smoke rising from his body as he fought against the presence that had forced its way into his body. It wasn't the same as the experience with Ehrenlish – this was many, many times worse. The spirit that possessed him permeated flesh and bone, curling around his heart like a serpent and leaving nothing but emptiness where his soul had once been. He raged against the spirit's icy touch, focusing all his will to force the presence from his body but making no impression whatsoever. Fell laughter echoed through his mind.

'Release me!' Malus groaned.

'Release you? But I've only just acquired you. Do you know how long I've waited for a servant like yourself?'

With a roar the highborn hurled himself at the crystal. He tore his sword from its scabbard and rained

blows upon the gleaming surface. Steel and crystal
rang like the clashing of bells, but when he staggered
back, his strength spent, the faceted surface was
unmarked.

'That's a poor way to treat such a fine sword, Malus.
If you keep that up you'll ruin the edge.'

'What are you?' Malus cried, frantic with rage.

'I? Compared to you, I am as a god.' A callous
chuckle reverberated through the room. 'Your kind,
with their rudimentary perceptions, would call me a
daemon. You could not pronounce my name if you
had a thousand years to make the attempt. For our
purposes, you may call me Tz'arkan. That will suffice.'

'A daemon?' Malus staggered at the thought. A daemon? Inside me? No. I will not allow it! The highborn
fell to his knees and dragged his dagger from its
sheath. He pressed the broken tip to his throat. 'I am
a slave to no one, be they daemon or god!'

'If you drive that blade home, mortal, you will not
only die a slave, but you will remain my slave for all
eternity,' the daemon said, its voice cold and grim.

'You are lying.'

'Strike then, and find out.'

The highborn's mind raged. Do it. He lies. Better to
die than to live like this! But doubt nagged at him.
What if he is telling the truth? What reason does he
have to lie? With a bestial growl Malus let the dagger
fall to the floor. 'You said I might remain a slave.'

'That's better,' the daemon said, approval in its
stony voice. 'Clever little druchii. Yes, I would make a
bargain with you. A trade: your soul for my freedom.
Set me free, and I will relinquish my hold on you.
What could be more fair than that?'

Malus frowned. 'I am no sorcerer, Tz'arkan. How may I free you?'

'Leave the sorcery to me, little druchii. You know the story of the temple, I presume? Of that worm Ehrenlish and his lickspittle cronies? You must know – it was Ehrenlish's screams I heard when the great storm was dispelled. How I have longed to hear that sound, Malus! I knew that sooner or later that fool's skull would turn up, but the way you used him to open the gate... it was glorious. For that, you have my gratitude.'

'Get on with it, daemon,' the highborn snarled. 'Unlike you, I can die of old age – or boredom.'

'Not within these wards, little druchii – at least, not for a very, very long time. But I digress. Ehrenlish and his cronies – vile, craven little slugs that they were – succeeded, at great cost, in trapping me in this crystal, many thousands of years ago.'

'Trapped you how?'

'How they did it is not important, Malus. It is enough to say that they did. They bound me to this place and made me their slave. I'm certain you can appreciate how horrible that was.'

'All the more reason for you to release me,' Malus snarled.

'Do not make light of my tragic circumstances, little druchii,' the daemon replied coldly. 'The five sorcerers drew upon my vast power to serve their own pitiful schemes. But they trifled with powers far beyond mortal ken, and that proved to be their undoing. One by one they met with terrible fates, until at last that fool Ehrenlish walled himself up inside his own skull and was lost to history for millennia. But the wards those fools laid upon me still remained. I curse their names for all eternity, but I will admit they did their work well when constructing this awful prison! As soon as Ehrenlish was gone I began clawing at the walls of my cell. I was able to amuse myself with the acolytes and slaves that the sorcerers left behind, but little else. Slowly, slowly, I was able to extend my reach a little further beyond my prison. Within the last hundred years I was able to extend the limits of my awareness to the walls of the temple itself. But I could go no further. The wards were too potent even for one such as myself.'

'So you admit you have your limits? Some god you are,' Malus sneered.

The daemon ignored him. 'The wards can be unravelled, little druchii. The sorceries involved are beyond the pitiful skills of any mortal sorcerer living today, but I know the words and the rituals that must be performed. However, I need a token from each of the five lost sorcerers – five talismans that can be used to undo the spells they once wrought. Each are potent magical artefacts in their own right: The Octagon of Praan; The Idol of Kolkuth; The Dagger of Torxus; The Warpsword of Khaine; and the Amulet of Vaurog.'

'What do I know of talismans, daemon? I am a warrior and a slaver, not some sorcerer or thin-necked scholar. These men died millennia ago. How am I to find these things, if they even still exist?'

'For your sake, little druchii, you had best pray they may still be found. Already the sands are running from the hourglass. Even as we speak your life is slipping from your grasp.'

Malus straightened. 'What! What are you talking about?'

'I have claimed your soul, Malus. Do you not remember? I hollowed you out like a gourd so I could fit the merest sliver of my essence into your frail little frame. That is how we are able to communicate right now, and how I am able to know your every thought. I am not one to let my servants go about unattended, you see.'

'Yet you are killing me? Is that it?'

'It is more fair to say that you killed yourself the moment you let your greed get the better of you,' the daemon said smugly. 'When I claimed your soul your body began to die. In fact, you would be dead right now if it weren't for my power. But not even I can halt the inevitable. If your soul is not restored within a year, your body will perish, and your spirit will be mine forever.'

'A year?' Malus exclaimed. 'I have only a year to find five long-lost relics? You ask the impossible!'

'Perhaps,' the daemon readily agreed. 'But there is no way to know until you try. And if you fail, well, I'm certain there will be others who will seek out the temple, especially now that the Gate of Infinity is no more.'

Malus ground his teeth in frustration. 'I could just stay here,' he said defiantly. 'You said yourself that I could linger here a very, very long time.'

'Oh, clever, clever little druchii,' the daemon said. 'You are right, of course. You could linger here for hundreds and hundreds of years, slowly shrivelling to a withered husk like those wretches you fought beyond my door. By all means, stay then. I will wait for another willing servant. Feel free to amuse your-self with the baubles Ehrenlish and his cronies heaped about me, though I must confess even this much gold loses its lustre after the first century or so.'

'Curse you daemon!' Malus snarled. 'All right. I will find you your trinkets!'

'Excellent! I knew you would come around sooner or later.' The daemon sounded as though he'd just succeeded in teaching a pet a demanding new trick. 'When you have found all the talismans you must return them here before the year is out, and I will take care of the rest.'

'And then you will free me?'

'Not only will I set you free, you have my oath that I will never try to enslave you again. And just to show you that I have your best interests at heart, I will reveal to you that one of the talismans, the Octagon of Praan, is very close by. I can sense it, even in my confined state.'

'Where is this trinket, then?'

'Upon the mountainside,' the daemon replied. 'The beastmen venerate it. At night I can hear their braying chants, calling out to the talisman for protection. Stupid creatures. Ironic that you may have to kill them all to pry their talisman of protection from their grubby little paws.' The daemon sounded inordinately pleased at the prospect.

Slowly and deliberately, Malus picked up his dagger and slid it back into its sheath. The highborn rose to his feet. 'I'll do whatever I must,' he said coldly, his willpower once again reasserting itself. 'In a year's time I'll return here, and we will finish what we've begun.'

'Indeed we will, Malus Darkblade. Indeed we will.'

'Do not call me that!' Malus seethed.

'Why not? Am I mistaken somehow? Darkblades are flawed things, are they not? Step before the crystal, Malus. There is something you must see.'

The highborn frowned in consternation, but after a moment he relented and stepped before the crystal.

'Good. Now look closely.'

The blue glow faded, revealing a crystal facet that gleamed like polished silver. It was like looking into a mirror—

And Malus saw what he had become.

His skin had turned pale as chalk. Distended black veins ran along the back of the hand that bore the ruby ring, disappearing beneath the wrist of his vambrace. They seemed to pulse with a steady flow of corruption. His eyes were orbs of purest jet.

'Gaze upon what you have become – a man with no soul, bound in service to a daemon. And you say you are not a flawed thing, Malus Darkblade?'

The daemon's laughter pealed like thunder as Malus fled from its prison.

MALUS FLED THROUGH the precincts of the temple, slipping in the dust of the dissolved mummies as he plunged down the ramp to the apartments of the doomed sorcerers. The bodies of the acolytes mocked him with their slack jaws and wide, staring eye sockets. They seemed to reach out to him as he passed, offering their knives or their hanging ropes. They offered him the charity of the damned.

His boots rang along the stone. He flew down the spiral staircase, feeling the heat of the magma on his face and fighting the urge to fling himself into the flames. When he came upon the mummified corpse lying on the steps he kicked the body into the lake of fire in his place, envying it its fiery plunge.

The stepping stones were waiting for him when he reached the bottom of the stairs, levitated into position at the will of the daemon upstairs. What a fool he'd been to believe that he had called them from the depths with the strength of his will! He crossed from one stone to the next with as little regard as he would have paid to the stepping stones of a river.

Beyond the plaza and the lake of fire, the statues of the gods seemed to laugh at his anguish, leering at his foolishness in assailing the lair of the daemon. This is what you get for spurning us, the abominable faces seemed to say. You and your Dark Mother. Did she hear your prayer in the stone halls above? Did she grant you victory over your foes?

He threw himself at the statues, howling like a fiend, but he had not the strength to throw those huge edifices down. If anything, the idols only seemed to mock him all the more.

Malus flung himself from the presence of the four gods, staggering through the ranks of the eternal servants. He dashed their obedient bodies into dust, screaming curses at their craven poses.

Distantly he could hear the sound of screams and the ringing clash of steel. Beastmen and druchii alike cried out in rage and pain. Malus drew his sword and ran towards the promise of battle.

Can I ever spill enough blood to drown the memory of my reflection?

Malus stumbled into the cold light of day and beheld the carnage at the temple gate. The beastmen had made a hole with their heavy, two-handed hammers, and dozens of corpses lay in mounds just beyond the breach. Two of the four nauglir lay dead, their bodies pierced and rent by the blows of sword and axe. A third trembled and bled from mortal blows that were slowly stealing away its life. Only Spite survived. Leaner and quicker than his fellows, he nevertheless bore a score of wounds across his armoured hide.

Malus's three retainers stalked amid the battlefield like carrion crows, their black armour splashed and streaked with the blood of their foes. They had cast aside their empty crossbows long ago, and held red, dripping blades in their hands. They worked with the dispassionate skill of butchers, peering among the corpses and dispatching any wounded that they found. There was no telling how many assaults they had already fought off, biding their time between each wave in the same fashion. They were so intent on their business that they didn't notice Malus until he was almost upon them.

It was Lhunara who saw him first. She was covered in gore, her hair matted and her face painted crimson like one of Khaine's murderous brides. There were scores of dents and creases in her armour, and she held a battered sword in each hand. Her expression was a mask of fatigue.

'You've come none too soon, my lord,' she began. 'They've tried to rush us three times now, and only just retreated. Between us and the cold ones we've killed close to eighty of them, but–'

The words died in her throat as Lhunara registered the change in her lord's face. Her eyes met his and they widened in horror. 'My lord, what–'

Malus howled like a wounded beast and buried his sword in Lhunara's skull.

Dalvar and Vanhir saw the blow fall and cried out in horror and dismay. The highborn leapt at them even as Lhunara's body was falling to the ground.

Nagaira's man moved to the left, his hand drawing back and snapping forward in a blur of motion. Without thinking, Malus swept his blade around and knocked the thrown dagger aside. He rushed at the rogue, snapping a blow at his head that Dalvar blocked with the long knife in his left hand. The rogue's right hand drew another long fighting knife and lunged in, stabbing for one of the joints in the highborn's articulated breastplate.

Malus caught Dalvar's wrist in his left hand and punched the retainer across the face with the pommel of his sword. Stunned, Dalvar stabbed for his throat but the thrust went a little wide, scoring a jagged cut along the line of Malus's jaw. The highborn snarled and thrust the point of his sword into the rogue's left armpit, where the armour afforded no protection. The point caught on the joint of the arm. Dalvar stiffened, his face going white with pain, and Malus leaned against the blade, grating against gristle and bone and sinking slowly deeper into the druchii's chest.

Dalvar shrieked and spasmed violently, trying to pull away, but Malus still held his other wrist in a death grip, keeping him in place. The rogue stabbed wildly at him with his dagger, but Malus's outstretched sword arm was in the way; the point of the retainer's dagger gouged him deeply at cheek, temple, ear and throat, but none could dig deep enough to kill. With every blow, every blossom of pain, Malus only pushed harder on his own blade. The point grated free of the joint, pushed past the ribs and sliced through muscle, lung and heart. Dalvar let out a strangled gasp, retched a torrent of blood and fell to the earth.

When Malus spun to face Vanhir, he found the retainer waiting for him several yards away.

'I want to look you in the eye when I kill you,' the knight said, showing his pointed teeth. 'I had much grander plans for your destruction, Darkblade – wondrous creations that would have taken years to end your miserable life. If I am to be denied those glories, I at least want to see the life flee from your pitiful eyes.'

Malus hurled himself at the highborn knight, raining a flurry of blows at his head, shoulders and neck. Vanhir moved like a viper, blocking each blow with the skill of an expert duellist. The dagger in his left hand rapped a staccato drumbeat against Malus's breastplate, vambrace and thigh, probing for weak spots in the armour. When the highborn drew back for another combination of blows, Vanhir's sword flicked out and laid a long cut across Malus's neck, narrowly missing the artery. The highborn was a skilled swordsman, but Vanhir was a master, an artist of the blade.

Now Vanhir pressed his advantage, alternating attacks with sword and dagger. Malus blocked the first sword but took a shallow knife wound through a gap in his right vambrace. He swept aside a lightning thrust – and then he flung himself onto the knight, sinking his white teeth into Vanhir's throat.

Vanhir screamed and writhed, smashing the pommel of his sword into the side of Malus's head, but the highborn would not be shaken off so easily. He bit deep, tasting a rush of coppery blood, then wrenched his head to one side and tore out the side of the knight's throat. Vanhir fell back, clapping his hands to the torrent of blood spilling from his ravaged neck, but it was a futile gesture for a mortal wound. Within moments the life faded from Vanhir's eyes, his gaze freezing in an eternal glare of unremitting hate.

Malus Darkblade threw back his head and howled like a maddened wolf. It was a cry so savage and unhinged that even the herd of battle-hardened beastmen, now advancing slowly down the road for their fourth assault on the gate, paused in fear and wonder at the sound.

The vision of Lhunara's face still hung before his mind's eye, tormenting him. The look of horror on her face when she'd realised his failure had been more than he could bear.

Malus staggered to his feet, wiping Vanhir's blood from his mouth with the back of his black-veined hand.

They had all served him faithfully and well, friend and foe alike, he thought. Better they die than witness his awful shame.

Chapter Twenty-two
BLOOD ON THE WIND

SPITE GROWLED AT Malus's approach. The cold one's eyes were glazed with pain and its flanks heaved with exertion. The nauglir dimly sensed something amiss with his master, yet could not understand what.

'Easy there, terrible one,' Malus said calmly, watching Spite's eyes carefully. If the pupils widened suddenly and his inner eyelids closed, Malus would be fighting for his life a heartbeat later.

'It's just me, Malus. We've done what we came here to do. There's blood on the wind and it's time to ride.'

For a heart-stopping moment it looked as though Spite had forsaken him. The nauglir growled again and his pupils widened, but then the beastmen advancing on the gate let out a ragged shout, distracting the great beast, and Malus took advantage of the moment to leap into the saddle. Spite grumbled and tossed his head, but Malus dug in his spurs and the cold one leapt forward obediently.

The highborn drove Spite right for the gate, kicking the nauglir into a run just as he reached the hole the beastmen had made. Malus leaned against Spite's neck and he still endured a fearfully close call as the cold one shouldered through the hole and scattered broken bits of stone in a wide swathe before him. Once they were through, Malus straightened in his saddle and spurred his mount into a charge, right into the face of the advancing beastmen.

In other circumstances the sight of a lone rider wouldn't have been enough to sway the mob of warriors. But they had been fighting a vicious, close-quarter battle at the temple gate and had seen three separate assaults hurled back by the crushing jaws and cruel talons of Spite and his kin. The sight of the onrushing nauglir caused them to waver, and the moment's hesitation was enough. Malus and Spite ploughed into them, hurling broken bodies left and right. The highborn slashed at upturned faces and throats, screaming like a banshee, and the beastmen fell back from the frenzied attack.

All but a familiar knot of huge beastman champions hefting large, two-handed weapons. Yaghan and his chosen warriors howled their war-cries and tried to rush at Malus, but the press of the retreating mob held the champions at bay for a few crucial seconds. The highborn hauled on the reins, whipping Spite's tail through the press of beastmen, then spurred the cold one into a run, breaking free of the disordered mob and racing headlong down the road of skulls. It took only moments for Yaghan to rally the beastmen with howled curses and oaths, but by the time the weary mob took up the pursuit, Malus was already around the bend in the road and well out of sight.

The highborn's mind raced, trying to force the horrors of the last hour from his mind in order to formulate a plan. Somhow, he had to sneak back into the beastmen camp and find where the Octagon of Praan was kept. He was sure that the only person who knew for certain where to find the relic was Kul Hadar himself. Slipping into the camp in broad daylight would be next to impossible. He would have to find a place to lie low for the night, and slip into the shaman's tent when the opportunity presented itself.

But first there was the matter of the howling mob on his trail.

Malus looked back over his shoulder. None of the beastmen had reached the bend yet, and there was another turn in the road just ahead. As the nauglir raced around the second turn, Malus hauled back on the reins. 'Stand,' he said, and leapt from the saddle. Then he unclipped Spite's reins and stowed them in his saddlebag. 'Run, Spite,' he said, looking the cold one in the eye. 'Hunt. Wait for my call.'

Nauglir were not bright creatures; some would even go so far as to call them stupid, but with enough patience and repetition, they could be trained to respond to simple commands. Spite knew these orders well; when Malus struck him on the shoulder the cold one trotted off, heading for the trees by the side of the road. He would make his way into the forest, looking for food and likely find a spot to lie down and lick his wounds. If things went well Malus could call for him later that night. If things didn't go well, it was better that Spite was free and able to hunt on his own.

As the cold one loped away, Malus sheathed his sword and dived into the underbrush on the side of the road closest to the herd camp. He stayed low and moved as quickly and stealthily as he could. Sure enough, within moments he heard howls nearby, and then the thunder of more than a hundred bare feet as the beastman mob ran past him along the road of skulls. If he was lucky they would run on for quite some distance before realising they'd lost track of their quarry. By then he hoped to be deep in the middle of the forest.

He was just beginning to congratulate himself on his tactics when he raced around an upthrust spur of rock and ran headlong into a beastman coming the other way.

Druchii and beastman went down in a tangle of limbs. Malus didn't know if the warrior was part of the mob that had been chasing him or not. He tore his dagger from its sheath and buried the blade in the beastman's chest. The warrior let out a bubbling moan and tried to hit the highborn with his club. Malus took the blow on his armoured shoulder and drove the knife again and again into the beastman's chest and neck. Within moments the warrior went limp, but already Malus could hear shouts coming from the direction of the road.

He gathered his feet underneath him and ran, holding his arm up in front of his face to ward off the worst of the brambles. He heard cries and howls behind him, and once again he was amazed at how easily the beastmen could move through the dense undergrowth. Malus ran on for another fifty yards and then slowed almost to a crawl, crouching low and looking for a fallen log or a depression in the ground he could hide in. After a few moments he found a dip in the ground that was partially covered by thick, green ground creepers, and he lay prone beneath them, struggling to control his breathing.

Within minutes there were sounds of pursuit all around him. Beastmen ran past on either side, grunting and growling to one another as they searched the woods for him. Malus lay as motionless as he could, still clutching the bloody dagger to his chest. The sounds of pursuit raced away to the north-west – and then Malus heard another beastman heading his way at a trot, moving directly in line with his hiding place.

There was no point moving. The searcher would either stumble onto him or pass on by. Malus lay on his back and listened.

Closer… closer. The warrior had to have seen the creepers by now – would he turn aside? Closer still. He wasn't turning away. Furred legs thrashed through the thick bed of vines. A hoof sank into the loam a scant two inches from Malus's thigh. In a burst of movement, the highborn sat up, grabbed the beastman by one of his curving horns and pulled him down onto the tip of his knife. The blade pierced the warrior's throat, plunging through and severing his spine. The beastman fell hard on Malus, spasmed once, and died without a sound.

The highborn lay there with the beastman atop him, warm blood flowing over his chest and pooling in the hollow of his throat. As far as Malus could tell, the larger beastman completely covered the parts of him that weren't already hidden by the creepers. Once his breathing settled, Malus rested his head against the cold ground and waited for night to fall. Within moments he was asleep.

MALUS AWOKE WITH a start, his breath misting in the cold night air. The body of the beastman had grown stiff; dried blood crackled faintly as the highborn moved. He slowly, carefully rolled the warrior's body off him and sat up, wincing at the stiffness in his limbs. The highborn looked around at the forest growth and for a moment his exhausted mind did not know where he was or how he'd gotten there. But then the throbbing pain of his wounds penetrated his consciousness, and he felt the sense of emptiness in his chest, and remembered.

He rose wearily to his feet and tried to take his bearings. In the distance he could hear the sounds of the herd and the crackle of bonfires. It sounded like a solemn gathering indeed, Malus thought with a merciless grin. Enjoy the bitter fruits of your victory, Kul Hadar. You should have never tried to match wills with me.

There was no way to tell for certain, but it sounded like at least half the herd's survivors had returned to camp. If Hadar followed the same ritual as Machuk had, he would be by the fire, drinking and eating with the rest of the herd until almost dawn. Malus would have to sneak to the edge of the woods and see if he could spy the imposing form of the shaman among the rest of the beastmen around the bonfires.

Then there remained the challenge of slipping through the camp undetected. Although many of the

beastmen would likely be intoxicated in the wee
hours of the morning, his silhouette would still give
him away as not being a member of the herd. He
needed some way to change his appearance.

Malus looked down at the body by his feet. He considered the beastman for a moment, then bent over
the body and began skinning it.

HE WORE THE beastman's skin over his armour like a
cloak. It hung poorly, but it only had to fool the herd
from a distance, and then only for a momentary
glimpse. Or so he hoped.

Malus crouched at the edge of the woods, scanning
each of the three bonfires as carefully as he could. As
far as he could tell, Kul Hadar was nowhere to be
seen. Not a part of the herd, are you Hadar? No wonder they eventually ran you off.

The good news was that he counted less than a hundred beastmen in camp. Between those lost to Urial's
riders and the terrible battle at the temple gate, the
herd had been decimated. Those that he could see
around the fire seemed well and truly drunk.

The highborn stepped from the woods and began
his ascent to Kul Hadar's large tent. He kept to the
shadows, moving no faster than a walk, and tried to
put tents and shelters between himself and the bonfires whenever possible. No one challenged him as he
moved deeper into camp.

As he approached Kul Hadar's tent, Malus noted
that the smaller satellite tents were dark. If those
belonged to Yaghan and his champions, it likely
meant that they were still out searching for him in the
woods. That would make his task much easier.

The highborn circled around to the rear of the great tent and pressed himself against the layered hides. He could smell wood smoke, and faintly heard someone moving quietly inside. Malus pulled out his dagger and, quietly and carefully, cut a slit in the hide long enough for him to be able to pry the leather apart and peer inside.

There was a figure sitting next to an iron brazier in the centre of the tent, facing the central door flap. He heard a faint murmur, like chanting. Kul Hadar was possibly praying to his gods for protection, or deliverance, or to pass the blame for the defilement of the grove onto someone else. Malus grinned fiercely to himself and began to slowly widen the slit, cutting carefully in the direction of the ground. When the slit was large enough for him to slip through, he let the skin of the beastman fall to the ground and crept quietly into the tent.

The interior of the tent was carpeted in thick rugs and hide-covered pillows; either Machuk or Hadar before him had lived like an Autarii Urhan, lounging like country lords on plump pillows. They muffled Malus's movements as he crept closer to the figure chanting by the fire. When the highborn was slightly more than an arm's length away, the sound of chanting suddenly stopped, and the horned figure tensed. Without hesitation, Malus leapt at the beastman, grabbing one horn and placing the dagger to the figure's throat. 'Not a sound, Hadar, or I'll slice you from one horn to the other.'

The cloaked figure let out a bleat of alarm and Malus knew at once that it wasn't Hadar he had caught. Within moments, hanging panels around the perimeter of the tent were pushed aside, revealing connecting entrances with the satellite tents ranged around the central tent. Yaghan and his champions rushed inside, weapons held ready. In their wake stepped Kul Hadar, clutching his staff and baring his fanged smile.

Furious, Malus cut the throat of the beastman he'd caught, stepping back as Hadar's decoy convulsed and bled onto the piled rugs.

The shaman was undeterred. 'When Yaghan and his warriors lost track of you in the forest, he came to me and asked what you might do next.' Hadar's horned head shook from side to side. 'I told him that if you weren't still running, it meant you would be coming back here. Predictable, druchii, predictable. What I do not understand is why?'

Malus grinned wolfishly. 'I'm here to deal with you Hadar,' he said. 'I'm looking for a talisman, something called the Octagon of Praan. I've been told you have it.' The highborn held out his hand. 'Give it to me and I'll share with you everything I've found in the temple.'

The beastman threw back his head and laughed, a coarse, braying sound. 'You amuse me, druchii. Here, I'll make you a counter-offer. Put down that knife and tell me everything you know about the temple, and I promise I won't skin you alive before I sacrifice you in the sacred grove.'

'An interesting offer, Hadar. Let me think about it a moment,' Malus said, and threw his knife at the shaman's head. Hadar knocked it out of the air with his staff, but by that point Malus had drawn his sword and was charging across the tent.

Yaghan roared, and the champions rushed forward. One burly warrior made to grab Malus, and the highborn gave him a backhanded swipe with his blade that severed most of the champion's fingers. As the warrior bellowed in agony, Malus reversed his stroke and ripped open the beastman's throat.

Another of the champions lashed out with a gnarled fist and struck the highborn just below his right temple. Malus's vision went red and spots danced before his eyes. Another set of powerful hands grabbed the highborn's sword arm and pinned it; the gnarled fist lashed out again and Malus received another stunning blow to the head. He felt his left arm being grabbed and pinned back, and then when his vision cleared Yaghan was standing before him, brandishing his enormous battle axe. The champion showed Malus the cruel edge of both axe heads, and with a swift movement he reversed the axe and drove the weapon's butt into Malus's midriff.

There was the sound of crumpled metal and an icy shock convulsed his body. The highborn looked down as Yaghan drew back the butt of his axe and pulled its four-inch-long triangular spike from the hole it had punched in his gut. Dark blood bubbled out of the hole, and then the pain hit, wiping everything else away.

Chapter Twenty-three
FEAST OF SOULS

THEY TOOK HIS swords and armour away and beat him with their fists until his robes and kheitan were soaked with blood. Blood still seeped from the wound in his gut, and the pain made any movement all but impossible. They lashed him to one of the thick poles in Hadar's tent, and the shaman questioned him at length about what he'd found in the temple.

Malus told him everything. He even overstated the amount of treasure waiting in the room with the terrible crystal. Let the beastmen kill one another trying to get there. If the Dark Mother was kind, Hadar would actually succeed, and Tz'arkan would claim him as he'd claimed Malus. Hadar said he didn't believe a word, and once again threatened to skin the highborn alive. Malus just laughed at him, which under the circumstances was torture in and of itself.

Soon he would be in the clutches of a daemon for all eternity, the highborn said. What could Hadar do that would possibly compare to that?

'You do not have to die as yet,' the daemon's voice echoed in his head. 'If you wish it, I can heal your wounds. I can lend you great strength and speed. I can–'

'No,' the highborn muttered.

'No? You're refusing me? You would rather suffer as my slave for all eternity?'

'Shut up,' Malus hissed.

A heavy blow rocked the side of his head. Pain exploded through his midsection, and Malus passed out for several seconds.

When he came to, Hadar was crouching on his knees, looking up at Malus. 'Don't die on me yet, druchii,' the shaman grunted. 'We still have some things to discuss before you go up the slope to atone for your sins in the grove. Now, what does Tz'arkan want with the Octagon of Praan?'

The highborn blinked slowly, trying to focus his thoughts. 'He wants to be free. The Octagon belonged to one of the sorcerers who imprisoned him.'

'All the more reason to keep it from him, then,' Hadar said. 'Praan was the great shaman who founded this herd, many centuries ago. The talisman is one of the herd's most sacred treasures.'

Malus wasn't listening. His head had drooped to his chin, and a thin stream of bloody drool trickled onto the rug. Hadar pushed the highborn's head back and thumbed one eyelid open.

'He's nearly finished,' Hadar told Yaghan. 'Take him to the circle. I must prepare myself for the sacrifice.'

As the champions untied Malus's bonds, Hadar retreated to the far side of the tent, where a copper bowl brimmed with clear water. The shaman began washing the blood from his hands and face, purifying his body for the ceremony to come. 'You know, Malus, for all the carnage you have wrought, I look upon you as a blessing from the gods. Truly I do. You brought the Skull of Ehrenlish, killed Machuk and opened the Gate of Infinity for me. Now you have given me priceless information about the dangers of Tz'arkan and the temple, knowledge I will use to approach the crystal on my own terms and bend the daemon to my will. And finally, thanks to your foolishness, I will cut your throat in the circle of stones, and your blood will purify the grove you so recently defiled.' He turned to face Malus as the champions prepared to carry him from the tent. 'I look forward to eating your heart at the bonfire later tonight, Malus. You have done a great service for me and my herd.'

Hadar's deep laughter accompanied Malus into the darkness.

MALUS LEFT A trail of blood behind him the entire way up the hill. His limbs were growing cold, and his vision came and went. He had never been so close to death before; he could sense it, just at the edge of his being, seeping into his body like a winter chill.

The daemon spoke inside his head every step of the way, offering to heal his wounds. The highborn savoured the subtle edge of desperation mounting in Tz'arkan's voice. The daemon might be telling the truth about his eternal servitude after death, but it was still clear to Malus that Tz'arkan would much rather keep him alive. He also found it interesting that the daemon couldn't heal him without receiving permission. What other limitations did he have? The thought quenched some of the pain he felt. It was good to have even a thin sliver of control over his own fate.

Yaghan and the remaining champions, four in all, carried him effortlessly up the mountain slope. The dark trees rustled hungrily as they passed, no doubt sensing the spilled blood on Malus's body. The standing stones had been shattered by the magical energies unleashed there earlier in the day, but the circle within was clear of debris. Someone, perhaps the surviving priests, had cleared the many bodies away. Many of them were probably being served around the cook fires downslope.

There was a handful of priests still clearing away debris outside the sacred circle. They bowed to the champions as Yaghan barked orders to his warriors. The beastmen stepped reverently into the circle and laid Malus on the stone, then retreated beyond its border. They hadn't bothered to bind him, and why should they? He was unarmed and nearly dead.

At least, for the moment.

Malus carefully opened his eyes. The champions were standing around the outside of the stone circle with their weapons grounded. Yaghan stood off to one side, watching both his warriors and the activities of the priests.

'Tz'arkan,' Malus whispered, the words coming forth in a faint hiss. 'You said you could heal me. Make me stronger and faster.'

'That is so. I can make you stronger and faster for a short time, but there will be a price to pay later. Do you wish it?'

'Yes,' Malus said, and hated himself for it.

Black ice raced through his veins, freezing his blood and causing his wounds to burn. Every muscle clenched at the pain; his shoulders and legs came off the stone slab and hung there for several agonising seconds. Then he collapsed against the stone, half-delirious with the absence of suffering, and when his senses cleared he realised that he was whole again. Whole and powerful.

He didn't want to think how much deeper Tz'arkan had sunk his talons into him after he'd made that request. He would pay whatever price he had to and count the cost later.

Malus slowly turned his head. He spied a large stone outside the circle, less than a foot from where one of the champions stood. As quietly as he could he rolled onto his side and scrambled for it.

It felt as though he was made of fine steel wire, light and strong. He all but flew the intervening feet over to the rock, and plucked it from the ground as though it were a pebble. The champion was just starting to turn, his eyes going wide, when Malus took the rock and crushed the beastman's skull. The champion's eyes bulged and blood flew in a lazy spray as the warrior toppled to the ground. Malus had the champion's great sword in hand and was rushing to the next warrior in line before the first one had hit the ground.

The next champion bleated out a warning and raised his axe as Malus struck, slashing the beastman along the midsection and cutting him in two without breaking stride. The highborn raced through an expanding cloud of blood and viscera and set his sights on the next warrior, who had stepped forward and raised his sword to parry the highborn's attack. Malus slipped effortlessly under the beastman's guard and disembowelled him with a swift slash of his blade, then left the champion clutching at its guts as he sought out the last of Yaghan's warriors.

The remaining champion was running towards him, axe raised high. Out of the corner of his eye, Malus saw Yaghan attempting the same, approaching from the side and a little behind the highborn. Malus focused his attentions on the beastman in front of him – and without warning the steel was gone from his step and the attacking champion seemed to leap directly in his path. The highborn howled inwardly. Cursed daemon and your paltry gifts, he raged.

'You asked for help and I gave it,' the daemon replied coldly. 'Ask, and you may taste of my strength again.'

Acting instinctively Malus ducked left and swept low with the great sword, just as the champion's axe plummeted towards his head. The beastman missed, and Malus's sword sheared off the champion's right leg at the knee. The warrior toppled forward with a scream, and Malus took two steps past and then spun to receive Yaghan's charge.

Yaghan came on like a charging bull, roaring a challenge and holding his axe high. If he hits me solidly, even once, I'm dead, the highborn thought. Without armour, the two-handed axe would split him like kindling.

Malus watched Yaghan approach, waiting until the axe started to fall before dropping the point of his sword and ducking to the left. The axe whistled into the ground less than a finger's width away, and Malus took the opening this presented by raising the point of the blade enough to stab deep into the champion's massive right bicep. The champion howled and swept the axe at Malus with a backhanded stroke that he barely ducked in time.

Before the highborn could fully recover, the powerful champion reversed his stroke and slashed for the highborn's head. Malus ducked lower still and threw himself forward, this time digging the point of the blade through Yaghan's thickly muscled thigh. Flesh and muscle parted easily before the sharp point, tearing a deep trench from front to back along the outside of the champion's upper leg.

The highborn propelled himself past Yaghan as quickly as he could – but not quickly enough. Another lightning fast backhand stroke made a glancing blow on his right shoulder, making a deep, painful cut. Blood poured in a hot stream down his arm and the highborn stumbled. Malus gritted his teeth and spun to face the champion while he tried to plan his next move.

Again, Yaghan dictated the exchange, rushing forward and knocking Malus's sword aside with a powerful blow that nearly wrenched the blade from the highborn's hands. But instead of remaining still, Malus rushed forward as well, so when Yaghan's backhand swing came again, the highborn was inside the weapon's arc and could not hit. Again, Malus threw himself past Yaghan, and again chopped at the champion's thigh in passing. Blood now poured down the beastman's leg.

Yaghan turned about and rushed again almost immediately, but he was slower now, and his swing a tiny bit less powerful. As he charged, Malus spun and suddenly thrust his sword at the beastman's face, causing the champion to check his advance instinctively. As soon as he did, Malus dropped the point of his sword and buried it deep into the champion's wounded thigh.

This time the leg collapsed out from under the beastman. As he fell, Malus raised his blade and rushed in, bringing it down on Yaghan's outflung left arm. The heavy blade chopped nearly through the thick limb, leaving it hanging by a thin strip of muscle.

Yaghan let out a bellow of anguish and fell forwards in a pool of his own blood. Yet despite his terrible wounds, the champion tried to push himself back upright with his one working arm. Malus raised his sword and spared the champion further anguish. The blade sang against flesh and bone and Yaghan's head went bouncing down the steep mountain slope.

A chorus of yells went up from the priests, almost immediately answered from the camp below. Malus thought he could make out Kul Hadar's bellow among the mingled cries. He had little doubt the shaman and the rest of his herd would be storming the grove in moments.

If he were going to claim the Octagon of Praan it would be now or never. Fortunately, Hadar had given him the one clue he needed to uncover its resting place. Where better to keep the most sacred relics of the herd?

Gripping the bloody sword in both hands, Malus ran for the cave at the top of the cleft and the holy sanctum within.

Chapter Twenty-four
THE DAEMON'S CURSE

THERE WERE TWO priests hiding just beyond the cave mouth; Malus stabbed one through the chest while the other pushed past him and ran braying down the slope. More crystal formations lent a greenish glow to the small, rough-hewn chamber. Scattered around the room were small altars to numerous beast-headed gods – minor deities, perhaps, that the herd worshipped in addition to the terrible Ruinous Powers that ruled the wild north.

In truth, the space wasn't so much a discreet chamber as it was an exceptionally broad bulge in a rough-hewn passage that led deeper into the mountain. Alert for signs of danger, Malus pressed onward.

The passage ran for more than fifty yards in more or less a straight line. The farther Malus went, the more he began to notice old, discarded bones – many cracked for the marrow within – and smell the stench of rotting meat. A guardian, Malus thought sourly. But what sort of guardian, and where is it hiding? More importantly, does it sense my presence?

Just ahead, the highborn could see more greenish light. The passage appeared to end in another small cave, lit this time by a glowing crystal that had been placed in an iron brazier instead of growing straight from the ground. In the pale glow Malus could see a broad shelf of natural stone along the far wall of the chamber. Resting on that shelf and gleaming in the greenish glow sat a large, octagonal medallion made from brass and affixed to a long chain. Runes covered the surface of the medallion, hinting at the power locked within.

'Yes – that's it! The Octagon of Praan! Seize it!' urged the daemon.

But Malus was far more interested in the stench of rotted meat that hung in the air of the small chamber. He crept carefully and quietly to the threshold and slowly surveyed the room. The highborn heard no sounds nor saw any movement.

That's strange, he thought. What is causing the smell? And then he saw the body of the stag heaped in a broken lump on the floor near the Octagon itself. Its back and neck were broken, causing the body to bend in opposite angles from one another. One side of a magnificent rack of antlers had been snapped off, and rested on the floor near the body. Both forelegs had been torn away at some point in the past, and the body rested in a black pool of rotting blood. Malus guessed it had sat in the cave for a week or more. Perhaps a sacrifice, he thought. Though those marrow-bones back there didn't crack themselves.

The highborn surveyed the room again. Nothing moved in the shadows. Maybe there was a guardian previously, and it was killed in one of the battles? The idea seemed plausible, especially since the chamber appeared quite empty. No time to waste, Malus thought decisively. I do know for a fact that Hadar will be here at any moment, and I don't relish being trapped in a dead-end tunnel.

Malus crossed the small cave, reaching for the talisman. When he was halfway across something huge and hairy landed on his back and knocked him flat onto the rocky floor. A knotted club smashed into the middle of his back, knocking the breath out of him. Another blow hit hard against his ribs and sent waves of fiery agony shooting across his chest.

The highborn tried to rise, only to discover that his attacker was sitting on his lower back and pinning him in place to deliver his blows. The club smashed down on his right shoulder next, and the pain of that atop the cut he'd received there, nearly knocked him out.

His attacker was in a perfect place to avoid the blows of the large sword in Malus's hands. Thinking desperately, the highborn reversed his grip on the sword so he held it underhand, and stabbed backwards as hard as he could. The point of the sword bit into flesh and his attacker let loose a savage howl that set his hair on end. It leaped off him, and when it did Malus raced quickly across the floor towards the Octagon. Panting in pain, he turned to face his attacker and his eyes went wide with shock.

If the massive guardian of the Octagon had once been a beastman, there was little resemblance left any more. The creature was massive, with huge, broad shoulders and short, trunk-like legs. The powerfully muscled body was covered in irregular patches of fur, and the stunted, misshapen head looked as though it had been made of wax and left half-formed. One bloodshot eye watched him intently.

Malus noted that the creature wasn't carrying a club. The damage it had done was with fists alone.

The guardian of the Octagon clapped a hand to the deep wound in its side and let out a howl that was part angry and part anguish. Without warning it turned and scrambled up the wall behind it, alighting on a rough ledge of rock that sat above the cave entrance.

For a split second Malus thought that the creature was just going to sit there and lick its wound, but as soon as it reached the ledge it let out a snarl and leapt at him once more.

With his back to the shelf there was no place to run. Had Malus been a beginner in the arts of combat he might have panicked. Instead he set the pommel of his great sword against the rock shelf behind him and pointed it directly at the creature's chest.

The guardian let out a wail and Malus struck the sword at a point just below its ribs. The broad blade drove itself up to the quillons in the creature's chest, spilling blood and bile in a torrent onto Malus in the heartbeat before the monster's bulk slammed against him. He hit the rock shelf hard and gasped at the pain that flared across his back. Then the creature let out a strangled cry and grasped the highborn's head firmly in one enormous hand. The guardian's other hand tightened on Malus's shoulder, and then the monster started to twist.

It was trying to twist his head off.

Malus gritted his teeth and tensed his neck, battering the huge hands with his fists, but it was like the chicken fighting the hands of the farmwife. He grabbed at the hilt of the sword and tried to twist it in the wound – anything to force the creature to release him. But the monster only howled in pain and redoubled its efforts.

Slowly, inexorably, Malus's head turned. When it reached the limit his spine would allow, it started to bend further. Pain shot along his vertebrae, and his vision dissolved into a white haze. The highborn started to shout, a single long, painful note as he felt his bones continue to flex and wondered how close he was to the breaking point.

Suddenly, the pressure eased, dropping off almost to nothing. Slowly – and equally painfully – Malus straightened his head, and the guardian's body slumped to the side. Its melted face was ashen, and huge quantities of its blood lapped against the highborn's boots.

Uncaring, the highborn sat down in the sticky fluid and tried to get his breathing under control. He'd been stabbed, cut and beaten dozens of times, but he'd never had to suffer an attack like that before.

'Get up,' the daemon urged. 'Hurry. Kul Hadar could be here at any moment!'

'Let him come,' Malus snarled. 'He can't twist my head off.'

'No. He puts his faith in axes,' Tz'arkan answered sarcastically. 'Now go.'

Malus climbed painfully to his feet and reached for the Octagon. 'Put it on,' the daemon said.

'Why? What does it do?'

'It absorbs magical energy. Spells directed against you will be consumed by the amulet, no matter how powerful. It is a most useful talisman.'

Suspicion warred with desperation in Malus's mind. What if the daemon were lying? Then again, could he afford not to take advantage of such a valuable talisman? In the end, the looped the chain over his neck with a barely repressed curse. The daemon might not be telling the truth, but neither would he put Malus in a position where he could no longer serve his interests.

With a great deal of effort, Malus recovered his sword and made his way back down the passage. His worst fears of facing Hadar and his mob at the mouth of the shrine turned out to be unfounded. They waited before the ruins of the stone circle, evidently unwilling to defile the sacred cave with further violence.

The highborn noticed with some surprise that Hadar had less than fifty of the herd with him. Is your support waning, Hadar, or has the herd gotten its fill of bloodshed for the time being?

The ones that did come, however, were the true believers. When they saw he wore the Octagon, the beastmen let out howls of anger and outrage.

'There are almost fifty of them,' the daemon said. 'You have neither armour nor mount. You will need my help if you are to prevail.'

'No,' Malus said angrily. 'I've bartered enough of my flesh to you today. You'll get no more.'

'You'll die!'

'Perhaps... and perhaps not. Now shut up and observe.'

Malus stepped from the cave. 'It appears I won't be serving your herd quite so well as you imagined, Hadar.'

'Remove the Octagon from your unclean neck at once!' Hadar roared, and the rest of the true believers howled their agreement.

Malus pretended to hold up the medallion between thumb and forefinger and study it intently. 'If this trinket is so sacred, and your faith so strong, why don't we put it to the test?'

For a moment Hadar didn't answer. The rest of the faithful eyed him expectantly, and the shaman knew he'd been trapped. 'What do you have in mind?'

Malus spread his hands. 'What else? I challenge you. If you win, your faith is clearly superior, and the medallion is yours. But if you lose…'

Malus and Hadar locked eyes. Finally, the shaman said. 'It is not worth considering, druchii. I will not lose.'

The druchii grinned. 'Then let us begin.'

'No!' Tz'arkan raged. 'You fool. You set no terms for the challenge!'

'Terms? What terms do I need? While I wear the Octagon, his magic can't affect me, and I fear that stick of his far less than Yaghran's axe. The advantage is mine.' And besides, Malus thought grimly, I want to be certain that, whatever else may happen, Hadar dies by my hand. He owes me a debt of pain.

Malus was already walking down the hill, sword held at the ready. Hadar shrugged out of his robe and hefted his heavy staff. His lips pulled back in a feral smile.

That's odd, the highborn thought to himself. What does he have to smile about?

Then Hadar spoke a string of words and the air seemed to warp around the shaman. His already imposing frame swelled even further, appearing far more powerful than before. Hadar roared like an enraged bear – and then barked out another string of magical words. By the time he'd finished speaking he had crossed the ten or so yards between himself and Malus.

The next thing Malus knew, the shaman's staff smashed against his sword hand and the great sword went spinning off into the grass. Hadar followed up with a backhanded swing that crashed into the highborn's chest and sent him flying in the opposite direction.

He fetched up alarmingly close to the dark trees, his ribs throbbing as though he'd been kicked by a cold one. It took a moment before he could breathe again, and in that time Hadar was standing over him, striking down at his head with his terrible staff. Malus summoned all his strength and leapt away barely in time.

'You lied to me!' Malus raged at the daemon as he ran headlong for his lost sword.

'No, I told you exactly what Hadar's limitations were. His magic can't affect you directly. You were the fool who thought you knew better than I in matters of sorcery.'

Suddenly a shadow fell over Malus, and instinct made him duck his head. Instead of killing him, the staff struck him across his shoulders and flung him face-first to the ground. His entire left arm was numb from the blow, and his right throbbed in agony. Worse, he was now several yards downslope from where his sword lay. Realising the danger in hesitating, Malus scrabbled to his feet and staggered forward, his right hand running through the grass before him as he tried to find something he could use as a weapon.

The faithful laughed to see their foe capering like a fool in the grove he'd defamed. Hadar stalked after him, summoning his power once more. 'You were stupid to challenge me in my place of power,' Hadar said. 'Here I can work my magic with impunity, drawing strength from the land itself. What do you have that can compare?'

'Let me help you,' the daemon whispered. 'I can give you the strength and speed to surprise him. Just say the word.'

'No,' Malus replied.

The staff smashed down on him again, this time striking the highborn in the lower back. Malus cried out in pain and fell face-first. His one good hand fumbled frantically through the grass – and finally closed on something small and hard.

Hadar rose above him, his staff poised to strike. 'I had expected better of the warrior who bested Yaghan,' the shaman said. 'But then, the earth is not your ally, is it?'

Malus rolled onto his back and snapped his right hand forward, fingers pointing up at the bottom of Hadar's jaw. The shaman had just enough time to register the motion before the small, charred boot knife punched through soft flesh and drove upwards into Kul Hadar's brain.

'Perhaps not, beastman,' Malus answered coldly. 'But from time to time she supplies me with what I need.'

The shaman swayed on his feet for the space of several heartbeats, then crashed to the ground.

I thought that knife had landed somewhere over here, the highborn thought as he climbed to his feet. Malus went and reclaimed his sword, ignoring the shocked cries and the horrified looks of the true believers. Then he turned on them, brandishing the point of the sword in their faces.

'Hear me, animals,' Malus growled. 'Your shaman is dead. Your champions are dead. Your relic has been plundered – all by my hand alone. Your herd has been broken – leave now, or try your faith against mine and perish, as Kul Hadar did. Now choose.'

The true believers stared at Malus for several heartbeats, clearly weighing their convictions. One beastman stepped forward, opening his mouth to speak, and Malus stabbed him through the throat. The rest fled, filling the grove with wails of despair.

Malus watched them go. Once they were lost from sight, he let the great sword fall to the ground and walked over to Yaghan's headless body. Bending down, he picked up the champion's fallen axe. Then, studying the black-boled trees carefully, he went to gather some wood for a fire.

THE LOGS BLAZED hotly in the stone circle, the heat reflecting from the slab and keeping the chill of the night at bay. Malus carved off another piece of meat with his boot knife and slipped the morsel into his mouth. It was tough and chewy, but by no means the most stringy meat he'd ever had. A little gamy, but that was all right, too. He sat back on his haunches and watched the northern lights dance overhead.

There had been much shouting and howls of despair in the herd camp throughout the afternoon, but as evening wore on the place fell silent. Malus wandered down from the grove – itself a great deal less demonstrative than before – and found the place deserted. He went through Hadar's tent and found it expertly pillaged. Except for his belongings – they sat in a neat pile on the dirt floor where rugs and pillows had once lain. Malus had armed himself, and, feeling more relaxed at that point, went into the woods to find Spite.

The nauglir now wandered near the bottom of the cleft, helping himself to Hadar's fallen champions. He'd let Spite eat his fill, and then begin the long trek south, back to the Hag. The daemon's words still echoed in his mind: *Already the sands are running from the hourglass. Even as we speak your life is slipping from your grasp.*

He had the Octagon of Praan, but that still left four talismans to go, and he hadn't any idea how to find them. And of the two people he knew who might have the information, one likely wanted him dead and the other had actively tried to kill him by sending him into the Wastes in the first place.

'Your sister sought to teach you a lesson,' Tz'arkan said. 'If she wanted you dead she would have kept you in the city where Urial could get to you.'

Malus bit back a curse. It was going to be a long time before he grew accustomed to the daemon's presence in the back of his mind. 'You may have a point,' the highborn grudgingly agreed. 'She may have expected me to turn back once the going became too dangerous.' He grinned. 'It appears my sister does not know me as well as she thinks.'

Then as he thought about the possibilities, his face grew cold. If that's true, then Nagaira never meant to sacrifice Dalvar and her men at all.

'Perhaps, but that assumption worked out in your favour, putting rest to a potential threat of betrayal. Simply tell her your warband was wiped out on the journey north. It is nothing but the truth.'

Malus nodded, but his expression was troubled. He'd lost a great many valuable resources during the journey. Some, like Lhunara, would be almost impossible to replace.

Yet the expedition hadn't been a total loss. He would return with enough wealth from the daemon's treasure chamber to pay off his debts and begin forming the power base he'd always needed...

'You are very free with my trinkets, Darkblade,' the daemon warned.

'If I'm free with your gold, you'll be free in turn,' Malus replied. 'I can't search for your relics if I wind up on the wrong end of an assassin's blade.'

Tz'arkan fell silent. Malus afforded himself a brief, smug grin. It was true that he'd left the Hag as a highborn and would return as a slave, but between now and then he would find a way to conceal the mark of the daemon's bond. As bad as his situation was, it still lent him advantages that no one else realised he possessed. He planned on making use of those advantages where they would do the most good.

He would overcome this setback. Eventually, he would be free again. He was capable of making sacrifices and suffering lasting torments if they brought him closer to his goals. That was the essence of who the druchii were – taking strength from darkness and making it their own.

The highborn leaned back against the burnt stump of one of the standing stones. He would find a way to rebuild his ties to Urial or Nagaira. The highborn was willing to pay whatever price was required. He was nothing if not a reasonable man.

Malus cut another slice of Kul Hadar's heart and chewed it thoughtfully, contemplating the future.

Glossary

Ancri Dam

Literally 'Heart of the Stag', an arcane talisman worn as a symbol of rule by one of the larger Autarii clans. Thought to possess potent magical powers.

Autarii

Translated either 'Shades' or 'Spectres', it is the name adopted by the druchii mountain clans north of Hag Graef. Superlative woodsmen and hunters, the Autarii are considered cruel and pitiless even by druchii standards.

Caedlin

A mask, usually of silver or gold, worn by highborn citizens of Hag Graef to protect their faces from the fog that sweeps over the city each night. Sometimes called a nightmask.

Courva

Root extract from a plant found in the jungles of Lustria. When chewed, it acts as a stimulant, sharpening the senses. It is believed to increase reflexes. Favoured by duellists and assassins. Mildly addictive.

Drachau

Literally 'Hand of Night', the title held by the six rulers of the great druchii cities as appointed by the Witch King Malekith. The drachau serve as the Witch King's lieutenants and his inner council, each fulfilling a specific function in that capacity. Traditionally the drachau of Hag Graef serves as the general of the Witch King's armies in times of war.

Druhir

The spoken language of the druchii.

Hadrilkar

Literally 'collar of service'. A torc worn by members of a highborn's retinue or followers of certain religious cults or professional guilds. The torc is typically made of gold or silver and etched with the highborn's family sigil.

Hakseer

The 'proving cruise' made by every druchii highborn upon reaching adulthood. Every highborn is expected to lead a yearlong raiding cruise to demonstrate his skill and ruthlessness and establish his reputation in highborn society. Oftentimes, success on the cruise depends on how much the family spends to outfit it. It is not uncommon, for example, for a drachau's son to take to the sea with a small fleet of ships at his command. The commander of the cruise keeps the lion's share of the plunder, as is customary on all raiding cruises.

Hanil Khar

The 'Bearing of Chains', an annual ceremony held in all six of the great druchii cities, where highborn families restate their oaths of allegiance to their drachau and present some form of tribute as a symbol of their fear and respect for him. The Hanil Khar marks the end of the raiding season and the beginning of the long winter of Naggaroth.

Hithuan

The druchii, with their passionate and murderous nature, have evolved a rigid etiquette of social space that allows the highborn to function socially without the near constant risk of bloodshed. Distance is measured in sword lengths; lowborn may not approach closer than three sword lengths (approximately twelve feet) without being summoned, while retainers may stand as close as two sword lengths from their masters. Valued retainers, lieutenants and lower-ranking highborn stand just out of sword reach. The closest, most intimate space is reserved for lovers, playthings and mortal foes. Hithuan does not apply to slaves, as they are expected to shed their blood at a druchii's whim.

Hushalta

A thick, acrid liquid also called 'Mother's Milk', made from plant extracts taken from Tilea and alkaloid substances found in the mountains of Naggaroth. The drink induces a deep sleep, characterized by vivid nightmares and lingering hallucinations after waking, though it also speeds the healing process for the druchii. High doses can result in memory loss and even dementia over a prolonged period of use.

Kheitan

A thick gambeson of leather and cloth worn over a dark elf's layered robes, covering his upper and lower torso. Typically worn beneath a coat of fine mail (in social situations), or an articulated breastplate (in wartime), the kheitan provides both added protection and insulation from the elements.

Maelith

Malevolent spirits, supposedly the ghosts of druchii who offended the Dark Mother and were consigned to haunt the earth until the end of days. They feed on the blood of the living and cannot be harmed save by the touch of cold iron. Occasionally used by powerful sorcerers as familiars and guardians.

Nauglir

Literally 'cold one', the druchii name for the huge, lizard-like predators found in the caverns beneath Hag Graef. Mistaken as large reptiles by humans, the nauglir are in fact a distant relative of the dragon, and are used by the highborn as cavalry and hunting mounts.

Raksha

One of the Autarii's many names for the restless dead. In this case, the name specifically refers to a vengeful ghost that preys upon the living.

Sa'an'ishar

A shorthand of the command 'Shields and spears!' – the standard druchii order for a formation to ready itself for action. Druchii lords often use the phrase as a general command for attention.

Urhan

Literally 'High One', the title of an Autarii clan leader.

Vaulkhar

Literally 'Maker of Chains', a title held by the warlord of a drachau's army. The title comes from the warlord's right of indenture – rather than killing or ransoming prisoners of war, he can enslave them if he so desires.

Vauvalka

Literally 'Shadow-casters', illegal users of the dark arts who can raise angry spirits and inflict them on a druchii's rivals – for a price.

ABOUT THE AUTHORS

Dan Abnett lives and works in Maidstone, Kent, in England. Well known for his comic work, he has written everything from the *Mr Men* to the *X-Men* in the last decade, and is currently scripting *Legion of Superheroes* and *Superman* for DC Comics, and *Sinister Dexter* and *The VCs* for 2000 AD. His work for the Black Library includes the popular comic strips *Lone Wolves*, *Titan* and *Inquisitor Ascendant*, the best-selling Gaunt's Ghosts novels, and the acclaimed Inquisitor Eisenhorn trilogy.

Mike Lee was the principal creator and developer for White Wolf Game Studio's *Demon: The Fallen*. Over the last eight years he has contributed to almost two dozen role-playing games and supplements, including the award-winning *Vampire: The Masquerade, Adventure!*, *Vampire: Dark Ages* and *Hunter: The Reckoning*. His short stories have appeared in the anthologies *Dark Tyrants, Inherit the Earth* and most recently Del Rey's *Crimson Skies*. An avid wargamer, history buff and devoted fan of two-fisted pulp adventure, Mike lives with his family in the United States.

WARHAMMER

GRUDGE BEARER

GAV THORPE

*Available now from the Black Library: an epic tale of
dwarfs, grudges and beer!*

GRUDGE BEARER

by Gav Thorpe

THE TWISTED, BAYING *creatures came on in a great mass,
howling and screaming at the darkening sky. Some shambled
forwards on all fours like dogs and bears, others ran upright
with long, loping strides. Each was an unholy hybrid of man
and beast, some with canine faces and human bodies, others
with the hindquarters of a goat or cat. Bird-faced creatures
with bat-like wings sprouting from their backs swept forward
in swooping leaps, alongside gigantic monstrosities made of
flailing limbs and screeching faces.*

*As the sun glittered off the peaks of the mountains around
them, the host of elves and dwarfs stood watching grimly as
this fresh wave of warped horrors swept down the valley
towards them. For five long days they had stood against the
horde pouring from the north. The sky seethed with magical
energy above them, pulsing with unnatural vigour. Storm
clouds tinged with blue and purple roiled in the air above the
dark host.*

*At the head of the dwarf army stood the High King, Snorri
Whitebeard. His beard was stained with dirt and blood and*

he held his glimmering rune axe heavily in his hand. Around him his guards picked up their shields, axes and hammers and closed around the king, preparing to face the fresh onslaught. It was the dwarf standing to Snorri's left, Godri Stonehewer, who broke the grim silence.

'Do you think there'll be many more of them?' he asked, hefting his hammer in his right hand. 'Only, I haven't had a beer in three days.'

Snorri chuckled and looked across towards Godri.

'Where did you find beer three days ago?' the High King said. 'I haven't had a drop since the first day!'

'Well,' replied Godri, avoiding the king's gaze. 'There may have been a barrel or two that were missed out when we were doling out the rations.'

'Godri!' snapped Snorri, genuinely angry. 'There's good fighters back there with blood in their mouths that have had to put up with that elf-spit for three days, and you had your own beer? If I survive this we'll be having words!'

Godri didn't reply but shuffled his feet in chagrin and kept his gaze firmly on the ground.

'Heads up!' someone called from further down the line, and Snorri turned to see dark shapes in the sky above, four of them barely visible amongst the clouds. One detached itself from the group and spiralled downwards.

As it came closer the shape was revealed to be a dragon, its large white scales glinting in the magical storm. Perched at the base of its long, serpentine neck was a figure swathed in a light blue cloak, his silvered armour shining through the flapping folds. His face was hidden behind a tall helm decorated with two golden wings that arched into the air.

The dragon landed a short way in front of Snorri and folded its wings. The figure leapt gracefully to the ground from his saddle, tall and lean, and strode towards Snorri, the long cloak flowing just above the muddy ground. As he *approached, he removed his helm revealing a slender face and wide, bright eyes. His skin was fair and dark hair fell loosely around his shoulders.*

'Made it back then?' said Snorri as the elf stopped in front of him.

'Of course,' the elf replied with a distasteful look. 'Were you expecting me to perish?'

'Hey now, Malekith, don't take on so!' said Snorri with a growl. 'It was a simple greeting.'

The elven prince did not reply. Turning, he surveyed the oncoming horde. When he spoke, his gaze was still fixed to the north.

'This is the last of them,' said Malekith. 'Well, the last for many, many leagues. When they are all destroyed we shall turn westwards to the hordes that threaten the cities of my people.'

'That was the deal, yes,' said Snorri, pulling off his helmet and dragging a hand through his knotted, sweat-soaked hair. 'We swore oaths, remember?'

Malekith turned and looked at Snorri.

'Yes, oaths,' the elven prince said, looking over his shoulder at Snorri. 'Your word is your bond, that is how is it with you dwarfs, is it not?'

'As it should be with all civilised folk,' said Snorri, ramming his helmet back on. 'You've kept your word, we'll keep ours.'

The elf nodded and walked away. With a graceful leap he jumped into the dragon's saddle and a moment later, amidst the thunderous flapping of wings, the beast soared into the air and was soon lost against the clouds.'

'They're a funny folk, these elves,' remarked Godri. 'Speak odd, too.'

'They're a strange breed, right enough,' agreed the dwarf king. 'Living with dragons, can't take their ale, and I'm sure

they spend too much time in the sun. Still, anyone who can swing a sword and will stand beside me is friend enough in these dark times.'

'Right enough,' said Godri with a nod.

The dwarf throng was silent as the beasts of Chaos approached, and above the baying and howling of the twisted monsters, the clear trumpet calls of the elves could be heard, marshalling their line.

The unnatural tide of mutated flesh was now only some five hundred yards away and Snorri could smell their disgusting stench of the storm wind. In the dim light, a storm of white-shafted arrows lifted into the air from the elves and then fell down amongst the horde. punching through furred hide and leathery skin. Another volley followed swiftly after, then another and another. The ground of the valley was littered with the dead and the dying, dozens of arrow-pierced corpses strewn across the slope in front of Snorri and his army. Still the beasts rushed on, heedless of their casualties, and they were now only two hundred yards away. Three arrows burning with blue fire arced high into the air.

'Right, that's us,' said Snorri. He gave a nod to Thundir to his right and the dwarf lifted his curling horn to his lips and blew a long blast that resounded off the valley walls.

The noise gradually increased as the dwarfs marched forwards, the echoes of the horn call and roaring of the Chaos beasts now drown out by the tramp of iron-shod feet, the clinking of chainmail and the thump of hammers and axes on shields.

Like a wall of iron, the dwarf line advanced down the slope as another salvo of arrows whistled over their heads. The scattered groups of fanged, clawed monsters crashed into the shieldwall growling, howling and screeching, their wordless challenges met with gruff battlecries and shouted oaths.

'Grungni guide my hand!' bellowed Snorri as a creature with the head of a wolf, the body of a man and the legs of lizard jumped at him, slashing at him with long talons. Snorri swept his axe from right to left in a low arc, the gleaming blade shearing off the beast's legs just below the waist.

As the dismembered corpse tumbled down the hill, Snorri stepped forward and brought his axe back in the return blow, ripping the head from a bear-like creature with a lashing snake for a tail. Thick blood that stank of rotted fish fountained over the king, sticking to the plates of his iron armour. The gobbets caught in his matted beard and made him gag. It was going to be a long day.

THE THRONE ROOM of Zhufbar echoed gently with the hubbub of the milling dwarfs. A hundred lanterns shone a golden light down onto the throng as King Throndin looked out over his court. Representatives of most of the clans were here, and amongst the crowd he spied the familiar face of his son, Barundin. The young dwarf was in conversation with the runelord, Arbrek Silverfingers. Throndin chuckled quietly to himself as he imagined the topic of conversation: undoubtedly his son would be saying something rash and ill-considered and Arbrek would be cursing him softly with an amused twinkle in his eye.

Movement at the great doors caught the king's attention and the background noise dropped down as the human emissary entered, escorted by Hengrid Dragonfoe, the Hold's gatewarden. The manling was tall, even for one of his kind, and behind him came two other men carrying a large ironbound wooden chest between them. The messenger was clearly taking slow deliberate strides so as not to outpace his shorter-legged escort, while the two carrying the chest were visibly tiring. A gap opened up in the assembled throng, a pathway top the foot of Throndin's throne appearing out of the crowd.

He sat with his arms crossed as he watched the small deputation make its way up the thirty steps to the dais on which his throne stood. The messenger bowed low, his left hand extended to the side with a flourish, and then looked at the king.

'My lord, King Throndin of Zhufbar, I bring tidings from Baron Silas Vessal of Averland,' the emissary said. He was speaking slowly, for which Throndin was grateful for it had been many long years since he had needed to understand the Reikspiel of the Empire. The king said nothing for a moment, and then noticed the manling's unease at the ensuing silence. He dredged up the right words from his memory.

'And you are?' asked Throndin.

'I am Marechal Heinlin Kulft, cousin and herald to Baron Vessal,' the man replied.

'Cousin, eh?' said Throndin with an approving nod. At least this manling lord had sent one of his own family to parley with the king. In his three hundred years, Throndin had come to think of humans as rash, flighty and inconsiderate. Almost as bad as elves, he thought to himself.

'Yes, my lord,' replied Kulft. 'On his father's side,' he added, feeling perhaps that the explanation would fill the silence that had descended on the wide, long chamber. He was acutely aware of hundreds of dwarfen eyes boring into his back and hundreds of dwarfen ears examining his every word.

'So, you have a message?' said Throndin, tilting his head slightly to one side.

'I have two, my lord,' said Kulft. 'I bring both grievous news and a request from Baron Vessal.'

'You want help, then?' said Throndin. 'What do you want?'

The herald was momentarily taken aback by the king's forthright manner but gathered himself quickly.

'Orcs, my lord,' said Kulft, and at the mention of the hated greenskins and angry buzzing filled the chamber. The noise quietened as Throndin waved the assembled court to silence. He gestured for Kulft to continue.

'From north of the baron's lands, the orcs have come,' he said. 'Three farms have been destroyed already, and we fear they are growing in number. The baron's armies are well equipped but small, and he fears that should we not respond quickly the orcs will only grow more bold.'

'Then ask your count or your emperor for more men,' said Throndin. 'What concern is it of mine?'

'The orcs have crossed your lands as well,' replied Kulft quickly, obviously prepared for such a question. 'Not only this year, but last year at about the same time of year.'

'Have you a description of these creatures?' demanded Throndin, his eyes narrowing to slits.

'They are said to carry shields emblazoned with the crude images of a face with two long fangs, and they paint their bodies with strange designs in black paint,' said Kulft, and this time the reaction from the throng was even louder.

Throndin sat in silence but the knuckles of his clenched fists were white and his beard quivered. Kulft gestured rapidly to the two men that had gratefully placed the chest on the throne tier, and they opened it up. The light of a hundred lanterns glittered off the contents – a few gems, many, many silver coins and several bars of gold. The anger in Throndin's eyes was rapidly replaced with an acquisitive gleam.

'The baron would not wish you to endure any expense on his account,' explained Kulft, gesturing to the treasure chest. 'He would ask that you accept this gesture of his good will in offsetting any cost that your expedition might incur.'

'Hmm, gift?' said Throndin, tearing his eyes away from the gold bars. They were of a particular quality, originally dwarf-gold if his experienced eye was not mistaken. 'For me?'

Kulft nodded. The dwarf king looked back at the chest and then glowered at the few dwarfs that had taken hesitant steps up the stairway towards the chest. Kulft gestured for his companions to close the lid before any trouble started. He had heard of the dwarf lust for gold, but had mistaken it merely for greed. The reaction had been something else entirely, a desire for the precious metal that bordered on physical need, like a man finding water in the desert.

'While I accept this generous gift, it is not for gold that the King of Zhufbar shall march forth,' said Throndin, standing up. 'We know of these orcs. Indeed, last year they were met in battle by dwarfs of my own clan, and the vile creatures took the life of my eldest son.'

Throndin paced forward, his balled fists by his side, and stood at the top of the steps. When he next spoke, his voice echoed from the far walls of the chamber. He turned to Kulft.

'These orcs owe us dear,' snarled the king. 'The life of a Zhufbar prince stains their lives and they have been entered into the list of wrongs done against my hold and my people. I declare grudge against these orcs!

Their lives are forfeit, and with axe and hammer we shall make them pay the price they owe! Ride to your lord, tell him to prepare for war, and tell him that King Throndin Stoneheart of Zhufbar will fight beside him!'

THE TRAMPING OF dwarf boots rang from the mountainsides as the gates of Zhufbar were swung open and the host of King Throndin marched out. Rank after rank of bearded warriors advanced between the two great statues of Grungni and Grimnir that flanked the gateway, carved from the rock of the mountain. Above the dwarfs swayed a forest of standards of gold and silver wrought into the faces of revered ancestors, clan runes and guild symbols.

The thud of boots was joined by the rumbling of wheels and the wheezing and coughing of a steam engine. At the rear of the dwarf column, a steamdozer puffed into view, its spoked, iron-rimmed wheels grinding along the cracked and pitted roadway. Billows of grey smoke rose into the air from the fluted funnel as the traction engine growled forwards, pulling behind it a chain of four wagons laden with baggage covered with heavy water-proofed sacking bound with iron cable.

The autumn sky above the World's Edge Mountains was low and grey, threatening rain, and yet Throndin was in high spirits. He walked at the head of his army, to his left Barundin carried the king's own standard and to his right marched the Runelord Arbrek.

'War was never a happy occasion in your father's day,' said Arbrek, noticing the smile on the king's lips. The smile faded as Throndin turned his head to look at the runelord.

'My father never had cause to avenge a fallen son,' the king said darkly, his eyes bright in the shadow of his gold-inlaid helmet. 'I thank him and the fathers before him that I have been granted to opportunity to right this wrong.'

'Besides, it is too long since you last took up your axe other than to polish it!' said Barundin with a short laugh. 'Are you sure you still remember what to do?'

'Listen to the beardling!' laughed Throndin. 'Barely fifty years old and already an expert on war. Listen, laddie, I was swinging this axe at orcs long before you were born. Let's just see which of us accounts for more, eh?'

'This'll be the first time your father has had a chance to see your mettle,' added Arbrek with a wink. 'Stories when the ale is flowing are right enough, but there's nothing like seeing it first-hand to make a father proud.'

'Aye,' agreed Throndin, patting Barundin on the arm. 'You're my only son now. The honour of the clan will be yours when I go to meet the ancestors. You'll make me proud, I know you will.'

'You'll see that Barundin Throndinsson is worthy of becoming king,' the youth said with a fierce nod that set his beard waggling. 'You'll be proud, right enough.'

They marched westwards towards the Empire until noon, the towering ramparts and bastions of Zhufbar disappearing behind them, the mountain peak that held the king's throne room obscured by low cloud.

At midday Throndin called a halt and the air was filled with the noise of five thousand dwarfs eating sandwiches, drinking ale and arguing loudly, as was their wont when on campaign. After the eating was done the air was thick with pipesmoke, which hung like a cloud over the host.

As Throndin sat on a rock, legs splayed in front of him, he admired the scenery. High up on the mountains, he could see for many miles, league after league of hard rock and sparse trees and bushes. Beyond, he could just about make out the greener lands of the Empire. Taking a puff on his pipe, a tap on his shoulder caused him to turn. It was Hengrid, and with him was an old-looking dwarf with a long white beard tucked into a simple rope belt. The stranger wore a hooded cloak of rough-spun wool died blue and he held a whetstone in his crackled, gnarled hands.

'Grungni's honour be with you, King Throndin,' said the dwarf with a short bow. 'I am but a simple traveller, who earns a coin or two with my whetstone and my wits. Allow me the honour of sharpening your axe and perhaps passing on a wise word or two.'

'My axe is rune-sharp,' said Throndin, turning away.

'Hold now, king,' said the old dwarf. 'There was a time when any dwarf, be he lowly or kingly, would spare an ear for one of age and learning.'

'Let him speak, Throndin,' called Arbrek from across the other side of the roadway. 'He's old enough to even be my father, show a little respect!'

Throndin turned back to the stranger and gave a grudging nod. The pedlar nodded thankfully and pulled off his pack and set it down by the roadside. It looked very heavy and Throndin noticed an axe-shaped bundle swathed in rags stuffed between the folds of the dwarf's cloak. With a huff of spelled breath, the dwarf sat down on the pack.

'Orcs, is it?' the pedlar said, pulling an ornate pipe from the folds of his robe.

'Yes,' said Throndin, taken aback. 'Have you seen them?'

The dwarf did not answer immediately. Instead he took a pouch from his belt and began filling his pipe with weed. Taking a long match from the pouch, he struck it on the hard surface of the roadway and lit the pipe, puffing contentedly several times before turning his attention back to the king.

'Aye, I seen them,' said the dwarf. 'Not for a while now, but I seen them. A vicious bunch and no mistake.'

'They'll be a dead bunch when I catch them,' snorted Throndin. 'When did you see them?'

'Oh, a while back, a year or thereabouts,' said the stranger.

'Last year?' said Barundin, walking over and standing beside his father. 'That was when they slew Dorthin!'

The king scowled at his son, who felt silent.

'Aye, that is right,' said the pedlar. 'It was no more than a day's march from here, where Prince Dorthin fell.'

'You saw the battle?' asked Throndin.

'I wish that I had,' said the stranger. 'My axe would have tasted orc flesh that day. But alas, I came upon the field of battle too late and the orcs were gone.'

'Well, this time the warriors of Zhufbar shall settle the matter,' said Barundin, patting hand to the axe at his belt. 'Not only that, but a baron of the Empire fights with us.

'Pah, a manling?' spat the pedlar. 'What worth has a manling in battle? Not since young Sigmar has their race bred a warrior worthy of the title.'

'Baron Vessal is a person of means, and that is no mean feat for a manling,' said Hengrid, 'He has dwarf gold, even.'

'Gold is but one way to judge the worth of a person,' said the stranger. 'When axes are raised and blood flows, it is not wealth but temper that is most valued.'

'What would you know?' said Throndin with a dismissive wave. 'I'd wager you have barely two coins to rub together. I'll not have a nameless, penniless wattock show disrespect for my ally! Thank you for your company, but I have enjoyed it enough! Hengrid!'

The burly dwarf veteran stepped forward and with an apologetic look gestured for the old pedlar to stand. With a final puff on his pipe, the wanderer pushed himself to his feet and hauled on his pack.

'It is a day to be rued when the words of the old fall on deaf ears,' said the stranger as he turned away.

'I am no beardling!' Throndin called after him.

They watched the dwarf walk slowly down the road, until he disappeared from view between two tall rocks. Throndin noticed Arbrek watching the path intently, as if he could still see the stranger.

'Empty warnings to go with his empty purse,' said Throndin waving a dismissive hand in the pedlar's direction. Arbrek turned with a frown on his face.

'Since when did the kings of Zhufbar count wisdom in coins?' said the Runelord. Throndin made to answer but Arbrek had turned away and was stomping off through the army.

THE SOLEMN BEATING of drums could be heard echoing along the halls and corridors of Karaz-a-Karak. The small chamber was empty except for two figures. His face as pale as his beard, King Snorri lay on the low, wide bed, his eyes closed. On one knee next to the bed, a hand on the dwarf's chest, was Prince Malekith of Ulthuan, once general of the Phoenix King's armies and now ambassador to the dwarf empire.

The rest of the room was hung with heavy tapestries depicting the battles the two had fought together, suitably aggrandising Snorri's role. Malekith did not begrudge the king his glories, for was not his own name sung loudly in Ulthuan while the name of Snorri Whitebeard barely a *whisper. Each people to their own kind,* the elf prince thought.

Snorri's eyelids fluttered open and his pale blues eyes were cloudy. His lips twisted into a smile and a fumbling hand found Malekith's arm.

'Would that dwarf lives were measured as those of the elves,' said Snorri. 'Then my reign would last another thousand years.'

'But even so, we still die,' said Malekith. 'Our measure is made by what we do when we live and the legacy that we leave to our kin, as any other. A lifetime of millennia is worthless if its works come to nought after it has ended.'

'True, true,' said Snorri with a nod, his smile fading. 'What we have built is worthy of legend, isn't it? Our two great realms have driven back the beasts and the daemons and the lands are safe for our people. Trade has never been better, and the Holds grow with every year.'

'Your reign has indeed been glorious, Snorri,' said Malekith. 'Your line is strong, your son will uphold the great things that you have done.'

'And perhaps even build on them.' Said Snorri.

'Perhaps, if the gods will it,' said Malekith.

'And why should they not?' asked Snorri. He coughed as he pushed himself to a sitting position, his shoulders sinking into thick, gold-embroidered white pillows. 'Though my breath comes short and my body is infirm, my will is as hard as the stone that these walls are carved from. I am a dwarf, and like all my people, I have within me the strength of the mountains. Though this body is now weak, my spirit shall go to the Halls of the Ancestors.'

'It will be welcomed there, by Grungni and Valaya and Grimnir,' said Malekith. 'You shall take your place with pride.'

'I'm not done,' said Snorri with a frown. His expression grim, the king continued. 'Hear this oath, Malekith of the Elves, comrade on the battlefield, friend at the hearth. I, Snorri

Whitebeard, High King of the Dwarfs, bequeath my title and rights to my eldest son. Though I pass through the gateway to the Halls of the Ancestors, my eyes shall remain upon my Empire. Let it be known to our allies and our enemies, that the death is not the end of my guardianship.'

The dwarf broke into a wracking cough, blood flecking his lips. His lined faced was stern as he looked at Malekith. The elf returned his gaze with a passive look.

'Vengeance shall be mine,' swore Snorri. 'When our foes are great, I shall return to my people. When the foul creatures of this world bay at the doors to Karaz-a-Karak, I shall take up my axe once more and my ire shall rock the mountains. Heed my words, Malekith of Ulthuan, and heed them well. Great have been our deeds, and great is the legacy that I leave to you, my closest confidant, my finest comrade in arms. Swear to me now, as my dying breaths fill my lungs, that my oath has been heard. Swear to it on my own grave, on my spirit, that you shall remain true to the ideals we have both striven for these many years. And know this, that there is nothing so foul in the world as an oathbreaker.'

Malekith took the king's hand from his arm and squeezed it tight.

'I swear it,' the elf prince said. 'Upon the grave of High King Snorri Whitebeard, leader of the dwarfs and friend of the elves, I give my oath.'

Snorri's eyes were glazed and his chest no longer rose and fell. The keen hearing of the elf could detect no sign of life, and he did not know whether his words had been heard. Releasing Snorri's hand, he folded the king's arms across his chest and with a delicate touch from his long fingers, Malekith closed Snorri's eyes.

Standing, Malekith spared one last glance at the dead king and then walked from the chamber. Outside, Snorri's son Throndik stood along with several dozen other dwarfs.

'The High King has passed on,' Malekith said, his gaze passing over the heads of the assembled dwarfs, across the throne room. He looked down at Throndik. 'You are now High King.'

Without further word, the elf prince walked gracefully through the crowd and out across the nearly empty throne chamber. Word was passed by some secret means throughout the hold and soon the drums stopped. With Throndik at their head, the dwarfs entered the chamber and lifted the king from his deathbed. With the body of Snorri's borne aloft on their broad shoulders, the dwarfs marched slowly across the throne chamber to a stone bier that had been set before the throne itself. Here they lay the king upon the stone and turned away.

The doors to the throne room were barred for three days while the remaining preparations for the funeral were made. Throndik was still prince and would not become king until his father had been buried, and so busied himself with sending messenger to the other holds to bear the news of the king's death.

At the appointed hour, the throne room was opened once more by an honour guard led by Throndik Snorrisson and Godri Stonehewer. As once more the solemn drums echoed through the hold, the funeral procession bore the High King to his final resting place deep within Karaz-a-Karak. There were no eulogies, there was no weeping, for Snorri's exploits were for all to see in the carvings upon the stone casket within his tomb. And his life had been well spent and there was no cause to mourn his passing.

On Snorri's instructions, the casket had been carved with dire runes of vengeance and grudgebearing, by the most powerful runelords in the hold. Inlaid with gold, the symbols glowed with magical light as Snorri was lowered into the sarcophagus. The lid was then placed onto the stone coffin and *bound with golden bands. The runelords, chanting in unison, struck their final sigils onto the bands, warding away foul magic and consigning Snorri's spirit to the Halls of the Ancestors. There was a final crescendo of drums, rolling in long echoes along the halls and corridors, over the heads of the silent dwarfs that had lined the procession route.*

Throndik performed the last rite, taking up a small keg of beer. He poured a tankard-full of the foaming ale and took a sip. With a nod of approval, he reverently placed the tankard on top of the carved stone casket.

'Drink deep in the Halls of the Ancestors,' intoned Throndik. 'Raise this tankard to those who have passed before you, so that they might remember those that still walk upon the world.'

BY MID-MORNING the following day, the dwarf army had left the World's Edge Mountains and were in the foothills that surrounded the Zhuf-durak, known by men as the River Aver Reach. From the cargo-loco the thudding of steam pistons echoed from the hillsides over the babbling of the river, while the deep murmuring of dwarfs in conversation droned constantly.

At the head of the column, Throndin marched with Barundin and Arbrek. The king was in a silent mood, and had been since the encounter with the pedlar the day before. Whether it was thought, or whether the king was sulking because of Arbrek's soft admonishment was unknown to Barundin, but he was not going to intrude on his father's thoughts at this time.

A distant buzzing from the sky caused the dwarfs to lift their heads and gaze into the low cloud. A speck of darkness from the west grew closer, bobbing up and down ever so slightly in an erratic course. The puttering of the gyrocopter's engine grew louder as the aircraft approached and there were pointed fingers and a louder commotion as the pilot pushed his craft into a dive and swooped over the column. Almost carving a furrow in a hilltop with the whirling rotors of the gyrocopter as he dipped groundward, the pilot swung his machine around and then passed above the convoy more sedately. About a half a mile ahead, a great trailing of dust that rose as a cloud into the air marked the pilot's landing.

As they neared, Barundin could see the pilot more clearly. His beard and faced were coot-stained, two pale rings around his eyes from where his goggles had been. Those goggles were now hung from a strap attached to the side of the dwarf's winged helms, hanging down over his shoulder. Over a long chainmail shirt, the pilot wore a set of heavy leather overalls, much darned and patched. The pilot regarding the king and his retinue with a pronounced squint as he watched them approach.

'Is that you, Rimbal Wanazaki?' said Barundin. The pilot gave a nod a grin, displaying broken, yellowing, uneven teeth.

'Right you are, lad,' said Wanazaki.

'We thought you were dead!' said Throndin. 'Some nonsense with a troll lair.'

'Aye, there's a lot of it about.' Replied Wanazaki. 'But I'm not dead, as you can see for yourself.'

'More's the bloody pity,' said Throndin. 'I meant what I said. You're no longer welcome in my halls.'

'You're still mad about that little explosion?' said Wanazaki with a disconsolate shake of the head. 'You're a hard king, Throndin, a hard king.'

'Get gone,' said Throndin, thrusting a thumb over his shoulder. 'I shouldn't even be talking to you.'

'Well, you're not in your halls now, your kingship, so you can listen and you don't have to say a word,' said Wanazaki.

'Well, what have you got to say for yourself?' said the king. 'I haven't got the time to waste with you.'

The pilot held up one hand to quieten the king. Reaching into his belt he pulled out a delicate-looking tankard, no bigger than twice the size of a thimble, so small that only one finger would fit into its narrow handle. Turning to the gyrocopter engine, which was still making the odd coughing a spluttering noise, he turned a small tap on the side of one tank. Clear liquid dripped out into the small mug, which the pilot filled almost to the rim. Barundin's eyes began to moisten as the vapours from the fuel-alcohol stung them.

With a wink at the king, the disgraced engineer knocked back the liquid. For a moment he stood there, doing nothing. Wanazaki then gave a small cough and Barundin could see his hands trembling. Thumping a fist against his chest, the pilot coughed again, much louder and then stamped his foot. Eyes slightly glazed, he leaned forwards and squinted at the king.

'It's orcs you're after, am I right?' said Wanazaki. The king did not reply immediately, still taken aback by the engineer's curious drinking habit.

'Yes,' Throndin said eventually.

'I seen them,' said Wanazaki. 'About thirty, maybe thirty-five miles south of here. Day's march, no more, if it's a step.'

'Within a day's march?' exclaimed Barundin. 'Are you sure? Which way are they heading?'

'Course he's not sure,' said Throndin. 'This grog-swiller probably doesn't know a mile from a step.'

'A day's march, I'm telling you,' insisted Wanazaki. 'You'd be there by midday tomorrow if you turn south now. They were camped, all drunk and fat by the looks of it. I seen smoke to the west, reckon they've been having some fun.'

'If we go now, we could catch them before they sober up, take them in their camp,' said Barundin. 'It'd be an easy runk and no mistake.'

'We don't need some gangly manlings, we can take them,' said Ferginal, one of Throndin's stonebearers and a cousin of Barundin on his dead mother's side. The comment was met with a general shouts of encouragement from the younger members of the entourage.

'Pah!' snorted Arbrek, turning with a scowl at the boisterous dwarfs. 'Listen to the beardlings! All eager for war, are you? Ready to march for a day and a night and fight a battle? Made of mountain stone, are you? Barely a full beard between you and all ready to rush off to battle against the greenskins. Foolhardy, that's what they'd call you if you ever lived long enough to have sons of your own.'

'We're not scared!' came a shouted reply. The dwarf that had spoken up quickly ducked behind his comrades as Arbrek's withering stare was brought to bear.

'Fie to scared, you'll be dead!' snarled the runelord. 'Get another thousand miles under them legs of yours and you might be ready to force march straight into battle. How you going to swing and axe or hammer without no puff, eh?'

'What do you say, father?' said Barundin, turning to the king.

'I'm as eager to settle this grudge as any of you,' Throndin said and there was a roaring cheer. It quietened as he raised his hands. 'But it's be rash to chase of after these orcs on the words of a drunken outcast.'

Wanazaki gave a grin and a thumbs up at being mentioned. Throndin shook his head in disgust.

'Besides, even if the old wazzock is right, there's no guarantee the orcs would be still around when we get there,' the king continued. There was a loud sigh of disappointment from the throng. 'Most importantly,' Throndin added, raising his voice above the disgruntled grumbling, 'I made a promise to Baron Vessal to meet him, and who here would have their king break his promise?'

As THEY MARCHED westwards to their rendezvous with the men of Baron Vessal, the dwarf army crossed the advance of the orcs. The sign was unmistakable; the ground was trampled and littered with discarded scraps, and even the air itself still held their taint, emanating from indiscriminate piles of orc dung. The most veteran orc-fighters inspected the spoor and tracks and estimated there to be over a thousand greenskins. Even with just eight hundred warriors, all that duty would spare from the guarding of Zhufbar, Throndin felt confident. Even if Vessal had only a handful of men, the army would be more than match for the greenskins.

As the evening twilight began to spill across the hills, several campfires could be seen in the distance along a line of hills. About a mile from the camp, the leading elements of the dwarf army encountered too men on the trail. Two horses were tethered to a small tree and a small fire with a steaming pot over was set to one side of the road. They were dressed in long studded coats and bore bulky arquebuses. Throndin could smell ale. They looked nervously at each other and then one stepped forward.

'Ware!' he shouted. 'Who would pass into the lands of Baron Vessal of Averland?'

'I bloody would!' shouted Throndin, stomping forward.

'And you are?' asked the sentry, his voice wavering.

'This is King Throndin of Zhufbar, ally to your master,' said Barundin, carrying his father's standard to the king's side. 'Who addresses the king?'

'Well,' said the man with a glance behind him at his companion, who was busily studying his feet. 'Gustav Feldenhoffen, that's me. Road warden, we's road wardens for the baron. He said to challenge anyone's on the road, like.'

'A credit to your profession,' said Throndin giving the man a comforting pat on the arm. 'Dedicated to your duty, I see. Where's the baron?'

Feldenhoffen relaxed with a sigh and waved towards a large tent near one of the fires.

'The baron's in the centre of the camp, your, er, kingliness,' said the road warden. 'I can take you, if you'd like.'

'Don't worry, I'll find him right enough,' said Throndin. 'Wouldn't want you leaving your post.'

'Yes, you're right,' said Feldenhoffen. 'Well, take care. Erm, see you at the battle.'

The king grunted as the road warden stepped aside. Throndin waved the army forwards again and passed the word to his thanes to organise the camp while he sought out the baron. Tomorrow they would march to battle, and he was looking for a good night's sleep before all the exertion.

The story continues in

GRUDGE BEARER
by Gav Thorpe

Available from www.blacklibrary.com

Go deeper into the action with the award-winning Warhammer Fantasy Roleplay!

The core rulebook provides everything you need to explore the gothic Old World and battle against the enemies of the Empire.

Warhammer Fantasy Roleplay
1-84416-220-6

Buy it now from *www.blackindustries.com*
or by calling + 44 (0) 115 900 4144